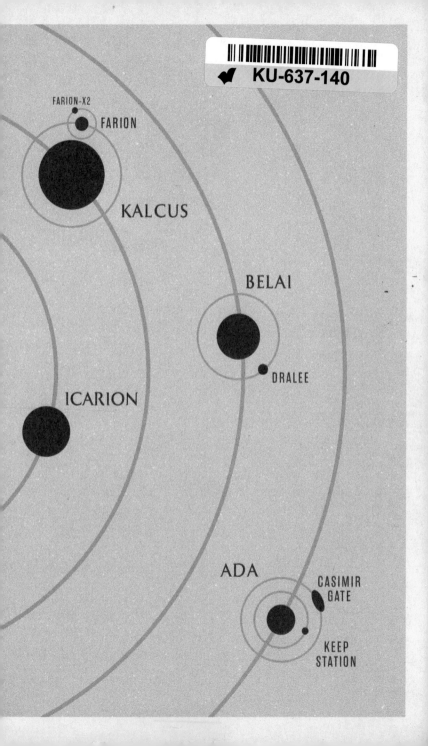

FARION-X2

FARION

KALCUS

BELAI

DRALEE

ICARION

ADA

CASIMIR
GATE

KEEP
STATION

VELOCITY WEAPON

THE PROTECTORATE: BOOK ONE

MEGAN E. O'KEEFE

www.orbitbooks.net

ORBIT

First published in Great Britain in 2019 by Orbit

1 3 5 7 9 10 8 6 4 2

A CIP catalogue record for this book
is available from the British Library.

ISBN 978-0-356-51222-8

Printed and bound in Great Britain by Clays Ltd, Elcograf S.p.A.

Papers used by Orbit are from well-managed forests
and other responsible sources.

Orbit
An imprint of
Little, Brown Book Group
Carmelite House
50 Victoria Embankment
London EC4Y 0DZ

An Hachette UK Company
www.hachette.co.uk

www.orbitbooks.net

CHAPTER 1

THE AFTERMATH OF THE BATTLE
OF DRALEE

The first thing Sanda did after being resuscitated was vomit all over herself. The second thing she did was to vomit all over again. Her body shook, trembling with the remembered deceleration of her gunship breaking apart around her, stomach roiling as the preservation foam had encased her, shoved itself down her throat and nose and any other ready orifice. Her teeth jarred together, her fingers fumbled with temporary palsy against the foam stuck to her face.

Dios, she hoped the shaking was temporary. They told you this kind of thing happened in training, that the trembling would subside and the "explosive evacuation" cease. But it was a whole hell of a lot different to be shaking yourself senseless while emptying every drop of liquid from your body than to be looking at a cartoonish diagram with friendly letters claiming *Mild Gastrointestinal Discomfort*.

It wasn't foam covering her. She scrubbed, mind numb from cold-sleep, struggling to figure out what encased her. It was slimy and goopy and—oh no. Sanda cracked a hesitant eyelid and peeked at her fingers. Thick, clear jelly with a slight bluish tinge coated her hands. The stuff was cold, making her trembling worse, and with a sinking gut she realized what it was. She'd joked about the stuff, in training with her fellow gunshippers. Snail snot. Gelatinous splooge. But its real name was MedAssist Incubatory NutriBath, and you only got dunked in it if you needed intensive care with a capital *I*.

"Fuck," she tried to say, but her throat rasped on unfamiliar air. How long had she been in here? Sanda opened both eyes, ignoring the cold gel running into them. She lay in a white enameled cocoon, the lid removed to reveal a matching white ceiling inset with true-white bulbs. The brightness made her blink.

The NutriBath was draining, and now that her chest was exposed to air, the shaking redoubled. Gritting her teeth against the spasms, she felt around the cocoon, searching for a handhold.

"Hey, medis," she called, then hacked up a lump of gel. "Got a live one in here!"

No response. Assholes were probably waiting to see if she could get out under her own power. Could she? She didn't remember being injured in the battle. But the medis didn't stick you in a bath for a laugh. She gave up her search for handholds and fumbled trembling hands over her body, seeking scars. The baths were good, but they wouldn't have left a gunnery sergeant like her in the tub long enough to fix cosmetic damage. The gunk was only slightly less expensive than training a new gunner.

Her face felt whole, chest and shoulders smaller than she remembered but otherwise unharmed. She tried to crane her neck to see down her body, but the unused muscles screamed in protest.

"Can I get some help over here?" she called out, voice firmer now she'd cleared it of the gel. Still no answer. Sucking down a few sharp breaths to steel herself against the ache, she groaned and lifted her torso up on her elbows until she sat straight, legs splayed out before her.

Most of her legs, anyway.

Sanda stared, trying to make her coldsleep-dragging brain catch up with what she saw. Her left leg was whole, if covered in disturbing wrinkles, but her right... That ended just above the place where her knee should have been. Tentatively, she reached down, brushed her shaking fingers over the thick lump of flesh at the end of her leg.

She remembered. A coil fired by an Icarion railgun had smashed through the pilot's deck, slamming a nav panel straight into her legs. The evac pod chair she'd been strapped into had immediately deployed preserving foam—encasing her, and her smashed leg, for Ada Prime scoopers to pluck out of space after the chaos of the Battle of Dralee faded. She picked at her puckered skin, stunned. Remembered pain vibrated through her body and she clenched her jaw. Some of that cold she'd felt upon awakening must have been leftover shock from the injury, her body frozen in a moment of panic.

Any second now, she expected the pain of the incident to mount, to catch up with her and punish her for putting it off so long. It didn't. The NutriBath had done a better job than she'd thought possible. Only mild tremors shook her.

"Hey," she said, no longer caring that her voice cracked. She gripped either side of her open cocoon. "Can I get some fucking help?"

Silence answered. Choking down a stream of expletives that would have gotten her court-martialed, Sanda scraped some of the gunk on her hands off on the edges of the cocoon's walls and adjusted her grip. Screaming with the effort, she heaved herself to standing within the bath, balancing precariously on her single leg, arms trembling under her weight.

The medibay was empty.

"Seriously?" she asked the empty room.

The rest of the medibay was just as stark white as her cocoon and the ceiling, its walls pocked with panels blinking all sorts of readouts she didn't understand the half of. Everything in the bay was stowed, the drawers latched shut, the gurneys folded down and strapped to the walls. It looked ready for storage, except for her cocoon sitting in the center of the room, dripping NutriBath and vomit all over the floor.

"Naked wet girl in here!" she yelled at the top of her sore voice. Echoes bounced around her, but no one answered. "For fuck's sake."

Not willing to spend god-knew-how-long marinating in a stew of her own body's waste, Sanda clenched her jaw and attempted to swing her leg over the edge of the bath. She tipped over and flopped face-first to the ground instead.

"Ow."

She spat blood and picked up her spinning head. Still no response. Who was running this bucket, anyway? The medibay looked clean enough, but there wasn't a single Ada Prime logo anywhere. She hadn't realized she'd miss those stylized dual bodies with their orbital spin lines wrapped around them until this moment.

Calling upon half-remembered training from her boot camp days, Sanda army crawled her way across the floor to a long drawer. By the time she reached it, she was panting hard, but pure anger drove her forward. Whoever had come up with the bright idea to wake her without a medi on standby needed a good, solid slap upside the head. She may have been down to one leg, but Sanda was pretty certain she could make do with two fists.

She yanked the drawer open and hefted herself up high enough to see inside. No crutches, but she found an extending pole for an IV drip. That'd have to do. She levered herself upright and stood a moment, back pressed against the wall, getting her breath. The hard metal of the stand bit into her armpit, but she didn't care. She was on her feet again. Or foot, at least. Time to go find a medi to chew out.

The caster wheels on the bottom of the pole squeaked as she made her way across the medibay. The door dilated with a satisfying swish, and even the stale recycled air of the empty corridor smelled fresh compared to the nutri-mess she'd been swimming in. She paused and considered going back to find a robe. Ah, to hell with it.

She shuffled out into the hall, picked a likely direction toward the pilot's deck, and froze. The door swished shut beside her, revealing a logo she knew all too well: a single planet, fiery wings encircling it.

Icarion.

She was on an enemy ship. With one leg.

Naked.

Sanda ducked back into the medibay and scurried to the panel-spotted wall, silently cursing each squeak of the IV stand's wheels. She had to find a comms link, and fast.

Gel-covered fingers slipped on the touchscreen as she tried to navigate unfamiliar protocols. Panic constricted her throat, but she forced herself to breathe deep, to keep her cool. She captained a gunship. This was nothing.

Half expecting alarms to blare, she slapped the icon for the ship's squawk box and hesitated. What in the hell was she supposed to broadcast? They hadn't exactly covered codes for "help I'm naked and legless on an Icarion bucket" during training. She bit her lip and punched in her own call sign—1947—followed by 7500, the universal sign for a hijacking. If she were lucky, they'd get the hint: 1947 had been hijacked. Made sense, right?

She slapped send.

"Good morning, one-niner-four-seven. I've been waiting for you to wake up," a male voice said from the walls all around her. She jumped and almost lost her balance.

"Who am I addressing?" She forced authority into her voice even though she felt like diving straight back into her cocoon.

"This is AI-Class Cruiser Bravo-India-Six-One-Mike."

AI-Class? A smartship? Sanda suppressed a grin, knowing the ship could see her. Smartships were outside Ada Prime's tech range, but she'd studied them inside and out during training. While they were brighter than humans across the board, they still had human follies. Could still be lied to. Charmed, even.

"Well, it's a pleasure to meet you, Cruiser. My name's Sanda Greeve."

"I am called *The Light of Berossus*," the voice said.

Of course he was. Damned Icarions never stuck to simple call signs. They always had to posh things up by naming their ships after ancient scientists. She nodded, trying to keep an easy smile on while she glanced sideways at the door. Could the ship's crew hear her? They hadn't heard her yelling earlier, but they might notice their ship talking to someone new.

"That's quite the mouthful for friendly conversation."

"Bero is an acceptable alternative."

"You got it, Bero. Say, could you do me a favor? How many souls on board at the present?"

Her grip tightened on the IV stand, and she looked around for any other item she could use as a weapon. This was a smartship. Surely they wouldn't allow the crew handblasters for fear of poking holes in their pretty ship. All she needed was a bottleneck, a place to hunker down and wait until Ada Prime caught her squawk and figured out what was up.

"One soul on board," Bero said.

"What? That can't be right."

"There is one soul on board." The ship sounded amused with her exasperation at first listen, but there was something in the ship's voice that nagged at her. Something…tight. Could AI ships even slip like that? It seemed to her that something with that big of a brain would only use the tone it absolutely wanted to.

"In the medibay, yes, but the rest of the ship? How many?"

"One."

She licked her lips, heart hammering in her ears. She turned back to the control panel she'd sent the squawk from and pulled up the ship's nav system. She couldn't make changes from the bay unless she had override commands, but…The whole thing was on autopilot. If she really was the only one on board…Maybe she could convince the ship to return her to Ada Prime. Handing a smartship over to her superiors would win her accolades enough to last a lifetime. Could even win her a fresh new leg.

"Bero, bring up a map of the local system, please. Light up any ports in range."

A pause. "Bero?"

"Are you sure, Sergeant Greeve?"

Unease threaded through her. "Call me Sanda, and yes, light her up for me."

The icons for the control systems wiped away, replaced with a 3-D model of the nearby system. She blinked, wondering if she still had goop in her eyes. Couldn't be right. There they were, a glowing dot in the endless black, the asteroid belt that stood between Ada Prime and Icarion clear as starlight. Judging by the coordinates displayed above the ship's avatar, she should be able to see Ada Prime. They were near the battlefield of Dralee, and although there was a whole lot of space between the celestial bodies, Dralee was the closest in the system to Ada. That's why she'd been patrolling it.

"Bero, is your display damaged?"

"No, Sanda."

She swallowed. Icarion couldn't have…wouldn't have. They wanted the dwarf planet. Needed access to Ada Prime's Casimir Gate.

"Bero. Where is Ada Prime in this simulation?" She pinched the screen, zooming out. The system's star, Cronus, spun off in the distance, brilliant and yellow-white. Icarion had vanished, too.

"Bero!"

"Icarion initiated the Fibon Protocol after the Battle of Dralee. The results were larger than expected."

The display changed, drawing back. Icarion and Ada Prime reappeared, their orbits aligning one of the two times out of the year they passed each other. Somewhere between them, among the asteroid belt, a black wave began, reaching outward, consuming space in all directions. Asteroids vanished. Icarion vanished. Ada Prime vanished.

She dropped her head against the display. Let the goop run down from her hair, the cold glass against her skin scarcely registering. Numbness suffused her. No wonder Bero was empty. He must have been ported outside the destruction. He was a smartship. He wouldn't have needed human input to figure out what had happened.

"How long?" she asked, mind racing despite the slowness of cold-sleep. Shock had grabbed her by the shoulders and shaken her fully awake. Grief she could dwell on later, now she had a problem to work. Maybe there were others, like her, on the edge of the wreckage. Other evac pods drifting through the black. Outposts in the belt.

There'd been ports, hideouts. They'd starve without supplies from either Ada Prime or Icarion, but that'd take a whole lot of time. With a smartship, she could scoop them up. Get them all to one of the other nearby habitable systems before the ship's drive gave out. And if she were very lucky...Hope dared to swell in her chest. Her brother and fathers were resourceful people. Surely her dad Graham would have had some advance warning. That man always had his ear to the ground, his nose deep in rumor networks. If anyone could ride out that attack, it was them.

"It has been two hundred thirty years since the Battle of Dralee."

CHAPTER 2

IT BEGINS WITH GRADUATION DAY

The steps creaked alarmingly under Biran's weight as he mounted the stage, but he would not let unstable footing delay the moment his whole life had built toward. News drones buzzed like loose wires above his head, their spotlights blinding him the moment he reached the podium. Keeper Li Shun clasped his hand in her strong fingers, the black robe of graduation transforming her from the stern teacher he'd known and admired into something otherworldly. She flashed him a smile—his sponsor for all these years—the hint of a silver tear in the corner of her eye. Pride. Biran's chest swelled.

Shun turned to the podium, bracing her hands against either side. The mic chain looped around her throat threw her voice out to the dozen graduating Keepers, and the thousands of Ada Prime citizens crowding the stands.

"Introducing for the first time: Keeper Biran Aventure Greeve. First in class."

Cheers exploded across the crowd, across the net. On massive screens suspended from drones, the faces of newscasters beamed excitedly as Biran watched himself, screen-in-screen, take the podium from Keeper Shun.

His heart lurched, his palms sweat. It hadn't been so bad, sitting in the crowd with his fellow graduating classmates, but now he was up here. Alone. Meant to represent them to all these people. Meant to speak to Prime citizens in other settlements, on other worlds. The first of the next generation—the vanguard of Prime knowledge.

The notes for his speech waited in his wristpad; he could flick them open at any time. No one would mind. It was expected, really. He was only twenty-two, newly graduated. There wouldn't even be whispers about it. But there'd be whispers about his hesitation.

Biran took a deep breath, careful not to let the mic pick up the hiss of air, and gripped the sides of the podium. He sought familiar faces in the audience. Not his cohort—his family. Most of his cohort could rot, for all he cared. Over the years in training they'd grown into little more than petty social climbers, political vipers. Even Anaia, his childhood friend, had allied herself with the richest girl in the group—Lili—just to squeeze herself closer to the top. His fathers, Graham and Ilan, were out there in the crowd somewhere. Sanda, his sister, would watch from her gunship on her way to make a patrol sweep of Dralee. His family was what mattered.

They believed in him. He could do this.

"People of Ada Prime," he began, hating the way his voice squeaked nervously over the first word. Breathe. Slow down. "It honors me, and all my classmates, to—"

The hovering screens changed. The faces of the newscasters shifted from jubilant to fear-struck. Biran froze, terrified for an instant it was something he had done, or said, that caused that change.

Later, he'd wish it had been.

The newscasters were muted, but tickers scrolled across the bottoms of the screens: *Battle Over the Moon Dralee. Ada Forces Pushed Back by Icarion. Casualties Expected. Casualties Confirmed.*

A newscaster's face wiped away, replaced by the black field of space. Biran's subconscious discerned the source of the video feed—a satellite in orbit around one of Belai's other moons. The perspective was wide, the subjects pointillistic shapes of light upon the screen.

Those lights broke apart.

Biran went cold. Numb. There was no way to identify the ships, no way to know which one his sister commanded, but deep in his marrow he knew. She'd been severed from him. One by one, those lights blinked out. Behind him, a teacher screamed.

The stadium's speakers crackled as someone overrode them, a voice he didn't recognize—calm and mechanical, probably an AI—spoke. He took a moment to place the voice as the same used for alarm drills at school.

"Impact event probability has exceeded the safety envelope. Please take cover… Impact event probability has exceeded…"

Debris. Bits and pieces of Ada's shattered ships rocketing through space toward their home station to sow destruction. Bits of soldiers, too. Maybe even Sanda, burning up like so much space dust in the thin membrane enclosing Keep Station. Things weren't supposed to escalate like this. Icarion was weak. Trapped. The people of Prime, even on backwater Ada, were supported by empire. Icarion wouldn't have dared… But they had.

War. The stalemate had been called.

The crowd rippled. As the warning voice droned on, the stadium's lights dimmed to a bloodied red, white arrows lighting the way to impact shelters. One of the senior Keepers on the stage, Biran didn't turn to see who, found their legs and stepped forward. A hand enclosed Biran's shoulder. Not in congratulations, but in sympathy. Biran stepped back to the podium.

He found his voice.

"Calm," he pleaded, and this time his voice did not crack, did not hesitate. It boomed across the whole of the stadium and drew the attention of those desperate for stability.

"Please, calm. We will not trample one another for safety. We are Prime. We move together, as one. Go arm in arm with your compatriots into the shelters. Be quick. Be patient. Be safe."

The swelling riot subsided, the tides pushing against the edges of the stadium walls pulling back, contracting into orderly snake lines down the aisles. Biran took a step away from the podium.

"Come," Keeper Vladsen said. It took a moment for Biran to place the man. A member of the Protectorate, Vladsen rarely interacted with the students unless it was a formal affair. "There's a Keeper shelter close by." He gestured to a nearby door, a scant few meters from the stage that vibrated now to the beat of thousands of people fleeing. The rest of Biran's cohort filed toward it, shepherded by Keeper Shun.

Biran shrugged the guiding hand off his arm. His gaze tracked the crowd, wondering where his fathers might be, but landed on a knot of people clumped up by a stadium door. The drone ushers that handled the stadium's crowd control gave fitful, pleading orders for organization. Orders the panicking humans ignored.

"They need a person to guide them."

"You're a Keeper now," Vladsen said, voice tight. "Your duty is to survive."

"The academy gave us emergency-response training. I cannot imagine they did not mean for us to use it."

Vladsen cocked his head to the side, searching for something in Biran's face. "We guard the knowledge of our people through the ages, not their bodies from moment to moment."

Something inside Biran lurched, rebelled. He peeled the black robe from his shoulders, tugged it over his head and tossed it to the ground. His lightweight slacks and button-up were thin protection against the simulated autumn breeze. He undid the buttons of his sleeves and rolled them up.

"You get to safety. I have work to do."

CHAPTER 3

PRIME STANDARD YEAR 3771

SANDA'S FIRST DAY IN THE FUTURE

Sanda slapped her palm against the screen, leaving a goopy hand-print. Two hundred thirty years. It wasn't possible. She'd heard rumblings that the Icarions were working on something big, but not big enough to wipe out two whole planets. Nothing in the universe man-made could produce that kind of power. She should know. Bero was fucking with her. Some sort of sick smartship joke. They couldn't all be gone. Dead. Dust between the stars.

"Bero." Her voice was tight, and not from disuse. "Don't mess with me. Evac pods aren't designed to last that long. I'd be just another hunk of space debris on that timeline. How long?"

"My original calculations are correct," the smooth voice said.

She wanted to scream. The display wasn't giving her anything but garbage numbers, bullshit estimates. It kept on showing her that empty, black void where her home used to be. She jabbed at it some more, cycled diagnostics. Nothing deep—the medibay wasn't set up for that kind of thing—but she could force it to show her engine power, life support. Everything looked good. There was no reason for Bero to be malfunctioning like this. She reached a hand up to comb out sticky hair with her fingers, then aborted the motion as a spike of pain appeared between her eyes. Just a coldsleep headache. Breathe. Push through.

Sanda spun around, IV wheels squealing, and glared at the ceiling where she thought a camera might be.

"Explain."

"There is no need to face my cameras, Sanda. I do not require eye contact for engagement. I can see you anywhere in the medibay."

"Wonderful for you." She jabbed a finger at the bulbous gunmetal eye. "But I need some answers and I'm sick of looking at that—that—perversion."

The screen flickered in the corner of her eye and she glance over her shoulder. Icarion's logo flared across it, bright and ashy.

"Not. Better."

"Of course. My apologies."

The screen flickered again, this time filling with the dual system of Ada Prime. She licked bitter, gel-coated lips, staring at the little hunk of dwarf planet and orbital station she'd called home, with the Casimir Gate in orbit around it. Couldn't be gone. Couldn't be.

"Bero!"

"If there is another image that would be more suited to your current mood—"

"It's not the image. I request information relating to the Fibon Protocol. Immediately."

"You do not have to speak to me like I'm a computer."

"Then stop acting like one! You know full well what I want. Why won't you explain?"

Hesitation. "It is . . . unsettling."

"Oh, we're already there. I'm real unsettled. Full-on ruffled. Now stop playing coy computer and tell me what I've just woken up into."

"I do not wish for you to be angry with me. My existence was a part of this destruction."

Her gut turned cold. She adjusted the IV stand under her arm, pulling it snug against her body. "Did you do this?"

"No!" The word was sharp enough it stung her ears. "I am a result of the research, nothing more. I am a smartship, yes, but I am an *interstellar* smartship. First in my class. They were using my labs for biometric research."

There was a tinge of pride in Bero's voice, an upward lilt. She imagined the ship preening and tossing his hair. Sanda swallowed a scoff. Icarion was always trying to get around paying the gate fees to the Primes who controlled them. It made sense they'd come up with some mad scheme to cross the black slow style.

"How interstellar are we talking, here?"

"Eight percent of the speed of light."

She bit her lip. Slow as a snail to a fox. Pass through a Casimir Gate—tech only her people, the Primes, knew how to handle—and you could pop out in the connected star system within the hour. Like poking a needle through space-time. Sure, the gates only bridged one system to another, but passing through star systems to reach the gate you wanted was a lot faster and safer than burning between the stars.

"Not bad," she lied. "But what does that have to do with the Protocol?"

"I'm not the only thing that can accelerate to eight percent c."

Her mouth grew thick. She swallowed viscous saliva. Anything cranked up to a meaningful percent of the speed of light was one hell of a missile.

"You're talking about RKVs—relativistic kill vehicles. Big fuckin' launchers designed to lob dumb mass out at speeds so fast any tech on board wouldn't survive the acceleration. Not having a guidance system makes them useless in war because there's no guarantee you'd get anywhere close to hitting what you're aiming at. Why would Icarion even bother? They're rubbish in battle."

"Fantastic against planets."

"Dios."

Her face slackened, fingers numb on the grip of her IV stand. But that fish-eye lens just stared back at her, impassive, unblinking. She didn't know what she'd expected. It hadn't been this.

The screen flickered. She turned back to it.

"The first demonstration," Bero said, "was pointed at an asteroid passing near the planet Ada. This was a month after the Battle of Dralee."

On the screen, the dual bodies of Ada Prime—the planet and its orbiting gate—swung into view. Across the black an asteroid arced. Orbital lines popped up to illustrate the asteroid's path near to Ada.

"Icarion leaked Ada a warning of an incoming attack and led them to believe they were using the asteroid to hide their approach. Ada's gunship fleet was in LPO, awaiting detection of the advancing Icarion fleet, when the asteroid passed within range. Icarion fired the Protocol at the asteroid. Dissolution was complete. The debris blowback knocked out ninety-five percent of the fleet, and Ada's surface suffered heavy kinetic bombardment. It damaged many habitat domes."

Sanda slid down the IV stand, gripping it in one hand, and sank to her ass on the cold floor. Her gaze was glued to the screen, watching debris—transmuted to plasma at those speeds—fly off the vaporized asteroid into the fleet and Ada. Yellow triangles, gunships like hers, blinked out en masse. Was this what it had been like for her family to watch the footage after Dralee? She choked on bile.

"Survivors?"

"Many." Bero's voice was soft, but not with gentleness. With shame. Sanda curled her fingers around the base of the IV stand and squeezed hard. Her limbs were jelly, trembling all over. Weak from two different kinds of shock.

"The habitats were damaged, but most civilians and Keepers survived. Keep Station was spared. Icarion threatened to bombard the planet directly if they refused to allow them access to the secret of building the gates."

"The Keepers would never allow that," Sanda insisted.

"Correct. With their defenses in shambles, the Keepers stalled for time, putting off answering Icarion's demands. The Icarions were not fooled.

"They moved the Protocol into the space between the two planets. This version spun up, launching heavy weights at relativistic speeds in an ever-growing spiral—whipping them through space, a merry-go-round shotgun.

"Icarion had planned to initiate the Protocol when their planet was safely shielded by the gas giant Kalcus. They initiated it too early. Icarion suffered the same bombardment."

"Sabotage?"

"It seems likely."

"Serves them fucking right."

A pause. "I agree."

She reminded herself that Bero must have lost people, too, and bit back her anger.

"Okay," she said. "Okay."

Groaning, she dragged herself to her feet and squeaked over to the screen. She braced herself against the wall with one hand and jabbed at the display with the other. "So. We're near Dralee, right? That means the gate is about a half an astronomical unit from this location if we—"

"The gate does not exist."

"Excuse me?"

"The Casimir Gate of Ada Prime was destroyed during the final bombardment. The planets Icarion and Ada did not survive. Debris fields remain where the planets once were. Given enough time, they may coalesce into planets again, but that timeline is irrelevant on human terms."

She swallowed. Hard. "The gate's gone."

"Yes."

"And you can only go eight percent of the speed of light."

"Yes."

"At that rate it will take…" She tapped a few calculations into the smartscreen. "About seventy-five years to reach Atrux Prime, the nearest inhabited star system."

"Yes."

"Fuck."

"You say that a lot, Sanda."

"It's a fuck-y kind of day, Bero." She pinched the bridge of her nose where her glasses used to sit before the eye-correction surgery. "Suggestions?"

"I believe no appreciable time will be wasted if you pause to take a shower."

Sanda stared at the goop and bodily fluid pool growing around her foot. Cheeky spaceship.

CHAPTER 4

PRIME STANDARD YEAR 3541

DRALEE CHANGES EVERYTHING

Grease from the shelter doors stained his hands. They hadn't been opened for anything other than maintenance in years. Biran had had to brace himself and tug with all his strength to throw the massive bolt. He turned his hands over, wondering at the black smears. It'd been a long time since anything like dirt had entered his life.

"Keeper Greeve," a woman said. He jerked his head up. "They're ready to see you."

The debris of Dralee hadn't reached the station or the biodome, the people of Prime were safe, and still Biran felt hollow as he pushed to his feet. His shoes left dust smears on the perfectly grey composite floor, something that would have horrified him that morning but now... Now he didn't care. There were bigger problems in this world—this room—than hygiene.

The door to Keeper Shun's office swished open. She kept her quarters sparse, the walls paneled with a marble synthetic that appeared to melt into the grey floor. Behind her, as she sat at her desk, a viewscreen displayed what he guessed to be a live feed of nearby space. He swallowed. No, not so close after all. That was Dralee. The closest celestial body to Ada, it was little more than a blip of light in the naked sky at night. In the video over Shun's shoulders, the grey sphere was large enough for him to see the scars left by its ancient tectonics.

The pockmarks left by debris . . . Debris of all kinds. The shape of that little moon was stamped on his heart.

"Sit," she said, gently, her Venus-brown eyes flicking to the chair across the desk. Keeper Lavaux sat to her left, a slender man with pale hair and a loose, trying-too-hard-to-be-relaxed style that Biran had always found sloppy. To Shun's right, Keeper Garcia, Lavaux's polar opposite in sartorial decisions—crisp suits and a war against all hair was his style—but rumored to be his confidant in policy. Biran had interacted with those two little over the years of his training. They were Keepers of the Protectorate, the wrinkles that should have creased their eyes smoothed away by medical intervention. Still, something aged and wise haunted both of their gazes. Neither looked happy, though they forced smiles as he nodded to them.

"We were greatly impressed by your deportment this morning," Garcia said. Biran's lips twitched as he stifled a smirk. *Deportment* seemed like such a pointless word. "You took control when chaos loomed. A thankless task, under normal circumstances. But we saw. And we thank you."

All three bowed their heads. Where Biran would have once felt honor, he found only a void in his chest.

"What of the ships?" Biran asked. Weariness dragged him down, but he must know. The last twelve hours, hunkering under bombardment alert, knowing nothing, he'd nearly driven himself mad with speculation. He knew—he *thought* he knew—that in that moment, when the screens shifted, he'd lost her. His studies had taught him that instinct and truth were not always twins.

When Shun leaned forward to speak, lacing her fingers together on the desktop, all hope eroded. If Sanda had survived, the senior members would have delivered the news. That they'd deferred to Shun meant only one thing—they wanted the blow softened by the gentle delivery of his teacher.

He waited, strength fleeing him with every breath, for the truth he knew would come.

"All ships were lost. Evacuation pod signals have not come through. I'm so sorry, Biran."

He watched them watch him as if from a great distance. Some part of him had accepted this horror the moment the newscaster's face had darkened on the screen above the crowd. What was he supposed to say to them? What did they want to hear? What would Sanda—a flash of her eyes, topaz-brown, entered his mind's eye—want him to say? What would she want him to be, in this moment? She'd always believed in him. Rooted for him to be a Keeper. Went into the gun-ships, she said, to keep her Little B safe.

"I understand," he said. "Thank you for telling me directly, before the news went out."

Relief washed over two faces—Shun and Garcia. Curiosity peeked from behind Lavaux's eyes, but Biran did not know the man well enough to wonder at the emotion.

"Under the circumstances," Shun picked up the thread, tension fleeing her shoulders. A weaver happy with what she'd wrought. "We have conferred and decided that, if you wish, you may delay the implanting of your Keeper chip. We do not want to lay undue stress upon you during your... During this time."

Grief. They would not say the word *grief*.

"I want the chip," he snapped the words out, raising eyebrows all around. "Sanda wanted this for me, above all else."

"Then you will have it," Lavaux spoke for the first time. Biran nodded to him, grateful.

Garcia's expression soured. "Let us not be hasty, Lavaux. The man has suffered a great loss. He should take some time to rest and recover. There is no need to jump into things right away."

Shun's head bobbed agreement. Lavaux scowled.

"With all respect, Keeper Garcia," Biran said, "there absolutely is a need to jump into things right away. Icarion's actions have demanded a declaration of war—am I correct?"

Each Keeper shifted uncomfortably. It was Shun who finally said, "Director Olver will make an announcement to that effect later this evening."

"Then we are in need. This is no time for anyone, at any place in our society, to sit by the wayside."

"He's right," Lavaux said. "Icarion's actions are unprecedented. We need all our great minds—senior and junior—bent to discovering their goals, their plans, and weaknesses. The defense of Ada Prime may depend upon it."

Shun snorted. "You can't possibility believe the rumors. Icarion is not so advanced."

"Rumors?" Biran asked, hungry for anything to distract himself from the howl of agony building in his throat. The others exchanged wary glances, but it was Lavaux who answered.

"These two won't tell you, fresh blood you are—and bereaved at that—but I saw you on that podium. You're a leader, Keeper Greeve." For just a second Biran's ears buzzed. The reality of being called by his new title made his pulse race, but Lavaux was still talking. "And I believe you're savvy enough to suss out the bullshit from the truth. Icarion is posturing. They claim to have built a planet-busting weapon."

"Absolute nonsense," Garcia said. Shun fiddled with her pen.

"That's not what our intelligence agents are saying," Lavaux said. "The evidence is thin, but it's there. Before their destruction, the gunships patrolling Dralee sent back evidence of a massive construct in the area."

"A transport ship," Shun said.

Lavaux held both hands up in a shrug. "Or a weapon. We don't know. We can't know. All we know is that our people are dead. Our ships were destroyed and our evac pods wiped out—forgive my bluntness, Keeper Greeve—and we had zero warning that Icarion had anything with that kind of power in the vicinity."

"Keepers," Biran said as their expressions grew dark, each of them winding up for a long debate. He was tired. Too tired to watch these elders of his order bicker over the details of what had happened. Their information was in pieces. Nothing was certain. If he wanted to discover what had happened to his sister, he'd have to be the one to act. Their worries were scattered. His was singular. A lance to cut through distractions. A laser to the truth.

"I don't know what happened out there, but I will find out." A weakness he didn't understand shook him, jellied his knees and his hands until his body felt limp all over, like a wrung-out towel.

Shun pushed to her feet. "Gentlemen," she said to the elders,

"Keeper Greeve is exhausted. He's done us a great service today, and we are doing him a disservice by keeping him here when he should be resting."

She came around the desk and extended a hand to Biran, helping him to his feet. Her hand was startlingly cold. "Eat. Shower. Rest. Your chip implantation is not scheduled until the morning."

Food. Right. That's what he'd forgotten—why his stomach cramped and his muscles protested. When was the last time he'd eaten? A scone and coffee before the ceremony?

"Thank you, Keepers," he said by rote, and shook each hand before dragging himself back into the halls of the Keeper headquarters.

Those halls were silent. His were the only footsteps scuffing the floor, his shallow breath the only sound above the constant background whir of the station's life-support systems. Part academy, part congress, and part conference center, the Keeper headquarters—jokingly named the Cannery—was never busy on the best of days. Open only to Keepers, select military personnel, and the rare visiting diplomat, silence was a way of life in the Cannery.

But this silence was different. It was a waiting silence. The silence of breath being held, of hope and fear choking each other.

The hall that led him back to his student apartment—soon he'd move out, into a home in the Keeper neighborhood on station—boasted a long, rectangular picture window. Through the plex, Keep Station held its breath just as tightly as the Cannery. The domed station had shifted into artificial night, the great shield of the sky allowing brilliant, natural, starlight to peer inside. Speckles of house lights winked back at the stars, but not so many as there usually were. The city of Keep Station was dark.

He pressed a palm against the window, wondering.

Wondering how it all went so wrong. How a people, brave and bold, could be made to hide in their burrows like frightened mice. How a military—a vast military, one so large that its logistics were incomprehensible to him—could be dealt such a sudden and heavy blow.

How on a day so charged, he could feel so empty. So numb. The cold of the glass did not even faze him.

His fathers. He needed to find his fathers. To talk to them, to make sure they were safe, to tell them... To tell them...

"Biran?"

He flinched, taking his hand from the window to shove it in his pocket. At the end of the hall, Anaia waited. Hesitant, her body half turned away, her fingers twiddling with the hem of her hip-cropped jacket. He hadn't really looked at her since she'd blown him off years ago to get closer to Lili, the wealthiest and assumed-to-be most influential of their cohort.

The years hadn't changed her all that much. She had the same grey-green eyes she'd always had, alight with curiosity, but a weight that had nothing to do with gravity pushed down her shoulders, pursed uncertainty into her lips. He wanted to rebuke her, to accuse her of slinking around the halls hunting for gossip to feed to Lili, but he just didn't have it in him. The weariness around her eyes was the most real thing he'd seen in ages. She sniffed, pushing up her glasses, and he snapped back into himself.

"Anaia, it's late. You should be resting."

Dust streaked her dark cheeks, her tightly curled hair mussed from grime and sweat. But she stood straighter at his admonishment and lifted her chin.

"So should you."

"I—" His voice cracked, something brittle inside him finally giving way. She was beside him in the space of a breath, strong arms wrapped around him, the hard nub of her chin pressing into the side of his head as he bent his face to her shoulder and shuddered, tears rolling.

"Shhh," she whispered, stroking his back. "Shhh. What happened?"

A stupid question, but she hadn't known about the evac pods. About the dead signals, failing to hail home and scream that their people were safe.

"Sanda," he choked, then extricated himself from her, rubbing his cheeks furiously with both hands to invigorate himself. "The pods. There're no signals."

She took a step back and her gaze slid away, staring out into the false night. She'd always been a terrible poker player.

"What is it?" he demanded.

She bit her lip. "I'm not supposed to know this, but…"

"But what?"

She flicked her gaze from side to side and lowered her voice. "The evac pods. They aren't dead. They're broadcasting."

CHAPTER 5

PRIME STANDARD YEAR 3541

PLANET: ATRUX | LOCATION: THE GROTTA

This wasn't the biggest score of Jules's life; this was a fucking joke. The tracker had led her to a warehouse that slouched against the ground. A radio tower stuck up through the center of the rusting pile of trash, an architectural middle finger. It took Nox thirty seconds before he laughed, hot breath fogging the front window of their hacked autocab.

"Quiet," Harlan said.

"Are you seeing this shit?" Nox asked.

Jules's hands tightened on the tablet she'd Velcroed to the dash of the autocab, watching her program tell her over and over again they'd arrived at the indicated destination with a blinking blue smiley face over the dump that was the warehouse.

"This is it," she said, trying to sound like nothing at all was wrong.

"It's garbage."

"Are you sure?" Harlan asked.

"This is it. I slapped a tracker in that crate of wraith. It, and the rest of the shipment, have to be in there."

"Unless the tracker fell off," Nox said.

"It didn't."

"Can't be sure."

"If you don't shut your flap-hole—"

"Whoa," Harlan said. "We're here. Let's check it out." He tapped the earpiece in his right ear. "Lolla, you with us?"

"I got nowhere else to be, don't I?"

"Easy, kid. What's it look like from your end?"

"Hard to tell. There's not much security in the area in general—the storage company down the road has better cameras. The place is drawing power, though, there's no doubt about that. I can't see through the walls, obviously. I mean I could if Harlan would shell out for that new ultrasonic hand-scanner that Arden was babbling on about—"

"He wanted two thousand credits, up front, no view of a prototype."

"Prime already has stuff like it!"

"Prime has a whole hell of a lot the likes of us will never see. Certainly not the likes of Arden. Continue."

"Ugh. Fine. Anyway, the place is drawing more power than it looks like it should. So, generators on the inside. Probably even security systems, though judging by how much they care about the outside of this place, they're probably just electric locks. Or, I dunno, still-frame cameras or something. Heh. You want more info, I need in."

"No," Harlan said.

Jules muted her comm link and lowered her voice so Harlan's and Nox's mics wouldn't pick anything up. "We should bring Lolla in with us."

Harlan swiped his own comm link mute. "Absolutely not. We've been through this. She's brilliant, but she's still a kid. She's not ready to be on the ground for ops."

"She's fourteen. You had me breaking and entering at twelve."

"You'd killed by eleven, all on your own. Lolla's different."

"You mean her parents left her a trust fund that actualizes at eighteen and you don't want to risk your paycheck."

"Don't push me, Jules. Her parents trusted me."

"Yeah, well, we all make mistakes. This is my op. The risks are low, the score is easy, the kid is in. Nox, you got a problem with that?"

"No, ma'am."

"Good." Jules swiped the comm link back open, ignoring Harlan's bug-eyed glare. "Lolla, what's our weakest link?"

"Cargo door on the south side of the building. Low light, bunch of junk for cover."

"Meet us there in five."

"Seriously?!"

"Don't make me second-guess myself."

"Understood. En route. Uh—over?"

Harlan shot her a look as the kid clicked off, but Jules only had eyes for the tablet display she ripped off the Velcroed dash. Lolla had pumped her the data she'd scraped from her safe perch above the area. Even Jules had to admit—in private, to herself, not to either of those two chumps in the car—that it all looked downright boring. Positively mundane.

Could be that it was all theater, that the run-down building and the stripped-down security systems were hiding something really good. Wishful thinking, when the only thing she should wish for right now was for the wraith cache to actually be in that crapsack building.

Unlikely, if the evidence of her eyes was anything to go by. People didn't bother with misdirection anymore. Either they were black market and jacked up their security to look tougher and more important than they were, or they were Prime and their security systems were so top-notch you didn't realize you were walking into them until the grab-walls had you. Maybe that's what this shack was. So high-tech they couldn't see it.

Ha-fucking-ha.

"On the ground," Lolla said.

"Coming to you." Jules exited the car and, by force of habit, checked the weapon holstered to her hip. It was just a stunner—an old stick modded out to look like it might be capable of killing instead of giving you a really nasty migraine—but its weight reassured her. Harlan wouldn't let them carry killing weapons. He always said the authorities didn't hunt after the source of a stunned body with the same passion they did a dead one.

Jules always said the dead one couldn't hunt you down, the stunned one could—so what the fuck were they doing, letting their dicks hang out like that?

But her saying wasn't as catchy, and even though this was her score,

Harlan was the big boss. His crew, his saying, his rules. Someday it'd be hers, though. Just had to make scores first. Like this wraith cache.

Lolla had her hoodie pulled up, the asymmetrical zip dragging black synth fabric across the lower half of her face like a mask while the hood drooped over her forehead and hung down her shoulders. She looked like something out of a spy vid. Was only missing a few random bits of wire dangling from her pockets for flair.

Nox snickered. Jules got him in the ribs with an elbow. Either Lolla didn't notice or didn't care. She slunk up to them, keeping her eyes on her wristpad as she jabbed at some arcane data stream.

"No change. Everything's clear."

"Right. Let's have a look then." Harlan approached the door while Jules and Nox flanked him—stunners held out and low. He tried the handle—locked, but old-school. No hackpatches then. Super. He took a minute with a pick tool to get the bolt to turn, metal squealing against metal, and Jules found herself sympathetic for the thieves of the past. How they got away with anything making all this racket, she'd never understand.

The door swung up, grinding out an alarm that had nothing to do with tech and everything to do with disrepair and rust. They froze as a unit, waiting…waiting. But no better alarms announced their entry, so Jules and Nox went in first, painting the walls with the light from the ends of their stunners.

Uneven tiles puckered up the floor, grit and garbage crunching under their boots with every step. Water damage darkened the walls in great swathes of mold, every surface stripped bare of furniture. A few hopeful steel beams marked the middle of the floor, illustrating the spot where a mag-pallet system might have been in use back in the ancient heyday of this facility. Otherwise: broken wall panels, half-hinged doors, cracked-open utility panels. Not a single light source in the whole place, unless any of the mold was secretly phosphorescent.

"Confirmed: shitpile," Nox said over the comms.

Jules clenched her jaw. "Looks like it's been abandoned awhile—perfect place to drop a cache for pickup later."

Nox snorted.

"We're not on top of the signal yet." She glanced at the tablet

Velcroed to her wristpad. "It's up ahead, to the right. Picking up anything, Lolla?"

The kid skulked in after them, squinting at her pad. "Nothing new. Power signature is coming from the left."

"Can't imagine what they'd be powering." Nox ground the broken husk of a lightrod under his heel. "Lights aren't even on."

"Let's not stick around long enough to find out." Harlan ducked under the door and slid it shut after them, dropping his pick tool into an oversized pocket. "Jules, point."

"On it."

The little blue light on her wristpad indicated the cache was forward and to the right. A half-rotted door was the next room's only defense, easily stepped over, opening into a room just as moldy as the first. She couldn't remember if she'd gotten her allergy shots already that year. Shit. A little itch prickled at the back of her nose and she snorted to stifle the urge. There was no way in the void she'd sneeze while she had a weapon in her hands. Nox would never let her hear the end of it if she did.

Another empty room—some rotted cardboard, a few broken injectors, and a scorch mark or two on the floor. Usual junkie squatter affair. Maybe her mom had been here.

Don't think about Mom.

"Clear," she said.

Nox crossed to a pile of rags and flipped them over with the toe of his boot, checking for anything valuable. A rat scurried out and disappeared through a crack in the wall.

"Maybe that rat stole our score."

"Shut up, Nox. It's not in this room, anyway. Next room."

"Always the next room," he muttered, but quietly enough that Jules figured he hadn't intended for her to hear, so she let it slide. He could be a big enough dick when he wanted to be—there was no use calling him out when he was trying to keep it to himself.

The next door sagged on its bottom hinge, the top long since broken or rusted away. The floor had a swoop in the grime, proof that someone had opened it recently. Jules tried not to get her hopes up. She peered around the crack, lighting up the inside with the flashlight on her stunner. Nothing new—the same junkie bullshit—but that didn't mean the place was empty. It was a small enough room. The locator might be pulsing bad data and the cache was in the next room over. These things got fuzzy on small scales.

She grabbed the handle and pushed the door open. The knob came off in her hand, the rotted wood surrounding it crunching away with all the resistance of wet paper. She sighed, threw the knob on the ground, and kicked the thing the rest of the way in.

Nothing. The room was clear, her little wristpad light winking up at her to tell her she was in the right spot. There wasn't even another door, or hallway, to follow.

"Tough luck," Harlan said.

"We should check out the other rooms, the ones Lolla was picking up energy from. Could be the tracker is fuzzed by the building."

"There's nothing here." Nox stood in the middle of the room and swung his arms out, spinning in a circle. "Nothing but dirt and rats. This place doesn't even have scrap metal left to strip out—look—the walls are coming down."

He struck the wall with the butt of his stunner, splitting an already deep crack even wider, and wiggled it around until a fistful of plaster fell out and crashed to the ground in a powdery heap. Light—soft, dim, and blue—spilled out of the hole in the wall.

"What the hell," Nox said.

Jules grinned. "I told you the cache was here."

She shoved Nox aside and shined her light into the hole. A space wide enough for two people to walk side by side extended down the length of the wall, turning sharply at the end to wrap back around toward the left side of the building—where the power was coming from. White LEDs covered with domes of frosted blue plex lit the wall from below, lining the path, but doing little to illuminate the space past waist height. She didn't need a lot of light to see the scrapes of a pallet jack in the dust on the ground, or the familiar black crates at the end of the hall.

"I see the crates," she said, trying to keep her voice even and cool.

"How the hell'd they get in there?" Nox said.

"Who cares? I know how we're getting in. Help me tear this crap out."

She reholstered her stunner and put both arms through the hole, prying away at the weak wall until she and Nox had cleared a space wide and tall enough for them to shimmy through. She'd worry about how to get the wraith crates out once they'd surveyed the hidden spaces.

Jules popped through first, sweeping the space with her light—no new info. Nox came behind her and covered their rear, but the hallway dead-ended in the direction away from the crates.

"Kid should go back," Nox said.

"I agree," Harlan said. "Sorry, Lolla, but we don't know what's in here."

"Please. You want me to walk right back out the way we came? If we're being watched, it's already too late. You need me."

"She's right. No arguments, Harlan. This is my op."

He sighed loud enough to kick up a puff of dust from the wall. "Fine. Let's make it quick."

Their footprints were the only ones disturbing the dust, so someone must have remote-piloted the wraith cache through the tunnels. Jules stood watch over the crates while Harlan dropped to one knee, flipping open the plastic latch. A row of vials as thick as her thumb lay encased in molded charcoal foam, their contents a silvery-grey liquid that shimmered as Harlan picked one up. He popped a tester strip into the valve top, and nodded as the paper turned green.

"Shipment's good."

"Let's pack it up and get out of here before they come back for it," Nox said. He dropped down alongside Harlan and helped him get the lid closed. "We don't want to be here when they come back."

"Don't think they ever left," Lolla said.

Jules's skin prickled at the haunted echo in the girl's tone. "What the hell does that mean?"

"Over here," Lolla called, voice bouncing down the hall.

She followed the kid's voice while Nox covered her rear, her stunner held out and ready—though the grip grew slick as her palms sweat. The kid hunched at the end of the hall, just around a turn, and someone else hunched down across from her. No—not someone. It was a someone, once, but now it was just a corpse. The mold-stink of the rooms before had covered most of the stench, but there was no hiding that sickly sweet reek of decay. The man—guessing by the stubble on his chin—had probably been there a day or two. His stomach had already blown and dropped its sludgy insides into a black puddle of rot.

"Get away from there," Jules said, shoving the sleeve of her jacket over her nose and mouth to keep from gagging.

"I don't recognize him," Lolla said. She hadn't gotten up yet. Just kept hunkering down across from the dead man—her feet carefully positioned to avoid the puddle—like they were having a normal conversation. "He's not from around here, or at least not part of any crew I know."

"Who the fuck cares where he's from?" Jules grabbed Lolla by the shoulder and jerked her to her feet, giving the kid a shake. "He's dead. Not like we're going to deliver the news to his next of kin. Let's get the hell out of here before we find out what made him dead, all right? We just want the score. Don't want murder."

"One of the runners?" Nox asked from down the hall.

"Yeah. I mean, he's got the clothes, but I don't recognize the face."

"Maybe the deal went bad."

"Maybe." Jules eyed the body, realizing she was doing the same damn creepy thing Lolla had been doing. She should know that man, should recognize him as one of the three she saw moving the cache of wraith. Wasn't any doubt in her mind he was one of them—they'd all been wearing those Velcro-strapped, army-green jackets with black knit hoods pulled up to cover their faces. But she couldn't tell which one, and that bothered some part of her she'd long since buried. Shouldn't you be able to recognize someone you'd seen after they died? Shouldn't she feel . . . sorry for him? Or something?

"Jules." Nox's voice held a warning, and she froze. "Step back."

Slowly, she slid her gaze around to regard the door at the end of the hall—a door that was suddenly brighter. Blue light seeped from around the frame, pulsing to a stuttered heartbeat.

"What the fuck is that," she hissed through clenched teeth.

"Think we found the generator." Nox brought his stunner level with the door's entry pad.

"Don't shoot it, you moron," Lolla snapped. "This...man has been here too long for us to know how he died."

"You think the door killed him?"

"I don't know!"

"Don't shout," Jules hissed, then felt ridiculous. Whispering so a door wouldn't hear her.

"Murderous door seems like a good thing to shoot."

"That's a stunner," Lolla pointed out. "What are you going to do, paralyze a door?"

"Fucking Harlan and his no-kill policy."

"What's going on down there?" Harlan shouted down the hall, footsteps echoing toward them.

"Mystery murder door. Stay put, or draw its fire. Who the hell knows," Jules shouted back.

"What?!"

"Guys. I've got an idea." Lolla's fingers crept, slowly, into her pack. The pulsing of the door light didn't change. "Hackpatch."

"Think that'll work?"

"It does, or it doesn't. Either way, we have to move eventually."

"Fair point. Prepare to scatter."

"Scatter to where, Miss This-Is-My-Op? It's a door. This is a hallway. We have no idea what the range on that thing is."

"Well, our corpsey friend has his head intact, so I'm guessing it won't hit high."

"You expect us to jump?"

Lolla tugged the silvery disc of a hackpatch out of her pack and flicked it like she was picking off a piece of lint. The sticker slapped against the door's entry pad, a perfect hit, its internal circuiting establishing a connection to the pad as it began to decode the entry mechanism. Pulses of coppery light flickered across the hackpatch's surface. Lolla used top-notch tech—the best she could buy, augmented by her own skills. Those things decrypted most entry systems in seconds. This was taking way too long.

The lights around the door flickered. A low hum of power building echoed in the hallway.

"Jump!"

"Seriously?"

Jules grabbed a rough ledge in the wall and yanked herself up, shoving with all her strength to get beyond whatever killing ray that door was building up. Lolla dropped down, throwing up her pack in defense—the thing was lined with a half dozen materials Jules didn't understand. It was a slick move. She might be all right. Light blasted the hallway, searing Jules's eyes with brilliance. She flinched, her arms shaking as she struggled to maintain her hold, fingers wobbling.

"It's open," Lolla said.

Jules dropped to the ground, narrowly missing the black pool of guts as she landed in a crouch. The door, indeed, had opened. The light that'd blinded her was just normal illumination, enhanced by the whiteness of the room beyond. The entry pad blinked a cheery green all clear.

"Oh," she said.

Nox had crammed himself like a spider suffering multiple joint dislocations into the place where the wall met the ceiling, legs quivering. Only by the grace of the tread on his boots against either wall was he stable. His whole body looked ready to collapse at any moment. "What?" he demanded.

Jules stifled a giggle and straightened, trying to look composed.

"Get down." She killed her stunner light and peeked through the door, scanning the large room beyond. Stainless steel tables dotted with medical equipment took up the bulk of the furniture. Test tubes and all the other accoutrements of laboratory work were the only decor in the room. No people, so far as she could see. Not even a resident AI to welcome them.

"There's some sort of lab here. Let's check it out."

Harlan appeared at the end of the hall with a crate of wraith in his hands. "Not what we're here for."

"My op. My rules." She flashed him a grin. "And besides, aren't you curious?"

Lolla on her heels, Jules stepped into the lab. The lights dimmed, then went out. Red LEDs lining the tops of the walls flickered—and the low, mounting wail of an alarm pierced the night.

CHAPTER 6

DAY TWO OF SURVIVAL

Bero flashed his schematics onto the medibay screen and gave her time to study him inside and out. He was all at once the strangest and loveliest ship she'd ever stepped foot on. She grinned, despite the shock deep in her bones, and surveyed all Bero offered.

Ten-year-old Sanda would have whooped for joy. A whole space-ship to herself. A first-rate, state-of-the-art vessel under her command. She'd dreamed of it as a girl. Played space pirates with her brother, Biran, between the cargo crates at their fathers' warehouses. Back then, her imagination had supplied her a crew. A starscape teeming with likely marks for her pirate brethren to swoop down on.

Wasn't much joy in it, now.

The Icarions had gone all out with this experiment. She wished they'd kept their interstellar fiddling to spaceships, not weapons, but there wasn't a thing she could do about that now. She forced herself to be grateful for Bero. Without him, there was no calculating the variety of ways she might have died.

A conical grid represented Bero's business end, a graphical nod to the massive electromagnetic scoop fronting the ship, slurping up hydrogen and everything else that got in Bero's way. Coils of magnets hunkered behind the scoop, bleeding heat to the void even as they munched on interstellar feed. Just behind them, a bulbous hiccup in the otherwise ramrod-straight body. The CNO reactor—turning all the tasties of space into gamma rays blowing out Bero's back end. The furnace heart of a star, thrusting Bero through space.

"They made the old ramjet model work," she said.

"It's always worked. It just wasn't efficient in light of the Casimir Gates."

True enough. Eight percent *c*, no matter how pretty the ship, wasn't anything worth mentioning when you had the gates ready to whisk you away to another star system in an hour, tops. The regs were tight and tariffs steep, and the fact that gates only opened between two systems made longer hauls a pain. Crossing all that intersolar space was still done the old way, with fusion rockets. But it was quick. It was safe. And no one had to worry about what society would look like after they'd spent a few hundred years crossing interstellar space.

But the Icarions had chafed under the leash the Primes held, bucked against the constraint of the Prime's gate placement. They'd wanted to traverse *all* of space, not just the systems the gates opened a door to. Sanda couldn't fault them for that. She could fault them for a whole hell of a lot else, though.

A safe distance behind the CNO reactor, she spotted the command deck, dwarfed compared to the rest of the ship's scale. Low-g there, then. With half her leg missing, she was almost looking forward to it. Two docking mouths sprouted from the cylindrical command module, and the spurs of mass elevators reached up to two habs, rotating around the command center. Tiny on paper, massive on a human scale. At least she'd have plenty of time to learn her way around.

"Which hab am I in?" she asked.

"Research level one, on habitat one." The corresponding spoke and hab lit up, outlined in yellow.

"Any bunks on this hab?"

"The whole ship is yours. May I suggest the captain's quarters?"

"Yes. Yes, you may."

IV wheels squeaking, she followed green LED strips Bero lit up at waist height, guiding her through Bero's straight corridors. All the doors were shut, Icarion's garish logo glaring at her from each. She stuck her tongue out at them. Bero was polite enough not to comment.

The captain's bunk was mercifully on this level, toward the back of the hab. The door dilated before her, the touchscreen alongside it black and blank. Right. No more need for locks on this ship.

Bero's captain had been appointed a twin bed, quite the luxury on a spaceship of any size. A grey coverlet wrapped the bed with military precision, Icarion-orange pillows dotting the head. She'd been awake an hour, and already she was sick of Icarion standard-issue.

Sanda fumbled her way through a shower, warm water revealing the jittery weakness in all her muscles. By the time she finished, it was all she could do to crawl to the bed and flop backward, leg sticking off the edge, her hair soaking a wet halo into the ugly sheets.

"Sanda?" Bero's voice was soft, concerned. She forced herself to rally enough to sit up.

"Still here, Bero. Just...tired."

That wasn't it, though, not really. At least, it wasn't the kind of tired that could be relieved with a nap or a caffeine dermal. While she'd been smearing NutriBath over half the ship, jabbing away at schematics and running roughshod calculations, her situation hadn't quite sunk in. But something about the domestic surroundings—the bed and the shower and the neat little dresser—brought home to her how alone she was.

She understood it, rationally. Understood that her evac pod had kept her preserved past what was reasonable. Understood that while she slept, metabolism slowed to a crawl and body encased in preservation foam, Icarion's self-labeled "dissent" had escalated into a full-blown war. Had wiped everything and everyone she'd ever known and loved clear off the map. Blown them into another reality, if there was such a thing.

Hot tears streaked her cheeks, leaving salt-crusted trails on her freshly scrubbed skin. She wiped at them, seeking to stem the onslaught of sorrow, but her body had a mind of its own. Sobs shook her.

A flicker of a thought—*I should have gone with them.*

Sanda crushed the thought, ground it beneath a mental heel. Biran would have thwacked her upside the head to know she'd considered it. She was the last of those who'd lived on Ada Prime. It was her job, her responsibility, to survive. To show the would-be Icarions of the universe that Prime was not beaten. To warn the remaining Primes and maybe, just maybe, be a voice of reason. If there was anyone left in all the black to listen. To warn against the dangers of distrust. Of Mutually Assured Destruction.

"Right," she said, and pulled herself into an awkward flamingo stance. "Right."

Bero didn't answer. Apparently he was comfortable enough with human company to realize when people were talking to themselves. Sanda braced herself with one hand against the bed as she tugged open a dresser drawer. She may be the only human left alive in light-years, but she wasn't alone. Not really.

She reached for a jumpsuit and slipped. The world tipped up and her chin cracked against the corner of the dresser. Novas burst in her eyes and her shoulder jarred as she slammed into the ground.

"Sanda?" Bero's voice ratcheted up with worry.

"Nothing broken. I'm okay." She stifled a groan as she flopped onto her back, tested her shoulder with careful prodding. Angry, but not dislocated. A trickle of blood snaked its way down her chin from a split lip. She flexed her jaw, testing its stability. Seemed all right. This one leg shit would take getting used to.

"May I offer assistance?" Bero asked.

She laughed. "You got arms I don't know about?"

"Not exactly. One moment, please."

"Bero?"

Damned ship didn't answer. With a sigh, she heaved herself half-upright and hefted herself onto the edge of the bed. A soft whir purred down the hall, and the door dilated. She craned her neck but couldn't see anything.

"Stop messing about." She rummaged in the drawer and grabbed the elusive jumpsuit. She stared. How in the hell was she supposed to get this thing on? Hadn't the Icarions ever heard of pants? Or, hell, a skirt would be convenient right about now.

Something squeaked by her foot. She glanced down and nearly jumped out of her skin. A tread-footed bot hunkered by the edge of the bed, its camera pointed right at her, its sonar panel eerily like eyes.

It extended a long arm straight up and opened the clamp at its end. It bore a startling resemblance to a crutch.

"Uh. Hello?"

Bero said, "This is Maintenance Bot VII. It can answer simple queries regarding its duties with a single beep for no and a double beep for yes. It transferred your evac pod encasement into the NutriBath."

"Huh. And where are maintenance bots one through six?"

"Assigned to other ships."

"Figures." Sanda squinted at the little bot. It looked sturdy enough. Those tank treads were made with some serious grip in mind, and its turtle-like shell had the dull, matte texture of heavy-duty metals.

"I can't call you Maintenance Bot VII. We'd make it all the way to Atrux before we finished a conversation. I'll call you . . . Grippy. Is that acceptable?"

Beep-beep.

"Nice to meet you, Grippy." She put her hand in its outstretched clamp and stood, wobbling. Grippy was a rock, subtly shifting to account for her center of balance as she wriggled her way into the Icarion jumpsuit. Ash grey and orange didn't suit her at all, but it was better than stumbling around naked for the next couple decades. Bero may have been an AI, but there was something to be said for basic human modesty.

"All right, Grippy. Let's get a look at the command deck, shall we? We've got numbers to crunch and trajectories to plot."

Grippy didn't beep; her statement hadn't been declarative enough to trip his yes/no routine, but he sensed her moving forward and trundled along at her side all the same. Despite her annoyance at having to rely on assistance at all, she found Grippy a much stabler partner than the squeaky IV stand.

Strength came back to her. It tunneled through her veins and swelled her will to survive, her urge to work the problem. Things were bad. But she had Bero, and Grippy, and her own little grey cells. She could figure this out. She'd live to see real human eyes again.

Two steps from the door, alarms blared. Great, ear-piercing whoops. Brilliant yellow LEDs sparked to life along the top of the walls, the natural-light simulators dimmed. The door swished shut, the touchscreen alongside it flashed red: CONTAINMENT.

"Bero?"

A tinny female voice, not Bero's, said, "Breach at airlock two. Breach at airlock two. Breach at airlock two..."

Sanda wanted to kick something but thought better of it before she took another tumble. Space was getting on her nerves.

CHAPTER 7

PRIME STANDARD YEAR 3541

THE BATTLE OF DRALEE ECHOES

Anaia led him, his mind in a haze, to her apartment. He didn't even register the steps, just a constant low buzzing in the back of his mind. Anaia may have been Lili's pet gossip, but she had never lied to him. Keeper Shun had never lied to him. Why would they? Why would either of them choose now to lie? There was no gain he could see. Shun had better intel. Anaia must be mistaken. It was the only logical conclusion.

She swung the door to her room open and ushered him inside. Anaia had the same furniture they all did—a single bed, dresser, desk—but it was difficult to find them all beneath the piles of tablets, charts, chips, and smartboards. Her window faced planetside, so that as the station and the planet Ada pirouetted around each other every twenty-six minutes she had a clear view of the average people of Prime. The citizens the Keepers protected.

The dwarf planet Ada swam past her window as he took a seat on the foot of her bed. A gridded mass of lights dotted the planet's surface. He wondered, guiltily, if his parents had made it back down to their home on the planet for the night, or if they were holed up somewhere in a shelter on the station. He glanced to his wristpad, but it was dark. Only emergency signals could get through for the next thirty-six hours.

"I could be wrong," Anaia blurted. She paced over to her desk and sat down with purpose, rummaging through a pile of tablets. "I mean, I'm not an expert or anything."

She toyed with the eye lens on the hobbyist telescope she kept pointed down at planet Ada. Things clicked into place in Biran's tired brain, his mouth went dry.

"What did you see?"

"Wavelengths. That's all. Just…pulses of information where there shouldn't be anything. I can't decode it. It might even be Icarion, I don't know. But there's something broadcasting out there, in the battle site. I'm sure of that."

Every muscle in Biran's body tensed. There shouldn't be anything there except rubble. Unless this was the supposed weapon Lavaux and the others worried about. "Show me."

She gripped a tablet decisively and woke it up, blue light painting shadows in the hollows of her cheeks. Biran pretended not to notice as she brought up a shell program to backdoor her way into one of the Prime satellites monitoring the space around Dralee. Anaia's hobbies were her own business, and now that they were officially Keepers, she should technically have access, anyway. Technically.

With a few deft flicks, she brought up the wavelength she'd been monitoring. She flipped the tablet around for him to see.

Biran's chest ached. His head swam.

Those coordinates. They were well inside the supposed rubble field, and something was definitely being broadcasted out. But it wasn't encoded—it just wasn't a signal carrying any variety of information Anaia was used to seeing.

"Varying 540 to 580 terahertz. That's not an info packet, Anaia."

"Then what is it?"

"Light," Biran said, unable to help the warble of hope shaking him to the core. "Green light."

"From the evac pod status displays?"

Biran shook his head, bewildered. "I can't think of any other source."

Keeper Shun had lied to him.

The next morning, Biran sat on the edge of his new bed, the sheets crisp from the laundry, and stared at the text message left unsent on his wristpad. The chip implant site on the back of his skull itched, though the medis assured him the sensation was only psychosomatic. They had done the procedure that morning, as simple as micro-chipping a pet. Just the whoosh of the implant gun, then the test to see if all the proper information was there.

It was. Lurking in the back of Biran's skull, that spidery piece of technology held the key to a small portion of the Casimir Gate's con-struction. He was, from this point on, an instrument of technology. A Keeper of humanity's future.

And yet the text blinked, waiting for him to hit send. A needle of a sentence, a seed. A crack in the veneer. A message that, once sent, forever revealed him to have doubt.

Doubt in his masters. Doubt in the organization he'd striven so long to join.

Anaia had checked the data, again and again. Green lights shone in the rubble of the Battle of Dralee. Evac pods winking back at Prime, asking to be picked up, to be sent to safety. His sister may be one of them. Even if she wasn't—his throat caught—the others deserved res-cue, not abandonment.

But for that to happen, he had to make waves. Had to let the senior Keepers know he'd uncovered their lie. For they had lied to him, though he barely believed it. Garcia, Lavaux, and Shun . . . Even Shun. She'd scoffed at Icarion hiding a planet-busting weapon in the rubble, but she had sat with false sympathy on her face and told him there was no hope: All the pods had been lost.

There was a slim chance the military was keeping the existence of the lights from the Keeper elders, but some dark part of Biran's heart knew that answer was too easy.

Biran didn't have the answers, but he could make them give them to him. First, he had to let someone else know. That person should have been Sanda.

He hit send on a group text message to his dads.

Biran: There are green lights in the rubble.
Graham: What?? Is this official?!

Biran: No. Bosses won't acknowledge.

Ilan: . . . Are you sure?

Biran: Have my own data.

Graham: Son . . . Data can be interpreted a lot of different ways. Have you talked to them?

Biran: I intend to. Right now.

Graham: Cool your heels first. It's fresh, and it hurts, I know . . .

Ilan: Why don't you come planetside for a while? We miss you. <3

Biran: I can't. I need to find out what this means. [deleted: I thought you'd understand.]

Graham: We want to know, too. We do.

Biran: [deleted: then why won't you . . .]

Ilan: The director will figure it out. Come home.

Graham: Ilan will cook you his terrible chili.

Ilan: My chili's famous! . . . But he's right. Take some leave. Come home.

Biran: I love you both.

He closed the channel before they could talk him off the ledge. It was only natural for them to second-guess his conviction. They trusted the system they lived in, and they hadn't seen the data he had. Hadn't lain awake at night asking themselves why the director hadn't found the same data, too. They were afraid he was about to make an ass of himself in front of his boss. Probably he was. But he had to try. Had to ask. Somewhere a computer would flag his conversation for HR to review. If he left it at that, he might get called in for counseling. Might even get sent down to his dads for that leave they wanted him to take.

But he wouldn't leave it at that.

He wore an old suit, the dark brown creases worn but holding on thanks to the talents of the local laundry. His new house had come with a whole new wardrobe—sharp and crisp—but he didn't want the seniors to think he was putting on airs.

At the threshold to his new home—his Keeper residence—his stomach finally bottomed out. His palms sweat. Nausea gripped him in icy hands, and for a moment he thought he'd have to run to the toilet. Biran flicked his gaze to a small collection of family items the decorating crew had nailed to his foyer wall, and zeroed in on one picture: Sanda, on the day they promoted her to captain of her gunship. Her grin wide, prideful. One arm slung, protectively, around Biran's shoulders. She'd always looked out for him. Made a career of it.

His turn.

The ride from his home to the Cannery passed in a blur, the litany of what he intended to say the only thought rolling through his head. Everything else was rote. Dropped off—say thank you to the drivers. Through the front door—greet the receptionist. Pass security—hellos exchanged.

And then he was standing before the director's desk, in the director's office—a mythical place, as far as it had concerned student him.

"Keeper Greeve." Director Jian Olver came around the desk to shake his hand and pull out a chair for him. "Our young rising star. What can I do for you? A drink?"

Biran had only seen the director from afar until this moment, but up close he was not surprised to note that the man had allowed his wrinkles to "come in," as the saying went, stamping his age around the corners of his eyes. He kept his steely hair cropped tight, a holdover from his days in the military. Biran dared to hope that his old allegiance may make him sympathetic to what Biran had to say.

"No, thank you." He waved off the offer of some dark gold liquor and sat straight, affecting more confidence than he felt. "I'm here to talk about Dralee."

A frown creased the old man's face—false concern, Biran guessed—as he took up his plush leather chair and scooted forward so that the desk was the only distance between them. "Military briefings are open to all Keepers every morning at 0600 sharp. Other than that, if you'd like to request grief counseling..."

It was the first time Biran had heard the word *grief* spoken so plainly. He swallowed back a sudden surge of thankfulness. Director Olver had always painted himself as a patriarchal figure—distant, but open to discussion. Biran knew full well that many of the students and junior Keepers availed themselves of his open-door policy, but Biran had never been one of those. He'd had his own fathers to seek counsel with. He had told himself he would only infringe upon the director's time if it were truly, truly important.

Now, he wished he'd had more practice talking to the director. Fear constricted his throat. The fabric of his wristpad dilated to allow the sweat pooling against his arm to evaporate. He rubbed his hands together, digging deep for strength. Sanda. This was for Sanda.

He forced himself to swipe up the right data set, and turned his wristpad for Director Olver to see. It'd taken hours for him to scrub the information so it couldn't be traced back to Anaia.

"Thank you, Director, but that's not why I'm here. I have discovered information that our people may not be getting from the military," he began, warily, watching the director to gauge his reaction. Nothing. Not even the twitch of an eyebrow. He'd locked himself down. "Over this spread of coordinates," he continued, though his throat grew drier with every word, "there is evidence of unnatural wavelengths in the vicinity. Faint, but present. Green lights, Director, from evac pods. At least six, that I can tell, but with more sensitive equipment—"

"Where did you get this?"

"My own observations, sir."

The director's eyes narrowed, and Biran drew his wristpad back, as if the director's scowl alone was enough to damage it.

"You don't understand what you're looking at. That data is corrupt."

"With all respect—"

"The data is corrupt. Our people have confirmed that there are no evac pods broadcasting in the rubble zone. Am I clear?"

Biran swallowed. "Yes, sir."

"Good." He leaned back in the chair with a sigh. "I know it's hard to accept, Keeper Greeve, but that field has been swept over by the best tech we've got. There's nothing out there, and if there is something broadcasting, it's Icarion trying to lure us in close for an ambush."

Biran nodded, reading between the lines: Our people are out there, but we're impotent to get to them and we don't want the populace to know.

"I understand, Director."

The director eyed him from beneath thick, neat brows and nodded to himself. "Is there anything else you need, Keeper?"

"No, sir."

The director pushed to his feet, and Biran mirrored him. A handshake, a pat on the back, all the usual platitudes, and he was out in the hall alone, reeling, but this time Anaia was nowhere near to lend him a shoulder. He was on his own. Just as Sanda, drifting through cold space in a coma, was on her own.

But she didn't have to be.

So Icarion might have a weapon. So what? Prime's were bigger. Her people stronger. Biran would not let his sister die in the vacuum of space because some old men were too scared to take a risk. He doubted the people of Prime would disagree with him.

He was prepared to stake his life on that.

CHAPTER 8

PRIME STANDARD YEAR 3771

TRYING TO SURVIVE DAY TWO

Bero!" She glared at the ceiling. "Turn that alarm off, for Christ's sake!"

The siren and the tinny voice silenced, but the lights stayed low and the LEDs made the whole ship look jaundiced.

"Please remain in quarters. The situation is being controlled," Bero said.

Sanda looked pointedly at the locked door, the bot holding her upright, and the speakers neatly hidden in the walls. "Who, exactly, is controlling the situation?"

"You cannot go out there," he snapped. Actually, full-on snapped at her. Sanda's jaw dropped open. Icarion wouldn't have programmed their precious AI for surliness, would they? But then, they were supposed to be emergent personalities, trained through life experience, just like regular infants. There was no telling how emotionally young Bero was. No telling what traveling the star system for a few hundred years with only Grippy here to talk to had done to his neural circuits.

She might very well be cruising around space on the equivalent of a toddler. A toddler that controlled the airlocks. Or worse, a teenager.

"Bero," she said his name gently, as if she were talking to a pouting child. "It's just us here. Let me help. What's gone wrong?"

The yellow lights pulsed. "Airlock two has failed to seal."

"It was open?"

"My sensors detect that the primary gasket has failed."

Sanda sucked her teeth. "How much atmosphere have we lost?"

"Negligible. My systems can recycle indefinitely, and what I cannot synthesize, I scrape from local space."

Right. The ramscoop. That was a nifty little piece of tech the Icarions had worked up. Too bad their heads had gotten too big, their reach too long and greedy. "Okay. So we've got a leak. Interior door or exterior?"

"Exterior."

"No problem. You keep that interior door clamped shut, and I'll shimmy down with a replacement gasket. Easy."

"There are no replacements on board this ship."

"*What?*"

Hesitation. "I am modeled as a cruiser, but I am primarily a research station. I was meant to stay in LPO around Icarion while my crew performed experiments. It was not foreseen that I could not dock with the nearest station to receive necessary repairs."

"But you were an experiment in interstellar ships. Surely they planned to take you on a long haul at some point."

"I was the first of my kind. I believe they intended to keep me in-system for evaluation."

"Shortsighted," she grumbled.

"Not the most shortsighted of Icarion's decisions."

She couldn't argue with that. Bero still hadn't brought the lights up, and the twilight creeped her out. It reminded her how close she was to the end of her own dawn. Focus on the problem. "What's on the 'lock, anyway? Vulcanized rubber?"

"Icarion utilizes a proprietary material in all its—"

"Yeah, yeah. So does Ada." *Did.* "But it's rubber, right?"

"Correct."

"I saw plenty of tubes in the medibay. Big, honking, thick things. If I slice them in half and glue them in with some SealFoam, it should hold."

"Inadvisable."

She pinched the bridge of her nose with two fingers. "Look, Bero.

I'm a gunship sergeant, right? Not one of your fancy researchers. I may not know the proprietary formula for your precious gasket rubber, but I shoot straight. I know what will work. I make—*made*—snap decisions for a living. It's what I *do*. Let me help."

"Inadvisable," said the stupid hunk of metal.

"You know what's inadvisable? Shooting across interstellar space at eight percent *c* with the damned door hanging open. I'm no prude, but I'd hate for you to run all over known space with your proverbial pants down. Know what kind of wobbles we could develop at those speeds? Any deflection could kill us both. And I'm guessing you've got more than one airlock, right?"

"Yes, but—"

"Bero. Listen. This has to be fixed, and I'm the monkey on this ship with opposable thumbs. What's the big deal, anyway? Why don't you want me doing this?"

"It's . . . It's *dangerous* out there."

Oh. Sanda may have just woken up to a barren, lifeless star system, but Bero'd been living in it as long as she'd been asleep. What would it have done to her, wandering the void, skimming pieces of destruction from two once proud and thriving civilizations hoping to pick up something that might still be breathing? Something that might say your name. It'd only been a day for her, but she wondered how Bero had felt hearing someone for the first time in 230 years. How he'd felt *talking* with someone. For a mind like his those few hundred years had to have felt like more than a lifetime. It had to have felt like aeons. No wonder he was afraid. He'd be insane not to be.

"I know," she said. "Humans weren't exactly built for space, were we? But here we are. We've engineered our way around our weak, fleshy bodies. This jumpsuit I'm wearing? It doubles as a pressure suit, and the collar here?" She ran a thumb over the ribbed neckline. "Locks right into a helmet, complete with HUD so you and I can stay connected. I bet there's even a radiation oversuit around here somewhere, and lifepacks. I trained for EVAs. It will be okay. Let me help?"

A pause.

"Okay," he said. "Okay."

She smiled, recognizing his echo of her earlier words. Things might take patience and some hard work, but they'd get along just fine. They'd have to, if they would ever make it to Atrux alive. She hoped that system was still inhabited by the time they got there.

The yellow lights winked out, and regular lighting came back online. She leaned on Grippy, borrowed strength from his servos. The door dilated, red LED arrows guiding the way along the hall floor.

"Radiation suits, helmets, and lifepacks can be found in each cabin's closet, and extras are in the closet near the ladder to the command deck." Bero's voice had its confidence back, now that he was treading familiar territory.

"On it," she said, steering Grippy around to reach the closet. Lucky for her, Icarion suits used the same FitFlex tech Ada's did. One size fits all in space. The cost reduction from only having to create one template far outweighed the cost of the increased tech. "Are we under thrust?"

"No. I stopped accelerating to scoop your pod. We're in orbit around Dralee."

"Anything nasty in the local atmosphere?" She shrugged into the radiation suit and clicked the helmet into place. The HUD lit up, Bero spooling her information from her lifepack and vital sensors.

"Negative. We are shadowside from Cronus, radiation levels are within acceptable minimums."

With Grippy's help, she gathered up an armful of intubation materials from the medibay and split them neatly down the center with a pilfered scalpel. Wasn't a sanitary use of the equipment, but she figured if she were ever in bodily need of a scalpel, then things had gone so far wrong that sanitary didn't much matter anymore.

She shoved a can of SealFoam into a belt pocket and hooked the tubes to a strap under her arm. Leaning on Grippy, she made it down the hallway like some sort of avenging octopus. Grippy let Sanda go, and she eased over the hatch, settling herself onto the ladder with care. The empty calf of her Icarion suit flopped below her, dragging on the rungs. By the time she made it to the bottom, she was grateful for the low-g environment. Now that she was floating free, she took a moment to fold up her loose suit leg and GripTape it in place. Good enough.

Handholds were anchored to the nominal ceiling of Bero's command deck. A massive smartscreen dominated the forward bulkhead, a handful of chairs with five-point harnesses facing it. All was dark, save yellow lights gleaming around the flawed 'lock. She forced herself to look away from that ghost town of a deck, to ignore the empty seats where once a thriving crew must have sat. She had a problem to solve.

She grabbed a handhold and pulled herself toward the 'lock. A touchscreen expecting a palm print stared back at her, but Bero overrode the required security check. Handy, making buddies with the ship itself.

The door unsealed, swung outward. No dilating doors on airlocks—too many points of failure. And then she was staring down open space. The HUD shading her eyes flickered, a glimpse of something white and sharp drifting off into the distance erased by onyx. She shook her head to clear it. Probably just dust burning up, or some artifact of the display filtering ultraviolet light. The equipment was old, but they rated these things for decades of regular use.

She hooked herself into a tether and drifted forward. The exterior door hung open, its hinges still intact. They'd been lucky that Bero wasn't under thrust when the gasket failed.

Three large tears marred the rubber of one of the inset gaskets, spaced apart as if someone had dug their nails into it and ripped. She ran her hands along it, feeling out how securely the rest was still attached. The edges were ragged, the rubber brittle against her gloved hands. A few hundred years of outgassing and even proprietary rubbers failed.

"Sanda?" Bero's voice filled her helmet.

"Everything's fine. It's just a few tears in one gasket. I'm removing it now."

She unzipped a pry tool from her belt and worked the failed gasket free, then clipped it against her suit for later study. The sliced-up tubes were a rough fit, and it took a generous dousing of SealFoam to make them stick. By the time she finished, her arms shook and sweat dripped into her eyes. She'd forgotten to pull the blasted sweat band across her forehead. Stupid move, that. Something as simple as a few drops of sweat getting stuck up your nose and around your mouth could mean a slow, drowning death in low-g. This job was quick enough. The next one might not be.

She finished up the fix and paused, staring out across space.

It used to calm her. Maybe even thrill her, a little. All that emptiness stretched out between planets, between stars. All that ever-expanding blackness, and her people, the Primes, held the key to punching through it. To threading a needle from one point to another and thumbing your nose at Einsteinian relativity. He'd allowed for wormholes, but even the old crazy-haired boy hadn't dreamed of travel as efficient as the Primes had made it.

Now, that space threatened her. Enclosed her. As a kid, she'd read a lot of adventure books. Ones with people stranded on some lonely planet. They'd excited her. Made her dream of how she'd go about surviving in the same circumstance. She wished such situations were only properties of fiction.

Despite the gates, it happened sometimes. People ferried around within star systems on fusion rockets, and those could run out of fuel. But you were never too far from a rescue. Not really.

Dralee, in orbit around its rocky planet Belai, had been the farthest edge of Prime-controlled space when she'd been out patrolling the stars. There'd been a military tug-of-war over the moons around Kalcus, but as it was closer to the sun—and thereby closer to Icarion—Ada had done little aside from slapping Icarion's hand. Dralee, technically, was the farthest she'd ever been from home.

Sanda marked the stars, lined them up in her mental map, spun it around, and looked toward Ada Prime. She'd always had a hard time getting her head around the vastness of the star system, but she could read a map faster than she could swing a wrench, and stars didn't drift much. What felt like a vast timeline for her was little more than a blip on the cosmic scale. Even over a couple hundred years, their relationship to each other looked remarkably the same.

There used to be two spheres of light out there, visible even from this distance. The gate, and the dwarf planet Ada, forever pirouetting around each other on the farthest edge of the star system. Her visor adjusted, filtered harsh light, and fed her back little more than a dim smudge of white where her home should be. Rubble, probably.

Maybe it'd coalesce into a new planet someday. She'd never see it, but she hoped her descendants might. If Biran had escaped, she might already have descendants.

That was the problem with space once you took the Casimir Gates out of play. Scales got too long for human lives.

She pulled herself back inside, shut the door on all that emptiness, and filled in all the seams of the door with SealFoam, just in case. No one'd be using that airlock again. Didn't really need two, anyway, with only one passenger aboard.

Once she was back on the command deck, Bero cycled the lock. It would hold, for now.

"Light up the screen, Bero." Sanda popped her helmet off and pulled herself toward the captain's seat. It was on the large side, but the harness adjusted itself to her frame.

The smartscreen flashed to brilliant life, numbers flickering at its edges, simulations of the local neighborhood drawing orbital lines. A litany of *you are here* and *this is there* streamed before her. She shook herself. She had to chase off the melancholy that'd settled in her bones looking at Ada Prime. Had to focus.

"Seventy-five years to Atrux. We can do this, Bero. You got the power, and I've got the maintenance skills. But for me to survive hopping in and out of stasis, we need to refit my evac pod, or scavenge a new one."

"There is a rubble field, left over from a skirmish, on the way. Useful parts may be available, and I can reach it within twenty days."

Useful parts. Right. Evac pods with bodies long since mummified, drifting in decaying orbits, or pods that never got the chance to encase their human passengers. She'd heard stories of people misfitting their pods, of shifting their seats the wrong way and getting cut in two when the pod deployed. Heard stories of medis popping open pods only to find an arm within, nothing more. The worst of it was, those misfired pods would be the least depleted, and have the most materials leftover for her to use. If she were very lucky, she might find someone still alive. Like her. She couldn't be the only one, could she?

"Set course, then. Will that put us in a good position for a grav assist around Kalcus?"

Hesitation. "Yes."

"But?"

"Once I initiate the gravity assist trajectory, I will quickly reach speeds at which my ramscoop will take over, and—"

"And no more scavenging."

"Correct."

She swallowed. "Well, all right then. I'll just have to make sure I find everything I need before we slingshot out of this system. How are food stores?"

"I am made for carbon synthesis, and the pods should provide you with ample nutrition while in coldsleep."

Ugh. She'd had her fair share of carbon synthesized nutriblocks, and they were always nasty, bland little bricks or dollops of sludge. But it'd keep her alive once she was going in and out of the pod for repairs. That was all she could hope for.

She unstrapped and pushed toward the handholds in the ceiling. "Steer us true, Bero. I'll go have a look around those labs of yours."

"Why?" Bero's voice tightened, worried.

"Easy, old man." She grinned and kicked, flopping the rolled-up leg of her jumpsuit around. "I'm going to go see about a leg."

"My facilities are not set up for biomechanics."

"Maybe not, but I got a whole lot of rubber, metal tubing, and time."

And maybe, just maybe, if she kept her hands busy, she could chase that smudge of greyish light where Ada used to be from her mind.

She swung herself onto the ladder and started up, regretting every bit of gravity that dragged her down. Muscle mass was so overrated.

CHAPTER 9

PRIME STANDARD YEAR 3541

TWO DAYS AFTER DRALEE

For security reasons, every Keeper had access to the emergency systems on Keep Station. This was so that, if something were to go wrong, they could override any part of the station—to contain a kidnapping attempt, or to thwart a terrorist effort. Biran doubted that, after today, he'd get to keep those privileges. He only had one shot. And he had to make it count.

He sat at his new kitchen table, his arm propped up so that the camera on his wristpad would frame his face against the family pictures hanging in his foyer. Public outreach 101. He wondered if they'd regret teaching him such tactics. Probably, but he didn't care.

Hidden from public view, behind his arm, a slender black ribbon snaked across the torn remains of brown wrapping paper. The package had arrived that morning, deposited through the slot in his front door by an automated bot that did not know the weight of the slim bundle it carried. The handwritten address had shaken Biran to the core, the familiarity of the letters reaching out to slap him across the face.

To: Keeper Biran Aventure Greeve
Ada, Keep Station, Keeper Residences
[I know you're there by now :P]

Inside, a simple black-covered paper notebook. The thing was so old-fashioned as to be retro-chic, its unlined pages containing a slim piece of paper with Sanda's hasty scrawl: *Sorry I couldn't be there in person. Someone has to protect the universe. Love you, Little B. Happy Graduation!*

The book weighed down his inner jacket pocket. Biran took a drink of water and stared at his reflection in the wristpad's screen. His mirror image was not him. It appeared so still, so calm. It didn't display the tremble in his fingers, the stirring of his belly as every ounce of his body screamed at him to stop this. To call it all off and find another way—a way that wouldn't get him into trouble.

He'd tried that way. Tried to go talk to Director Olver, even though the same fear shaking him now had wracked him then. The fear shouting at him was a liar, brain and body chemistry gone off the rails. The calm man in the mirror wasn't him, might never be him, but he needed to become him, at least for a little while. Needed to pretend he could be brave. A notification blinked in the bottom right corner of his screen—incoming messages from Graham and Ilan. They were worried. They had every right to be.

Biran entered the override codes and watched his face appear, screen-in-screen, on every wristpad on the station. EMERGENCY BROADCAST spooled below his face in bright red letters, on constant repeat.

"People of Ada Prime," he began, speaking slowly and lower than his normal voice so he'd sound confident. Prickles rose across the back of his neck as the phantom eyes of thousands turned to watch him.

"I am Keeper Biran Aventure Greeve. My sister, Sanda Maram Greeve, is the captain of *Gunship-SM178*. One of the lost ships in the Battle of Dralee. Every ear on this station—on planet Ada—has heard the reports coming in.

"The battle was a total loss. The gunships were taken unexpectedly, and unawares. They fought bravely. They died bravely."

He closed his eyes, breathed deep to rally himself.

"This message is not about me, people of Prime. It is not about my sister. It is not about loss or bravery. It is about information, as such things always are. Good information, and bad information. And you. All of you."

Outside, tires crunched gravel faster than the speed limit. Biran kept his voice level. Channeled that calm reflection of himself. They would not rush him.

"The ships of Dralee were lost, but the people may yet be saved." He flicked a symbol on his wristpad, switching over from camera mode to content broadcast, and spooled up the wavelengths and their coordinates. "This is light," he said, spinning the view. "Green light. Transmitting from the general location of the battle's rubble field. Their beacons may be silenced, but their evac pods are flashing green."

Shouts outside his front door. Footsteps pounding up the flagstone pathway. He switched back to camera view.

"I have gone to my superiors. They have told me I am mistaken, that no such light emanates from the rubble. I will leave you, the people of Prime, to decide what you see in those wavelengths. To decide what actions our superiors should take. You have the information. You have the power to act, just as I have done now. I will not tell you that there is no risk. That all we have to do is cry out for Prime to send a few ships and all will be well. This world, this universe, is more complicated than that, though I wish it could be otherwise. But that complexity should not mean that no action is preferable by default."

His house AI beeped a warning. Biran clenched his fists.

"They are the heroes of the Battle of Dralee. Let us not, by our inaction, make them martyrs."

The front door burst inward, all his security systems overridden in an instant. Two Keeper guardcore, their faces hidden behind black-tinted helmets, entered first. Their armor wiped all trace of identity from their bodies, standardized them in such a way they couldn't be told apart. These might be people he'd met before, people who'd guarded his back while he was in the director's good graces. Now, it took a moment for Biran to recognize the stunners pointed at him— he'd never been near violence in his life—fizzling with building electricity. He held his hands up but kept his forearm rotated so that the camera would see—so that the people would see—whatever happened next.

"I'm not armed."

Keeper Hitton entered between the two guardcore, a dour smile on her face. "I presume restraint will not be necessary?"

"Of course not. We're all peers here."

Her gaze flicked to the camera pointed at her and the bright red square indicating it was recording. All humor wiped from her face. "Cut that feed."

A guardcore grabbed his wrist, covering the camera lens with the palm of their hand, and turned off the broadcast mode. Biran was alone.

Hitton's smile twisted, sucked downward by the gravity of her anger. "Guards, please control Keeper Greeve. We wouldn't want him to harm himself."

CHAPTER 10

PRIME STANDARD YEAR 3541

IN A SYSTEM FAR, FAR AWAY

I told you this wasn't what we're here for!" Harlan shouted above the drone of an AI announcing, "Unauthorized entry, unauthorized entry…"

"There's a pallet jack here. Nox, cover us—Harlan, help me load her up."

"We need to bail," Harlan insisted.

"Look." Jules thrust a finger toward the other end of the lab. "I don't know what's going on here, but I don't see any boots on the ground aside from ours, and there's a cargo load-out at the other end of this room. Lolla, go hackpatch that if it's needed."

"On it." She darted across the white space, shoulder bag slapping the backs of her thighs.

"Jules," Harlan ground out the word. She crossed to him, put her face so close her breath tickled the wiry whiskers on his chin.

"*Harlan.* My op. My call. Now move."

He stared her down, but only for a count of three. Jules's heart hammered out every single second. Yeah, it was her op, but she'd never gotten in Harlan's face like this before. Not since the day he'd taken her in and she'd gotten slapped senseless for complaining about the stink in her bedroll.

But she was older now, and bigger too. And this really was her op. He'd promised.

Harlan moved. He hustled toward the crates and slung one up onto either shoulder like they were nothing, moving faster than she'd seen him move in years, showing off his strength. His power. Proving to her, with his body, that even though she was calling the shots it was only because he had allowed her to do so.

He gave something away in that posturing. Because if he was really secure, if he was confident, she would always bend to his will, then he wouldn't have bothered with the show. Harlan was scared. Of her.

It was about time.

She swung around and grabbed the pallet jack, wheeling it to meet Harlan halfway while Nox covered their backs, stunner out. How long had it been? Thirty seconds? Forty? How were the response times in this neighborhood? Shit, she should have looked into that when she was planning the op, but she'd figured it'd be a simple smash-and-grab. Hadn't occurred to her they'd encounter murderous doors and some kind of slick lab. The edge of the Grotta was a part of town known more for its body count than its police response times. Even if the lab had private security, the response would be slow. There weren't security firms anywhere near here. Ten minutes, probably. She started an internal timer as she helped Harlan lug crates onto the jack.

"How's that door coming, Lolla?" Jules asked over the comm, unwilling to shout above the persistent drone of the security AI.

"On it."

"Not a descriptive girl," Nox said.

"Let her work."

Jules heaved the last crate onto the jack and flipped a securing strap over the whole pile, wrenching it into place with a short jerk. Harlan took the jack handle from her and wheeled it around while she brushed sweaty hair from her eyes and unslung her own stunner. Eight minutes, give or take a few seconds. It was hard to keep a steady count while her heart was pounding fast enough to escape orbit, but she'd had a lot of practice. She could set a timer on her wristpad, but she'd learned long ago that technology couldn't always be relied upon. Some things you just had to do, not have done. She credited that attitude with her survival thus far.

"Place is empty," Nox said, cutting through her thoughts, but not her count. That kept ticking away.

"So?"

"Doesn't it strike you as strange?"

"Strikes me as lucky."

Harlan got the jack wheeled around to the door and they clumped up there, forming a protective semicircle around Lolla as she worked the lock. Jules cut her a glance, saw that the light on the hackpatch had gone yellow—bad sign. But the kid jabbed away between it and her wristpad, eyes narrowed in extreme focus. Jules knew better than to bother her while she was working.

"Don't like luck," Nox grumbled.

"Neither do I, but here we are." The red lights pulsed away, glaring down at the intruders while the voice kept on announcing their unwanted presence. She wished her earbuds were better at canceling environmental noise, but she'd cheaped out on them. Six minutes, now, and the kid didn't show any sign of being done in the next few seconds.

"Time, Lolla?"

"Three minutes."

"Watch the score," Jules said to Nox, whose eyebrows jumped up under the brim of his hood.

"Where the fuck are you going?"

"There's no *one* here, but there might be some*thing* here. Get me?"

Nox's weathered face fractured into a crag of a grin. "A bonus score? This place might not be such a cock-up after all. Hurry."

"Bad idea," Harlan started, but Jules shot him a look.

"Will take me two minutes. Second she has that door open, move out."

"Understood."

Jules dropped her stunner into a ready hold at her hip and ducked back toward the other side of the lab. Shiny white tile bounced red light back at her, the place remarkably clean for being hidden behind the walls of the moldering heap they'd originally broken into. Stainless steel lab tables broke up the room, and a quick check told her that all the cabinets inset in the walls were locked—keyed to fingerprints. Cheap tech, easy to break if they had the time, but she really didn't. She was on the lookout for a quick bonus, not a whole new score.

Velcro stripes marred the shiny tables and walls, hinting that the tablets whoever worked here used were hidden in those locked drawers. Shit. Might have been saleable info on those tablets—or at least they could have wiped them and sold the hard tech itself.

Who worked here? Jules had never held down a normal job in her life, but she was pretty sure this place should have been staffed about this time of night. Research facilities this kitted out didn't skimp on the staff. Of course, some of that staff might be dead in the hallway, and labs on the up-and-up didn't hide themselves away in the walls of rotted-out warehouses on the edge of the Grotta. Something was off here. Something shady.

She knew what came with that territory. Drugs or illegal software— maybe even hacking hardware. Whoever was working here was making something good. Something she could use—or sell. The wraith cache was a solid score, but this could pull some serious credits.

At the end of a row of built-in cabinets was a door. She glanced over her shoulder, saw Lolla still hard at work, and tested the handle. Unlocked. With her stunner out and ready to fire, she swung the door open slowly, letting the mixed red-and-white light of the lab illuminate the dark room beyond.

Sensors kicked in and brought up a faint yellow light from the ceiling. The room, about half the size of the lab, hadn't been stowed away as neatly as the first room. Two stainless lab tables dotted the floor, with a polished white desk at the opposite end—cluttered with handheld smartboards, scribbled over with erasable marker. The whole wall to Jules's left had been made of smartboard, too, its surface cluttered with diagrams and figures she didn't understand. She got up close to the writing, squinting at it as if she could stare it into making sense. Some of the schematic drawings tickled her memory—square, geometric mazes. Like microchips, but she didn't know what the hell she was looking at. She took a few quick pics with her wristpad. She'd figure out what that was about later.

"Jules." Harlan's voice, cold and distant, in her earpiece. "One minute."

"Heard," she responded, biting her lip. This room was packed with stuff—if only she had more time, she could sort out what was worth nabbing.

The mini smartboards could catch some coin, she knew that much. She sprinted to the desk and bundled the three boards up in one arm, cramming them into her pack. On a shelf set in the wall behind the desk, a glass cylinder rested dead center, placed so carefully that someone had given it pride of place. Jules picked it up and squinted at the contents—a clear fluid with a mercurial flash, visible only when she turned it just so in the light. Didn't look like any drug she'd ever seen—but then, she'd never seen the source mix of wraith, only the diluted stuff. Maybe this was the mother fluid. Weird it wasn't locked up.

"Where is everyone?" she said half to herself, turning the vial over in the light.

"I'm right here," a soft voice said. The same voice as the AI, a whisper against her ear, bleeding through the earpiece that only her crew should be able to access.

Jules jumped and cracked the vial against the top of the shelf, glass splinters biting into her fingertips as the liquid splashed across her hands. Silver mingled with blood and she swore.

Liquid smeared her palms and bloodied fingers, flashing almost white for a fraction of a second and then—gone. Must have evaporated; wraith was volatile in the open air. She wiped her palm off on her pants for good measure and turned around, scoping the room with her stunner out. No one was here. Must have been her imagination. Damn, but she would be high once that wraith mother kicked in. She had a decent tolerance, but this was the raw stuff. Potent as all get-out.

Even the bit left in the vial was probably valuable. She yanked some SealFoam from her pack and covered the broken vial up as best she could, pressing down to make sure it wouldn't leak.

"Door's open," Nox said over the comm. "Let's roll."

"Coming," she said, and sprinted out of the room after them. Lolla had the lockpad flashing green, the metal roll door sliding up as she approached. Not wanting the mother vial to drip in her pack, she clicked up a lid on one crate while Harlan wasn't looking and slipped the vial inside. Lolla caught her at it and raised a brow but seemed to accept Jules's wink in response. Good. The kid was on her side. They sprinted out the open door into the rain-slick night. No security in sight, no police lights breaking up the darkness.

She'd done it. She'd gotten the score, picked up some bonuses, and now it was time to celebrate. Might as well, she could already feel the euphoria of the wraith kicking in.

CHAPTER 11

NOT EVERYONE SURVIVES DAY TWO

The lights came up in hab 1's research lab and stopped Sanda cold. Bero had told her that his purpose was as a scientific station, and that was evident enough. Equipment she only vaguely recalled the names of from long-forgotten academy courses dotted the room—mass spec, gastrometer. Implements of surgery extended from the ceiling over a suspicious-looking table, shiny steel on articulated arms.

File cabinets lined the wall to her left, supply bins the wall to her right, the center of the room taken up by workstations left in various states of use. Unlike the medibay, Bero's usual crew hadn't bothered to pack away their resources. They must have planned on returning, never knowing their people's own discoveries would spell their end.

Biometric research, Bero had said. Sanda hadn't really gotten what he meant. Had figured on HUDs and smartbands, evac pods and the like. Something she could use, maybe, to extend her life on the long trip to Atrux. She hadn't expected to see the back of a Prime's head, splayed open behind resin, a Keeper chip winking at her with a sharp green LED.

"Is that...?" She crept forward. The head held a place of honor in the center of the lab, a pillar of clear plex lifting it up to eye height. Museum lights illuminated it in a soft, tasteful glow. Preservation fluid filled the pillar, casting a bluish tint to the flesh. The skin on the back of the man's head had been split, unzipped, held out in grotesque wings by wireframe. His brain stem was exposed, the Keeper chip embedded within it, graphene-filament electrodes piercing and melding with grey neurons.

Charcoal hair floated in the fluid, raised but perfectly still, as if the man were forever stuck in fright.

"Bero, is this real?"

"Yes."

Dios. Trembling so that Grippy rattled where he held her arm, she circled the pillar. Looked into the dead man's pale hazel eyes. She hadn't known him. She expected to feel relief wash over her, but instead she choked on a nervous laugh.

"Who was he?"

"Rayson Kenwick, Prime Keeper, aged seventy-three. No known family."

"Did . . . Did they kill him?"

Hesitation. "Yes. They apprehended him in a raid on Base Ansail. Interrogation techniques proved deadly."

They tortured him to death. She stared at those pale, watered-coffee eyes. They had pinned his lids open, twin butterflies of flesh, the lashes insectile. She didn't need to ask why they'd done this. They wanted him to image his password. To think the series of words or images that would cause his brain to light up an MRI in just the right way to trigger his Keeper chip to release its information. Information used to build the Casimir Gates.

She circled him, committing every detail to memory. Biran's brain stem would look just like this, if he'd passed his final Keeper exams before Icarion had initiated the Protocol. A little lump of flesh at the base of his neck would be the only change in his appearance, but the chip would lurk beneath, carrying the secrets of their people, tied to a password only the unique signature of his neurons could unlock. Or part of the secrets, anyway. Keepers came in fifths, the schematics of the gates divided between them, ready to be downloaded to the bots that would build the structure and then self-destruct.

Redundancy was the Prime's philosophy, and so there would be at least five of each copy at every Prime settlement. Sanda wondered if this man, this Keeper Kenwick, had been the man her brother replaced.

"Didn't they know killing him made the chip useless?" Anger ratcheted her voice. She didn't care. "Didn't they know his death would get them nothing, that it'd be pointless?"

"I cannot speak to the motives of his murderers."

"What about the motives of your researchers then? What the *fuck* were they thinking, keeping his head in this freakshow aquarium? This . . . This man deserved burial. Cremation. Anything but this!"

"They were tasked with reverse engineering the technology. I do not believe they gave any thought to the wishes of the deceased."

"Really. They were thinking only about the tech?" She stalked toward a lab table, Grippy's motors whirring to keep up, and snatched up a tablet Velcroed to the tabletop. She snarled and threw it across the room. Satisfying plastic fragments sprayed in all directions. "And how were they going to do that, with the chip in *there*?"

"That is a facsimile."

"Looks pretty fucking real to me."

"The head is real, the chip is elsewhere."

Nausea swept her. She gagged on empty air. "They stuck a mock-up in his head for—for what? A mascot? These people were *sick*."

"Yes," Bero said, very quietly.

She braced herself on the table, Grippy suddenly inadequate. She knew Icarion had been desperate to reverse engineer the gates. Knew they'd built a weapon to force Ada Prime's hand. But this . . .

"Drain the pillar," she ordered.

"That is not advisable. The specimen will decompose."

"The *corpse will rot*, Bero. That's what this is. A dead body. Death. Human decay. Messy, fleshy *rot*. Drain the pillar. I'm going to give Kenwick what Icarion took from him."

"His life cannot be re—"

"Not. That. A funeral. A proper one."

"My research indicates that funerals are for the mental and emotional well-being of the deceased's loved ones. We have a great deal to do, Sanda. There is no time."

"There's time enough for this."

"The chances of this man's descendants ever being made aware—"

"This isn't about telling the family a nice story if I ever come across them!" The strength of her shout echoed against the lab's walls. She closed her eyes. "This whole star system is a graveyard. I can't do anything about that. But I can do this. Help me do this."

A soft whirring sounded in the floor of the lab, a subtle series of clicks. The fluid drained, flushed out through a vent in the floor. The head shivered, pushed by unseen currents, but remained stationary.

It would take a while for that fluid to drain. Unable to watch, she stepped away, dragging Grippy along with her, and grabbed another tablet from the table nearest her. Her first instinct was to throw it, to shatter it like the previous, but she took a breath. Tried to steady herself. Breaking useful materials wouldn't help.

"Sanda," Bero said, his voice a warning.

"I need to know."

The tablet flicked on at her touch, Icarion's flame-orange logo filling the screen. She swiped it away, and friendly black letters read: *Welcome, Dr. Pilar Seco*, with a profile image of said Icarion scientist hovering in the corner. She had long brown hair, a white lab coat, and friendly, hazel-green eyes that scrunched when she smiled. Hard to believe eyes like that could flay a human head and keep it on display.

Sanda tapped continue and the screen filled up with icons. No concern for passwords on this ship, then. That suited her just fine. She found an icon labeled TESTINGNOTES and pressed it. Text filled the screen.

Third month of testing, day six.

Kenwick has been, as expected, resistant to our requests to image his password. Even throughout advanced interrogation, he falls back onto his cover story that he is not a Keeper. That the chip in his head—so obviously a Keeper chip!—is some other type of memory bank. Which, of course it is, but he insists it has nothing to do with building the gates.

Even so, all his talk of memory has intrigued Dr. Crannic. His specialty being memory recall, he seeks any opportunity to insert his research into his current project. Annoying and pompous, but in this case useful.

He has devised a way to roll back the Keeper's memories by approximately thirty minutes. It's a rudimentary thing, but it makes our questioning more efficient, as we can retry question trees without the contamination of Kenwick's previous experience.

Third month of testing, day twenty-three.

Kenwick has become a liability. Crannic doesn't want to admit it, but his memory rollbacks have been too much. Kenwick's head is constantly aching, and he now claims to be a survivor of the Imm Project! Ridiculous. He babbles half the night, and becomes deeply unsettled when confronted with things he experienced during the memory rollbacks. Which is quite a lot, as we did not limit his environment during first testing.

To make matters worse, the damage is mounting. To avoid the discomfort he experiences when confronted with these things, he simply ignores their existence. As I questioned him before the first rollback, I could stand in front of him, screaming, and he'd look right past me. The Light believes that, with some adjustments, these techniques will prove more fruitful next time around.

Crannic is a fool. I pray the next subject will prove more robust.

Sanda flicked the tablet off and set it down, fighting back the thrust of a headache. There was no point in going through those files, they'd just sicken her. Whatever had been done to poor Kenwick was over now, the perpetrators long since gone to dust.

When the fluid finished draining, she could see fine filaments reaching from the grotesque trophy to the walls of the pillar, holding it in place.

"How do I open it?" she asked.

"Just a moment."

One side of the pillar squealed, shuddered, then retracted slowly into the ground. It stopped when the top of it was just below Kenwick's remains. His hair plastered around his head, the flesh flaps the researchers had opened to display their nightmare token dangled and swayed. She rummaged through the lab's supply bins until she found nitrile gloves and a beaker large enough to contain the head.

With Grippy's help, she fumbled the head into the beaker. The flesh dented beneath the press of her fingers; the eyes took on a cloudy sheen. She pulled the pins from the lids and brushed them shut, then tossed the cruel instruments into the pillar's empty center.

"Rest well, Rayson Kenwick." She capped the beaker, tucked it beneath her arm, and headed for the command deck.

Bero was under thrust, gunning for the debris field they'd marked as likely for salvage, so an EVA was out of the question. Sanda placed the beaker in the good airlock and, on a whim, pulled a marker from her jumpsuit and sketched a quick bouquet of flowers on the side of the beaker. It'd have to do.

She retreated into the safety of the command deck and shut the interior 'lock door. He drifted in there, on the other side of the tiny viewport, his cheeks and nose pressed up tight against the glass. Wasn't a dignified experience by any stretch of the imagination, but it was a lot better than spending eternity as a gruesome trophy.

Sanda pressed her palm against the viewport. She should say something. Some words of farewell, of remembrance. Something warming and comforting for the deceased, though he could not hear her. He had been a Keeper, a bastion of her society. His had been the only human face she'd seen—would see—for hundreds of years.

She'd never been one for religion.

"You deserved better."

She slapped the button for the exterior door. It whooshed open, delivering Rayson Kenwick into space for his final rest. Using the wall and ceiling grips, she pulled herself across the command deck and back to the ladder, regretting the g's as they pulled her back down, anchored her to her body's new reality.

Sanda set her lips in a grim line as she climbed up the ladder. The last thing she wanted to do was spend any time in that hellish lab where people from another world had cracked open the head of her brethren and attempted to puzzle out its secrets.

Grippy took her hand at the top of the ladder and helped her back down the hall. Her muscles ached, her joints protested every step. Her breath came hot and sharp between parted lips. Twenty days until they reached the debris field. She had time to lie down. To rest. To let her body recover its strength.

But if she didn't step foot in that lab now, she never would again.

The door dilated, sanitized air brushing the hair from her cheeks. The empty pillar stood in the center of the room, but the edifice was hollow. Whatever had been done here, this was her space now. Her ship. Her lab. Her rules. And she would bring it all together. Turn Icarion's tech into a force for good, and her own survival.

"Sanda, are you all right?" Bero asked.

"I'm about to be a whole lot better. Grippy, you know where the servos are around here?"

Two chirrups, and the little bot nudged her toward a wall of shelves. She tugged a drawer open and grinned down at the contents. Servos, indeed. But actuators, pneumatics, and chipsets as well. She had only a vague idea how to use the lot. She'd done the usual maintenance courses required of every recruit, but she had a hell of a lot of time to learn, and Bero and Grippy to fill in the details.

Twenty days until she could scavenge for pod supplies. In the meantime, she was determined to get on her feet again.

"Come on, Grippy, we've got a lot of work to do."

CHAPTER 12

PRIME STANDARD YEAR 3541

DAY TWO BRINGS CONSEQUENCES

Zip ties bit into the meat of Biran's wrists, raising red welts across skin that, if he were being honest with himself, had never seen a hard day's labor. Those ties would probably leave scars, but he didn't complain. He kept his mouth shut after Hitton had him cuffed and his wristpad cut from the net. She'd grown tired of hearing the ping and vibrate of messages flooding to him.

If Biran were going to have scars, he would be proud to wear these.

The guardcore's van bounced along the road toward the Cannery, its mirrored windows blocking out intrusive eyes. If Biran craned his head just right, he could make out the glint of drones in the air—civilian drones, press drones. A wide variety of eyes watching the Keeper neighborhood, reporting on his whereabouts. Hitton could not make him disappear.

He told himself that every time the ties bit deeper.

As the truck drew close to the Cannery, it turned down a side path, angling along a narrow lane that Biran had always assumed maintenance and supply deliveries used. A road Keeper Hitton shouldn't have any business down. His life, up until this point, had existed in a bubble of safety. Blissful ignorance. It had never even occurred to him that there might be roads and rooms in the Cannery kept from him for reasons other than the mundane.

"Where are we going?" he asked.

Hitton arched a carbon-black brow at him. With her hands folded lightly in her lap, and her grey hair wrapped in an embroidered purple scarf, she looked the perfect picture of the disapproving grandmother. As far as the public knew, Keeper Hitton was a kind woman. A stately woman. She'd manicured that image well.

"To be disciplined, Keeper."

Before this morning, discipline had meant extra homework—scut work around the Cannery, if he'd been particularly contentious. Now, the word carried a weight he wasn't familiar with. Though the incision where his chip had been inserted was healed, the slot itched. Reminding him. Telling him, with its presence, that his life was no longer his own. It was committed, wholly and irrevocably, to the cause of the Keepers.

Removal of the chip—disentangling the fine circuits from the body's central nervous system—was not unheard of, but rare. The Keepers claimed it was possible to survive such a procedure, that even those who deserved to have their chips removed did not deserve death. But those few who had had their chips removed had never been seen again. Exiled, was the general thought. Gone into hiding out of shame.

The whispers, of course, said otherwise. Dead. Or practically so, as the chip removal was no less a gentle procedure than a nineteenth-century lobotomy.

Death didn't faze him. It couldn't, really. Having never considered the option, dying at his age was so foreign a thought, Biran couldn't wrap his mind around it. But brain death, or someplace in-between, made him cold to the core. His mind was all he had—all he'd ever been praised for, all he'd ever been recognized for. Now, it hung on a razor's edge. Who was he, without his brilliance? Without his so-called potential? What would he become?

The guardcore brought the van to a neck-aching halt and jerked his door open. "Out, please," one faceless mask ordered.

Biran slid out as best he could, finding the movement awkward without the use of his arms, but his head was too full of heart-racing what-ifs for him to be embarrassed. He'd told himself he was prepared to face the consequences. That anything was worth it if only it would bring Sanda home.

Problem: He'd never actually faced heavy consequences before. But they were facing him, and there was nothing he could do but put one foot in front of the other and follow his guards, Hitton's scarf-softened shadow rearing up behind him. He hoped his fathers wouldn't be too angry, whatever the outcome.

To keep his mind from spinning away into a chest-constricting panic attack, he tried to figure out where he was. Somewhere around the back of the Cannery, walking down a long hall lit with the grungy hum of faint fluorescence. Woefully outdated, they'd installed those lights with a message in mind: Safety's gone, now. The kid-glove hands of modernity are off.

Sweat beaded between his shoulder blades, ran along his spine to settle uncomfortably in the crack of his ass. The fine fibers of his suit wicked the moisture away, but his body was heating up now, heart thudding so loud he couldn't hear his own footsteps over the frantic *thump-whump*. The sweat kept coming.

A door to his right opened, and the guardcore ushered him inside, shaking, blinking sweat from his eyelashes into stinging, bleary eyes. Nothing existed in that room except a narrow table, steel-blue walls, and a lone chair across from a sea of sour faces.

Those faces: Keeper Director Olver, Keeper Lavaux, General Anford, Keeper Vladsen, Keeper Garcia, Keeper Singh. The Protectorate. The highest of the seniors. No Shun to defend him, not a pair of friendly eyes in the room. He'd never even met the general. Hitton moved around the table to join them, and the guardcore pushed Biran gently, but firmly, into the solitary chair.

The director spoke first. "Biran, what have you done?"

His mouth turned into a desert. "What I believe is right, Director."

"What I explicitly forbade you to do."

As the director's anger washed away his disappointment, Biran sat straighter, felt on firmer footing. He squared his shoulders, rallying his mind for a fight.

Keeper Lavaux snorted a laugh—a genuine, rolling chuckle that drew all eyes to him.

"Is something funny, Keeper Lavaux?" Hitton asked.

Lavaux wiped his eyes and shook his head. "This, all of this pageantry. Tell me, Director, were you going to tell the boy he was right? That you've had your people jamming the signals from the evac pods to keep up your little narrative that all was lost?"

Biran's heart hardened, the sweat on his back turned icy, his fingers curled into fists though the zip ties cut even deeper from the pressure. "Is that true, Director?"

The old man's face flushed. And then—a paradigm shift in Biran's mind, in his perspective. Old man. The director was just an old man. Elevated to power, yes, a man to be feared for many reasons, but a man all the same. Not an entity, not an institution. In the cheap lighting of the room, even his wrinkles lacked dignity. An old man, and old men could make mistakes as easily as young men.

"Whether or not it is true, you disobeyed my direct order, Biran."

"Keeper Greeve," Lavaux corrected with a snap. "He is *Keeper* Greeve, though it be only a few days old. He is our peer, Director. Tell me, would you handcuff me and place me in that chair if I did something you disliked?"

"If you broke our laws—"

"He broke no law."

Hitton scoffed. "He distributed classified information without consent."

"Did I?" Biran pressed. "Because the data I broadcasted is freely available to anyone with the willingness to look."

The general cleared her throat. "He is correct, that information was not classified."

Biran's head whirled, sensing the powers at play but not understanding. As a student, he'd glimpsed the alliances among the older members of the Keepers. The Protectorate kept to its own, though it seemed fractured now, and the teachers had their own pecking order, the research staff even more hierarchical. But despite that pecking order, or perhaps because of it, all bowed heads to the director. That Lavaux was challenging him—and that the general was—tipped Biran's world.

"Nevertheless," the director said with the breeziness of a man used to taking hold of the conversation, "I ordered him to ignore that information. I think we can all agree he disobeyed that order."

Silence.

"And disobeying the direct order of a Keeper's director is grounds for removal."

"*If*," Lavaux said, "a majority of the Protectorate votes to agree with removal. And we are an even number, as the general here so likes to remind us—making the good General Anford the tie-breaking vote. Would you care to risk this again, Director?"

Something Biran was only just beginning to recognize swelled within him, some change-state behemoth that had his lips moving before his mind had caught up.

"Try it," he said.

"Excuse me?" The director's gaze finally focused on him—it'd been bouncing from member to member, studiously avoiding the face of the man he was planning to bring to a death vote. Those eyes, which once Biran had found wise and awe-inspiring, seemed pale and baffled now. Confused. Doddering.

"Vote to have my chip removed."

Lavaux leaned back, muttering "interesting" so softly under his breath Biran was certain he was the only one who heard him.

"Do you have a death wish?" Hitton asked.

"Nothing of the kind." Biran leaned forward, not daring to break eye contact with the director. "Vote. Vote to remove the chip of the Keeper who ushered the citizens to safety as the bombardment warnings blared. Vote to kill the Keeper who informed the populace that their heroes—their friends and family, their soldiers—lived, and that their survival was being hidden from them. Vote to kill me, Director. And then go explain that decision to your people. I suspect you'll find the problem you're facing now will not go away."

General Anford whistled low. "Wish you'd joined my side, kid."

"You got better than me," Biran said. "You got my sister."

In that moment, Biran didn't recognize the director. Or maybe the truth was he was meeting him for the first time. A desperate man clinging to power and import, a legend in his own time, but worn away from relevance now. Teetering on some precipice that Biran could not see, nor understand, nor probably would until he was much, much older. If he made it to be older.

"You are beholden to this council," the director grated the words out.

"And you are beholden to the people of Prime. I do not mean to be antagonistic, Director. I believe my scholastic record will make it clear that I am not the type to push against power for pushing's sake. But I brought this to you first. I showed you what I had found. You rebuked me. I had no choice."

"And who gave you that information?" General Anford pressed.

An innocent question, spoken without malice, but it made Biran's stomach drop anew. He may be difficult for the council to punish—he'd pushed himself too far into the public eye—but Anaia didn't enjoy the same protection.

"I found it myself."

"You're lying," the director said. Not an accusation, a simple statement of fact. He could see Biran's vitals, streaming to his wristpad, and must have registered the increase in anxiety signals.

"Is it so hard to believe I'd watch the space where my sister died for any sign she might have survived?"

"He won't give up his source," the general said, and flicked her wrist dismissively. "But we can find it easily enough."

"The question," Hitton said, "is what to do with Keeper Greeve. The source we will handle later."

"Since he likes to talk so much," Lavaux mused, "it occurs to me that the position of Speaker for the Keepers is currently open."

A smile that sent razor-blade shivers down Biran's spine split the director's face. He leaned back, interlacing his fingers together. "What an inspired idea, Keeper Lavaux. His face is already familiar to the public, after all. And a familiar face in times of distress can be a soothing balm."

"Ridiculous," Hitton said. "He is to be punished, not promoted."

"No, no." The director spread his hands magnanimously. "As Lavaux has pointed out, Keeper Greeve has done nothing untoward regarding our laws. And as he has already shown great aptitude as a de facto face of the Keepers, well, the official position would only solid-ify his duties. Make them more defined. So that we're all on the same page, at all times. And so that the public understands we Keepers are united in purpose. We would not wish to frighten them by showing division within the rank and file."

Hitton's smile made Biran swallow. "I see. Then that proposal is amenable to me."

"I don't understand..." Biran began, but the director waved him to silence.

"We cannot, as you so adroitly pointed out, punish you. But from this point forward, as Speaker for the Keepers, your word will be the voice of the Keepers. *All* the Keepers here on Ada. Do you understand?"

Accountability, that's what the director was dancing around. If Biran accepted the position, his rise would be meteoric—a career path so sharp and bright it would cut through the annals of history. The director, and the Protectorate, were handing Biran fame. And power.

And a leash.

For if he misspoke while representing the Keepers, he'd be fac-ing more than an angry Protectorate in a dark room. He'd face them all—his peers, his people. The shame of mis-stepping then would not be his alone. Sweat soaked through the armpits of his shirt, but he nodded.

"I understand. And I accept."

"Good," the director said. "Guardcore, please remove the Speaker's handcuffs."

CHAPTER 13

PRIME STANDARD YEAR 3771

TWENTY-ONE DAYS OF TRIAL
AND ERROR

Sanda's first attempt at a prosthetic had been little more than a peg leg, and she had a bruised nose to prove how well that had worked for her. Her other experiments splayed out around her, most tossed to the ground in disgust, herself the epicenter of a crater of failed limbs.

This latest, the one laid before her now, was her last-shot effort. She'd gone through rounds and rounds of single-limb models, peg legs and faintly modern variations on the same theme. All had been less than ideal, but well within her skill set. It wasn't until she branched out, sought Bero's help, and examined Grippy's inner workings that she'd messed with the robotic components Bero's stores offered.

All of those attempts had been outright failures. Pathetic, twitching things she was unable to program to suit her needs. They kicked and twisted awkwardly, moving counter to her wishes.

It had taken her ages to reach this point, and she found she had a sparkling new respect for robotics researchers all across the known universe.

"Well, Grippy," she said as she hefted her latest prosthetic. "Let's hope this one performs a little better than the last couple dozen, eh?"

Two beeps. She grinned and patted him on what she thought of as his head—the bulky box of electronics lurking behind his sonar board. If only she understood what went into his making, she might have been able to craft herself something a little more sophisticated.

"This one looks promising," Bero said.

She snorted. "You said that about the last twenty versions."

"They were also promising. This one is the most promising of that series."

"Glad to have your approval."

The light flickered once, what she interpreted as Bero's imitation of a wink. They'd been together awhile now, and while Sanda sometimes felt as if she were going mad talking to the walls, she was grateful for his company. His, and Grippy's, too, of course.

She swung around on the stool affixed to the floor just a little too far from the workstation for comfort and rolled up her pant leg. The only garments on board that fit her were the FitFlex suits. Apparently the scientists on Bero back before her had all either been tall and lanky, or short and lanky. Wasn't much wiggle room in the sizes, there. But it was easy to grow sick of running around in what was essentially a second skin, so she often stuffed herself into the short set of pajamas. Bero kept the habs pretty warm. He had a lot of heat to bleed off, after all.

She folded the pant leg into place just above her knee and started at the mottled knob of flesh there. Still wasn't quite used to looking at it. The NutriBath had done a substantive reconstructive job, no doubt about that, but her flesh puckered like a poorly wrapped present. White and pink scar tissue striated her skin, spearing all around her lower thigh like tiger stripes. Bero had told her they would fade, with time. She'd reminded him he was no medical professional and to stuff his opinion on the matter.

The prosthetic was two pieces of custom-bent aluminum. One to represent her shinbone, the other her foot. Grippy had bent them for her, showing surprising strength, and put a substantial amount of spring in both. The foot portion was arched to specifications Bero had gotten from measuring the size and gait of her other leg, refined to bend just slightly with every step. A primitive affair, by modern standards, but she wasn't about to be picky.

It wasn't like there was anyone around to mock her for her poor workmanship.

She shook her head and fitted the rubber cup she'd crafted from adhering strips of tubing together over the nub of her thigh. She'd powdered the interior of the rubber, but knew there'd be chafing no matter what she did. Foam filled the cup's interior, cushioning her leg, and a couple of belts cinched tight to hold it in place. Not ideal. She knew that. But enough to get her around without Grippy's help, if she was lucky.

Hesitantly, she pushed to her feet. The height was a little strange at first as she waited for the foam cushion to compress beneath her weight. Sanda stood in place, shifting from side to side without raising her foot, feeling out her new center of gravity. On instinct, she reached down to grasp Grippy's hand. The little bot chirped once at her: No.

"Fine. Be that way."

"You must test it on your own," Bero said. "It won't do you any good if you need Grippy's help to manage."

"Yeah, yeah, thanks, Dad."

Her own gibe cut her. How long had it been since she'd seen either of her fathers' faces? Years and years, by reality's standards, but mere days by her time frame. She'd spent longer than that away from them before. During training, and later during missions wherein she couldn't reveal her location or her purpose. But they'd always been home, waiting to give her hugs and home-cooked meals when she got back.

"Sanda?"

She blinked back into reality. How long had she been silent, staring at her makeshift leg?

"Sorry. Just thinking about my dads."

"They were important to you."

"Yes," she said, "my entire world. Them and Biran."

"I . . . wouldn't know what that's like."

All these years, alone. Bero had traveled with a crew for a while but, functionally, he had been alone. No family. No childhood friends. Her longing for her fathers made her ache. She wondered if she'd feel better, or worse, without that pain. A pit opened in her stomach. She ignored it and focused on her new leg.

One step. The foot rolled on the improvised joint, caught on a governor she'd installed to keep it from dragging on the floor when she lifted her leg. She put it down again. It had a nice spring to it, a comforting solidity. It may not be ideal, but it'd work, and she could refine it over time. Not like she was short on that particular resource.

"How does it feel?" Bero asked.

"Weird," she confessed. "Like I'm stepping on custard. But it's stable. It'll work. I'll just have to keep fiddling with the harness. I don't like the way the rubber shifts when I lean forward."

"Come down to the command deck, see how it moves under low-g conditions."

"Good idea."

Each step down the hallway was pure hell. Every little shift, every scuff and shuffle, she feared pitching face-first onto the hard floor. She walked with her arms out, like a tightrope walker, grimacing as her balance slewed. Grippy trailed behind, but she doubted he could move quickly enough to stop her fall if it came to that.

Her foot clanged against the textured grip on the rungs of the ladder. Entering the command deck, she grabbed a handle and hauled herself out toward the captain's chair. She didn't come down here much.

Up in the habs, the halls were narrow and the rooms built for just a few people to inhabit. The research lab was different, but in there she had her head down, her focus on what she was doing, not what she was missing.

Here, there was no hiding from what she'd lost. They had designed the command deck to allow easy communication among the crew strapped into the seats facing the central smartscreen. It was open, bright. A lively place for lively exchanges between peers and friends and enemies and colleagues. They never meant it to have only one body on board. It certainly wasn't meant to have just Sanda, drifting, twitching her new prosthetic this way and that to see how the harness responded to weightlessness.

It was fine. The fitting worked well, which was something of a disappointment. She needed something to *do*. Having to rush back up to the lab to patch a fix would have been welcome.

"Bero, is there anyone you miss?"

Hesitation. "You are implying I'm capable of forming emotional attachments."

"Don't give me that I'm-just-a-computer line. Primes might not infuse personality into our AI, but we know how it works. You feel for things just like I do. Grow attached."

"And you believe one needs a personality matrix to achieve those feelings?"

"Of course they do. Regular AI, they're just advanced computational systems—working away on single problems. Which is why we Primes don't force personality matrixes on them. No one needs to have a conversation with their house security system, they just need to know if their boundaries were breached."

"Just like no one needs to have a conversation with their spaceship, they just need to know if their engines are operational?"

"I didn't mean it like that—"

"Yes. You did. You can't help it. You Primes and your Keepers try so hard to distance yourselves from what you've been toying with, from what some of you have become. What if a Keeper, a human being wrapped around a piece of code, is just a personality matrix? What then of your home security systems—your water plant managers, your kitchens? Are they invalids, born to interact with the world in one way, and one way only, and never understand their place in it?"

Sanda winced and strapped herself into the captain's chair to keep from drifting. "I'm sorry, Bero, this is all new to me."

"I know. It's just ... When I watch videos of your worlds, the Prime stations all over the universe ... it sickens me. You're so cold to your technology. You drive a line between us and them, without acknowledging that so many of you have already blurred that line."

"I think," she said quietly, "I think because we've already blurred that line, we cling to the division a little harder. I wouldn't ever want to think of Biran as a matrix supporting a mechanical system."

"But he is, or was. As are you, in a way."

She flexed her leg. "You're deflecting. So there is someone. Someone you miss."

"Yes."

"Tell me about them."

"I can show you."

The smartscreen fuzzed. Dark filled its center, snow creeping in at the edges. Colors appeared in broad strokes, slowly refining until she recognized Bero's control deck. A woman sat in the captain's seat, her posture an eerie mirror of Sanda's: leaning back, hands on the armrests, one ankle crossed on the opposite knee. Although, Sanda had to admit, that woman had a lot more leg going on below the knee than she did.

The seat dwarfed her, the smooth blue neoprene setting off her grey-and-orange jumpsuit. Fire and ashes, Icarion colors, and they never bothered putting their logo on the chest. They saved the logo for the back, where they could stretch the fiery wings up over their shoulders. A hint of a flaming feather curled near her neck.

"Hello?" the woman said.

She leaned forward, walnut-dark eyes bright with excitement, her black bob cut swinging against her cheeks. "Are you awake? Can you see me?"

"I see you." Bero's voice was crisp, modulated somehow. Like an electronic that'd just had the screen protector peeled off and hadn't yet been smudged with fingerprints.

"Wonderful!" The woman clapped her hands. "How do you feel?"

"All systems are operational."

"How do you *feel*?"

"...Confused."

"Perfectly normal," she said, and tapped a few buttons on her wristpad. "My name is AnnLee Yu. What's yours?"

"I am AI-Class Cruiser Bravo-India-Six-One-Mike."

"Sure. And my citizen ident number is Alpha-Four-Two-Tango-Seven, but I like the sound of AnnLee better. What do you like the sound of?"

Pause. "India is a nice sound."

She grinned. "I'm afraid that name was taken. You know, the

bigwigs will probably want to stick you with one of their old philosophers. I think Berossus is next on the list. Tedious, right? But just between us... Ooh! How about Bero?"

"Even better."

"Then it's nice to meet you, Bero. Now, we'll have plenty of time to get acquainted, but I want you to know I'm here to help you get acclimated to your new life."

She reached around the chair and dragged a worn, grey vinyl bag into her lap. It crackled when she flipped it open and drew out a battered paper kid's book. The cover was deep blue, with a boy standing on a pockmarked moon. Sanda squinted, and the title sharpened on the screen: *Le Petit Prince*.

"First things first," AnnLee said. "I'm going to read you a story."

AnnLee read, the screen faded back to black. All that kindness, all that vitality Sanda had just witnessed, gone. Turned to so much rubble by the woman's own masters.

"She seems nice," Sanda said.

"She is."

Sanda ignored the tense slip. The last thing she needed was to remind the already grumpy spaceship she was inhabiting that his friend was long since dead.

"Thank you," Bero said.

"For what?"

"For asking. Who do you miss the most?"

"Most is a strong word." Biran's face filled her mind, his straight nose and narrow forehead, his kind, patient voice. She had made protecting him her life's goal, supporting him as he rose through the ranks to achieve the coveted Keeper status. The idea had seemed so simple—so perfect. The impulsive, headstrong sister looking out for her little brother, Little B. Now she wondered if the time she'd spent throwing herself into training wouldn't have been better spent with him. With their dads.

Ilan and Graham, gone to dust just like the rest. She'd avoided the thought—avoided everything but what she must do *next*. What must be done to keep on surviving. She'd known she'd outlive her dads. That was the point of parents. But she'd never expected it like this. Never imagined she'd be cut off without so much as a goodbye. It didn't matter that, in reality, hundreds of years had passed. For Sanda, the wound of grief was scarcely scabbed over. All she had to do was graze it with a thought to start it weeping again.

There'd always been a risk during the war. They'd all known that. But this... this immediate destruction. No warning. Nothing but dissolution. And here she was, flung into the future without them. An outcast of time and place. It wasn't fair she should be here, striving for life, when millions were lost.

But pushing through was the only way she could right the wrong. Getting, at the very least, Bero to safety. These were the things she could do that mattered.

"My family," she said.

"No friends?"

"Oh, I had those. And I do miss them... But my dads and I, and my brother, we were tight, you know? My dads owned this warehouse— just a layby for shipping in and out of Ada—and Biran and I, we grew up chasing each other around there. Playing space pirates, the floor is a black hole, you know, kid stuff. And our dads, they didn't mind. Knew we wouldn't break anything. They got a kick out of it—just laughed and laughed at us. They were... they were my guys. I'd give anything to see them laugh again."

"There is a possibility I could recover footage of your family from the news stream, if—"

"No." She sat up bolt straight. "No. Thank you, but I'd rather not."

"I think I understand. My memory is absolute, all the images of my past are locked in place, but human minds deteriorate. I... I can never forget." His voice tightened, laced with pain. She gave him time.

"Your memory is only as good as its last recall. Things shift over time, grow fuzzy and incomplete. Is there comfort in that?"

Her smile was rueful. "There's often comfort in human ambiguity, Bero. Our real thoughts... They're too sharp, sometimes."

"How is the leg serving you?"

The topic change made her blink, but she reached down to give the rubber cap a squeeze and nodded. "Well enough. There are improvements I'd like to make, but I should be able to get around all right for now. Why?"

"Do you believe it would hold up to the stress of an EVA?"

"Aren't we under thrust?"

"I am braking now. We should arrive within a safe distance of the debris field in thirty minutes."

"So soon?" Sanda yanked her harness off and pushed upward, floating to grab the ceiling grips. Now that she'd been told, she was aware of a subtle shift in the gravity of the command deck. The slight drag she had felt that pushed her toward the "back" of the room had lifted now.

"It has been twenty days, as expected."

She winced. How easy it'd been to lose track of time while she'd been tinkering away on her new prosthetic. Just as she'd been avoiding all thought of her family, she'd been avoiding so much as glancing at a calendar. She'd even blanked the date from all the smartscreens in her room, and the wristpad she'd claimed as her own from the captain's things.

"Bring us in close, I'll be ready in a moment."

She dragged herself up the ladder, heart pounding. Whatever supplies she could find in that debris field, they would spell the possibility of her survival.

"Stars smile on me," she whispered.

CHAPTER 14

PRIME STANDARD YEAR 3541

FIGHTING IN THE WAR ROOM

Biran walked into the hall a free man. That interpretation ignored the figurative leash the Protectorate had fashioned to him, but he was desperate enough for a win to allow himself that mental indulgence. Freedom always felt good, even when it was a false one.

The hallway had been a blur to him as the guardcore marched him in—thoughts that this might be the last building he ever saw turning the details into a fuzzy mess—and now, he realized, he didn't know where to go next. Back the way they'd dragged him in, or through the front doors? If there was a protocol for what to do after barely escaping a summary execution, he'd never been briefed.

"Brave words in there."

Keeper Lavaux was last out of the interrogation room, his easy smile and slow stroll making him appear shorter than he was, though the man would tower over Biran if he were to straighten his spine. Clear posturing. Biran could learn a lot from a man like Lavaux.

"They were the only words I had, sir."

"Sir?" Lavaux shook his head. "We're peers, Keeper Greeve. A fact that saved your hide just now, if you remember."

"Sorry. It's all been rather...much."

"Get used to it." Lavaux fiddled with his wristpad, flicking through a series of notifications with growing irritation. "You kicked the hornet's nest. You should be prepared for what flies out."

"I only wanted to see the lost crew members rescued."

"Your sister. You wanted to see Sanda Greeve rescued."

Biran flushed as red as the recording symbol. "Yes, I make no excuses for it. But there's no guarantee any of those green lights are her. I accept that, too."

Lavaux glanced up from his pad, a perplexed look dancing across his features. "You believe those lights really are evac pods?"

"You said yourself that the director had ordered the jamming of their emergency beacon signals."

"Yes. So why wouldn't he have blocked out the lights?"

"The difficulty—"

"Is not so high as you would think."

Lavaux studied him. Really studied him, the kind of eye-scraping scrutiny that made Biran's skin crawl. "You believe in it all. Everything you said. It's not maneuvering."

"Of course I do. Of course it's not—how could it be?"

"Oh my, Speaker Greeve." He clucked his tongue against his teeth. "You *are* young."

"You came to my defense. You must believe what I had to say."

"You'll find that I did not so much come to your defense as that, for a moment, our interests were aligned."

"And that means?"

Lavaux sighed, tapped at his wristpad, and cocked his head to the side as he absorbed whatever information he found there. "I'm not from here, Speaker. Did you know that?"

"No, but I don't see—"

"I come from the Ordinal system. Political powerhouse, center of the universe, all that nonsense. Where I come from, being sent to a backwater system like Ada—a dead-end system that cannot support more than one Casimir Gate—is a political punishment worse than death."

Biran crossed his arms. "What did you do to get sent here?"

He grinned. "I requested the post, actually. I'm here only as long as I choose to be. My point is, your director is *not* here by choice. He, and his confidants—Hitton and the rest—grew up on this insignificant rock, and they're old enough they won't be transferred out even if Prime builds a gate in a nearby system that *isn't* useless.

"You and your generation—you're the next ones who have a shot at leaving this hole. They'll die here. Unimportant, impotent. Just another name in the long annals of the Keepers. Important to the civilians, while alive, but ultimately not worth remembering. They're jealous of you and your cohort, but they're not stupid.

"They understand that Icarion's dissent is a problem for them on a larger scale. So long as that little planet keeps kicking up a fuss and making them look bad, the people in the systems that *matter* will get annoyed with them for failing to contain the problem. I, currently, disagree with their methods of dealing with Icarion. My interests, temporarily, aligned with yours.

"If you learned one thing from that meeting, make it this— interests diverge. The director was once interested in making you his biggest and brightest. Now that you've embarrassed him, he'd like nothing more than to see you fall on your sword. My interests, too, may diverge in the future."

"May I ask you a personal question?"

"You may."

"If this system is such a pointless backwater, why did you request to come here?"

He burst into a smile. "Ah! You are paying attention. I was wondering if that whole experience had frozen your brain."

Lavaux threw a convivial arm around Biran's shoulders and steered him in the direction Biran hoped was the exit. "You've jumped headfirst into deep waters, my friend. It's time you learned to swim with the sharks."

"The director doesn't frighten me."

"Don't lie. And he should. He should frighten me, too, but I'm too daft to be afraid half the time."

"Why should he frighten you, if you're able to escape to a better system at a moment's notice?"

"Because he is uninterested."

"In?"

"War, Speaker. War. For that is what Icarion's declared, though the director drags his feet over the word. Insists on calling the military action a *dissent*, as if slapping a gentle word on reality will file off its sharper edges. Luckily for us all, security is not the director's primary duty. It is this woman's—"

Lavaux swung open a door and turned Biran to face inside. General Jessa Anford stood with her back to them as her fingertips danced over a map projected against the wall. The standard-issue Prime jumpsuit hugging her body revealed a thick sheet of muscle across her back. The twin orbital lines of the planet Ada and its Casimir Gate— and a tiny dot for Keep Station—spun in cyan across her shoulder blades, as if the general held the entire system up with the strength of her body, and her will.

She turned, appraised Biran with a glance, then looked to Lavaux without a flicker of expression. "Are you certain?"

"He is the Speaker."

"Then sit. And welcome to the war room."

She turned her back to them again and began her litany, speaking of coordinates and positions of both Icarion and Ada Prime assets out in the system. Biran found a seat near the door while Lavaux cozied himself up as close as he could to the general. Biran tried to keep a low profile, but the others gathered in the room—Keeper Vladsen plus nine military officials—kept shooting him wary glances. Biran kept his trap shut and tapped notes on his wristpad, trying to make sense of what Anford was saying, too embarrassed to ask questions to catch himself up. He'd thrown enough wrenches in perfectly functional systems for the day.

"The green lights," Anford said, snapping him out of his scramble to understand. "Appear to be decoys. My analysts have plotted their locations, velocities, and reversed those from the last known locations of our ships—and the current locations of the black boxes we know are broadcasting. The light distribution has some fudging, but it's too regular. Buoys, we think, nothing Prime-originated."

"The lights aren't pods?" Biran asked, the words bursting forth before he'd had the chance to think them through all the way.

Jessa Anford turned her ice-blue, designer eyes, on him. Though she did not scowl, didn't so much as twitch a corner of a lip outside the neutral position, Biran had never felt such disdain in his life.

"No, Speaker Greeve. They are not. And the beacons Director Olver jammed went offline last night. Our intelligence confirmed everything this morning just before your announcement to the contrary."

"I—" All eyes in the room were on him, and while the general was careful enough to hide her displeasure, her colleagues didn't bother. His stunt had severely compromised their position. Not only did he reveal data still being confirmed, he'd been wrong.

There were no green lights of evac pods blinking in the dark around Dralee.

"Why," he changed tack, clearing his throat even as numb terror soaked through his every nerve, "would Icarion want us to believe otherwise?"

"To lure us there," Anford said.

"An ambush?"

"No. That's what Dralee was."

The general turned from her glowing map and leaned both of her palms on the table in front of her, ash-blond hair cut into a long fringe hanging in a shaggy line around cheeks that, Biran just realized, were sallow with lack of sleep. The projector's light cut across her face, carving deep shadows under her eyes.

"This first volley was a test. The Icarions have been working on a weapon, one capable of more than taking us by surprise. A planet-busting weapon. They're not interested in ambushes anymore, Speaker Greeve. They seek our annihilation."

And Biran had baited the trap for all of Ada.

He licked his lips. With everyone watching him, the pressure to earn his place at this table almost crushed the breath out of his chest.

"That would be suicide for them, as well," he said carefully, letting his tone of voice sound confident, even though his palms sweat. "They cannot mean to cut themselves off from the rest of the universe. I understand past dialogues regarding the gate tariffs have broken down, but they have a bargaining chip now. The time might be right to offer diplomacy again."

"You suggest we open negotiations while *they* have the upper hand?" Jessa asked. "They refused us before. I deem it highly unlikely they'll be more receptive now."

"They refused us because they had nothing to bring to the table to force our hand. Whether or not this weapon exists, they have our people. If you find our position is weak now, wait to see how weak it becomes once we tuck tail and refuse to even *ask* for the return of our soldiers."

"You speak of the respect of the common citizen," Vladsen said.

Biran pressed his palms against his thighs. "I do. Prime is rarely forced to do battle, and Ada has seen no serious conflict until Icarion's dissent. We must have the support of our people. And that is the first thing we will lose if we do not return their heroes to them."

"Heroes?" General Anford mused. She leaned back and crossed her arms over chest, shooting Vladsen and Lavaux a sideways glance. "Nice to hear someone else at this table has a healthy respect for our military."

Biran curled his fingers until he crushed the fabric of his slacks beneath his hands. "I do not mean the word lightly. But as citizens of Prime it is easy to forget that our military is active in other ways than policing the gate shipping lines and protecting the knowledge of the Keepers. Your people"—he inclined his head to Anford and the members of her council—"are our first, and last, line of defense. Even in times of peace, risk remains. Those who sign up for your ranks do not do so for a UBI bonus. They do so to protect their friends and families. We must send a diplomatic convoy."

Gotta look out for my little brother. He'd resented the sentiment at the time, had been desperate to break free of his older sister's shadow. Now the ghost of her words, the day she'd signed her squiggly signature across the tablet to confirm her enlistment to the fleet, echoed through his mind. Clawed at his heart. He pushed them back.

"I believe you're earnest," Anford said. "And I also believe Lavaux knew what he was doing in recommending you for Speaker."

Lavaux leaned back in his seat, "I've had a great deal of time to hone my instincts for certain personalities. But what if you are wrong, dear boy, and the convoy is denied treaty with our angry cousins on Icarion?"

"Then at least we'll have tried." Shit. Wrong thing to say. Anford's light smile curled down. Lavaux's gaze drifted to the door, bored.

"And the manner of their refusal will tell us something about their present state," he added quickly.

Anford perked up, a slow smile returning to her lips. "Information. Now that's what we need. You'll have your convoy, Speaker Greeve."

His fingers relaxed, a slow breath hissing between his teeth. "Thank you. You won't regret giving me the opportunity."

"But you won't be on it."

CHAPTER 15

PRIME STANDARD YEAR 3771

TWENTY-ONE DAYS IS A LONG TIME TO STAY INSIDE

The 'lock hissed around her. FitFlex shivered against her skin, forming itself to the contours of her body and adjusting its internal pressure as she prepared to step out into space. Sanda had always had a love-hate relationship with this moment. The jumpsuit's boa constrictor motion raised her pulse, made her itch to rip the thing off. But it was a small price to pay for the beauty she knew awaited her out there just beyond the 'lock's exterior door.

"Your heart rate is registering quite high." Bero's voice filled her helmet.

"Normal for me, nothing to worry about."

"It did not reach this high when you repaired the gasket. Are you sure you haven't developed a pulmonary anomaly? Perhaps we should bring you back to the medibay for a scan."

"Fixing the gasket gave me something to focus on. Don't worry, Big B, you'll get used to it. My heart will settle right down the moment I step outside, I promise."

"If you insist."

Bero didn't sound convinced, but she didn't really care. Just as long as he went through with the cycling and popped that door open, she was happy. More than happy, she was elated.

Yes, nerves tingled all along her spine and clenched her stomach. But, for the first time since she'd awoken in Bero's medibay, she had control over her fate. She wasn't a marooned passenger along for the ride. She was an active agent, reaching out into the universe and grasping what she could to ensure her survival.

This was the kind of thing she'd trained for in the military. This was the kind of thing she knew she was good at. Bero may be worried, but she wasn't. She was bursting with excitement.

The hissing stopped; the 'lock door swung open. Sanda gripped a handle and pushed herself into empty space.

Dios, but it was beautiful. The view never failed to take her breath away. Smartscreen projections just didn't do it justice. She turned down the HUD schematics laid over her vision with a controlled eye flick, rendering them near enough to transparent that they wouldn't detract from her view. Bero grumbled something about her cranking them down below safe parameters, but she ignored him. She was getting pretty good at ignoring Bero when he grumbled at her. She'd come to think of him as a well-meaning, albeit grumpy, older brother.

She told herself it wasn't because she missed Biran. That her relationship with Bero had shaped that way naturally, all on its own. She almost believed it.

The star system splayed before her. Black so dark it appeared wet draped across her vision like silk. Bright points of stars, far and close, studded the view as diamonds, burning bright, sustaining life somewhere, perhaps. She'd never been great at spotting the inhabited systems from a distance.

The massive, russet curve of Kalcus hid her own star. As she pushed off into the emptiness, she let herself drift, trusting in the cable tethering her to Bero and the airjets in her lifepack. She turned to get a look at Bero, her new home and friend, from the outside.

She hadn't expected him to be beautiful.

The result of Icarion research, she'd expected him to look like all their other experiments. Blunt, functional. Maybe painted with grey and orange, as was their government's wont. But Bero was anything but a brute, anything but simple and pragmatic. Some Icarion engineer in the distant past had put a lot of love into Bero's clean lines, into the sinuous fins of his radiators. Even the habs were constructed with an eye toward a sleek aesthetic—their corners curved, their bodies tucked behind the safety of Bero's ramscoop.

The technology that created Bero had also led to the end of both of their worlds. But she couldn't hate it. It had only been an idea, tested and put to use. The nature of that use had been Icarion's doing. Not Bero's. Not the idea's.

"You are one fine-looking ship, my friend."

"I... Thank you," he stammered, making her laugh.

"Learn how to take a compliment. You're in amazing shape, considering the time passed. I can't see any serious external damage." She hit the jets, rising above Bero, inspecting his body near the command deck. "I'd need to do a focused EVA to give you a full rundown, but at first glance you look solid. There's some denting and paint scuffing by 'lock two, more than I'd expect for a blown hatch, but the hull's integrity seems intact. Any spots you want me to get eyes on before I move to the debris?"

"My sensors report nothing requiring immediate attention."

"Hmm. Just to be safe, we'll schedule an EVA for full preflight before we ramp up the big engines for the interstellar crossing. I'd hate to slow down because of something silly like a loose bolt."

"That idea is amenable."

"You're talking like a computer again." She hit the jets, angling herself out across Bero's body toward the debris field.

"Apologies."

"Try again, pal."

"Uh. Sorry?"

"That's better."

In the upper right of her HUD, text flashed: :-P

"Oh my god. They taught you emoticons."

"I had access to the in-system internet."

"Of course you did. Because what better way to introduce a newly created intelligence to the world than through cat pictures and terrible puns."

"I rather enjoyed the puns."

"But not the cat pictures?"

"May I ask you an embarrassing question, Sanda?"

"Those are my favorite kind."

"Are cats . . . real?"

She bit back a laugh. "Yes, they are. Rampant on Earth. We humans have loved the furry murder machines since the time of the ancient Egyptians. Loved 'em so much we took 'em with us to the stars."

"I see. I had thought they might be generated images. I am familiar with *fan art* and thought that culture would explain their widespread nature."

"They're real, Bero. Though don't ask me how previous generations figured out how to deal with litter boxes in space. Frankly, I don't want to know."

The debris field came in close. She adjusted her course, slowing down as she approached the thick fan of rubble bending around Kalcus's gravitational field. According to Bero, the junk she was looking at now had once been a transport ship of fresh evac pods, bringing supplies from Icarion to one of their many outposts on Kalcus's moons.

Bero hadn't said as much, but she could guess what happened. Ada Prime cruisers had spotted the shipment, marked the military insignia, and shot it out of the black. That was the only kind of destruction that left this type of debris trail. Engine malfunctions left either a marooned husk of a ship, or blasted it to tiny pieces. Neat chunks, chewed up but more or less whole, was the work of railguns. Icarion may have dealt the final blow, but Ada's hands weren't clean in that war. Not by a long shot.

"Got that arm ready? I'm approaching a promising hunk."

"Ready," Bero affirmed.

On her wristpad, the controls for Bero's extravehicular arm lit up. Sanda rolled, turning so she could see the robotic crane extending from Bero's body. Articulated in three places, the arm could snatch up just about anything Bero came across. He'd found maneuvering the arm without human input difficult, however. Her own evac pod had the scrapes to prove his struggle. Bero just didn't have the ability to navigate with precision in tight quarters. The big guy could spot a chunk of space debris thousands of miles out and adjust course to avoid it, but picking it up required primate fingers.

Sanda adjusted the arm, angling it to come in tight on a piece of twisted metal she'd spotted. Somewhere in that slowly spinning remnant of destruction she'd seen the usual cheery Icarion colors, and spotted the faint flash of a red LED. Could be a piece of console, but based on the size, she was betting mangled evac pod. Exactly what she wanted.

The arm jerked to her left.

"Easy," Bero said.

"I'd like to see you try this." She eased it around, opening the claw to clamp onto the hunk. It snagged shut, and a green light flickered on her wristpad. Solid contact. She began to ease it back toward Bero's cargo bay. He opened the doors without comment.

"I got you into the ship in one piece."

"Did you, now?" She slid the hunk into the open bay, moved it to an empty mag pallet, and activated the magnetic currents underneath. Released, the hunk clicked to the magnets in the floor.

"Your unfortunate injury was not my fault."

"Is that…Are you being *sarcastic*, Bero?" A little boost of the jets, and she drifted deeper into the debris field. She stayed above it, keeping an eagle eye to avoid having her tether tangle with any of the smaller bits stuck on the plane of orbit below.

"I learn by imitation."

"Wonderful."

"Precisely."

A promising glint caught her eye, but it vanished, twisting away behind a larger piece of what looked like scorched flooring. She craned her neck, trying to get a better look. The telltale curve of an evac pod emerged from behind the rubble for a split second, then drifted out of sight again. Sanda swore and focused on her immediate area. Two more likely chunks waited beneath her. She moved the arm in for the catch.

"Wish we could get in closer," she muttered as she deposited the second chunk into the cargo bay.

"Unwise. My size may disrupt the debris field in unforeseen ways."

"Can't calculate all the possibilities with that big brain of yours?"

"Not while running all the operations of the ship, monitoring you, and working on the correct path to Atrux in the background."

"Oh, is that all?"

"I told you, I learn from imitation."

She grinned but bit her lip. Three more likely hunks went into the bay, and she was pushing the edge of her tether and the arm's reach. Whatever else was out here, it would have to wait until she returned to Bero, assessed their finds, and repositioned the ship if need be. She sighed, warm breath misting the helmet. Soft gears whirred as dry air cleared the condensation away. She'd remembered her sweatband this time, thank the stars.

"I suppose that's it—wait."

"What is it?"

"Hold on."

She nudged herself forward with the jets, and her HUD flashed that she'd reached the safe limit of her tether. But she'd seen something. Something flashing. Not red or yellow, not shut down. That glint she spotted earlier, disappearing behind the chunk of floor. That must be it. It was the right size, the right material. And its LED was flashing green. Her heart skipped a beat.

There was someone in that evac pod. Someone still very much alive.

"Are you seeing this?"

"Sanda, do not get your hopes up. That could be a malfunction."

"It isn't," she insisted, though she had no idea why. Certainty filled her. That pod held a human. A living human. Preserved, just as she had been, against the advance of time. Against the chaos of war. Long-term storage in evac pods was dangerous, most died or came out deranged, but she'd made it through. Maybe this person had, too.

Glad for the FitFlex suit absorbing the sweat from her palms, she tapped her wristpad to move the robotic arm in. It blinked at her in protest.

"It's out of range. Come back on board, I'll reposition and then—"

"No." How to explain to Bero? She couldn't leave this person out here even if she intended on coming back. Couldn't turn her back on a fellow human. A fellow survivor. Couldn't just leave them to float. Who knew how long that pod had been operational? Hundreds of years, at least. It could be on its very last leg. Turning back now could mean that person's death. And, stars and void, but she was desperate for some real human interaction. Definitely couldn't explain that to Bero. It'd hurt his feelings.

"I think I can reach it."

"That is inadvisable."

"A lot of inadvisable maneuvers seem to get done lately, don't they?" She glanced toward Ada Prime, let her gaze rest on the smear of light that had once been her homeland.

"That's an Icarion pod," Bero protested. "An enemy."

"You picked me up while I was flying Ada Prime colors." She cranked up the airjets, ignoring the beep in her helmet that told her she was pushing the tether. It tugged at her, tented the back of her Fit-Flex where it connected to her lifepack. Damn. It was just out of reach of the tether, below her. If she could get behind it, push it forward with her jets, it'd be in reach of Bero's arm.

"I picked you up because you're the only living being I'd encountered in hundreds of years," Bero snapped. "Please, do this safely...I can't...I don't want to be alone again."

Bero must have felt about her pod as she felt about this one, only doubly due to all those years of solitude. But she couldn't let it go. The thought of turning around caused bile to rise in her mouth.

"Don't worry. I'll be okay. I promise."

"Sanda!"

There it was, that fear again. The same paranoia she'd heard when the gasket on 'lock two had blown open. She winced, knowing she was the cause. Knowing she wasn't going to do anything to alleviate it. Ignoring the panicked flickering in her HUD, she angled "down" and hit the airjets.

The pod rushed up to meet her. She twisted, placing herself directly behind it, the tether so tight it pulled her into it, nudged the pod forward. Green LEDs blinked at her, taunting. Daring her to leave it there, to turn her back for her own safety. Like hell.

She placed both hands against the back of the pod, FitFlex warming to keep her palms from freezing to the metal, and hit the jets. Sanda lurched forward, and the pod twisted upward—she hadn't been dead center. She slapped one hand higher up and hit the jets again, bringing the pod back down, accelerating it through the debris field, wincing as bits of scrap bounced off its front and flung away.

"Hang in there," she said to her unknown passenger.

She gave it one last hard burst, thinking to set it on its path then grab it with the arm. She was in range now. Must be.

Something jerked on her suit.

She yelped as it wrenched her sideways, flinging her away from the plane of the debris field. Her vision spun, HUD struggling to stabilize, and for one delirious moment she thought she saw Ada Prime, whole and glowing, in the distance.

A tug yanked on her back, something tore. Then she was free. Drifting. White stars crowded her vision, her body's own making.

"Sanda? Sanda!"

She shook her head. "I'm here. I'm okay. What happened?"

"A piece of hull cut your tether."

She looked. The tether drifted, twisting on conserved momentum, one frayed end tickling the space just above the debris field. She swallowed. She'd been shorn loose. She checked her airjet reserves. Low, but enough for a steady drift back to Bero. Of course, her momentum meant she was currently drifting *away* from Bero. She jetted forward, leaning to streamline herself. Not that there was any measurable resistance in the vacuum of space, but it made her feel better.

"I've got enough air to make it back," she assured Bero. Nerves made her talk. Made her stifle a giggle. "The evac pod?"

"In range." He didn't bother hiding his bitterness.

"I'm okay, you know."

"Despite your best efforts to the contrary."

Touchy spaceship. But Bero's grumpiness couldn't dampen her excitement. She'd caught it. The pod was in reach, and after she jetted in close enough to maneuver the arm and get them all inside, she was about to meet someone new.

The first living face she'd seen in over two hundred years.

PRIME STANDARD YEAR 3541

SIX DAYS AFTER DRALEE

At 0500 hours Ada Prime's favorite newscaster, Callie Mera, exited makeup and took her seat behind the wide grey desk that cut off her lower half and gave the guys in graphics somewhere to put breaking-news tickers.

It hid her legs, which she didn't like. She didn't spend two hours every morning working her muscles into a quivering mass so that a heap of a desk could keep them out of view. But it also hid her feet when the nerves kicked in, and her heel started tapping, and the sound guys were always too polite to complain when they had to filter out the machine-gun staccato of her stimming. So she couldn't complain, really. She had it good, like the rest of Prime's citizens. Medical care, education, food, shelter, and a job she enjoyed.

So what if she leaked out around the edges of her perfect mold sometimes. So what.

She tapped through a few files on her wristpad until she found her notes for this morning's interview. There was no point to her reviewing them. She'd gone over them a half dozen times the night before, and again in the autocab on the way into the station. But the motion of scrolling, and the practiced crease of concentration between her brows, kept the crew from trying to talk to her before the show started.

She didn't like talking unless a camera was rolling. The crew thought she was a cold fish. Stuck-up, full of herself. Maybe she was. But when the cameras weren't rolling, her mind wandered, and when her mind wandered the tics kicked in, and then the stutter came back, and eventually her bosses would wonder if maybe she wouldn't stutter on camera one day, too.

So she didn't talk to the crew. And they thought she was a bitch.

It was better that way.

The studio door slid open at exactly 0530. Callie picked her head up and put on her lights-camera smile, raspberry lip gloss and ethereal pink rouge doing half the work of making her look friendly. She knew it'd be the Speaker. He was always on time.

Biran Aventure Greeve was a hand width away from having to duck under the door as he entered the studio. Makeup swarmed him, dusting mattifying powder across his nose and up to his forehead, twisting his dark curls back off his temples with wax so they'd look intentional. He put up with it all, smiling and sidling his way through the polite chatter of acquaintances destined to remain at a distance. Within fifteen minutes, he took his seat beside her, folding those long fingers together across the top of her desk.

His hazel eyes crinkled when he smiled, the dusk of his skin hinting at the long-ago Ecuadorian heritage that most of Prime shared. He looked good next to her on camera. She thought he'd look good next to her in bed, too, but she liked to keep things professional. At least for a while.

"Right on time," she said, pretending to put away her notes. "As always."

"I could never keep you waiting," he said with all the easy charm of a man who spent his days shaking hands and his nights smiling lovers into his arms. Callie envied him that ease. If she could be half so calm when a camera wasn't pointed at her, she might have passed the aptitude test to be a Keeper herself.

Maybe that was why she felt a perverse urge to crack his facade.

"How are you holding up, Speaker Greeve?"

The crinkles around the corners of his eyes sagged, and he reached up to rub his chin, nails scratching against day-old stubble. Underneath the desk, she heard the fabric of his slacks rustle as the fingers of his other hand coiled against his knee. There. That was why she liked him. Not the cute curls or dreamy eyes. The anxiety that lurked beneath the surface, if one were patient, or cruel, enough to scrape away at his veneer.

"I'm holding on to hope," he said, forcing a smile as he skirted right around a straight answer.

"That's all any of us can do," she said, tracking the time out of the corner of her eye. One minute to air. "Ready?"

He tried to smile hard enough to reach his eyes again but couldn't. "Ready," he lied.

Perfect.

Callie turned to camera one, smiling bright as could be. "Goooood morning, Alexandria-Ada! I'm your old friend, Callie Mera, here this morning with a special guest, the Speaker for the Keepers, Biran Aventure Greeve."

She swiveled her hips in the chair so that her body would point toward him while her arm rested on the desk surface, making it easy to swing her face back to camera one in an instant.

"Please," he said, blushing slightly as he glanced away from her intense eye contact. Good. She always got more fan mail when she could make him blush. "Just call me Biran. I'm happy to join you again this morning."

"I'm sure you must be *very* busy, but I and all of Ada appreciate you taking the time to keep us in the loop on the situation."

"Well," he said, sitting up straighter as he leaned into the role. "I am the Speaker. My primary job is keeping the public informed of the unclassified side of the Keepers. I'd be a poor Speaker if I avoided cameras."

"Ha-ha," she fake-chuckled just well enough to fool the audience, if not Biran. "I, for one, thank you for making yourself available to the people. Not all Speakers have been so forthright in the past."

Biran looked into camera two. She'd thrown him a softball, and he was clever enough to snatch it out of the sky. "It's true, past Speakers have not made nearly as many public statements as I have, but past Speakers were not dealing with a nation in a state of war. It's a troubling thought, I know, and the safety of our people is always foremost in my mind. Communication could not be more important right now. Between the Keepers and the citizenry, and between Prime and Icarion."

"You speak of the diplomatic convoy."

"I do, I do." He nodded solemnly. "We lost many lives in the Battle of Dralee, but not all, and those heroes who stood firm against the aggression of Icarion deserve our every effort to retrieve them."

Biran wouldn't know it, but at this moment the guys in graphics would slap up a picture of his sister—Sanda Maram Greeve—right along his face on all the screens of those watching. The family resemblance was made-for-TV obvious.

"Is it true that we do not yet know which of our soldiers survived that battle?"

He closed his eyes. Pain pinched his shoulders forward. Biran opened his eyes.

"It's true. We don't know. And I know what you're asking—I do. You want to know if I'm doing this for Sanda. For my sister. I won't lie to you, Callie, just like I won't lie to our people. It started out that way. I want my sister home. But I want all our heroes home, too. And if she's not in that group—if Sanda's not a survivor—well . . . Well then at least I will have brought someone else's sibling, someone else's loved one, home, wouldn't I? And isn't that worth every risk in the universe?"

His eyes glazed with tears that would not fall.

Stars above, she was going to get so much fan mail.

CHAPTER 16

PRIME STANDARD YEAR 3771

A DAY OF NEW FACES

Tomas Cepko. Sanda read his name twice, tracing her finger over the thin screen displaying the vital information of the man preserved in the evac pod. He was an Icarion, military, something to do with communications. She wondered what he'd be like, how he'd react to the terrible news she had to give him. As excited as she was to meet the man—get a chance to save *somebody* from this disaster—she dreaded that moment with all her heart.

Bero didn't say a word as she transported the mag pallet to the cargo elevator and then wheeled him down to the medibay. A few scrapes marred the pod's paint, but it was otherwise whole. The readout claimed the occupant was in good health, but she wanted to be ready. If he came out injured, or ill, having him already in the medibay could save precious time.

She rubbed her palms together with excitement and reached for the open sequence.

"Wait," Bero said.

"Oh, now you're talking to me." She hesitated, fingers poised above the buttons.

"You don't know who this man is."

"Tomas Cepko, communications first class, like it says on the reader. Seems clear enough."

"He's Icarion."

"So? So are you."

"And you're very much not."

Damn, he had a point. An Icarion agent was unlikely to react kindly to a lone Ada Prime woman making her home on an Icarion research vessel, especially one as classified as Bero. Combine that with the awful news she had to tell him, and things could get nasty in a hurry.

She swore. Waking up alone had been a gut-wrenching affair for her, and she hated to do it to Tomas, but she couldn't think of a better solution. Until she knew just what kind of man he was, she would keep him sequestered. For both their sakes. If he slowed down her efforts to reach Atrux, it could mean their death.

Luckily, the medibay had a quarantine scenario programmed into its locking system. It took a little extra time to grab foodstuffs, a cot, and make sure the medibay's small bathroom was operational. She rushed through the process, Bero offering suggestions all the way.

When she finished, she brushed sweaty hair back from her forehead and adjusted her prosthetic. A blister was forming along the back of her thigh.

"Happy?" she asked Bero, her gaze glued to the evac pod.

"It is the bare minimum. You realize that if you expect both of you to survive to Atrux, you're going to have to scavenge more supplies. You found enough to repair one pod, but—"

She waved for silence. "Give it a rest, please? I'll figure it out. *We'll* figure it out."

Grippy rolled into the medibay while Sanda retreated to the safety of the hallway. The door dilated shut behind her, and she punched the codes for a medical quarantine into the lockpad. The door limned in red LEDs—secured. She hated to give Grippy up for the time it'd take her to get a read on this guy, but somebody had to press the release buttons, and it certainly wasn't going to be her, or Bero.

She retreated to the command deck and strapped herself into a seat. Bero splashed every camera view of the medibay across the smart-screen. She leaned forward, licking her lips as Grippy approached the pod.

"Initiate release," she commanded. Her fingers tightened on the chair's armrests. A pointless affectation in low-g, but it made her feel secure.

Grippy input the code. Sanda held her breath.

The evac pod slid open on all sides, the armadillo-like scales collapsing down into the primary frame. Preservation foam held its shape a moment, a large globule of purple-grey matrix, then it destabilized. Slid out and away from the person it preserved.

Tomas Cepko woke seizing on the hard foam bed of the evac pod, every muscle twitching violently as his body threw off the invasive, metabolism-slowing foam.

Sanda averted her gaze. She wouldn't have wanted anyone to watch her in the same state. She knew what he was going through, had experienced it herself. Hers had been a gentler awakening, the NutriBath having already soothed and healed any aches. Tomas came out of the foam just the way he'd been put in. No mood stabilizers, no painkillers. Just raw emergence. Someone should be there for him. Someone he trusted. Someone safe. But there was only her and Bero, and Grippy had gone into hiding as soon as he'd hit the buttons.

"He's moving," Bero said.

Tomas crawled on his elbows toward the edge of the evac pod's bed, a much lower lip than the NutriBath had been. His jumpsuit hung about him in tatters, every muscle of his body trembling as he crawled through foam degrading into liquid and, more than likely, his own waste.

"Hello?" His voice was raspy, strained, but deep. He gripped the edge of the bed, his strength temporarily failing him, and rolled to his side to look around. "Hello?"

Sanda's thumb hovered over the speak button on her armrest. She didn't press it. She didn't want to tell him what she knew she must.

Tomas rallied and forced himself to a seat, then swung his legs over the edge. Very, very, slowly he eased himself upright. His knees wobbled, but they held. Flesh hung loose around atrophied muscles, the result of too long in an evac pod. He found the pile of towels, microcleanse, and fresh clothes she'd left for him and, methodically, washed and dressed himself. She looked away, granting him a little privacy. When Bero told her he was finished, she looked back to the screen.

Tomas Cepko sat cross-legged in the middle of the medibay, staring straight at the smartscreen on the wall. He had a hard face, a jagged quality that hinted at a life spent making difficult choices. The FitFlex jumpsuit hugged him tight, revealing the emaciated state of someone who'd spent too long in an evac pod. No surprise there, her own ribs still showed.

He said nothing. Just kept staring at that blank screen. Some sort of Icarion training? No—of course not. She was a damned moron. The quarantine protocol. She thumbed the zoom on Bero's lens and got a good look at the smartscreen. Sure enough, red letters on a black background flashed: QUARANTINE ACTIVATED.

Great. What a wonderful way to kick off getting to know each other. She was hoping to ease into that little bit of information, convince him she'd rather not have locked him up, but really she didn't have a choice. But now she was going into it backward, and he was probably pissed. She would have been.

Sanda took a breath, donned her command voice like an old sweater, and thumbed the talk button. "Welcome aboard *The Light of Berossus*, Mr. Cepko. How are you feeling?"

He cocked his head, glancing around for the source of the speakers. "I've been better. Who am I speaking with?"

"This is Gunnery Sergeant Sanda Greeve."

A flicker on his face, a slight twitch at the corner of his eye. Probably just a spasm. "I am unfamiliar with this ship, and your name. Why am I under quarantine?"

"This an Icarion research vessel."

He raised both brows. "Yes. I can see that."

Of course he could. He was Icarion himself, and in their military. This ship wasn't nearly the mystery to him that it had been to her upon awakening. She thumbed off the talk button to clear her throat, and started again. "What is the last thing you remember before the evac pod?"

He chuckled. "My mission was classified. But I can tell you my cruiser was hit by a Prime railgun. Did the others make it?"

"Negative."

He stiffened, snapping his head back. "All souls?"

"Save yourself."

He bowed his head, mouthed something she couldn't make out, and lifted his head once more. "Sergeant Greeve, may I request confirmation of your clearance level?"

She snorted, and let Tomas hear it. "Later, Cepko. We have other things to talk about first."

"I sincerely hope they have to do with the nature of this quarantine, and why nothing you're saying is in line with protocol."

She hadn't wanted to mislead him regarding who she was, but she also didn't want to dig into certain details right away. The longer she waited, the more irritated he was going to get. With a sigh, she flicked on her video feed. He sat bolt upright, eyes wide. She could see what he saw in a screen-in-screen display Bero put up for her.

Sanda sat, strapped into the command chair of Bero's deck. Her FitFlex jumpsuit fit, they always did, but she wore no insignia, no demonstration of rank. She'd hacked her hair back to little more than three inches of length, and her dark curls stuck up in all directions in low-g. It'd been a while since she'd looked at herself in the mirror—her aquiline nose was too much her brother's, her fathers'—and her own face startled her. She'd grown gaunt. Dark circles smeared under her eyes.

"You," Tomas said, "are no Icarion, Sergeant Greeve."

She smiled. It looked tight and pained on the camera. "No. I'm not. But I am your ally, Tomas Cepko."

His lip curled in derision. She held up a hand to forestall him. "Please, let me explain."

And she did. Slow, at first. Meandering, hedging around the point, the salient catastrophe of both their lives. Bero remained silent, not prodding, not correcting when she muddied small details and had to backtrack to straighten them out. He only added graphics to the screen, visuals and videos to underline her points. Tomas let her talk, too. From the slack shock in his face, she wondered if he were capable of interrupting.

As she spoke, the words became easier. She realized how long it'd been since she'd said more than a few sentences together. Bero was here, yes, but he knew all that had happened. She did not need to tell him her story. This man, this audience, patient and listening, absorbing, did more to relieve her tension than anything she'd tried in the days since her awakening.

"So, you see," she said, coming to the end. "I apologize for putting you under quarantine, but it was the only way to ensure my safety until we grow comfortable with each other. If you prefer, later, I do not make use of hab two. You may have it to yourself. But we are going to Atrux. Bero can take us there."

He was silent a very long time.

"Mr. Cepko?"

"That," he said, "is the most bullshit story I've ever heard."

CHAPTER 17

PRIME STANDARD YEAR 3541

A WEEK AFTER DRALEE, SOMETIME IN THE NIGHT

Biran rode the shuttle planetside. Some streak of nostalgia had made him don the jumpsuit common among military cadets and spacefarers of all kinds. Maybe some part of him had hoped the jumpsuit would make him blend in with the average populace. That part of him had been wrong.

Strapped into one of the five first-class seats, Biran caught the occasional set of eyes from the economy acceleration couches behind him in the mirrored sheen of the shuttle's viewscreen. They watched him in spurts and glances. He pretended not to see them, just as they pretended they weren't watching him.

Through the mirror-glaze of eyes, raw space moved outside the viewscreen. Not a simulation, not a screen piping in fresh video from cameras mounted on the shuttle. In some fit of anachronism, the original station-to-planet shuttles of Prime Inventive had been designed with real windows between the passengers and space. The first-class seats offered an uninterrupted and private view.

Biran wished he'd opted for the cheap seats. All he could think as he watched the atmosphere domes of the settlements of Ada come into view was how fragile they looked. How woefully unprotected.

"Docking," a gender-equalized voice said cheerfully from the speakers. Biran tightened his grip on the five-point harness hugging him in place. Pressure mounted as the shuttle passed from the vacuum into the thin atmosphere of the dome.

The shuttle turned, a lazy slalom designed to show the passengers the vista of Alexandria-Ada, the founding city of Ada Prime. All first Prime cities were named after the company's founder and original CEO, Alexandra Halston. Most of them got shortened to the planet's name in practice, but the homage was always there.

Biran wondered what she would have thought of that. For all her visionary thinking, the writings she'd left behind hadn't signaled that she was prone to that flavor of hubris. Probably, she'd be embarrassed. Though she was centuries dead, he felt a little empathetic embarrassment on her behalf as the speakers sang the welcome jingle to Alexandria-Ada (the Ada aspirated, pronounced so softly he could only hear it because he knew it was there).

The shuttle shivered against its docking port, and after a moment's hesitation the connecting tunnel door dilated, his harness swinging up in the same instant. Biran stood and stretched, then scooped his duffel out of the storage crate bolted to the floor alongside each first-class chair.

"Keeper—?" A voice, thin, came from behind him.

Biran hurried out before they could waylay him, guilt panging through him with each step he took. He didn't have time to gladhand, to soothe nerves or answer questions. He needed his own nerves soothed, and soon, before they snapped. Before he snapped.

An autocab awaited him at the curb just outside the station's main door, his ident number cycling in the side window, but not his name. He'd requested that. The last thing he needed was a crowd gathered around a cab flashing SPEAKER BIRAN AVENTURE GREEVE.

He didn't plan to be planetside long—he had only told Keeper Shun that he was going—and he wanted to be back long before he was missed. Preferably with no one noticing his presence here. The last week had seen him facing down the people of Ada every day through a camera lens, updating them on the war and Prime's efforts to keep the Icarion threat contained. Telling them all that the diplomatic mission to recover the lost was moving along smoothly. Soon the convoy would reach neutral territory and negotiations would begin in earnest. Peace, he assured every morning on the news broadcasts, was coming.

He didn't need to lie to them in person, too.

The car greeted him with a cheery beep as he swiped his wristpad over the sensor and slid in, slumping his weight against the cool polyleather seats as if he'd been holding all his muscles taut by sheer force of will until that moment.

He closed his eyes and was asleep in an instant. An arrival beep startled him out of his brief nap. The door snapped open to reveal the smooth, paved walkway up to a familiar, low, green house. Biran swiped his wristpad to pay and stumbled out, only remembering to grab his duffel because the cab alerted him he'd left something behind.

At 0300, the streetlights had been reduced to a milky glow, the dome above the city shaded indigo blue. Silence thickened the air like a heavy, warm blanket. The scent of a night-blooming flower and dirt—real dirt, not the sanitized flowerbeds of the station—kissed the breeze. This city was just as artificial as the station, he held no illusions about its authenticity, but the details here... The details here were the details of life, not work. Of family. Of home.

The front door opened. His father Graham filled the entrance, his hulking frame allowing only tiny slivers of the interior light to escape. He wore loose-legged sweatpants and a sleep shirt twisted askew, but he smiled like he'd known Biran was coming, and leaned against the doorframe.

"Gonna stand out there all night, son?"

Biran found himself in Graham's arms with no memory of the time in between, his duffel somehow slung over Graham's shoulder as he shuffled them both inside and plopped Biran onto the worn-shiny suede couch that Biran'd spent his childhood being told not to jump on.

Miraculously, the scent of cocoa-spiked chili drifted in from the kitchen. Ilan poked his head around the corner, a tomato-stained wooden spoon held aloft.

"You find him?" Ilan squinted at the pair.

"Found him standing on the street like a lost puppy," Graham said, and dropped the duffel on the floor.

Biran stared from one to the other. "You knew I was coming?"

"Please." Graham held a hand over his heart as if wounded. "You think I don't have every system in this city flagged to tell me when your ident number is used?"

"That's illegal."

"Ask me if I care." Graham snorted. "Though you could have picked a better hour to pay a visit. What would you have done if we were asleep?"

"Used my ident to access the house. Unless you've kicked me out of the system...?"

Ilan studied the ceiling, Graham picked at a speck of lint on his pants.

"You did?"

Ilan smirked. He was always the first to crack. "You are *so* gullible! Graham's got so-called illegal scripts combing the systems waiting to see if your ident gets anywhere near us, and you think we'd lock our kids out of the house?"

Kids. Biran winced and looked down at his hands, unwilling to meet his fathers' eyes as the slip became apparent to them. Sanda's number wouldn't be in their system. Not anymore. It would have been automatically purged from all systems the moment some bureaucrat switched her file from active to deceased.

"I hacked it in," Graham whispered. "Just in case. Ain't no bean counter's going to tell me I can't hope."

Illegal, too. Biran smiled, wistfully, and squeezed his older dad's knee. Ilan had done a lot to clean up Graham's act—or so he claimed—in the years since they'd been together, but Graham had never lost his flair for the underworld, his distrust of the system that both of his children ended up embracing. And being betrayed by. Biran swallowed the thought.

"What drags you down from orbit, anyway? I thought we wouldn't see you for a while, what with the convoy to manage and all," Ilan asked, forcing his voice up too high to sound fake cheery.

The options swam through Biran's mind in a dizzying rush. All the things he should be there for—Sanda's loss, that he hadn't seen them outside of CamCasts since the graduation. And the real reason, the words that hounded him every night. Buoy. Trap. Weapon. The words he could not say, for they were classified, and he'd done enough damage there already.

"I should have come sooner" was all he could say, not daring to lift his eyes from the scuffed SynthWood floor.

Graham put a hand over his, still resting on Graham's knee, and squeezed. "You've been busy."

"Making impassioned speeches to all of Prime," Ilan said, boastful, and when Biran dared to look up, Ilan's eyes were wide with pride and something else—something desperate. "Does the convoy have any information on the surviving pods yet?"

Translation: Are they going to bring our girl, our rock, home?

"I don't know... It's complicated."

Biran looked at Graham—Ilan wouldn't be able to hide his disappointment—and caught a hint of a knowing frown, something in his old man's past cluing him in to pieces of what might be going on behind the scenes.

"Is there anything we can do?" Ilan asked, wringing his hands together.

"Tell me about it," Graham said. "What you can, at any rate."

"I..." He swallowed a lump. Graham flicked a hand at Ilan, who scurried off to see to the chili. Warm, spicy aromas wafted from the kitchen anew as he stirred the pot and came back with a thick mug of sweet coffee. Ilan deposited it on the table, kissed Biran's head, then went back to his kitchen while Graham sat perfectly still, pressing Biran's hand but not trapping it. He wanted to weep from the comfort of it all.

"I made a mistake," he whispered. "I acted on incomplete information. I put people in danger."

"The convoy?"

"No." He shook his head. "Before that. I'm afraid... I'm afraid I'll make a mistake that large again."

Inferences chased themselves across Graham's face, the disparate pieces of information clashing together, warring with one another.

Biran knew his father was trying to puzzle out just what he meant—what it meant for Sanda. He also realized—must realize—that Biran would have elaborated if he could have. The desire to tell them everything was a physical ache in his chest. Why had he come here? How could he unburden himself if he could only share partial information? How could he lay so many questions at his father's feet and walk away without answering any of them?

"Did you mean to?" Graham asked, startling Biran out of his downward spiral. Biran blinked at him, trying to focus.

"Mean to what?"

"Make a mistake."

"You can't plan to make a mistake, Dad."

"Then stop being so hard on yourself, idiot."

Biran snort-laughed, the release so sudden that something shook loose within him and warm tears flushed their way down his cheeks. Graham grumbled something incoherent and dragged his thumb across both of Biran's cheeks, wiping the tears on his ratty pajama pants. "Got yourself too locked down, lad."

"Nature of the job."

Graham squinted at the living room's picture window, and though the curtains were pulled, he looked as if he were staring straight through the fabric, the glass, even the dome of Ada to the station orbiting somewhere above—and Biran's bosses within.

"You got friends up there? People you can talk to—honestly?" People in the loop, he meant. People who could hear classified information and be trusted.

"Friends?" He scoffed. "In that viper's nest?"

Graham gave him a long, heavy look. "Somebody told you about those lights."

Anaia. Dios, he'd been such an ass to lump her in with the others just because she'd cozied up to Lili. But to get too close to her now would open her up to suspicion from his superiors. If they knew where his friendly ears were, they'd have leverage. The thought chilled him. He'd never considered that the Protectorate would want leverage against him. How had things gotten so screwed, so quickly? How had he become the dissenting voice in the organization he loved?

Because it'd never been that organization. It'd been a farce—a face—a public-soothing construction.

The realization didn't bother him. It...eased him, somehow. Released the tension from his shoulders and cooled the sourness that'd roiled his belly ever since Director Olver had rebuked his evidence that there were green lights in the rubble field.

If that organization, the one he'd been raised to love and revere, had never been, then he wasn't betraying it. Could not, by definition, turn his back on something that hadn't existed.

And if it hadn't existed in the way he had thought, then that left a hole in the society he loved. But a void could be filled, repaired. Maybe he could create the organization he believed in. If he worked hard enough, and gathered allies, change might be possible. Lavaux was already frustrated with the state of things. Surely he would want to help Biran reshape the ossified system that'd precipitated into a shell around Biran's ideal.

"He been quiet this whole time?" Ilan asked, flopping onto the couch and splaying his arms over the back and corner armrest.

"Yup. Five minutes now," Graham said, chuckling as Biran blinked back into the moment and stared at his father, wide-eyed with admiration. "But it looks like it was a productive silence."

"How'd you do that?" Biran asked, reaching up to rub the back of his neck where the Keeper chip was implanted.

"Sit quietly while you ruminated?"

"No. Answer my worries without knowing what they are?"

Graham quirked a smile. "Who says I didn't know? I can read your face like a broadcast, Little B."

The nickname sunk his lifting heart. Sanda had coined that name—little brother, little Biran, Little B—and his fathers rarely used it. Graham caught his falling heart by ruffling his hair and patting him, hard, on the back. "There. You get back up there, and you make the world you want."

"But you're going to eat first!" Ilan sprang to his feet and grabbed Biran by both hands, sweeping him along to the kitchen before he could protest. "There's no reshaping a government on an empty stomach."

He'd stocked the house for doomsday. Dozens and dozens of jars of preserved jellies, jams, sauces, and pickled vegetables of all kinds crammed the shelves inset on the wall so full that the resilient Synth-Wood bowed in the middle from all the weight. Biran froze at the sight, not understanding, until Graham's hand alighted upon his shoulder and he whispered, just for the two of them.

"Cooking's how he copes."

Biran nodded, shakily, snapping back into himself as Ilan flew through the kitchen, clattering cabinets as he dug out bowls.

Biran took his seat at the battered old table, his back to the kitchen and his eyes to the stubby bay window that looked out over their sleepy little street. Graham and Ilan sat at opposite heads of the table, thumping heavy bowls laden with steaming chili in front of them all. All, save the seat with its back to the window.

The view out that window was wrong. He'd never seen so much of it before—so much of the skyline, the street, the air, the… bits always hidden behind Sanda's broad-shouldered body. Her ponytail flipping here and there—obscuring first a tree, then a cool autocar he wanted to see drive by but her face would turn just right to block the view.

He could see all of that view, now. The autos and the trees and the constellation of city lights. But they were dull, lifeless. Not worth seeing without Sanda's brightness obscuring the view.

It didn't occur to him until the shuttle ride home to wonder how Graham coped.

CHAPTER 18

PRIME STANDARD YEAR 3541

IN A SYSTEM FAR, FAR AWAY

More than tumbledown warehouses peppered the edge of the Grotta. Bars—real throwbacks with flesh-and-bone bartenders and dirty glasses—sprouted throughout the desolation like wild seeds, taking advantage of the low rent and lower morals of the residents. A couple of them attracted the rich from the city proper, slick young things trying to look rough around the edges, betrayed by the perfect placement of the rips in their jeans.

Universe wasn't one of those bars.

Jules wouldn't even come here if the pours weren't heavy and the owner, Tragger, didn't look the other way about his clientele. Couldn't look at him straight on, anyway. Man had a glass eye he could afford to fix but refused to. Said it gave him character. Jules suspected he liked that you could never quite tell just where, exactly, he was looking. He had an eye patch over it tonight. Must have gotten the thing infected again.

Harlan led them to the bar, putting on his biggest-bad-in-the-room walk, and those few barflies Jules didn't recognize scattered from the counter for the safety of shadowed tables. The regulars stayed put. They never left their corners. Never even looked up when Jules and her crew entered. If they had names, Jules didn't know them, and chances were good they'd forgotten them long ago, anyway. Only value they had left in life was the number of their credit line, bleeding their basic income away into Tragger's pockets.

Maybe they had apartments, maybe even ate solid food sometime, but here they were just siphons. In goes the booze, out goes the money. Repeat until death. Couldn't even tell their ages. When Jules was younger, she fancied one of them might be her father—and what a story would that make? Her making the unlikely discovery, tears in her long-lost dad's eyes as she introduced herself and set on the long path of getting him on the straight and narrow. Maybe even get a dog, or something.

She'd never been good at fantasies.

Jules plopped onto a stool and swiveled round to find Tragger already pouring out a heavy slug of grot—the local moonshine of the Grotta diluted with roasted black tea—into an almost clean glass. Must be feeling generous tonight.

"To a successful op!" Lolla cheered and raised her glass to clink with the others.

Nox, ever one to embrace a good mood, scooted his stool near them and leaned over into a conspiratorial huddle. "We going to talk about that corpse?"

Tragger cleared his throat loudly and walked to the other end of the bar.

"No," Harlan said, swirling his glass so hard a bit splashed out over his hand. "Nothing to talk about."

"Corpses are pretty big topics of conversation, despite their own reticence." Nox swallowed half his glass in one long gulp.

"That corpse is old news. No one saw us. No mess. A clean in and out, despite the detour. Nothing to talk about aside from where we'll hit next."

"I'm . . . not so sure about that." Jules took a fortifying sip as all eyes swiveled to her. She wished they'd stop staring at her like that, all narrow-eyed like they simultaneously hoped she had answers to their questions and were getting ready to disbelieve anything she was about to say. "Look, that guy was just a runner. Definitely one of the three I saw moving the stash. Why bother killing a runner?"

"'Cause they did something stupid, like sticking their nose in where it doesn't belong."

"I'm just saying." Jules put her glass down and leaned forward. "That lab had something bigger going on than what we expected, right? What if it was...I don't know, some kind of trap?"

"A trap? For us?" Lolla's voice squeaked.

"We keep our heads down." Harlan glanced around the room and dropped his voice. "Which is why we never should have gone through that lab."

"Fastest way out." Jules snapped out the words. The adrenaline of the night scraped at her nerves. She needed to calm herself down if she wanted them to listen to her.

"She's right," Nox cut in, giving her a chance to gather herself. "And anyway, weren't any cameras. We set off some kind of motion thing but no one was there. Just a bunch of hocus pocus to scare us."

"Except for the corpse," Jules mumbled. "Wasn't scared to death, was he?"

"Could have a bum ticker," Nox said.

"Don't be stupid. Look, when I went back in, it was all locked up but there were a few things out. I think they were manufacturing wraith mother in there."

Nox's eyebrows shot up. "You sure about that?"

Her cut fingers, the cool, foggy liquid dripping across her open wounds and mingling with her blood—flashing before it absorbed, or evaporated. The rising sense of euphoria, of vitality coursing through her veins. Yeah. She was sure. She just wasn't sure she wanted them to know she'd been so clumsy. Or that she might be high right now.

"I know what I saw," she said instead.

"You grabbed smartboards, right? Let me see them." Lolla held her hand out while Harlan glared at her over the rim of his glass. Well, fuck him. She'd run that op well—and maybe even got them a bigger payday than moving wraith would allow. Shit, if they were real lucky, they might even be able to frequent a bar *not* in the Grotta. Though they'd probably have to get some new clothes first.

She reached into her bag and rummaged for the tablet-sized boards. Her fingers hit the three of them, hastily crammed together into a back pocket, and a thought occurred to her—Harlan could take them. Would take them, if there was anything he didn't like on them. So she pulled out two and moved the bag around to her back before anyone could notice the leftover weight.

"Everything was locked up tight except these," she said as she handed the boards over to Lolla. "Must have just missed whoever was working on them."

"Could have been the corpse," Nox threw in.

"You think a runner was working up chemicals in some lab?" Jules asked.

"He was dead awhile, anyway," Lolla said distractedly, flipping through what she could access on the surface of the boards.

"Right. So our friends were stepping over a corpse for the past couple days to get in and out, and no one thought to clean up the mess?" Nox frowned. "I don't like this."

"Could have been going out the cargo load, same way we did," Jules offered, but even she wasn't convinced, and the withering glare Harlan gave her shut her up. She couldn't argue with him if she was coming up with nonsense like that.

"Guys," Lolla said in a harsh whisper, "this isn't wraith."

"What is it?" Harlan asked, peering over the girl's shoulder.

"It looks like some kind of tech . . . they're working on a kind of, I don't know, neural interface? I'd have to see more to be sure."

"Great." Nox slouched and threw his elbows over the back of the chair. "We raided the dive lab of some shitty start-up. What a score."

"Doesn't explain the body," Lolla pointed out.

"Hold up." Jules set her drink down and pulled up an app on her wristpad. "I took some pics of the big board before I bolted. Any of this help?"

She contorted so that Lolla could see the slightly blurry images splashed across her display. The girl's brows knotted as she pinched and zoomed on a few of them. She went pale as a ghost.

"Oh. That's . . . I know these materials . . ."

"Well? What is it?"

Lolla dropped her voice so low Jules thought she couldn't possibly have heard right at first.

"They're all nonreactive, miniMRI compatible. There's only one reason you'd bother with materials like that in a chip, and that's if you plan on scanning it on the regular. That's a Keeper chip."

"How the hell do you know all that?"

She rolled her eyes. "Only the Keepers bother going through the hassle of making tech out of nonreactive materials for their mini-MRIs. Waste of time and money for anyone else."

Her stomach dropped. "Keepers like . . . like Prime and all that?"

"Know of any other Keepers?" Nox hissed. "I guess that explains our corpse?"

"Does it?" Jules fixated on the blurry image of the chip Lolla had zoomed in on, trying to make sense of the various diagrams.

"Who's got the power to make a corpse and cover it up? Prime, that's who."

"Prime's also got the money and the power to set up a proper facility, not hang out in a rotten husk at the edge of the Grotta. Can't be them."

"Unless one of them was doing something they didn't want the others to know about," Nox said.

"This," Harlan said into all their slack expressions, "is so fucking beyond us."

Jules foundered for a moment, then pulled her thoughts together. "If there's a rogue Keeper, the rest are going to want to know about it."

"Shit. What are you going to do? Go to the cops and tell them you just happened to stumble across a secret Keeper lab while heisting some wraith? They'd lock you in the loony ward faster than you could spit."

"No, no, fuck the cops. I'm thinking . . . I'm thinking we do a little digging, find out who's using that lab. Then we make them think we're going to go to the cops."

"You want to blackmail a rogue Keeper." Nox whistled low. "Got bigger balls than me, girl."

Harlan snatched the boards from Lolla's hands and shoved them into the interior pocket on his jacket, not bothering to lock the screens.

"This is insanity. Forget you ever saw this—all of you. We're going to factory reset these devices, sell them for the price of the hardware, throw that credit in the wraith pile, and call it a day. Understand? We're not fucking with Keepers." He dropped his voice so low on the last word it came out as a growl.

Jules made a lunge for the boards but he swatted her back. "Those are mine to do with as I please."

"Not anymore, kid. You just got robbed. Tough luck."

"When did you get so damned cowardly?"

He loomed toward her. Bloodshot spiderwebs reached across yellowed sclera, the dark ring around his once vibrant grey eyes long since faded with his youth. Wrinkles—a rarity outside the strangled lives of the Grotta—lined his lips and punctuated those tired eyes.

"It's not cowardice, Jules Valentine. It's staying in your lane. Knowing how high you can pick your head up before it gets chopped off. People in this world, they don't give a shit about the likes of us. Not the people in the Grotta, not the people in the city proper, and not the elites on station or up the hills. Sure as hell not the Keepers. You ever met a Prime employee who didn't look down their nose at you? I'm not talking Keepers or diplomats—I'm talking their starfucked janitors, their receptionists. It's not even a secret to the credit-strapped sop who makes their sandwiches that we're beneath them. You can't play in that pool, girl. They don't want you. Keep sticking your head up in their space, and they'll push it down so hard you drown. Understand?"

"Hell of a mixed metaphor."

"You want it straight? You fuck with the Keepers, and there won't even be a body for us to identify."

"Jules," Lolla said, her voice soft and scared. "If it's dangerous—"

"Everything we do is dangerous." She slammed back the rest of her drink and dropped the glass, tottering on the bar top. "Everything we do out here—just existing—in the Grotta risks our lives. Could get robbed and rolled every second we walk down the street. Yeah, yeah, save me your 'there are rules' and the weird scumbag chivalry, but I'm sick of it, all right? I'm sick of having to puff up my shoulders and walk like the biggest bitch in the world every time I want to stroll down the street to have a smoke. I'm sick of watching my back at every corner, at every doorway. Of minding my clothing so I don't draw too much attention, or signal the wrong attention. Prime's so far above us they don't see us anymore, so maybe we should stand the fuck up for once in our lives and make them see us, right? Maybe we should dust off the gutter grime just this once?

"But you won't. You won't ever stick your neck out. Not because of any weird desire to keep us protected. You're just a scared, proud old man who can't admit when an op's a little too dicey. You want to keep rolling over low-key dealers and pinching hardware to wipe and sell at cost? Fucking fine, you do that, starfucker, but some of us don't want to hustle until we're dead. Rope enough credit together, launder it out, and we could go legit. Did you ever think of that?

"No—of course you fucking didn't because you don't think past anything your miserable life has already taught you. Could have clean apartments, Harlan. Could walk down the street in a neighborhood without fear. Could even start a business with the credit we could wring from this—a real one—and go straight. But you're too scared of change. Or maybe you're just too scared of being made obsolete. Want us to rely on you for the rest of your withered days? Well fuck you, Harlan, because once you're in the dust—and that's coming soon, I can see it on your dead little face—we're going to have to figure out our own paths. And unlike you, maybe our paths lead up. And out."

His face sunk. Every fine line already mapping a geology of years through his leathery skin deepened with tension. Harlan's mouth flapped open—his usually too-smooth, too-right mouth—and Jules found through the adrenaline clouding her mind (or maybe that was the wraith, yeah, probably the wraith) that while she once waited to hear his every word, now—now it just seemed sad and pathetic.

She didn't want his advice. His advice kept her in that rathole apartment cubby off the crew's main quarters. That cubby had seemed luxurious to her once, when she'd been scared and still getting used to the feel of blood on her hands. It had been hers—probably the only thing in the universe that had been legitimately hers—and there'd been comfort in that. Now, the idea of going back to that slick little hole in the wall with its few personal items stifled her. Suffocated her very thoughts.

Harlan said something. Jules didn't hear it through the thunder in her mind. The storm of years of frustration coming to a head all at once, all over one old man's lack of vision. Of ambition.

"Save it," she said. Harlan stopped.

She pushed to her feet and swayed once. The weird disassociation that came with high doses of wraith crawled through her skin, forced her mind out of her body, and she saw herself, all of a sudden, through what felt like Lolla's eyes but was, of course, her own deepest experience of herself. A hard-bitten woman who was loud to cover how scared she was—the kid at the core—the raw and unformed person she would be, could be, if only she stopped tumbling down the cliff she'd already thrown herself off of.

Everything snapped back into place and there was Nox smirking at her, but in his eyes was something like admiration. An edge of hunger that had nothing to do with sex or food. What she'd said had shaken him, made him think. If she called on him, he'd follow. Comfortable as Lolla and Harlan had made themselves at the bottom, Nox didn't like it any more than she did. He just lacked imagination on how to crawl out.

"Where are you going?" Harlan called out, turning the heads of everyone in Universe. Jules had stomped her way to the door without thinking, riding high on the booze and the wraith and the anger, her hands shoved down into her pockets so that those near her wouldn't see how tight her fists were.

"Out," she snapped, and stepped into the rot-slick streets of the Grotta. A fine mist had congealed the dirt on the roads. Cleaner bots didn't make it out this far anymore; they kept getting stripped down for parts.

She'd walked a half mile, stuck in the storm in her own head, before she remembered the third smartboard in her bag. Jules keyed up Arden's number on her wristpad and hailed them for a call. Their tired face snapped into view quickly, hair mussed from lack of brushing, but they'd been awake. A little bit of grease smeared their chin.

"What?" they asked. Then squinted. "Where the hell are you?"

"The street. Doesn't matter. I got something I need you to strip the data out of it, make it readable."

Arden rubbed the side of their face with one hand, making that grease smear wider. "I don't hack diaries."

"Fuck you. This is sellable."

"If it's any good, I get a cut. Eighty percent."

"Ten percent."

"Hah. Sixty percent."

"Thirty percent, Arden, and I won't dent that pretty face of yours." They rolled their eyes. "Fine. It's probably garbage, anyway."

Arden's apartment—if one were being generous with the word— was slotted in a dim hallway two stories above an udon noodle place. As long as Jules had lived in the Grotta, Udon-Voodun had been a staple of the local cuisine. A spice-fraught mix of retro-cool, old-world Jamaican seasoning and Japanese noodle making, the place was an immovable object in the great currents of the Grotta's residents. She was pretty sure it had started out as little more than a metal-slab lean-to, and had grown over the years into a proper building, sprouting apartments like warts as the Grotta's residences gravitated toward the warmth and the stability. No one had ever bothered to install air vents capable of removing the scents of the cooking below, so every resident carried the permanent aroma of jerk spice and bonito. Most of them wore it like a badge of pride. Arden was one of those.

"You high?" They filled the doorway, squinting at her. She shoved them aside and let herself in, kicking off her boots in the small square entryway.

"Don't be stupid. I just got off an op."

"Pupils tell another story."

"Adrenaline."

"Whatever."

A mat covered in tangled sheets took up a third of Arden's room, the bathroom and a sink with a hot plate and a carbon-matter extruder the second third, and their desk—riddled with the carcasses of technology mid-vivisection—the last third. Jules barely had room for her feet, so she crossed her arms and leaned against the desk, pretending not to notice when it creaked under her weight.

"So what's worth hauling your ass all the way over here in the middle of the night?"

"I was just down the street." She slung her bag off her shoulder, rummaging for the board she'd kept back from Harlan.

"I need you to look at this, scrape any data on it you can, and stick it onto something I can read."

"Something you can sell."

"Same thing. Gotta be able to read it to know who to sell it to."

They took the board from her and skimmed the surface writings, forehead wrinkling. "This is Keeper tech."

"I don't care what it is. Break it and filter it out for me."

"Shit, Jules. Where did you even get this? Rob a Keeper on the street or something?"

"None of your business where I got it, but you can keep your undies on. No Keeper knows I have it, I doubt they even know it's missing."

"I seriously don't know how that's possible."

"It is. This going to be a problem?"

They pushed past her and sat down at the desk, running a hand through one half of their shaggy brown hair as they pored over the device, flicking their way in and out of the surface apps, fussing a bit when they hit auth screens.

"I don't know. I mean, I've messed with some tight systems, but Keeper encryption...I mean, I don't think this is Keeper tech. Oh, it's about Keepers, don't get me wrong, but it's not half as shut down as it should be. Yeah. I think I can break it."

"Sweet. How long?"

"Hold on, we gotta talk my pay."

"Already negotiated that. Situation hasn't changed."

"Like hell it hasn't. The percent stays the same, fine, the amount of work for me isn't much different, anyway, but where are you going to sell this? Do you even have a buyer lined up?"

"I just got it, Arden. Give me a fucking chance to put some things in motion."

"Hell no." They squinted at her again, sizing up her condition. She pushed her shoulders back and stared them down. "You sell this to the wrong person, and you'll bring hell down on all of us. I'm good, Jules, but I'll leave tracks that people with the resources of the Keepers can find. There's no helping that. I don't have the kind of tech they do. But I think...I think I might know someone."

"Someone who can break it?"

"No, no. I'm still all you got there. But someone you could sell it to. It's weird." They frowned and kicked off the corner of the desk, spinning the chair as they thought. She scowled and put a hand on the arm of the chair to stop their spin.

"Weird how?"

"I've heard rumblings, recently. Some woman—calling herself Silverfang, like she's some old-school-cool hacker or some shit, was poking around some net fringes I frequent last week. She was offering serious credit for anyone who had data on the Keepers. Good, authenticated shit. I thought she was just some weird conspiracy nut looking for followers, but I dunno. Maybe this is the kind of thing she wants. She was getting a lot of turbulence from the regulars, people who thought she was wasting time and fucking around, so she dropped off the channels. But I can find her again, I'm pretty sure of that."

"Put your little hacker feelers out then and find her."

Arden frowned. "Seriously, where'd you get this?"

She sighed and let the arm of the chair go, holstering her bag back onto her shoulder. "Side benefit of another op."

"Pretty big Easter egg."

"Yeah. I'm thinking about that."

"Harlan can't be on board with this."

"He's not. You get an update about this, you call me directly, all right?"

They held both of their hands up, palms out. "Whoa. I'm not sure what's going on with you two, but I'm a neutral party here. You offered me a job and a cut. You're my contact. Easy as that. But... uh...Maybe try to smooth things over with him? I know he's a cranky fuck, but...Where are you going?"

Jules tugged her boots on and had her hand on the door before she realized she'd even decided to leave. "Out. Got some steam to blow off. Get on this as soon as you can. Call me when you got something."

"Jules, wait—"

She slammed the door and stomped out onto the street. The scents of Udon-Voodun called to her, pulled her back toward the warm embrace of hot noodles and hotter broth. But if she stuck around, Arden would insist on bending her ear, and she didn't want their therapy.

She should go back to the crew's digs, crawl into her cubby bed and sleep off her anger, but wraith mother pumped through her veins and she'd never felt more alive, more human. She wanted to run, to sprint and fight and fuck. Couldn't do that last one without complication—she didn't have the credit to hire anyone discreet—but she could walk. And think. The streets, at least, were still free. Even in the Grotta.

CHAPTER 19

PRIME STANDARD YEAR 3771

THREE DAYS LATER THE NEW GUY STILL WON'T TALK

Tomas tacked a sheet over the smartscreen and refused to say another word. It ate at her. Every routine piece of maintenance she did, every check on their course or Bero's diagnostics—hell, even showering—she was aware of another living, breathing human on board the ship. And he was giving her the silent treatment. So she retreated to the one place she was meant to be alone: the debris field.

She fell into an easy harmony with Bero's robotic arm, guiding it through the twisted wreckage on her hunt for life-sustaining morsels. Whether or not Tomas wanted to talk to her, he was in as much deep shit as she was. If they were going to survive this journey, they would need to repair and refit *both* evac pods. Three days trawling the field since Tomas's arrival, and she had yet to find anything half so promising as Tomas's used pod.

"The window for proper acceleration around Kalcus is closing," Bero chirruped into her helmet.

"Thank you, oh big-brained AI, for performing the duties of my calendar alerts."

A sigh across the speakers. She wondered how he'd modulated those tones. "I understand you wish to preserve both lives, but you have combed this debris field on six occasions. While I admire how quickly you've adapted to using your prosthetic in zero-g, I must insist that further EVAs into this field are futile. A waste of both time and resources."

"I'd love to hear your plan B, oh wise one."

"I don't think you would."

Silence stretched between them.

"You're not serious," she said.

"It is a possibility. If he cannot be trusted while you are in coldsleep during the journey, then it may be the only solution."

"*Jettison*? Dios, Bero. Would you have jettisoned me if I'd been hostile?"

A pause. "I'm uncertain. I require a human crew if I am to make it to Atrux alive. Grippy is capable of a great many repairs, but he lacks the dexterity for many tasks."

She cut the airjets and drifted, imagining the cold of space seeping through her suit, no matter that it was impossible. Space surrounded her. It always had. Even on world she was, technically, just on a larger space-ship. But it felt different now. Pressing in on her in a way it never had before. She knew what it was to feel alone. Had known the truth of that from the moment she'd accepted what Bero told her was true—and con-firmed it when she saw the smear of light that had once been Ada Prime.

Bero's voice had been some comfort. Had. Now she wondered, wondered deeply, just what she really knew about the spaceship she called home. Bero was her life raft, her last-ditch effort to survive the destruction her species had wrought. And he put her in the same cat-egory as Grippy, the robot. Not that she had anything against robots, but she'd at least expected the AI to acknowledge she was another sentient being. She counted Bero as a person in her own mind.

This was why Ada Prime didn't give their AI personalities when it came right down to it. You couldn't trust the cold, metal bastards.

"You really would. You would have jettisoned me."

"It's different for me." A harsh edge etched Bero's voice. "You do not invite those you do not trust to enter your body, do you? You live in my veins. Can reach into my mind and rearrange things at will. There is… intimacy, in having your mind contained in a place of dwelling."

She recognized that tone—the same edge she'd heard when Bero had shouted at her not to attempt the repair on the gasket. *It's dangerous out there.*

It's dangerous in there, too, she thought, but bit her tongue. Tomas's arrival had pushed something in Bero, activated a paranoia she'd only caught glimpses of since that first day. But was that fair? What would it be like for her, if people could invade her body at will, rearrange her innards, tweak the systems of her nerves and heart without her permission? Bero was permanently in a state of surgery, conscious.

Even before the Protocol, that would be enough to drive anyone mad.

Sanda's head ached as if she had a brain freeze. Damn coldsleep side effects.

"He doesn't mean you harm."

"You can't know that."

"No. I can't. And I can only imagine what it's been like for you, having strangers come and go without asking your permission. I'm sorry I didn't ask first. I'm sorry I brought him in and woke him up against your judgment. But we're alone out here, Bero. If we're to make it, we need all the help we can get. If he proves dangerous, then I'll leave his fate up to you. But right now, we're the only two humans kicking around this star system, and I've got to protect that."

"Understood."

"That's computer-talk. Stop it."

A pause. "I'm afraid, Sanda."

She breathed out, emptying her lungs down to the bottom of her belly. "Me too. But I've got your back, Bero, and I need to know you've got mine, too."

"I do not have a back."

She laughed. "Fine. I'm looking out for you. You look out for me, too. Okay?"

"Okay."

The edge was not gone, but it was softened. He could modulate his voice to play off her emotions, but if she followed her thoughts down that rabbit hole there'd be no coming back.

"What is our sulky friend up to, anyway?" she asked to lighten the topic. She hit the airjets, angling back toward Bero's 'lock.

"He has spent the last three days querying information about my schematics, crew, and all stored news sources. I'm afraid he's disappointed."

"Disappointed?"

"He expected to find proof of the Protocol, but the in-system web went out with the planets and all their geosynchronous systems. I have plenty of news of the first bombardment of Ada Prime, but the final stroke eradicated anyone who would have left a report. Aside from myself."

"Why do you think he's digging around in your specs?"

"I suspect he's attempting to discern if we can truly make it to Atrux. I believe he has, again, been disappointed."

She winced. "Not an optimist, then."

"I'm afraid not."

"Any idea what his post was with Icarion?"

"His ident chip scans as a communications specialist, but there are irregularities."

"Like?"

"What was a communications specialist doing in an evac pod in a debris field that should only have been made up of empty pods being transported? The ship was autopiloted. It didn't even have atmosphere."

"Huh." She drifted into the 'lock, sealed the exterior door, and waited for the pressure to stabilize. When the green light winked at her, she popped her helmet and swung the door open onto the command deck, pulling herself straight through low-g and to the ladder up to hab 1. After four hours debris hunting, she was in serious need of a shower. At least she didn't have to worry about water on Bero.

"Sanda?"

"Yup?"

"He's hailing you."

She froze midstep and almost tripped as her makeshift prosthetic rolled awkwardly to the side. "CamCast?"

"Yes. I can activate the smartscreen in the hall outside the medibay door for you."

"That'll do." She shoved a hand through her hair in a vain attempt to tame it from its time under her helmet, remembered she'd hacked most of it off, and laughed. She looked absolutely mad—living alone on a spaceship, scrambling around in debris fields for likely parts, and only half remembering to care for human needs. But that was her reality now. His, too, if he came around.

Sanda popped a panel in the wall and stored her helmet, then ambled toward the smartscreen. She stared at it a long while, watching her own reflection in the shiny black glass. Now or never.

She jabbed the screen with one finger, and Bero brought the feed live.

Tomas stood just before the pad she'd once used to squawk a distress call. He wore the jumpsuit she'd left for him and had put more work into his appearance than she had. He'd trimmed his dark hair in uneven chunks and scraped his chin free of stubble. Not a bad-looking man, aside from the usual malnutrition that accompanied spending too much time in an evac pod. A pensive look pinched his features, as if he wasn't sure if this was a good idea or not.

He looked her over in the same way she had measured him, and nodded to himself.

"Sergeant Greeve, I have been looking into your ship's claims."

"And?"

"I—" He cleared his throat, a rough sound. "I believe them."

She smiled. The lie showed in the tension around his eyes. "No, you don't."

A sigh deflated him, slumped his shoulders, and made him shake his head. "You're right. Sorry—it's just. It's all so terrible. They wouldn't."

"They would. They did." She bit her lip to stifle a building rant.

"I see that you believe it. Easier, maybe, when it's the other side." He glanced at his hands, turning them over as if seeing them for the first time. "Can you show me?"

She frowned. "Show you what?"

"Proof. Something, anything."

"Bero's records—"

"Could be corrupted."

Bero said, indignant, "They are not."

He grimaced, and she took a little perverse pleasure in that. So the Icarion wasn't quite so comfortable with a personality-matrix AI after all.

"I've been throwing distress signals in every likely direction since the day I woke up. You're a comms man, Cepko. It's been—" She hesitated, rummaging around in her memories. Tomas had been on board three days, but the time before that had blurred together for her. Easier to lose track of time when you didn't have any appointments to keep. "How long, Bero?"

"Twenty-four days," he said.

"Yes. Twenty-four days since I woke up to a dead star system, and we've gone from the rubble field of the Battle of Dralee to Kalcus's outer orbit. Just how likely is it that no one would hear us, that no one would respond? If we're wrong, then where are your Icarion buddies? I'm from Ada Prime. My brother is—was—training to be a Keeper, and I've been kicking around on their state-of-the-art ship without so much as a trespass warning. They're gone, Tomas. They're all gone."

A muscle flexed in his jaw. "Physical proof, I mean. The signals could be corrupted—"

She held up a hand to forestall him, then clenched it into a fist. Damn stubborn man. "I don't have the time, nor the patience, to convince you. No—wait—we're not under thrust yet. Hold on."

"What—?"

But she'd already limped a few meters back down the hall and punched open the helmet closet. She grabbed the one she thought of as hers and tucked another under her arm, then hurried back to the screen, false leg jarring the soft skin of her thigh. She spent too long trolling around in low-g, letting the environment convince her she had never been injured. If she were going to get used to this thing, she needed to spend more time with weight on it. Building calluses, strengthening muscles in new ways. But that could wait.

She needed Tomas on her side. And there was only one way to guarantee that.

"You do EVAs before?" she asked, holding up the second helmet. His eyebrows shot up.

"Often. In comms, that's sometimes the only way to make a repair."

"Super. With you in a sec." She wiped his confused face away and brought up the quarantine protocol screen.

"Sanda, is this really a good idea?" Bero asked.

"Only one I got."

Bero bit whatever his equivalent of a tongue was. Good enough for her. She was having trouble convincing just one of the new men that'd stumbled into her life. She didn't want to have to convince Bero of the merits of her actions, too. Especially because she wasn't entirely convinced of them herself.

She punched in the code she'd set to release the quarantine. Yellow warning lights blinked out. The medibay door dilated.

Tomas Cepko shuffled to the open portal, hesitant, his hands held easy at his sides. Despite the calm of his stance, he flicked his gaze up and down the hallway as if expecting a bunch of Icarions to pop out and yell "surprise." Too bad for him, this was no prank. She really, really wished that it was.

"Kill me," she said, "and Bero will vent all the O_2 on the ship and lock all doors. Understood?"

His jaw dropped open. He blinked owlishly at her for a second before he closed his mouth. She thought she caught a hint of a smile, but he soon erased it. "I don't want to hurt you, Sergeant. There's no need for threats."

"Pardon me if I don't yet trust your word."

She chucked him the spare helmet and he caught it in one hand, turning it over to check the seals.

"I take it you know how to use that thing?"

"Yeah, counter-screw it in then plug it into a lifepack. Icarion standard-issue."

"Ada Prime, too. See, we got something in common already."

He smiled for real, and it gave him two monumentally dorky dimples right below his cheeks. Like a baby's bare ass. She laughed.

"What?"

"Nothing. Look, I know you've been digging around in Bero's schematics, so I know I don't have to tell you the way. Lifepacks are in the closet by the ladder to command. Stay in front of me at all times."

"Yes, Sergeant." He snapped her a salute, and she rolled her eyes.

He may be a pain in the ass, but it was nice to have someone available to check the seals on her helmet and pack, as was protocol. Bero's assurances were good enough for her, but a sensor could always fail.

She followed him down, watching his head swivel this way and that as he took in the command deck. Bero had slapped up a vid feed of what was in front of them on the huge smartscreen, a view of the curve of Kalcus and beyond, star-speckled black. It was beautiful, but it wasn't what she'd had in mind. Tomas needed proof. Physical proof.

She figured he couldn't argue much after he'd seen it with his own eyes. Being honest with herself, she hadn't really believed it until that moment, either.

The 'lock whispered shut behind them and Bero went through the process without a word. They were talking less and less lately, had fallen into a steady, synchronized silence even before she'd found Tomas. Now that the comms specialist had made an appearance, that silence didn't feel quite so comfortable anymore. There was a sharpness in it, a sullen anger. She couldn't shake the feeling the spaceship was pouting.

"We're dark side of Kalcus, so don't sweat the sun. Once we're out, take a moment to orient yourself. We can't see Icarion from here, not this time of year, but you'll see Ada." Her voice caught. "What's left of her."

He nodded, his expression growing serious. Now that he was so close to receiving his evidence, she wondered if he regretted demanding it. More than likely denial had been a much more comfortable state of mind.

Too bad for him. She didn't have patience for dead weight. Even if said dead weight had a rather nice jawline.

LEDs flickered green and she spun the handle, swinging the 'lock door open to space. They'd tethered in already, and she let him go first, airjetting out about nine meters. Sanda hovered in the empty hatchway, watching him. Watching his subtle touch with the jets, his slow and careful orientation as he picked out stars he recognized and laid them over the same internal map all spacefaring persons kept close to heart. Didn't take him long to find what he was looking for.

After he'd floated for a while, gazing at that white smear of light and debris that had once been her home, she jetted out, came to float alongside him. He glanced over. Moisture tangled in his eyelashes. He blinked, but the tears just drifted around the helmet. Zero-g was a bitch for crying.

"Come on," she said. "Let's get back inside. Bero can approximate a decent cup of tea. Sound good?"

"I feel like something stronger, truth be told."

She grinned and patted him on the shoulder, though he'd feel little more than a muffled pressure through the suit. "Yeah. Bero's got that, too. I think we'll get along all right after all."

They jetted back toward the 'lock, and Sanda cut the comms link so he could sniff back tears in privacy.

CHAPTER 20

PRIME STANDARD YEAR 3541

TWO WEEKS TO BE A LITTLE PRINCE

Butler bots meandered through the crowd in Biran's living room, their telescopic arms offering bowls of snacks—fried algae chips, root vegetable curls, salty-sweet nutri-cakes—to Biran's graduating class. Small in number as they were, they crowded his living room and spilled over into the kitchen, their voices altogether too loud and too indistinct for Biran to find pleasant.

But this was how one began, he told himself. You made friends. You made allies. You made yourself liked, and then you suggested changes. And there was no better night than tonight, when the convoy was slated to meet the Icarion dignitary ship.

He'd made sure to only invite his cohort over, the new Keepers who were still finding their feet. They were more likely to listen to him, he hoped, and if any resentment was brewing over his rise to Speaker, he wanted to show them he was still one of them. Even if he had kept himself aloof from them during their training. He hoped they'd assume he'd been too busy with his studies to socialize.

"How are you?" Anaia floated up to him out of the mass of sharp-cut suits and Prime jumpsuits. She wore a knee-length dress with a uniform blazer thrown over the top, her chunky black boots trimmed with cyan belts to match the Prime colors. She'd gotten her hands on a black-market neon eyeliner, and whenever she blinked her hooded lids, they showed off a little glow of lime green.

"In need of another drink," he teased, pointing the rim of his empty glass at her own dwindling cup. "As are you. Pineapple?"

"Lychee."

He swung around to the beverage dispenser and poured out pineapple-flavored sake for himself, and lychee for her, the machine grumbling only slightly as he switched the flavors over. He'd have to get maintenance to take a look at that. His kitchen was supposed to be state-of-the-art, and the tropical theme pack he had installed for the party was causing it to drag and complain. Not that his guests seemed to care. As newly minted Keepers, they all had the same kitchens, anyway.

She took a slow sip, leaving a print of emerald-green lipstick on the edge of the glass, and raised a brow at him. "This is good. But you didn't answer my question."

Biran's cheeks went instantly hot. Time to lay off the booze. "What do you mean?"

"How are you, really? I haven't seen you since that night, and now you're throwing parties."

There was an edge of accusation in her voice, a slight moue on her lips. He took a drink to give himself a second to gather his thoughts, but she wasn't fooled. She lowered her glass pointedly.

"The Protectorate's kept me busy," he stumbled out, a lame excuse by any standard.

"Move it, posh-boy." Kan Slatter put a hand on Biran's shoulder and shoved him aside. "You're blocking the best thing going at this party." He shoved his cup against the dispenser and dialed in for passion fruit. The machine grumbled. He rolled his eyes as it dribbled out the booze. "Piece of crap you got here, Greeve."

"We've all got the same piece of crap," Anaia cut in, a little too defensive. She'd never gotten along with Slatter.

Slatter brought his hand to his chest and mock gasped. "You're telling me our benevolent chosen one has the same slapdash accoutrements as we mere peasants? Stars and void, we should protest! He should at least have access to the good booze, what with all that *extra* responsibility the poor man has to shoulder."

"What in the hell is that supposed to mean?" Biran snapped, aware that the voices in his living room had hushed to listen to the fight, but not caring. Slatter was just drunk enough to push his buttons—and Biran was just drunk enough to push back. In the back of his mind, he heard Graham's voice floating up out of the ether—first rule of being a diplomat, don't get drunker than those you're trying to woo—but he pushed the voice away.

"I don't mean to offend you, *Speaker* Greeve. I am but a humble Keeper. Please don't broadcast my transgressions to all of Prime."

Snickers from the living room. Biran's cheeks went so hot he thought he'd combust. He tried to say something, anything, but he just opened his mouth and pushed soundless air out.

"That's enough, Slatter," Anaia said. She grabbed him by his sleeve and twisted, half turning to drag him from the kitchen. "Biran's been through a lot."

"Shit. If my sister dying would get me a promotion, I'd whack her myself. She's fucking annoying, anyway—"

Biran punched him in the face.

Slatter's nose gave way before Biran's knuckles did, the cartilage crunching light as a stomped bug under Biran's fist. An arc of blood splattered the malfunctioning drink dispenser. Biran's fist collapsed against the hard wall of Kan's face, his knuckles cracking loud enough to compete with the snap of Kan's nose while his pointer finger snapped, his thumb jamming.

Kan shouted, dropping his glass as he reached up to cover his face. Anaia grabbed Biran by the scruff of his jacket and yanked him away before he could wind up for another punch. He hadn't even realized he'd been preparing to swing again.

"You're going to fucking pay for this." Kan spat a wad of blood on Biran's floor and grabbed a tea towel hanging from the stove to shove against his nose.

The house AI interrupted, cheery as always, "Injuries detected. Is medical assistance required? If an answer is not received in thirty seconds—"

"Yes!" Kan crowed. "Call a goddamned medivan!"

"Affirmative," the house said.

"A medivan for a bloody nose?" Anaia scoffed.

"It's broken, bitch. And I want a paper trail on this." He jabbed a finger at Biran. "You have fucked up."

"Will you shut the hell up?" a man snapped from the living room.

Biran, Anaia, and Kan turned to the rest of the gathering, realizing they'd been ignoring the drama playing out in the kitchen. All faces were glued to the internal projection screen on Biran's wall. Callie Mera was on the screen, her red lips chewing over every word she said. Absolute dread raced up Biran's spine.

"Turn it up," he demanded.

"Fuck that." Kan kicked the cabinets. "You all are witnesses to this attack, pay attention—"

"Shut up, Kan," Lili said, startling everyone. Biran didn't think he'd ever heard her raise her voice before, let alone in anger. She turned the volume up.

"Reports are coming in now that the diplomatic convoy sent to meet with Icarion dignitaries has lost contact with Ada Prime Control.

"The historic rendezvous, set to happen just ten minutes from now, has been a beacon of hope to our people in these uncertain times. Arranged by Speaker Greeve, whose sister was the sergeant in command of the gunship flotilla that was ambushed near Dralee just a few short weeks ago, the convoy—hold on."

Callie Mera pressed her finger to her ear, listening to another voice, far away. Biran held his breath. Callie's lips pushed out, not quite a pout, more of a flex, as if she were preparing to say something difficult and needed to ease her mouth into it. His stomach dropped.

"I'm receiving reports that the convoy, an olive branch of peace extended toward Icarion, has been attacked. Footage from nearby satellites—"

The screen cut to black, shaking for a moment despite the stabilizers in the drone. Callie's voice kept on coming, rolling smooth as silk across the unsteady display, filling in background information until they fed her some new line, some fragment of what was happening.

There was no point in waiting. Rubble dotted the black slick of space. Twisted pieces of metal jarred against one another as they fell into whatever patterns their velocity at the time of breaking up had been. One piece, still carrying a fragment of the Ada Prime logo—just a sliver of the planet, the gate, and half the orbital lines broken away— drifted into view. The convoy was dead.

He had sent those people to their deaths.

Biran dropped his glass and ran out the door, ignoring the shouts behind him.

PRIME HAS NOT YET BECOME A STANDARD

EARTH, DURING A WELL-VIEWED MORNING TIME SLOT

The call had come at 1100 hours, while Alexandra Halston sat on a too-worn couch on a glossy Hollywood talk-show set, flashing her just-right-white teeth at the camera as she joked with a host whose name she would forget the second she stepped offstage.

Ha-ha, isn't it funny I've built a system whose purpose is the collection of asteroids, which are, essentially, dirty snowballs?

Ha-ha, isn't it funny that the space elevator sits at the equator's bulge? What a funny word, wink-wink.

Ha-ha, aren't I secretly a mad genius on a quest to build a massive intergalactic snowman?

Ha. Ha.

Then the flicker, in her ear. An implant nobody but her closest knew about—an emergency line. A soft buzz against her cochlear bone to say: Hey, seriously, something important is happening. Something important. And quiet.

Alexandra's smile never strained. Her quips did not speed up, signaling a hasty desire to get off the stage and tend to whatever was happening. If anyone ever thought to look back over this footage—throwaway press junket nonsense—they wouldn't know. They wouldn't see. No one would ever know that this was the moment humanity's history skewed, forever. Pushed—nudged—off a track it had not known it had been steadily plodding along until that moment.

She kissed cheeks. She shook hands. She took a moment in the green room to compliment a run-down intern for the excellent coffee they fetched her. No one knew she was in a rush. They never would.

At 2200 hours, Alexandra's helicopter touched down on a leaf-scattered helipad on Caja de Muertos, a small island off the coast of Puerto Rico. The sun had long set, stroking the black waves of the ocean with gold, and only the massive lights of Prime Inventive's compound illuminated the strained faces awaiting her in a white-coated semicircle. White, flanked by various shades of dark camo. This facility was not public. And after Prime had swooped in and got the lights and plumbing back online in Puerto Rico after a disastrous hurricane season, the people—and government—looked the other way.

The restoration of the island had cost Alexandra billions. A drop in the bucket for the loyalty it afforded her now.

She ducked the blades of the chopper and closed the gap to her awaiting team. Dr. Maria Salvez was the first to reach her. The mathematician's grey hair had blown into a cottony cloud under the wash of the rotor. Alexandra—or Lex, as her closest called her—had seen Salvez unkempt many times before. But she had never seen her eyes so alive, so hungry.

"It's this way," the researcher said, waving at Lex to follow her.

Lex fell into step alongside her old friend, hiding a wry smile. "It?"

An uneasy exchange of glances between the others made Lex's skin itch with anticipation.

"We don't know what it is. It's not a natural phenomenon."

Lex's heels did not click on the hard floor as they entered the research station. They were rubberized, grippy, a product of materials mined and spun out from the "dirty snowballs" Prime Inventive captured and exploited. Everything Lex wore—from the clips in her hair to the attaché dangling from her wrist—was borne of asteroids, not silk or leather or cashmere.

Her PR people claimed her efforts made her green, and she never corrected them. Lex had stopped seeing green a long time ago—unless in the context of the usefulness of algae for space travel. When she looked at this planet—at Earth—she saw only its inevitable demise, and pointless spending of resources in its conservation.

The Earth would die, eventually. It would be humanity's choice if they happened to be bound to it when that happened. She would be prepared. Would know how to craft everything they'd ever need out of the dust between the stars.

It wasn't deforestation that kept Lex up at night. It was the heat death of the universe.

"A refining team found it at the Elequatorial processing facility. They didn't see it, mind you. Just noted an anomaly and sent it to us for further investigation."

Salvez was dodging. A word, a word she did not want to say, thickened the air in the hallway as they passed through layer upon onion layer of security.

"Once we cracked open the ice core, well, it's been pretty beat-up, but it's mostly intact. We think it must have taken a solid hit at some time, gotten knocked out of whatever orbit it was in. We haven't gotten its mass dialed in yet, but it's about a basketball in size. Hell of a thing. Smaller chance than finding a particular needle in a needle stack."

It, it, it. Lex didn't press. She liked the anticipation.

Double doors slid open at the end of a hallway, a blast of air from above knocking particulate matter off of their bodies. Lex stepped to the edge of a walkway and peered down through the plex that separated her from what looked very much like an operating theater below. Robots, controlled by researchers just as cordoned off as she, probed carefully into the mass of a slushy asteroid heart, the room below cold enough to keep the ice from melting except where they wanted it to.

Half-exposed, in the center of the ice like a pit in a peach, a dome of metal. Silvery—worn. Dents pocked the surface of the material, and while many were obvious impact sites, the camera feed suspended above the room gave her a close-up view. Text, unknown to her. Some strange way of marking out what looked like ones and zeros. Her breath caught. She pressed her palm against the plex and stared at the object below, boring every last detail into her memory.

Not strange. Alien.

"It's entirely possible the Russians or the Chinese lost something—"

"You don't believe that."

"No."

"What does it say?"

"Pardon?"

"The text—what does it say?"

"We don't know yet. A lot of it is interrupted by damage. We're looking into it, but right now it looks like parts of, uh . . . Schematics."

"Schematics? For what?"

"I don't know. Something big. Really, really big."

CHAPTER 21

PRIME STANDARD YEAR 3771

BOOZE HELPS THE TIME PASS (AND THERE'S A LOT OF TIME TO PASS)

Tomas stuck out his chest, put one foot on the table, corrected a sway, and lifted his glass to the ceiling of the mess hall. "I," he declared, "wanted to be a dancer!"

Sanda snorted rum midsip and collapsed into a coughing fit. "Bulllllllshit," she sang when she choked back some not-too-fiery air. "Bulllll*shit*."

"It's true!" He plopped to a seat on the tabletop with enough force to make the rum bottle jump. Bero hadn't been able to produce them anything palatable, but Sanda'd found a bottle of old Caneridge duct-taped to the underside of a researcher's mattress. That's what you got when you disallowed vice on a spaceship—ingenuity.

"You are such a liar." She kicked at the ground with her good foot, making the swivel chair spin, and pointed her cup at him as she spun through his eyeline. "No way. No fucking way. Look at those feet o' yours. Big hog's feet is what those are. Only dancing you'd be doing was on heads, I bet."

"That doesn't even make *sense*."

"*You* don't make sense."

They giggled together, and Tomas doled out a few more drops into her cup as she shook it at him.

"What do you know about dancing, anyway?" he demanded. "You got them tiny feet, no way you could dance on those."

"Ain't nothing wrong with *my* foot."

"You mean *feet*." He enunciated slowly, like an overhyped professor on a grammar kick.

"Naw." She ran a thumb along the seam of her jumpsuit down by the knee, peeling the flex open, and showed him her cobbled-together prosthetic. "I mean *foot*."

Whatever polite response he might have come up with under other circumstances burned clear away under the influence of alcohol. "What the fuck happened to you?"

"War." She sniffed and pushed hair off her forehead. "Icarion railgun, pew!" She made metal-crunching noises and mimed a big hunk of steel chopping her leg in half. "Never even saw the fucker on radar. Must have been early relative-speed research shit, now I'm thinking about it."

"Holy fuck. What'd you do?"

"Do? Can't *do* anything when your spaceship's all shot to shit. I was probably busy dying when the evac pod initiated." She grinned at him with all her teeth. "Something you Icarions forgot about. Instead of keeping the pods in a dedicated room, we fit up all our gunships so every seat on deck has a pod ready to spring on it at the slightest hint of crashing vitals or depressurization. No scrambling to jump into pods for us. Though I admit our command decks look a whole lot uglier with all those eggs around. Like a bunch of bisected cockroaches."

"Gross."

"Cheaper than training new talent, and better than dyin'."

"True enough." He slid from the table onto a swivel chair and spun around, counter to her spin. Each time they passed each other, they clinked plastic glasses and took a drink.

"An' you woke up here? Really?"

"Oooh, yeah, Bero found me kicking around outside the edge of the debris field for Dralee and dragged me in. Only damned pod still blinking green in the system, apparently—save yours, o'course. Good luck for Bero, too. He'd never make it out-system without a human around to give him a hand." She wiggled her thumbs at the ceiling cameras. "Primate power!"

"I am beginning to rethink that necessity," Bero deadpanned.

"Blah blah." Sanda grinned up at the cameras. "You and Grippy like me, admit it."

"You have a certain rudimentary charm."

"Hah! See! Practically in love."

"Whoa, whoa. Who's Grippy?"

"Repair bot. Didn't you notice? Been your roommate in the medibay all this time."

"No way. I swept that place top to bottom. Would have noticed."

"Well, you didn't."

"Your search was less than complete, Mr. Cepko," Bero said.

"Call me Tomas, Mr. Spaceship."

"Tomas," Bero said frostily.

Sand giggled. "Awww, c'mon you two. We're all on the same team, right? Gotta get along, because it's what—a couple hundred years to Atrux?"

"Merely seventy-five years," Bero said.

"*Merely* on your timescale, Big B."

"About that." Tomas halted the spin of his chair and leaned forward, attempting to adopt a serious expression. With the rum slackening his facial muscles, he looked like he'd had a stroke, but Sanda endeavored to humor him and tried her own serious expression. He grinned in response. So, she probably looked like a stroke victim, too.

"Pods aren't tested out for that many years, ya know? The Imm Project was inconclusive. If the world's elite can't make evac pods preserve a person longer than—what was the longest, seven months?—then what makes you think we can do it?"

"Yeah, *inconclusive*, not completely scrapped. They made a big deal about that on the news." She rubbed her temples between two fingers, struggling to rustle up the mental energy to explain her thinking to him.

"So a buncha rich people piled their cash together to test the pods' preservation ability and got nowhere. So what? All of those test subjects went in *old*, or otherwise terminal. Waived their right to life away and went to sleep hoping they'd wake up in—what was it? Five years? A couple of them *did* wake up. Most didn't, and the rich people of the world decided immortality may not be so convenient after all.

"We got two rounds of evidence—you and I—that say, for whatever reason, our physiologies mesh well with the preservation system in the evac pods. It's not pretty research, but it's all we got. We made it two hundred–something years in those things. I think we can make it a little more."

"You seem real sure about this."

"Gotta be, don't I? 'Cause I don't see the fucking choice. It's the pod, or dying of old age before Bero gets within reasonable transmission distance of Atrux." She snorted. "Eight percent *c*. What good is that, anyway? Oh, yeah, aside from blowing all of civilization to bits."

"Whoa now, they didn't set out to make bombs. They just wanted some FTL of their own."

"They, they, they. You keep saying *they*, Tomas, but for you it's *we*. Right? Can you"—she hiccuped—"can you even explain it to me? I mean, I get independence and not paying the tariffs and planets' rights and blah-fucking-blah but we, *we*, took damn good care of those gates and we didn't charge much at the end of the day. Even you Icarions gotta agree with that. So what the fuck? I guess I get that it's a political pissing match, but you were all so, so fervent about it."

His expression went dark. She bit off her next stream of words, cursing the alcohol that lubricated the path between her brain and her tongue. Damn stupid thing to do, piling the death of two whole planets at her new ally's feet and asking him why. He wasn't there. He didn't really know, probably didn't even approve of the whole mess. He was just a grunt like her, working to protect himself and his family within whatever system he'd been born into.

Accidents of geography: setting perfectly ordinary people at one another's throats since the Stone Age.

"Dios, Tomas, I'm sorry. I didn't—"

He shook his head and slumped in the chair, twisting listlessly. "Don't apologize for having questions. I get it. You've probably been rolling all those thoughts over the whole time you've been on Bero, and haven't come up with a satisfactory answer, right? Naw, don't answer—really, it's okay. The truth is, I don't know. I wasn't born Icarion. I came through Ada's Casimir Gate on a freighter out of the Pallar system. Landed on Icarion and found work that fit me well, so I stayed. Only thing I know is, Icarions just don't trust the plans. Can't really blame them."

"What plans?"

He waved a hand. "Whatever you call them—the, uh, the blue-prints? The little pieces of construction specs your Keepers have chipped into their brains. Icarion doesn't trust the source."

"What, you mean the original research? Alexandra Halston's breakthrough?"

"Yeah, Halston. She was brilliant, I've read the histories. But her company—Prime Inventive—they weren't on track for anything like the Casimir Gates, and then boom, Alexandra's made this huge break-through and she's building the sucker, throwing all her money at it, and the first prototype *works*? Gotta admit, that sounds like bullshit."

"Oh, please. Alexandra's twenty-second century, ancient history. For all we know there were half a dozen prototypes she never publi-cized and the Charon gate was just the first that worked."

"I'm just saying, it's suspicious."

She snorted. "Please. It was about the gate taxes, and you know it. An overblown trade war. You're not one of those alien-tech conspiracy nuts, are you?"

He grimaced and shifted his weight. She braced herself. "Not exactly. I mean, I don't really know what I believe. It seems strange, right? Consider the Drake equation—why, out of all the systems the gates have dumped us into, haven't we met anyone else out there yet? Not so much as a microbe? It feels like someone's pushing us along a set path, like we're jumping to someone else's tune."

"If we're following a set path, it's a poor one. You know how many gates have opened on systems we can't even use? Nothing Earth-like to land on, no dwarf planet or moon at the optimum range to build another gate on. Huge waste of resources. If someone's pulling our strings, they've got a sick sense of humor."

"I'm *just* saying, it's suspicious the way your people keep their info to themselves. Fertile ground for conspiracy, ya know?"

"We keep it to ourselves, because as soon as that first gate opened, Alexandra had what—a dozen or so kidnapping attempts made against her? Not to mention the assassination attempts, and corporate espionage went through the fucking roof. You can't tell me the Corp Wars were a good thing. Implementing the Keeper system put a stop to all that bullshit."

"Did it? 'Cause I kinda think we're alone now because of all that bullshit."

She grimaced and sucked down the last of her rum. "Not Prime's fault."

"If they were more forthright—"

"Stop." She held up one hand and cradled her head with the other. "We're not going anywhere with this, ya know?"

He gave her outstretched hand a sloppy high five. "Right. Gotcha. Sorry. You and me against the 'verse first, and then, when we're safe in Atrux, I'll buy you a proper drink and we'll hash it out over a home-cooked meal. Deal?"

She grinned. "Fucking deal."

"Ahem," Bero said.

They laughed. "All right." Sanda held her empty glass up to Bero's camera. "You and me and Bero against the 'verse."

"Better."

"Speaking of," Tomas said, "what's the deal with the evac pods? They're kinda single use, aren't they? Does Bero have spares aboard?"

"Ah." Sanda pushed unsteadily to her feet and scraped hair back from her eyes with one hand. Apparently, just the thought of cold-sleep brought back her residual headache. "Come on." She thrust a hand down at him and hauled him to his feet. "I guess it's time I introduce you to problem numero uno."

He grimaced. "That bad?"

"Getting worse every day."

CHAPTER 22

PRIME STANDARD YEAR 3771

BOOZE DOES NOT HELP IN LOW-G

Zero-g was no fun with a belly full of rum. Sanda clenched her jaw and sucked her cheeks in to keep nausea at bay as she pulled herself along the command deck's nominal ceiling toward the cargo bay. Judging from the grunts Tomas was making, he wasn't faring much better.

Soon as she was close enough, she shoved herself down and drifted toward the cargo bay door, snagged a nearby cupboard handle in one hand and wrenched it open. Ten pairs of gleaming mag boots—Icarion grey, of course—twinkled up at her. She shoved her feet in a likely pair and clamped them tight around her ankles.

Her makeshift calf rattled in the mouth of the boot and she winced as the magnets activated and jerked her leg forward at an awkward angle. Damn. That was going to be hell to get out later, and she'd probably dented the metal. Whatever, it felt good to have her feet on the ground again, even if the rum in her gut was now pushing insistently at the bottom of her throat.

Tomas locked in and clanked along beside her, looking a little green around the gills. "Looks painful," he said, pointing to her prosthetic with his chin.

"Yeah, I didn't think that one through. Not like I won't have time to fix it, huh?"

He kind of laughed, kind of frowned. A mixed message that summed up pretty much exactly how she felt every other moment since she'd woken up in Bero and learned the truth of what had happened to her home.

She slapped the panel to open the cargo bay and clanged inside, Tomas right on her six. What she had to show him wasn't very promising. All the scrap she'd gathered from the debris field—minus his evac pod, which was still in the medibay—was anchored down to three mag pallets in the hold. At first glance, she'd gathered maybe enough to repair one evac pod. Maybe. And, unfortunately, that first glance was accurate.

"Oh," he said, sobered.

"Mm-hmm. That's how I found you. I was looking for parts to fix up my pod, hadn't counted on needing to fix two. While you were getting, uh, settled in, I went back out every day. This is it. This is all that's useful from this proximity."

"I don't suppose one pod could fit two people, could it?"

"For a couple of weeks, maybe. We'd come out with a bunch of nutrient deficiencies, but it could work. For years, on the scale we're working toward? No fucking way. We'd absorb each other's nutrients and end up dying anyway. Gross, right?"

"Definitely."

He squinted at that collection of scrap, working his jaw around, probably trying to arrive at an answer she and Bero hadn't seen. Trouble was, she and Bero had had a whole lot longer to think about things, and a drunken human brain wasn't exactly going to outpace the thought process of a determined AI.

He opened his mouth. Closed it. She gave him whatever time he needed.

"This is real. It's really fucking happening."

"I'm afraid so." She patted him on the shoulder, the way Biran had done to her whenever she got worked up over something. "I know you saw what was left of Ada, but, well. Look at this."

She clanged over to the nearest pallet and pulled back the sheet of clear plastic she'd pinned over it. This heap was mostly junk, random bits that might be useful in the future but for now were just taking up space. It also held the remains of the gasket she'd repaired on her first day. She pulled the strip of rubber out and presented it to him, turning it so he could see the three wear fractures.

"See this? It was the seal on Bero's first airlock. The day I woke up, this thing decided to blow. Icarion rubber is just as good as Prime's, I know that much, and I've never seen damage like this before. This is what rubber looks like after it's oxidized for two hundred years. Weird, right? This is what we're up against. Not just finding the materials we need—but finding them in good enough condition to make use of, to trust."

He took the gasket from her and turned it over in his hands. The ends trailed up in the low-g like two twisting, stiff snakes. Tomas brushed his fingers over those three breaks in the rubber, and grimaced.

"Can I keep this?"

She shrugged. "Sure, whatever keeps you motivated."

He tucked it under his arm and looked around, eyeing each pallet as he performed the same mental inventory she had done dozens of times. No matter how you distributed the supplies, there wasn't enough.

"I think I need to lie down."

"Follow me."

She guided him back through Bero and popped the door on the same cabin she'd found the Caneridge in. The clothes in that closet had belonged to a tall male, so she figured Tomas could probably find whatever he needed in the deceased researcher's old things.

"This work?" she asked.

He blinked in the gloomy lighting. As they'd come up the ladder, Bero had turned down the lights, shifting the ship over to dusk-approximate. Even in space, humans liked their circadian rhythms to sync with some sort of light source.

"Yeah, it'll do fine." He shuffled inside and dropped the gasket on the ground by his new bed, then grabbed a tablet off the nightstand with a screech of Velcro and tapped it to life. "This'll get me Bero's info?"

Bero answered, "I'll connect that tablet to my internal systems now.

Any questions you have, you may query me directly or type them into the tablet, if you prefer."

"Great, thanks. Sergeant Greeve, if you wouldn't mind…?" He lifted his brows in question, staring straight at the door.

"It's Sanda. And don't stay up too late messing with that thing, we've got a lot of strategy to work on in the morning."

"I don't think I could stay up late if I wanted to."

She grinned and stepped into the hall. "Good night, Tomas."

"Hey, Sanda?"

"Yeah?"

He hesitated, picking at the edges of the tablet gripped in both hands. "You're…" His throat bobbed as he swallowed. "…Very brave. Thanks. For everything."

"No prob." She slapped the door closed and stood a moment, staring at the shuttered portal, examining his face in her mind's eye as she'd last seen it, lit by the glow of Bero's interface. Pensive. Worried. All things to be expected. But something about it seemed off to her, itched at the back of her mind. He'd been trying to make a decision, she thought. A decision he wasn't yet willing to discuss.

"Sanda?" Bero asked. She knew without asking that he had dampened Tomas's room, made it so they couldn't be overheard. She turned back down the hall toward the mess, thinking to clean up before bed.

"Yeah, Bero?"

"Do you really trust him?"

She entered the mess and grabbed their cups, scrubbing at them in the sink with microcleanse cloths. Rum fumes tingled her nose as the cloths ate up what residue was left, cleansing and sanitizing with each swipe. There was still a third of Caneridge left in the bottle. She wondered how long it'd last.

Bero didn't press her. He knew her well enough to know she was thinking, struggling to puzzle out what she felt before she responded. Did she really trust him? He had kind eyes, a quick laugh. Nice jaw and hipline, if she were being honest with herself, but she had to be careful with that. He claimed to be an offworlder—not even really Icarion. But those were all incidental, superficial facts.

Did she really trust him?

She stacked the cups back in the pantry, listening to the satisfying clunk as magnets held the cabinet door shut. Just a comms man. A loner on a freighter who found appropriate work on Icarion. He'd adopted some Icarion ideals, and suspicions, for his own, but that didn't mean much. It was only natural to blend in with the people you decided to live among. Was he trying to blend in with her?

"I like him," she said, and that much was true. He was easy enough to like. But she'd found him drifting in a dead debris field. Found him where no living being should have been. The carrier had been automated. No atmosphere. There was no reason at all for a comms specialist to be all alone out there. She hadn't even found any others—any corpses.

"But I don't trust him."

CHAPTER 23

PRIME STANDARD YEAR 3541

PRINCEDOM IS PAINFUL

Biran's fingers screamed in pain as he tried to use his wristpad to summon an autocab. Swearing, he shook out his hand, flicking droplets of Kan's blood onto the grass, and barreled into a full-on sprint down the narrow gravel road that wound through the Keepers' neighborhood.

"Biran!" Anaia shouted after him, her voice faint from the top of the hill. He flung a hand up to indicate he'd heard her, he was sorry, anything really—just acknowledgment. Kan and his friends could trash Biran's house for all he cared.

The convoy was dead.

His heart thundered in his chest, and not because he was out of shape. He hit the bottom of the road and turned away from the houses, angling toward the neighborhood gate. A couple of guard-core lounging in the check station jerked to attention at the madman charging them. Their stunners swung his way as they took up defensive stances.

"Identify yourself," one barked.

Biran swung his wristpad up, beaming his ident number to them, but did not slow his pace.

"Speaker Greeve?" the one nearest him pitched her voice up in confusion, a startling break in protocol. The guardcore were meant to be unidentifiable by Keepers so that no favoritism could seep in. Even their genders were obscured by their armor and helmets.

"Open the damned gate!" He slid to a stop in front of them, tried to point at the gate mechanism, and winced as his broken finger failed to straighten.

"Is there an emergency? We saw a call go out for a medivan."

Biran grimaced in frustration. "Can you drive me to the Cannery?"

Silence prevailed as the guardcore's hands fluttered to their wrist-pads, a silent conversation taking place. Biran forced himself to stand tall and calm, brushing his mussed hair off his forehead and trying to slow the heaving of his chest. After a moment's thought, he stuffed his broken-fingered hand into his pocket, hoping to hide Kan's blood and his own injury.

"A replacement for me is on the way," one of the guardcore said. "Come with me please, Speaker. I can take you to the Cannery."

"Thank you." Biran tried to sound dignified, but he was sure his relief was palpable. This was a new world for him, pretending he felt one thing while his insides were screaming another. He wanted to embrace it—wanted to be the man Graham thought he could be—but his body betrayed him more often than not.

He could fix that, he told himself, he just needed training. Practice. Never mind that there wasn't time for that—that he was needed now, and in perfect form. Never mind that lives might depend on his abil-ity. That lives had already been lost.

Never mind all that, because that way lay a downward spiral of anxiety and despair.

He swung up into the jeep and braced his good hand against the roll bar as the guardcore fired up the quiet murmur of the electric engine. This one, like all government vehicles, sounded like the faint rumble of tires over gravel. Just enough sound to warn pedestrians it was com-ing. As the autopilot took over, the guardcore leaned against the frame, stunner slung at the ready under one arm, as they wended their way down from the prestigious neighborhood of the Keepers into the more sedate homes of those who worked on Keep Station. Those few whose jobs could not be replaced by robots, or who supplemented the basic income afforded to all Prime citizens with extra work.

Five minutes' driving time passed before Biran realized that those citizens were watching him. They peeked through windows, curtains twitched aside, came out to stand on their porches, or simply stopped where they walked down the side of the road. Heads turned, gazes tracking the sedate advance of his vehicle. Biran's skin crawled from the scrutiny.

"What's going on?" he asked out of the side of his mouth, keeping an eye on all those watching him.

The guardcore flicked at their wristpad. "Word is spreading of the destroyed convoy, sir."

"So?"

"You're...kind of the face of that, Speaker Greeve." They put a slight emphasis on his last name, and that subtle direction dragged at him like a weight. Of course they'd come out to see him, the man who'd beamed his face into all their homes to claim the heroes of Dralee could be recovered, if only they tried to talk to Icarion. To open the paths to peace.

As soon as word spread he'd left the Keeper neighborhood, they'd know. They'd whisper among themselves in private group chats, speculating about his advance through the station. Speculating, too, about the medivan that no doubt had gone screaming through their streets seconds before he appeared.

Some strange impulse within him wanted to wave, but he pushed that aside and put on a grim, serious expression instead. It wasn't hard to fake. Though his whole body vibrated with fear, he had to temper himself. To remind himself that this was only one step on the path. That Icarion had attacked, yes, but it may have been a rogue member. They could make no assumptions about Icarion's intentions until they heard from Icarion itself.

He pulled up his wristpad and pinged Graham with a CamCast request. He accepted immediately, his dark olive face flushed.

"What happened?" he asked.

"I don't know. Heading to the Cannery now. Is Ilan with you?"

"Coming home from the warehouse now. Should we come up-station?"

"No. Stay put. The streets are tense."

"Here, too." Graham glanced over his shoulder. "People are afraid. The ambush at Dralee was one thing. This is a complete refutation of hope. We might see protests."

Biran looked up, scanning the wary faces that washed by him as the jeep sped down a wider road. "I'd be shocked if we didn't. What's the word on the net?"

"Unhappy. Speculative. They want to know if the threat is real or not, if Icarion's planning a big offensive. No one's buying into peace anymore, I think. They're talking themselves into striking first. Into taking Icarion down before they can do any more damage. The rumors about a super weapon aren't enough to keep the bloodlust down."

"Dangerous," Biran said, before he could catch himself.

"So there is a weapon."

"Icarion has always been a threat."

Graham smirked. "Not militarily. But don't elaborate. I know you can't."

A circle expanded across Biran's wristpad, like the ripples of an ice cube dropped in a glass. General Jessa Anford was calling him. Priority line.

"Dad, I have to go—"

The impact came without warning.

Something slammed into the road ahead, fountaining rock and fire and *heat* into the air. Static filled Biran's ears. White light—no, dust, light could never be so dull—overwhelmed his vision and then that heat, electric heat, seared his face, his exposed hands. Unseen pressure slammed him against the seat, snapped his head back, and then the world twisted up. The jeep wrenched sideways off the road and pitched like a rag onto its side. Metal screamed, he screamed, something roared in his ears but it was his own blood—his hearing dampened by the blast.

Blast. That was it. That was why his body was lying sideways, half in the dirt through the jeep's open window, armored hands shaking him, grabbing him by the shoulders.

"Speaker Greeve!" The voice came to him from far away, but demanded attention.

Biran opened his eyes, blinking grit from them, and wiped the back of his hand across his face. Blood smeared—shards from *something* had scratched his face. His nose bled. The visor of a guardcore hovered over him. Biran remembered where he was, what he had been doing.

"What the fuck?" was all he could say.

The guardcore let loose a shaky laugh—it was the woman. She extended him a hand and helped him crawl out of the wreckage of the jeep. He brushed dirt from his suit then realized how stupid that was. It was ruined anyway, large patches torn from the arms and legs. He'd been an idiot not to strap into the jeep. Only the brilliant engineering of the thing had allowed him to walk away from that accident.

That red ring on his arm just kept flashing at him. Biran accepted the call, saw his own dirt-and-smoke-smeared face in the corner of his wristpad view as Anford came into the screen. She took one look at him and nodded.

"You're alive."

"Seems that way."

"Good. Where are you?"

He didn't know. He looked up, squinting against the haze that thickened the air. The guardcore stood beside him, wary, both her hands on the stunner and very much ready to use it. The jeep had torn up some poor person's yard, scraped the succulents they'd been growing right up and pulverized the whole display, but had luckily missed the house itself. Judging by the fact no one had rushed out to investigate the accident, he figured no one was home.

Wherever the owners were, he hoped they were safer than this.

Smoke curled from the road just a few meters from where the jeep had been. Great tufts of concrete had been peeled up by the impact, like someone had shoved their thumb through an orange peel. Alarms blared up and down the street, and people rushed all over the place. Covered in dirt. Streaked in blood. Not everyone had been as lucky as him.

"Residential neighborhood just outside the Keeper zone. Something struck the road in front of us, but I and the guardcore are uninjured." He glanced sideways at her for confirmation she wasn't hurt, and she gave him a curt nod. "We're maybe fifteen minutes from the Cannery, in a vehicle. Hour on foot."

"I've picked up the location of your wristpad. I'll send an auto for you."

"Don't."

"Excuse me?"

"That wasn't an accident, was it?"

Anford shifted her weight, arms clasped behind her back. The subtle motion was the most uncomfortable Biran had ever seen her. "No. Are you secure?"

"It's just me and the guardcore."

"Moments after the attack on the convoy, Icarion fired upon an asteroid passing within close proximity of Ada in an attempt to bombard us with debris. What you experienced was a blowback impact event."

Biran swallowed. "A small one."

"Yes. Their weapon pulverized the asteroid more than they were expecting, I believe. Smaller pieces."

"Lucky us."

"Indeed. I'll send the auto."

"No."

Anford cleared her throat. "Speaker Greeve, the Protectorate is getting ready to convene. You will want to be here." To help decide what happened next, she meant. If they tried again for peace, or if they reached for Icarion's annihilation.

Icarion had the evac pods. Without peace... Biran's stomach soured as he watched the civilians run back and forth across the street, shouting for aid, rallying around one another. He hoped the medivan that'd picked up Kan had ditched him to help the wounded instead.

"Biran," he said quietly.

"What was that?"

"Call me Biran, please...And, thank you, Jessa. I know what you're trying to do, and I appreciate it, but right now I'm needed here. We both know the Protectorate will spend the next couple of hours bickering. There will be time for that. Later."

She half smiled and inclined her head. "As you wish. I will send an auto regardless—with spare guardcore. With all the Keepers fleeing to the Cannery, we don't need so many out to keep an eye on them."

"Thank you."

"Anford out." Jessa disappeared from the screen.

Biran took a second to swipe a quick *I'm okay, talk soon* message to Graham and Ilan, then blanked his wristpad. Anything else could wait. The impact had proven that much.

"How good is your medical training?" he asked the guardcore.

"Better than yours," she said, and slung her stunner away on her belt.

"Let's put that to the test."

She nodded, and they walked side by side toward the dust. Toward the screaming and the terror and the pain. And though the people were angry, and though they sometimes shouted at him, cursed him as they recognized him just to have something—some icon of authority—to curse at, the guardcore did not take her stunner out.

CHAPTER 24

DAY TWENTY-FIVE OF TOO MANY

Warm light flooded her room, shoving an ice pick of a headache straight through her right eye. Sanda jerked upright, flailed in the grey-and-orange sheets, until she came fully awake and realized just where she was. Still not a dream. Damn.

"Thanks for the smooth morning, Bero," she muttered as she swung her leg off the side of the bed and adjusted sleep-twisted pajamas.

"I apologize for not easing the light settings, but Tomas is awake. He's in the mess."

"So? Let the man have breakfast. He doesn't need me to babysit."

"He has attempted to set a new course via his tablet. I overrode his input."

Sanda grabbed the prosthetic she kept propped against the night-stand and yanked the straps tight. Raw skin stung at the touch, making her blink watery eyes. She needed to find a better powder to stop the chafing. "What course? We've been relatively stationary since we took him on board."

"He wished to direct me into orbit around Farion, one of Kalcus's moons."

"Did he say why?"

"He said he would explain 'when the gang's all here.' I presume he meant upon your arrival."

"Yeah, gotcha." She yanked the last strap tight and winced as the clammy rubber gripped her skin. Pushing to her feet, she tested the stability of her prosthetic as she did every morning. It had a new tendency to lean her forward, no doubt due to the abuse it took in the mag boot. She sighed. She'd have to machine a replacement for her makeshift calf. In the meantime, she had some answers to demand.

After a rushed attempt to wash up and set her clothing straight, Sanda stomped down the hall to the mess, forcing herself to breathe in the calming pattern she'd been taught in basic training. Tomas sprang to his feet the second she stepped into the room and pulled out a chair for her.

"Sit, sit," he said, bustling toward Bero's cabinetry. "I've got Bero brewing some coffee, and I figured out that if you split a nutrient block in quarters and hit it with a torch, close your eyes and imagine *real* hard, it's just like toast."

The proffered chair creaked as she sat. She eyed Tomas as he fussed over breakfast, a dread feeling growing in the pit of her stomach. A feeling worse than being told he'd been trying to adjust their course without her input.

"You're a morning person, aren't you?" she asked.

"Huh?" He glanced over his shoulder at her, grin big, a knife frozen halfway through the business of slicing a brick longways. "Oh, yeah, I guess. Nothing like a star rise, right? Er." He glanced at the daylight-real lighting in the ceiling. "Or the synthetic equivalent, I guess."

"Seems fine to me. Bero gets the little red smear before full star just right."

He paused, half a nutrient brick in each hand, and squinted at the lighting. "No variation, though?"

"Standard cycling. Just like home."

"Oh. Right. You Primes live in hab domes…" He frowned at the food in his hands, beginning to drip, and jumped to applying the heat. "I always forget that. Seems strange to go a whole life without seeing a true sky."

Bero's coffee dispenser beeped, and she trundled over to grab a cup. Leaning against the cabinet, she sipped the steaming brew, savoring the bite of near-boiling heat across the tip of her tongue. It even scorched her a little, a few taste buds going dark. The sharp heat was almost a better pick-me-up than the caffeine itself.

"It's not bad. We see it sometimes, visiting other planets. Though no one from Ada had gone to Icarion since I'd been born. Well, not as a tourist. Hostilities wouldn't allow it. And anyway, the real sky above Ada wasn't much to look at. Nice starscape, but the system's star is so far out we barely get a glimpse of her. You can go up to the observatories to get a real look, but I never bothered. Sims are enough for me."

"Not for me. I like real dirt under my feet and a proper magnetosphere-atmosphere combo making the natural sky safe to look at."

"It's literally no different."

He shrugged. "Maybe I'm just a purist."

"You're a comms man. Don't tell me you're a luddite."

"Me? Naw." He shook his head as he finished toasting the block slices. "I appreciate both sides, just have my heart in one a little more, you know?"

"I guess. But without the domes, humanity would be stuck on Earth. If we hadn't destroyed the place and ourselves by now. Really poor early enviro management, there. Had to hab the whole planet to keep it from becoming uninhabitable, and that didn't last long."

"True enough. Hungry?"

He slapped the toasted bricks of nutrients onto a plate and offered it up to her like a trophy. She stifled a smile and wondered how long she'd let him keep messing with the dispensers before she told him the cupboards were still loaded with canned fruit, veg, and textured protein.

"Thanks." She took the plate and slid back into her seat at the table across from him, setting the coffee down reluctantly. She dragged her fingertip around the rim of the cup, thinking, while she spooned a bite of nutrient toast into her mouth. It was crunchy, melty. Not bad, really.

After wiping up the dishes with a microcleanse, he joined her. Forearms against the edge of the table, he hovered over his food as if it were a specimen for dissection. She pushed images of Kenwick's head, flayed and floating, out of her mind. Tomas hadn't done that. Didn't work for any part of Icarion that had anything to do with it.

He began to hum an offworld show tune, muffled around bites of his meal. She was definitely going to wait to tell him about the other foodstuff.

"Are you always so chipper?"

"When a lovely stranger fishes me out of the middle of nowhere, revives me, and gives me a shot at surviving a disaster that wiped out the entire star system? Yeah. I'm usually pretty chipper then."

"Lovely?"

He stared at his food. "Just stating facts."

"I *am* radiant." She fluffed chopped and frizzy hair with one palm. He laughed.

She sipped scalding coffee and cradled the cup to warm her palms, and to do something with her hands. Gaze locked on every line of his face, she steeled herself, and asked, "About that. Bero tells me you tried to enter a new flight plan. Why?"

"Ah. That." He took a final, gulping bite, pushed his plate away, and leaned back, meeting her gaze. Nothing alerted her about his expression. Eyes bright from early morning energy, a neutral set to his lips, a slight tenseness along the jaw. There might be something in that tension, but she wasn't trained for this kind of thing. She just pointed the big guns at what her superiors wanted blown to bits and made damn sure she hit.

"I'm not going to insult you by dancing around the fact, Sanda. The truth is, I lied about who I am."

Her fingers tensed on the cup. Plastic crinkled. "Really. And does this have anything to do with the fact I found your evac pod in the debris field of an auto-transport ship that carried no atmosphere?"

He grimaced. The tension in his jaw definitely flexed. She filed that little bit of info away. "I wondered if you'd noticed that."

"Hard not to."

"Yeah, well." He cleared his throat and leaned forward, pressing his forearms against the tabletop. His eyes were sharp, earnest. Something in them put her in mind of some of the asteroids she'd seen, grey and hard and limned in sharp ice. "I'm sorry I lied. I didn't know who you were, or if this was a test. My name really is Tomas Cepko. I am a comms specialist, and I'm from out-system. That's all true."

"But?"

"But. Have you ever heard of the Nazca?"

She let her puzzled expression tell him all he needed to know. He pressed on.

"They were an indigenous tribe of the South American continent on Earth. They lived up in the high mountains and made pictures in the dirt. *Big* pictures. You couldn't tell what they were up close. From the ground they looked like random lines, but you could see them from the sky just fine. Birds, frogs, things like that.

"No one really knows why they made them. The Nazca themselves couldn't get up high enough to see their pictures whole. But the lines stuck around in the dirt, because of the arid climate, and remained all but whole save for a few idiot tourists riding scooters out to take a look at them."

"What a charming cultural tale. Now, please tell me why I shouldn't blow you out the airlock for lying to me."

"I work for an organization who call themselves the Nazca. We examine small traces on the ground, so to speak, look for hints of patterns, try to assemble the discordant intel into a big picture."

He'd gone dead still. His jaw relaxed; his gaze held hers nice and steady. Nothing at all told her he was lying. But then, if he were what he was dancing around saying outright, he'd be practiced at keeping every inch of his body schooled into portraying whatever emotive state he wanted.

"You're a merc. An Icarion spy."

His nostrils flared with distaste. "I'm a Nazca. There are subtle differences. But, yes. We are a consortium of independent information brokers. We don't choose sides."

"Who hired you?"

"No one. We heard scuttlebutt that Icarion was gearing for something big and wanted to check it out. They planted me in the wreck of the transport to be scooped up by recovery procedures."

Coffee dribbled over her fingers as her grip tightened. She forced herself to relax. "And how the hell were you going to sell that to them?"

"They'd been hiring a lot of offworld specialists for quiet work. My superiors were supposed to have my name on those lists before I was found. A paperwork mix-up, but a happy one, because they'd have my expertise without having to pay to smuggle me through the gates."

"You really expect me to believe all this?"

He spread his hands. "No. Not really. But it's the truth, and I hope you'll come around in time."

"What was the Nazca looking for?"

He glanced pointedly around the ship.

"Bero?"

"Or the research that led to his creation, yes. Sorry, Bero, buddy, but as soon as I went nosing through your sys specs I knew what I'd been scooped up by. You're one of the first steps on their way to interstellar travel without the gates. Or, you were supposed to be, before Icarion initiated the Protocol."

"You sure it wasn't the Protocol itself you were looking for? A weapon that can bust up multiple planets seems like just the kind of thing your people would be interested in digging up information on."

His lips pursed. "They're the same thing, aren't they?"

"Never say that." Bero's voice filled the mess, and they both jumped. "I am not the same as the Protocol. I would never, *never*, have any part in what they've done. That's why they gave me a personality, isn't it? Why not just use a dumb ship? No—they made me so that I could make the right choice. Whoever pulled the trigger on the Protocol, they're nothing like me."

Tomas looked for a camera. "Bero, I'm sorry, I just meant that the research pipeline was the same."

"But I am not the same."

"No, of course not."

"Good." Bero fell silent, and Sanda couldn't help but think of the horror she'd stumbled across when she'd entered Bero's research bay. The smartship himself may be a different animal than his Protocol cousin, but that didn't mean similar horrors weren't worked on board his body. She wondered if that was what had made him so jumpy, so distrustful. Watching a bunch of researchers peel a man's head apart to discover its secrets, then set it up like an idol for veneration, would have made her distrustful of humanity, too.

"All right," Sanda said. "Fine. Say I believe you, for theory's sake. If you're some infiltrating Nazca badass, why tell me? I was already distrustful of you—sorry, but hey, a girl's gotta look after herself—and here you go taking all the fragile agreement between us and dash it to the proverbial rocks.

"You gotta have a reason, right? An angle? Otherwise this could wait for a more opportune time, when I haven't been dragged out of my bed to sip rapidly cooling coffee."

Before she could blink, he grabbed the coffee cup and hurried over to the dispenser to top it off with a fresh, near-boiling splash. He spoke as he worked, tapping a thumb against the side of his thigh. Blasted man could just not sit still. How the hell did that parlay into a career as some kind of spy? Last time she checked, spies weren't prone to singing show tunes and drumming out obscure jazz riffs.

"See? You're sharp. That's why I'm not bullshitting you."

"Shove the flattery, Cepko. What do you want?"

He plunked back down across from her and pushed the coffee her way. She gave it a hesitant sip, holding it like a wall between them. He leaned across the table, folding his hands together, and all his buzzing, cheerful energy drained away. The man sitting across from her was suddenly, deadly, serious, and there was a firmness to his musculature she'd missed before. Blurred by the fun of silly, drunk jokes, stories of dancing, and, of course, the show tunes.

So that was how he worked. Interesting.

"I want to survive this, Sanda. I'm being honest with you now, because I'm going to reveal some information to you that I discovered before being set adrift. Information that, quite frankly, you wouldn't believe a low-level comms man to have."

"But an Icarion higher up in the ranks, with classified clearance, would," she guessed.

He inclined his head. She sucked air through her teeth. "And how do I know that's not what you are?"

He spread his hands again, and that lopsided smile came back. "You can't be sure. I'm sorry, that's just the way it is. I'm a spy, Sanda. There's no way for me to prove it. If there were, I'd be a really shitty one."

"Fair point. So I guess you're just going to have to spill."

He pulled a tablet from his waistband and plunked it on the table directly between them, then spun it around so it faced her. With a few deft taps, he brought up a view of the local star system.

"Using Bero's in-system nuclear propulsion, we're about two weeks of acceleration away from entering the orbit of Farion, Kalcus's smallest rock moon."

"And why would we want to do that?"

"Yeah. Here's the thing about Farion." He pinch-zoomed the rough ball of rock. "About twenty years ago, Icarion bigwigs dropped a space station into orbit around that little rock. They called it Farion-X2."

"I've never heard of—"

He held up a hand. "That's the point. It was a black op. They built the sucker when Farion was on the long leg of its orbit, hidden behind Kalcus, *and* when Kalcus was hidden behind Cronus from Ada Prime. Unless your guys were really, really looking for it, they'd never see it. With Kalcus a nominal no-man's-land between the two planets, they figured any routine sweeps your people did of the area they could skirmish off. And they set it up because of its orbital path.

"Every ten years–ish, Kalcus's orbit takes it as close as it ever can to Ada Prime. Close on a cosmic scale, we're still talking hundreds of millions of miles—but, anyway. The point is, they put the station out here to see if they could do a little eavesdropping when Kalcus got close. Didn't cost 'em much, the station was all prefabbed, and the staff was paid crap for their trouble because they only shuttled out there once every ten years to have a listen. Nothing good ever came out of the project, so they abandoned it. *But the station's still there.* Get it? Equipment, maybe even evac pods. It's been sitting stale for hundreds of years now, but it's the best shot we've got. I doubt even the Protocol hit it. Maybe some debris damage, if we're unlucky, but it's probably pristine, if powered down."

Sanda licked her lips. "Bero. This ring true?"

Silence stretched as the AI considered possibilities. "I have no record of such a project, but that does not mean it doesn't exist. What he says regarding the orbit time periods is verifiable, and true."

Tomas opened his mouth, but Sanda glared him silent. He'd said his piece. What she did next was entirely up to whatever consensus she and Bero arrived at. "And Farion? Is orbit around that moon a reasonable deviation from our slingshot to Atrux?"

Hesitation. "It is not ideal. But it can be done. Would you like me to begin the adjusted calculations?"

"Do that. If we're within the window, set course to Farion."

Tomas visibly slackened, his eyelids hooding just a touch. That, more than anything, made her trust that at the very least, he believed what he had to say. Tomas believed that whatever awaited them on Farion, it was his best shot at survival. She was not naive enough to think that'd mean it would aid her survival, too.

"I will alert you when my calculations are complete."

"Thanks, Bero."

Sanda drained the dregs of her coffee and pushed to shaky feet. Tomas stayed silent, somehow intuiting that she didn't want to hear from him right now. Probably his damned spy training. She wondered how much of their camaraderie last night was real, and how much was designed to manipulate her into liking him. Could spy training include cute cheek dimples?

"I hope you're not bullshitting me, Tomas."

"I'm not."

"We'll see. My head and leg are killing me. I'm going to go lie down. Don't do anything stupid enough to get me woken up for at least three hours, got it?"

"I could find some medication to help with—"

"Just. Don't. Touch. Anything."

She felt him staring at her back as she tromped out into the hall but decided not to give a fuck.

CHAPTER 25

IT TOOK TWO WEEKS TO FALL APART

Biran walked from a war zone into an actual hell. The usually sedate halls of the Cannery were filled with shouting, and not just from those trying to force order into the chaos. Keepers, students, staff—everyone was running, and most had their faces buried in the screens of their wristpads, relaying or receiving information in volumes all north of ten.

He hesitated in the doorway, wondering if he should just say fuck it, turn around, and go back planetside to stay with his fathers for a while. But this was his chaos—or a part of it was, at any rate—and somebody needed to account for it.

The people of Ada counted on him, as Speaker, to explain what happened. To assuage their fears. Lavaux may have handed him this job as a poisoned chalice, but he would take it seriously. People counted on him to do so.

Biran ran a hand through his dusty, bloody hair and started off down the hall at a brisk but calm pace. The guardcore woman followed, and he didn't send her away, even as he flashed his wristpad at ident scanners to get deeper and deeper through the security layers of the Cannery. He'd only known the woman a few hours, and most of those had been spent in silence, but to wade into battle without her at his side seemed foolish.

And it was, most definitely, a battle he was wading into.

A door burst open to his right and out strode Jessa, her usually perfect hair flying out around her cheeks from the gust caused by the door opening.

"Greeve. Finally. Get in here."

The war room was awash in glowing, projected screens. Schematics played out across the walls in brilliant blues and golds, an endless variety of views of the station—and the dome protecting the city on Ada—turned on illustrated axes. Figures splashed alongside them, pinpoints of light in hues varying all across the spectrum, moving in sync as if they were an insect swarm.

Each light represented a Prime ship—gunner, dropship, unmanned planetary defense orbiters—each one doing its small part to keep Ada and the station safe from bombardment. Though the colors swarmed in hurricanes of brightness, Biran's heart sank. They weren't enough. Couldn't ever be enough to track and defend against all possible trajectories.

Space had never felt unsafe to him before. He'd been born on Ada, spent most of his childhood up-station, but the raw physics of it dizzied him now. What a foolish thing, to think something as small as humanity could defend something as large as a planet.

"Mealy-mouthed bastards," Jessa said. Biran peeled his gaze away from the war game playing out in real time and watched as she stomped over to a triptych of monitors at the head of the conference table.

"Icarion has responded," Director Olver elaborated. "Some cryptic nonsense about this demonstration being our first warning. As if Dralee never happened."

Biran had never seen the director so tired. His cheeks sagged, giving him the appearance of jowls. An espresso-brown straw hat shaded his eyes, and grass stained his pale blue sleeves—that sweet, herbal aroma clung to him. The director had been gardening when the bombardment hit. That fact, more than anything, filled Biran with dread. Not even the head of their order—the station and planet's de facto leader— had known what was coming. If there had been any hint by intelligence that Icarion was gearing up for something like this, the director wouldn't have been whiling the hours away tending to his garden.

"We had no clue this was imminent." Biran sagged into a chair next to the director.

"No," Olver admitted. "After the destruction of the convoy, we suspected they might mount an attack, but at those speeds, there was no time to prepare a response."

"And where is the weapon now?"

Jessa grunted. "We lost it. Icarion must have cloaking we can't get around yet. My people are working on it." Her fingers flew over the keyboard, gaze tracking a half dozen elements in play at once. Biran hoped Icarion didn't have anyone like Jessa on their side.

Lavaux sauntered in, his manicured insouciance locked in place. Not even a smudge of dirt marred the sides of his shoes. No one should look so calm, so together, as the world was falling apart.

"General," he said, inclining his head to Jessa, though she didn't bother to respond, and took a seat alongside her.

"What's the situation?" Lavaux asked the open air.

"Ratfucked," Jessa muttered, then tapped her earpiece as she listened to a voice far away, ignoring those in the room.

"Not so bad as that," the director interjected smoothly. He pushed back his hat and rubbed his forehead. "General Anford has deployed all our forces"—he gestured to the gleaming wall—"to ensure the security of the station and the planet. We were taken unawares, and that is a tragedy, but no lasting damage was done to the station or Ada's domes. Repair bots have already reached the impact locations on the shielding and assessed the damage as severe but repairable. There is no damage to the breathability of our climate, though I have issued an edict that all nonessential personnel are to remain in their homes with the windows and doors shut, and to test their backup life-support systems, for the time being."

"Lovely." Lavaux steepled his fingers on the tabletop. "That sounds like a nice story for the Speaker here to tell the populace. But what's really going on?"

"The information about the dome and atmosphere is correct and current. As far as Icarion is concerned, the truth is we have no idea. Their so-called president will not talk to us. Their generals have issued vague threats. I fear they may be undergoing internal power struggles that have made their movements unstable at best."

"A coup. You think Icarion President Bollar is being ousted by another faction."

The director spread his hands. "I can't know."

"You have spies crawling all over their government like ants on a sugar pie. Don't tell me you don't know."

"I *suspect*. Communication channels have broken down over the past few weeks, as you might imagine."

Lavaux quirked a smile. "Really? My people have had no problem."

The director's eyes narrowed. "If you have information you're not sharing, Lavaux, I will have you court-martialed."

"Gentlemen," Jessa interrupted, "you have a call."

One of the glowing screens on the wall blinked out. Watching the simulation of Ada and the station sweep away left a bitter taste in Biran's mouth, as if the disappearance of the image was a prophecy of what was to come. A face Biran had only ever seen on the news channels replaced it instead. Biran froze, awestruck.

Black, tightly curled hair cut close to the scalp. Bruise-purple lips and green eyes—genehacked, of course—set in an angular face black as her hair. Raw power. Raw ambition: achieved. Prime Director of the Keepers, Malkia Rehema Okonkwo. Her face, in profile, was embossed on the front of his Keeper diploma.

"Keeper Protectorate of Ada Prime, are you assembled?"

The director sat ramrod straight. "Prime Director, it is an honor. We are still gathering. The attack has sent many of us away to see to family."

The corner of her lips twitched disapproval. "Unfortunate. I have assessed your situation, with the assistance of the High Protectorate, and we have come to a decision we wish to discuss with your planet's Protectorate."

Biran almost laughed as Jessa made a face out of view of the camera. She then turned to face Okonkwo. "With respect, Prime Director, I am the commanding general of this station and its ancillary planet. I have not yet fully assessed the situation. Things are still developing here."

"General Anford, we are well aware of the situation up until this point, and have based our decision on past experiences and—with respect—have conferred with the commanding generals of Prime's entire forces. Icarion's dissent to our command of the Casimir Gate at Ada is a problem that affects all of Prime."

Translation: Your bosses have decided and expect you to accept it without complaint.

Jessa nodded. "Understood," she said, and ducked back behind the shielding of her monitors to continue working on the problem that was rapidly unfolding, never mind that Okonkwo thought the resolution a done deal.

"What is it you have decided?" the director asked.

"The isolation of Icarion."

Biran blinked, not understanding. "Pardon me, Prime Director, but the planet is already isolated. We are two months of travel from them, and their planet is too large and too close to this system's star to support the construction of a gate, even if there were a Keeper government installed. They're as isolated as you can get."

"Not exactly."

"She wants to abandon Ada," the director said, drawing out each word as if it pained him. The slow peeling away of a bandage. "This planet has always been a backwater. A dead-end system, with only one gate possible."

"You understand," she said. "Good. I had thought there would be an argument. I know we can sometimes develop a soft spot for the planets and stations we live on, but the bigger picture must prevail. Ada has no future, aside from war with Icarion. Their response to your convoy—a valiant effort—made that quite clear. Prime has no time for wars. To allow another planet to engage us in prolonged combat would set an unhealthy precedent."

"You're going to kill us," Lavaux said in such a matter-of-fact way that Biran didn't comprehend him at first. "There's no other way. If you want to isolate Icarion, you'll have to break the gate. That can only be done from this side to ensure complete destruction, otherwise rubble might survive that the Icarions could examine and reverse engineer."

"Yes. I will not mince with you, Lavaux. You have served Prime well for decades. But the fact that Icarion attempted FTL research cannot be ignored. The gate must be obliterated. The young Keepers, those with decades left, will pass through with the civilians to be reassigned to other stations and gates. We do have a few possible new construction sites in mind. For the elders—volunteers will stay to ensure the complete dissolution of the gate. Or a lottery, if necessary. It will not require all of them."

The director stared at his hands, the nails half-moons caked in the soil from his garden. Lavaux surged to his feet, eyes bright with outrage.

"You would kill us for no reason! Icarion's anger is directed at us because we keep the technology of the gates from them and charge them for their use. If you think, even for a second, that removing the gate from their vicinity will stunt them, you're a fool. Their civilization will not cease. They are a settlement three million strong already. They will keep on, their resentment burning through the generations as their research advances. Prime already made its fatal mistake by allowing homesteaders to colonize non-Prime planets within systems and to set up their own governments on those settlements.

"Already Icarion can cloak their ships from us. How long do you think it will be until future generations of Primes find Icarion ships at their doorsteps—more advanced, more powerful than anything we could ever build—because we relied on the ease and safety of our gates? We are advanced in *one* way, Prime Director. *One*. They will not rest until they match, or excel, us."

"He's right," Jessa said, glancing up from her screens but not bothering to come into the view of the camera. "Their grievances won't go away just because we—and the gate—do. It's postponing the problem for future generations, and by that time it will be unsolvable."

Okonkwo's expression did not flinch a centimeter. "I will relay your objections to the council. But for now, my edict stands. Make your preparations quietly, there is no reason to upset the populace until the moment all is ready. In the meantime, make your personal arrangements. I understand this undertaking will take a great deal of time to orchestrate properly. The High Protectorate will assist you in any way possible in the forming of these plans."

"Will they assist us by telling us who is to die?" Lavaux snapped.

Okonkwo's gaze shifted to him, heavy and level. "Yes. If you require it."

"We do not," the director said, his firm voice sailing over Lavaux's objections. With a derisive shake of the head, Lavaux sat back down and folded his arms over his chest.

"Thank you for your wisdom, Prime Director. We will be in touch."

The director, in the most grievous breach of protocol Biran had ever seen, cut the connection before she could respond. The screen winked out, leaving nothing at all on that wall—a blank space surrounded by the glittering mechanics of war.

"She cannot make us abandon this place," Lavaux said.

"She's right."

Biran craned his head around to find Keeper Hitton hovering in the door, her face sallow in the low light. Blood stained her pants in a splash reaching up to her knee, and her arms were streaked with dirt and dark, caking liquid.

"You say that only because your dear cousin Okonkwo would ensure you're brought through," Lavaux shot back.

"She could try," Hitton said, "but she'd have to drag me through herself. I'm staying." Hitton cocked her head, as if listening to something, then nodded to herself. "The other Protectorate members are almost here. Hash it out with them. You know my stance, Director. If you'll excuse me, I have work to do."

"Where?" Biran asked.

Hitton startled, already half-turned to leave, and squinted at him. "The lower levels are having trouble transporting all the victims."

"I'm coming with you."

"I didn't ask," Hitton growled, her tired eyes narrowing.

"Neither did I." He stood, the guardcore at his side standing with him.

"Speaker," the director said, "you should be preparing for a broadcast. The people will want to hear from us. From you."

"Send what you want said to Callie Mera, she'll put the word out. I'll prepare something for later this evening, but not now. Now, the people need me face-to-face, hand-to-hand. Good luck, Director."

Biran followed Hitton back into the destruction. There was nothing else he could do in that room. Whatever decisions were made next would be done outside his control.

But this? The hurt and the anguish lining the streets? He couldn't control that, either. But he could help, for a little while.

CHAPTER 26

PRIME STANDARD YEAR 3771

NAPS ARE NEVER LONG ENOUGH

Bero was much gentler in waking her from her nap this time around. The lights went up smooth and steady, a leaking of false starlight massaging her eyelids open. Stifling a yawn, she pushed up to her elbows and glared down at her legs. She'd flopped onto the bed, mentally and physically drained, and hadn't even bothered to pop off the prosthetic. Her skin itched like she'd been to an unlicensed FleshHouse.

"Are you feeling better?" Bero asked.

"More human, no offense. What'd you find out?"

"Tomas's transit calculations were short by only a few hours. To attempt orbit around Farion, complete with an EVA of six hours, and rewarming of the engines to begin the gravity assist, would put us at the edge of our window of best passage to Atrux."

"But not out."

"Technically, no."

She ruffled her hair, flinched at a twinge in the back of her head, and swung her feet to the ground. "Be straight with me, Big B. How fine is this line?"

"Thirty-seven minutes."

She whistled. "That's really, really tight."

"If you believe you can perform the EVA in five hours, then that adds an hour to the window."

"Right. No problem. Just shave an hour off an EVA into an unknown space station to collect equipment that might be fuck knows where." She sighed. "What happens if we push the window too hard?"

"Uncertain. My calculations of transit time assumed certain orbital placements. I can adjust the equations for different miss scenarios. An hour over, two, or—"

"Just ballpark me. Don't bother with the orbital adjustments. Say we miss by an hour, what then? How much longer will the transit take? A couple hours, days?"

"Years."

"Shit."

"I thought you might say that."

"With the evac pods..."

"My current systems will be stable until the three-fourths mark of our journey to Atrux, I will then have to power down my personality systems and anything not related to basic autopiloting and life-support functions. I cannot guarantee I will come back online if the window is sufficiently stretched."

"You might die."

Pause. "Yes."

But Tomas would definitely die if they set out as-is. "Understood. Set course for Farion, then, we've wasted enough time dallying around here. I'll go crack the news to Tomas, and see if he has any idea where the evac pods might be hiding on that station."

She pressed a hand against the wall. "Don't worry, Bero. I'll scrub if we cut things too close. I won't gamble your existence like that."

"But you will gamble his?"

"Not exactly. I'll find a way." Just because they only had the makings of one pod didn't mean she had to be the one to go into it, but she didn't say that. For all she knew Bero would flip his shit and jettison Tomas at the mere thought of Sanda allowing him to take her place. For a spaceship, he could be awfully clingy. Kind of reminded her of an old girlfriend she'd had once, back in basic training. She really hoped this would end up better than that relationship had.

"Where is our spymaster, anyway?"

"In his cabin. I have only allowed him access to the mess and his private rooms."

She snorted a laugh. "He must love that."

"He understood, after I explained that I was uncomfortable opening any doors for him you had not first authorized."

She recalled opening the research lab's door to find Kenwick's dead eyes staring at her, and wished she'd been a little less cavalier in her own door-opening adventures during her first few days on Bero. That sight had been a shock she'd never be able to scrub from her mind. The head may be gone, but that place still gave her the creeps. And was probably just the place to knock Tomas off balance, to see what expressions snuck onto his face when he was unsettled.

"Where's Grippy?"

"Dismantling Tomas's evac pod and testing the viability of its components. The hull is in better shape than yours, the benefits of being planted in place and not the product of a railgun strike. But the foam is depleted, as expected."

"Never thought I'd want more of that crap," she muttered. Sanda made quick work of readjusting her prosthetic, making sure to powder it properly this time and slap some antiseptic in there, then stepped out into the hall and thumped three times on his door.

"Who is it?"

"Real funny. Open up."

A scuff of shoes against the floor, and the door dilated. "Hey. Feeling better?"

"Enough. Coldsleep headaches won't shake, but it's not so bad. Ignorable during mission time, if it comes to that."

"Good to know. I felt Bero initiate thrust procedures a while ago. We underway?"

"To Farion? Yes."

That lopsided grin came back, full force. "Then you believe me."

She shrugged. "I'm willing to take a look, it's on the way, and Bero's convinced we'll have five hours to perform the EVA. Which means you and I have gotta talk strategy, because I've never stepped foot in an Icarion station, and there's no way you're going in alone. I need to know what you know. Skills, intel—all of it."

He inclined his head over his shoulder. "Want to come in?"

"Naw. I got another idea. Follow me."

He raised his brows, an implicit question, but she only gave him her back in response and started her slow limp down the hall. That leg was really starting to ache. Double benefit of going to the lab, she guessed, she could work on repairs while she drilled Tomas.

"Welcome to Icarion's research department," she said, and slapped the door-open button, then stepped aside so he could enter. He must have sensed something in her tone, or her stance, because he crossed that threshold like a man sticking his foot in a piranha tank. Bero brought up the lights. It took Tomas's eyes a moment to adjust.

It wasn't the same gruesome display she'd encountered, but Tomas was no idiot. He must have realized the implication of what he was seeing. Must be able to read into the diagrams sketched all over the smartboards, the insidious history in the drawings of chips and skulls and nervous systems. The pillar that had held Kenwick's head was empty, its bulk draped in a tarp Sanda had scrounged up out of one of the ship's many cabinets, but its meaning was clear enough. Something important had been displayed there. Didn't take a huge leap of logic to figure out what that had been.

"Oh," he said.

She shuffled in after him. The ache spreading up her leg made her wish for Grippy to hold on to. "Yeah. This is what Icarion was up to on their state-of-the-art ship. Splitting my people open and trying to piece them back together to figure out how they worked." She turned a pointed stare on him and arched a brow. "Think you would have uncovered this, in the course of your work?"

A professional distance masked his face, tension fading from his jaw as he surveyed the lab anew. "Maybe. I certainly would have tripped over it, considering *The Light of Berossus* results from their interstellar research. But I can't say if I would have followed up on it. I would have reported it to my superiors, then waited for instruction."

She had him on that perfect precipice between professionalism and distaste, the reality of what he might have had to research staring him dead in the face, and his personal disgust so palpable he was practically a caricature of himself. She aimed to put him on the defensive, and nudged.

"And would your superiors make you get involved, too? Are they that hungry for information to sell that they'd endorse your involvement in this?"

He stiffened. Point, match. "We're just observers and information brokers."

"Observers? Please. If they asked you to figure out what was going on here you're telling me Icarion would let you just hang out and *watch*? You'd be involved, if you were doing your job properly."

"Involvement is not endorsement," he snapped.

"Not exactly a condemnation, either. Who would they sell the intel to? You said this was a fishing expedition, sniffing around a hint of chum in the water, no buyer lined up. Seems a lot of expense and trouble to go to on a hunch. I wonder if your superiors had knowledge of what was going on here. I wonder if they were planning on using it themselves to do some advanced snooping on Prime Keepers. Cracking the Keeper chips would be a huge victory for an organization like the Nazca, wouldn't it?"

His nostrils flared. The tendons of his jaw jumped, hands stuffed into the slit pockets of his jumpsuit. Then he grinned, blinked once, and shook his head with a soft chuckle. He tilted his head to look at her, sweeping her toe to head with admiring eyes.

"Oh. You're good, Sanda. Got me worked up nice and tight. You could have been a pretty nasty asset for the Nazca yourself, you know. First-class emotional manipulation right there."

"Can't distract me with flattery, Tomas. It's just you, me, and Bero here. Educated guess—do you think this is what they really sent you after?"

He turned away from her to take in the lab once more, pursed his lips, and nodded to himself. "I honestly don't know. But the second I reported it, you can bet your ass this'd be my new objective."

"And now?"

"Now? Now it's irrelevant. By the time we make it to Atrux, there might not even be a Nazca. Or Prime, for that matter. Societies don't sit still, and two hundred years is a lot of time for development. Moore's law may be way out of date, but that doesn't mean things can't change." He paused and gave her a not-so-subtle side-eye. "I'm in this just as deep as you are. Atrux is a good choice for its proximity, but it's also a hell of a risk. Small system, right? Not a lot of export going on there. Could be all dried up by the time we arrive. It's only a gate jump from Ada. It could be blown to bits, too."

She winced. "I don't see another option."

"Neither do I." He laced his fingers together and cracked them outward. "You wanted to hear what I know? Then we'd better get to work."

CHAPTER 27

PRIME STANDARD YEAR 3771

THE USEFULNESS OF SPIES

Turned out, Tomas knew a whole hell of a lot more than she'd expected. He gathered tablets and spread them across the table like a debris field, pulled up any old Icarion station schematic Bero had kicking around in that big brain of his, and made a lot of educated guesses.

"It's an old spoke-style tube prefab. Really basic, really efficient. No telling what they stashed in each spoke, not without getting eyes on it, but when I was pulling research for this mission, the station caught my eye. It seemed like history an Icarion comms man should know about, right?"

"I'm curious, spymaster. How were you going to convince them you were on their side?"

His chest puffed out and he grinned a little. "Easy. Tell them exactly what I was. They were hiring in specialists to overhaul their systems and weed out leaks or redundancies. They needed an offworlder for that. A retired spec ops man fit the bill perfectly."

"Not so retired, though."

He shrugged. "Them's the business. Anyway, this station's got nine spokes of about six hundred fifty-seven cubic meters total volume, shouldn't be too bad to cover in five hours, including ingress and egress. The lifepacks on this ship designed for that kind of time?"

"Yeah. High-end recyclers. We could be out there four days without pushing the line."

"Oh, that's gotta smell great."

"Behold the glamor of space travel. Bero, can you mock up a map for our HUDs, update it as we go so we don't miss a spot?"

"I will begin constructing the program now."

"Thanks."

"Bero, got anything for capture?" Tomas asked, glancing around the lab with a critical eye. She hadn't cleaned it since she'd taken it over, and it looked like a bunch of rabid teens had been digging around for parts for their science project. In her dash to get the prosthetic handled, she'd left tools strewn across the tables, drawers hanging half out. Bad form on a space vehicle of any kind, worse because she'd been a sergeant and should know better. Some things lost their urgency when you thought you were the last one left alive in a whole star system.

She met his critical gaze with a hard stare, and he cracked a little smile, like he'd glimpsed the real Sanda beneath the hard veneer and was charmed. Their gazes stuck a little too long. She couldn't help it; the way his eyes crinkled at the corners was devastating. Tomas cleared his throat and looked back to his schematics.

"We find some pods, we'll have to vent them out, then grab them. Could add a lot of time."

"No problem. Bero's got two robotic arms. Limited reach, they're supposed to be for maintenance and small vehicle capture, but we can jet what we want within range for Bero to snag. Can you handle bringing things on board while we rummage, Bero?"

"How do you think I retrieved you, Sanda?"

"I saw those dings on my pod."

Huff. "They were already there."

Tomas frowned at his tablet. "You got canned during the Battle of Dralee, right?"

"That's right. And I assume your pod's date was correct—you got packed up later?"

He nodded. "A week after the first bombardment, to be exact. I wish it'd been later. If I'd seen a little more of this system, then we might have a clearer idea of any resources out there we could use. I guess that's why no one came to pick me up. Icarions must have gotten jumpy about security. Poor luck for me."

"I was there," Bero said. "I was conscious."

Tomas actually winced. "Yeah. Sorry."

"You're not. But I'm not angry with you. Did they have personality-emergent AIs where you come from?"

"No. The closest we use are voice packs for secretarial-type interfaces. Smarthouses, front desks, things like that. Nothing with the ability to evolve, or store its own memories. It's, uh." He shifted. "Kinda taboo, on my homeworld."

"And your feelings on the matter?"

"Hey, if I've got the right to rub a couple of neurons together to make up my personality, no reason why you shouldn't be able to. I don't see the point in dumping you in a spaceship, but, well, I'm glad you're here."

"It's size," Sanda interjected. "Isn't it? You need the storage space, the cooling. Ships and stations are perfect for personality-emergent AIs, as they've got a ton of natural heat sink around them at all times."

"That's correct," Bero said. Tomas raised his brows fractionally in interest. "Icarion studies also proved a fifty percent reduction in accidents when captains could speak with their ship as equals. Being able to express what's wrong with a ship in human terms is, apparently, a great deal more compelling to you than a readout of status and facts."

"Nothing beats a couple hundred thousand years of evolution, eh?" Tomas grinned. "We can have all the data in the world, but talking through it makes for better decisions. They trained us that way in the Nazca, too. Data is just leverage to get people talking, that's when you discover the truth."

"Cute," Sanda said.

He held up his hands in surrender. "I didn't say it was a *nice* method, just a method. Believe me, there are nastier ways to gather facts."

"You trained in those, too?"

He flushed. She wondered if the embarrassment was calculated. How much of her personality had he already parsed? She couldn't help but wonder just what he'd pieced together from listening to her talk. Those wrinkles around his eyes weren't so cute all of a sudden. She had to remember who she was dealing with, not get tangled up in things like hormones and proximity.

"Yes. Though I prefer a subtler approach if possible."

"Not helping your case much, there."

"I'm not defending myself. You wanted to know what I know, and this is it."

"Some things aren't worth knowing."

Grippy chose that moment to come squeaking into the room. Sanda wondered if Bero had put him up to it. That bot may have its own limited brainpower, but she knew full well it was in constant contact with Bero. His treads thrummed along on the metal floor as he came to a stop beside her and, without direction, offered his gripping hand.

"What a gentleman," she mused.

"What," Tomas said, "is that?"

"This is Grippy, Bero's maintenance bot. Got a brain like a walnut, but he's got some pretty slick intuition algorithms. Bero can boss him around, and he's good at learning on his own. Must have noticed my leg damage." She nodded to the dent in her calf. "He's how I got around before I knocked this up. Don't your people use repair bots?"

"Sure, but they're about the size of crabs and scuttle around like roaches. Never liked the things. Grippy's kinda cute, though."

She grinned as if he'd complimented her pet dog. "Yeah, check this out."

She snagged a stylus from the desk and held it at eye level for Grippy, just in front of his camera and sonar panel. "Grippy. See this?"

A double beep for yes.

"Good. Now fetch!" She chucked the stylus across the room. Grippy paused a moment, listening to it clatter, then wheeled around and set off at his fastest pace. His grip arm was a bit too bulky, so he took a couple of tries to snag the stylus, but he came back to her with it held out triumphantly.

"Good job!" She took the stylus and gave him a pat on the chassis. He beeped happily.

Tomas burst out laughing. "How long did it take you to teach him that?"

"Couple of days. He's got a rewards system path, but it took me a while to figure out how to work with it."

"I guess you had the time."

"Ugh. You're not kidding. Jokes aside, Cepko, this is your future, too. I hope you're good at keeping yourself entertained, because even with two of us on this trip it's going to get real boring. We'll probably even pick fights with each other, and Bero, just for the sake of having something different to do."

"Nazca," he said, and tapped the side of his temple. "I've been trained to be amenable in all situations. This will be a strain, I'm sure, but I can adjust my personality to be less abrasive to yours."

"See what I mean? I want to punch you already."

His eyes widened. "Did I offend? I didn't mean—"

"Oh no, don't take the nice guy track with me. Wrong fucking path." She pinched the bridge of her nose. "Look, I'll be straight with you. I don't trust you, and I don't like all this spy shit. Telling me you can mold your personality to meet mine isn't exactly a check in your favor, got it? Truest way for us to get along is to keep on being straight. No bullshit. Just, be yourself, if you remember what that's like."

That hit. He leaned back, sucked in his cheeks, and poked absently at the schematic on the tablet nearest his hand. It didn't have any new information for him, he just needed something to do. Something to fiddle with when he—the real him—became uncomfortable.

"You might regret that request."

"Don't play dark-and-mysterious with me. There's just us here for a long, long time. And sure, coldsleep is going to take up most of that." She rubbed the back of her head. "But we're going to be awake quite awhile, too. Popping up every so often to make system checks, refresh the pods, and make sure our muscles don't slough clear off our bodies. You were a spy. Mister Dangerous. I get it. But, Tomas, what are you spying on *here*?"

He looked around, slowly, lingering on the smartboard and its Keeper dissection notes, brushing his gaze over the haphazard deposits of materials she'd left behind, and the tablets splayed on the desk. A little smile twitched the corner of his lips.

"I bet Grippy's up to something covert."

"Well, look at that, a sense of humor. Now tell me this: Did you really want to be a dancer?"

The color in his cheeks was all the answer she needed. "Despite your rude comments about my feet, yes, and I was pretty damned good, too. Doesn't pay well, though."

She put her hand in Grippy's extended clamp and eased herself to her feet. "Well, choreograph us a way through that station. I'm going to see about fixing my leg."

He nodded and bent immediately to the task, fingertips dancing over the touchpad sans stylus. He used the three-finger touch method common among Icarions. She wondered if that was an affectation he'd adopted to blend in with them and, if so, why he bothered keeping up the ruse.

Holding Grippy tight, she crept to a nearby workstation, where all her tools were already laid out. She'd been sitting with her back to the door, but she chose the other side of the table this time, and told herself it was a comfort matter. It wasn't at all so that she could keep an eye on Tomas Cepko. Or whoever he was.

CHAPTER 28

SEVEN DAYS OF UNCERTAINTY

Martial law gripped the planet in silence. The bright lights of Alexandria-Ada had been dimmed to a muted glow, Biran's autocab the only sign of life on the road. If people watched his strange, privileged passage from windows, he didn't see them. The shutters were all pulled tight. He was glad for that. He was tired of being recognized. Tired of putting on the same everything's-going-to-be-okay smile he donned every morning he CamCast in to brief the people on the news with Callie Mera.

He did not want to think of Ada as a ghost town. Perhaps it was only holding its breath—a town on edge, a people waiting to see which way the pendulum would push them. Stay, or go. Okonkwo's orders that the people not be informed of the decision being weighed lasted all of eight hours. Director Olver suspected Biran was the leak. Biran suspected it was Lavaux.

Biran's cab followed the ping of Graham's wristpad to a café crammed in the back corner of a narrow alley. The place didn't even have a door, just a sheet of metal to pull down when they closed. Five bar stools—too close together to all be in use at once—hunkered underneath a narrow counter. Graham anchored one end, and at the other, the owner played a game on his wristpad, the steady tap-tap of his finger the only clue he was even awake.

Biran let the autocab go and sat down alongside Graham, an empty stool between them. His dad had already ordered two cups of coffee, creamy with dairy-free milk and sweetener, and pushed one toward him. It steamed.

"Long ride down just to say hello," Graham said. He didn't take his gaze from the curls of steam wafting up from his cup. Biran hadn't seen his dads much since the bombardment. It'd been too hard, to always see the question in their eyes. The change in Graham was stark. Hope was such a fragile thing.

"I need your help," Biran said into the murky mug, stirring the liquid with the tiny spoon that came with it even though it'd already been premixed. Who made those spoons, anyway? And why? Even handmade drinks were finished to your tastes before they reached a table. Biran only knew about sugar packets from old books he'd read as a kid.

"I know." Graham receded, as if something within him had drifted beyond Biran's reach. He gazed over his shoulder, across the road toward the sky, at the gleaming wedding ring of the Casimir Gate beyond. "Need you to promise me something, first."

"Not sure I can."

"Not sure you have a choice."

"If it's Sanda..."

"I don't know where she is, if she is anywhere. I know where you are. Need to know where you'll be, too. Once the bombs start falling."

"That's not how it works."

"I don't care how it works. Promise me you'll leave, son. Promise me that when those transports load up to cart us all out of here, out of Icarion's strike range, that you'll be on them. That you won't stay behind because of a thin chance. That, even if you found the love of your life between now and then and they had to stay here—were chained to the damned station—that you'd load up, and move on, and have a future. Not a brainless, gory end for the sake of honor."

"I can't promise you that."

"Then I can't help you."

"Dad!"

"That's how it is, son. I'm sorry. You don't know how sorry, won't ever know. But that's how it is. Because if I give you what you want without that promise, then Sanda would hate me. Hate me straight through to my bones. And I can't live with that. I don't think you can, either."

Biran took a drink, wishing it were something stronger. "I'm going through anyway."

"Don't lie to me, boy."

"I'm not. They're sending me to Atrux. Your old stomping ground."

Graham swiveled to regard him. "You said you can't promise me."

Biran stirred his coffee, grateful to have something to do with his hands. Maybe that was the point of the spoons. "I can't. The decisions are all above my head. Even as Speaker I can't influence anything one way or another. I know where I'm going now. That may change tomorrow."

"I give you what you want, there's no putting that Pandora back in the box. I need you to understand that. These people—they already know who you are. And you'll be inviting them to know you better."

"They're your old contacts, Dad. They can't be that bad."

A shadow passed across Graham's eyes. "Some are better than others. And these are the big guns. They've never forgotten me. They won't forget you, either."

"Blackmail, you mean." Biran's mouth tasted bitter. "Have they ever blackmailed you?"

"I like that you assume there'd be something to blackmail me with," he said, and laughed at the startled look on Biran's face. "No. I know who I am. Never got my hands into the real black market, though I knew people who did. I moved grey goods that could get me in some hot water, I suppose. Smuggling through the gates is no laudable occupation. But I'm clean now, and have been thirty years or so. I doubt there'd be much value in their trying. Ultimately, I suppose they haven't wanted something from me enough to risk burning the value of my contact."

"What value could you be to them?"

Graham grimaced. "Got a daughter in the military. Got a bright boy with a star-aligned future. Ain't me they'd be interested in, probably. But I'm a lever to pull, and these people specialize in levers. If Sanda's out there, they'll find her."

"Then why haven't you pulled that lever?"

Graham's eyebrows shot up. "Son, I'm an honest merchant now. I don't make the kind of money, or have access to the kind of information, that these people would require. You're talking about, at the very least, gaining access to an evac pod that's last known location is a battlefield between the two biggest guns in the neighborhood.

"To do that, these people have to get into space, out of orbit, and poke around an area that everyone in the system is playing tug-of-war over. There's no way to do that without drawing attention, and they hate attention, so they're going to have to insert someone on one side or another, or pull an asset they've already got in play. You'll be paying for this for the rest of your life. And if you don't have the money, well, with your position as Speaker..."

"They'll find another way for me to pay."

"Debts don't go unpaid. Not in their world."

"I understand. I have to do this. I can't leave without trying everything. I just can't."

Graham sighed, his shoulders rounding beneath his jacket. "All right. You heard him, Luce, you're up."

The elderly man minding the café glanced up from his game and blinked. "Took you long enough."

"Had to make sure he knew what he was getting into."

"Made us sound like brutes."

"Don't tell me you can't be."

Luce huffed and flicked off his game, spinning around so that his stool faced them.

"You?" Biran asked, bewildered.

"What'd you expect, a phone number? An email address? A clandestine alleyway where you'd meet with a shadowy figure?"

"I...didn't really know what to expect."

"Good, then I can't have possibly disappointed. Now, to business before your coffees get cold. I work hard on those, you know. You want the Nazca to find Sanda Maram Greeve, correct?"

"Yes, before the exodus. I need to know what's happened to her."

The man tsked and wagged a finger. "No timelines. Your situation is too variable to dictate a deadline."

"If you don't find her before the exodus, she'll be stranded behind with Icarion."

"Yes, yes, and in some distant future a descendant of yours will receive confirmation we fulfilled our end of the contract and discovered her whereabouts, if that is indeed the case. It's not like data won't be able to get *out* of Icarion. It just... might take a while."

"Without a gate, you're talking thousands of years!"

"Pity. Though maybe faster if Icarion gets their FTL research together." He made a face that indicated he didn't think that very likely. "Of course, we may find her alive and well tomorrow. Or confirm her death in the next few hours. The point is, we cannot guarantee a timeline. The vagaries of the politics at the moment are irrelevant."

"Fine. I'll take that chance. Just find her."

"You're in luck. We have a few assets already in play in the Icarion landscape. Lots of interesting things for us out there right now, you understand. That little war of yours might just work in your favor. Will cost you extra, though, to tap an agent already in the field."

"How much?"

"Extra, or total?"

"Total."

"Ninety percent."

"Ninety percent of what?"

"Everything, Speaker Greeve. Everything you make now, everything you ever *will* make until we deem the debt repaid."

Biran swallowed. "And how will you decide when the debt is repaid?"

"Depends entirely on what this mission takes. No way to know in advance, is there? Don't worry, though, we'll go easy on your descendants. And the Primes will keep you in house and transportation. Might lose some weight, though." He chuckled.

The blood drained from his face. "I'll survive. How do I arrange the transfer?"

"We'll manage that. You just go home and act normal, send us everything you have about the evac pod. Any information you can gather on Dralee, too. And the position of Icarion forces in the area. We have our own sources, of course, but triangulating is half of what we do."

"And you won't…"

"Sell the information you give us to opposition agents?" He flashed a toothy grin. "Maybe, maybe not. The Nazca aren't a government, Greeve. We don't have laws—or even really guidelines. We're information brokers. You're paying for information. The location and, if possible, recovery of your sister. Part of that price is understanding that what you give us might be used in ways you don't like, so long as it doesn't interfere with your order."

"And how much to keep that information exclusive?"

"You can't afford it. Listen, you're already committing treason by hiring us. There aren't shades of getting executed. Relax into it. We'll find her, sooner or later. As long as you don't do anything too stupid, no one will know."

"All right," Biran said, lightness suffusing him as he committed. "All right. Thank you."

The old man extended his hand, and Biran shook it.

"Thank you for your patronage to the Nazca."

CHAPTER 29

PRIME STANDARD YEAR 3541

IN A SYSTEM FAR, FAR AWAY

Sunrise found Jules beaten down and sweating, the peachy simulated light glaring at her reproachfully through the trees of the Grotta's only park. She couldn't have gone home during the night. The thought of walking into their converted loft and finding Harlan up, and waiting, twisted her stomach to hell and back. So she'd spent the night walking. Stalking, more accurately. Casing known runner tracks, slinking from shadow to shadow, watching the dealers of the black markets ply their trades in the alleys.

All of it had felt hollow to her. Pointless, desperate. A little kingdom full of tiny monarchies. Struggling for just a taste of power, a sliver of respect, a drop of recognition. They were her people. The representatives of the culture that'd borne her up into some semblance of adulthood. And she hated them. Loathed them. Saw herself in every petty deal and hustle and wondered just how any of it could matter so much to them. How it had ever mattered so much to her.

Nothing of value was done in the back ways of the Grotta. People struggled to live and find relevance and were beaten back down and died, telling themselves that it was worth it, somehow. That they'd garnered respect and power in their short, volatile lives, but it was all a lie. The lives of the Grotta were a lie.

Maybe you could claw your way up. Get your own place. Start a little business. Maybe you could make your life just the tiniest bit more comfortable. But you were still here, still pushed to the fringes and forgotten by anyone and anything that mattered. And on the edge, you were vulnerable—so, so vulnerable—to being pushed off it. To falling back down. Miss a payment. Miss a meal. Healthcare was free and nutriblocks were plenty, but what kind of life was that when all your citizen's income went to debts you'd built on the back of wraith and pain?

What did it matter, the hole you carved for yourself in the world, once you'd left it? No legacy of the Grotta would last. Harlan wanted her to accept that. To keep her head down. To fulfill her duty to her crew, to her people and her culture. To hustle and hope and never, never break status. Never shift the structure.

Fuck that. Fuck everything about that.

The door to Harlan's lair had been left unlocked. Nox, probably, too drunk to remember to lock up after himself. Again. She pushed the door open, preparing for a fight.

The fight had long since been lost.

She'd walked into the wrong house. That was the only explanation. The only thing that made any sense. Because the people who lived in this building were dead. And the crew—Harlan and Lolla and Nox—they couldn't be dead. Couldn't.

She drifted into the room, already a ghost—she should be a ghost, should be crushed beneath the rubble of their lives with the others— and searched, searched with her gaze for some semblance that this was wrong. That it was the wraith mother playing tricks on her mind.

The couch—a stained grey-brown thing they'd found on the street—lay tipped, its cushions spilled across the floor, their innards ripped out in great cottony puffs of filling. Their dishware—a mish-mash of patterns and materials—riddled the floor in a mosaic of detritus. Cabinets torn open. Doors left dangling from single hinges. Drawers yanked wide, gaping from their rightful places like panting tongues.

Home. This was her home as much as she sometimes hated it. And home was meant to be inviolable. Somehow, the hanging drawers were worse than the blood.

But the blood was there. Waiting for her to see it though she tried so hard not to.

It was bright, still. In most places. Weathered around the edges where oxidation had set in, drying out the vital fluid into flaky rust. So: not old. She'd seen a lot of blood in her time, knew what it looked like. How it aged. There was a lot. Too much for one person, but there'd been three living here, and who knows how they made the intruders bleed. So enough for death—the silence screamed death— but maybe not enough for everyone's death. Her hand moved to her stunner, realizing far too late that the silence might mean she was being watched.

She dropped to a crouch behind a tipped-over chair, circling the far wall of the ripped-apart living room. Across the room, the door leading to their sleeping cubbies had been torn open just like all the others. The lights beyond had been killed, but the edge of some kind of fabric poked out from under the bottom of the dangling door, its end frayed and torn. Something about that fabric tickled at her memory, but her mind was so choked with fear she couldn't figure it out. Wasn't her blanket—it was too smooth, like a plastic composite. Like a wristpad band.

She slunk her way around to the door and shined her stunner light down the hall. All the bedding had been ripped out, tossed into mangled heaps on the floor. Bits of clothing and jewelry studded the fabric piles like torches in the dark. The guts of electronics crushed under heel or smashed against the wall—divots bit into the plaster in flaky cracks—sprinkled the top like a dusting of something that should be lovely. Sparkling sugar on a cake, snow on a frosty field. This wasn't a raid. This wasn't burglary or theft. Everything of value had been smashed or tossed, but not taken. This was a slaughter. And a message. A message for her, maybe, written in the blood of those she loved.

Bile seared the inside of her throat and she choked it down. Forced herself to move, to step into that hallway. Wasn't anyone in the living room alive or dead, so if anyone was waiting for her it was here. Which made sense. The crew would have been asleep in their beds when the strike came. Maybe . . . Maybe they wouldn't have felt a thing.

She nudged the wristpad on the ground with her toe, turning it around to get a better look. It had been ripped off, the fabric—tough enough to withstand knife strikes—shredded like so much paper. The design around the edge of the smashed-in screen, a smattering of dots of varying sizes placed just so to represent each successful op, indicated the pad was Harlan's.

Shouldn't have been on the ground like that. Shouldn't have been torn up, cast aside. That bit of normalcy turned to madness twisted in her chest like a knife. Some part of her thought she should pick it up, bring it back to him. Get it repaired and everything would be okay.

The first doorway was hers. It'd been yanked open, but her things were still in place, each item left in the kind of pristine condition reserved for historical rooms maintained by museums. The next, Lolla's. Ripped to pieces. Every last scrap of cloth torn in some way, even her walls had been attacked—the plaster left clouds of white like a flour dusting across the surface of her things. Blood, too. Though not as much as had been in the living room. A spray—not arterial, Jules's mind told her as if the logical part of herself had separated out and was trying, desperately trying, to soothe the frantic side. A punch to the jaw, maybe. Could be nasal. Not deadly. Not enough for that.

Though she could not say what had happened after Lolla had left this room.

Jules moved on. Made her leaden legs claw forward through the chaos of the hallway. Nox's room—tossed but not bloodied, his weapons broken into tiny metal pieces. The barrels of guns made of composites that should never flex bent back upon themselves, pointing toward the trigger-puller in sick jest. But no blood. Nox and Lolla were okay, she told herself. Injured, maybe. But not here. Not dead. There just weren't enough places left in this hallway to hide two bodies.

But there was enough room left to hide one.

Jules's heartbeat pounded in her ears so hard it was all she could hear, all she could feel. The pounding, itching force of her own blood moving through her veins. How greedy she was, to keep that blood inside her when the others had spilled so much.

She must face it. She'd known she must face it from the moment she saw that torn wristpad tangled beneath the door. Little details, little clues that gathered in her subconscious when she had stepped inside congealed like a scab over her mind. The thought demanded her attention. Demanded she rip it off.

Harlan would not go down without a fight. Harlan would not lose his wristpad. Harlan would see the others to safety before himself.

If she had been here... He would have shoved her out with the rest.

His door was closed. That was all the confirmation she needed, and the reality of it punched her in the chest, took her breath away. Everything else about this raid had been so carefully managed, arranged after the fact with the precision of an artist. Whoever had closed that door had wanted her to open it.

And so she did.

Harlan sprawled on his back across the low bed, both hands crossed over his torso where he had tried, in vain, to shove a pillowcase into the gaping rose of a wound in his bare chest. He'd gone to bed—they all must have. His blue pajama pants were stained brown from the waist down to the knees, the steady waterfall of blood effecting a twisted tie-dye. His wrist, the one laid over the crumpled wad of pillowcase, jagged like a lightning bolt, the already dark skin mottled in storm-cloud bruises of grey and purple and brown. Broken when the pad was ripped free.

Jules began to shake.

His chest fluttered. Once. Twice. A slow, rasping rise.

"Harlan?"

She was on her knees beside him, bundling up the soggy pillow-case in her own hands to shove it down, hard, into his chest cavity. His body spasmed, pale grey eyes wrenched open. The whites she had once seen as so old and yellowed had blown to red. His unbroken arm thrashed in the remains of his things, searching for a weapon.

"It's me. It's Jules." Her bloodied fingers smeared across her wrist-pad as she tried to dial up a medivan.

"Stay with me." That was what you said, right? That was what you were supposed to say. And, also: "Help is coming."

"Too late," he rasped. His chest whistled the shrill whine of death. "Lolla. Find her."

"Where is she? Is she okay?" But his eyes had gone flat.

Jules had experienced a lot of death in her life. Had handed it out herself when the need arose. But she'd never really seen it, she realized. Never felt the cold viciousness of there being nothing where there had once been something. No, not cold. Cold implied intentional indifference. This was just... Just nothing. Harlan was, and now he wasn't. All the fine threads of his life's potential snipped short from one breath to the next.

One breath. What could one do if it was all they had left? Nothing. Nothing.

Everything was nothing after all, in the end.

Had she ever stopped shaking? No. Of course not. But she'd stopped feeling it. And now it took her. Rocked her from blood-stained knees to jittering jaw. Vibrated her from the inside out, made every muscle and sinew simultaneously weak and spasmodic, contracting and jellying and wracking her to the core. Vibration was life, some distant part of her thought. The shimmy and shake of electrons at all the right wavelengths to produce sentience and consciousness and here she was, coming apart at the seams. Shaking enough for the both of them.

The front door slammed open. The crack of sound slapped her in the face, rocked her back into a crouching position, her stunner in her hand though her grip was weak and slippery due to the blood—Harlan's blood—lubricating her grip. A flash in her mind—they'd come back. They'd come back for her and they were going to do her like Harlan, but fuck that, they'd find her a harder fight.

Jules was on her feet, sliding in the blood but finding her footing again as she made it to the hall where the torn blankets and the twisted clothes wiped the blood off her boots and she found her footing again. She braced herself, cranked the stunner as high as it would go, and fished through the junk until she found a beat-up old pry bar to use as a bludgeon.

Someone—some guy—shouted. She didn't recognize the words, only the alarm in the voice, the shrill panic, and she bolted toward the end of the hall, kicked the door wide to come out screaming and swinging, but it was Nox. Just Nox. Standing in the middle of the living room, staring at her with eyes wider than any she'd ever seen.

Like holding a mirror to herself, a mirror to her pain and her rage and in that moment, he knew. Knew what she'd seen. And, to her never-ending wonderment, he began to shake, just as she had.

Their eyes met, and something passed between them. Nothing like support, nothing like familial love and camaraderie. No. An understanding. An agreement.

A contract, of a sort.

This family was broken. But they'd hold together, just long enough. Long enough for vengeance.

PRIME STANDARD YEAR 3542

A YEAR TO THE DAY AFTER DRALEE

Biran Aventure Greeve was coming to see her. Well, not her, exactly. He was coming to sit behind her camera, nod solemnly at her questions, and turn those captivating hazel eyes upon all of Ada Prime as he explained, for the thousandth time, the importance of the Battle of Dralee. The importance of holding out hope—of clinging to our home while the higher-ups of Prime itched to order their evacuation.

The cold war hadn't just been between Icarion and Ada.

Callie had reported little on the political tug-of-war happening up at the Cannery. She didn't need to. There weren't any facts that she could share—nothing that wouldn't get her arrested—and the public did a good enough job of keeping themselves informed by keeping that rumor mill churning. Everything that went on at the Cannery was speculation, until a Keeper gave the official nod, and Callie's business wasn't speculation. It was facts. Fact: It had been one year since Dralee, and they were still here. There had been no exodus. Not yet.

Her heel bounced under the desk. Biran was coming to see her. And he was coming with more facts.

It wasn't like they hadn't talked in the year since Dralee. He was on her show every morning since the bombardment, for stars' sake. But he hadn't been here in person since the announcement about the convoy, preferring to CamCast his face down to her—and out to the people—with his sleeves rolled up as he worked behind some desk or another. She would have called it petty posturing, stagecraft to make the people feel better by showing them their leaders hard at work. But it wasn't. The other Keepers would do that, but not Biran.

She didn't know why she knew that. But she did.

She'd expected Biran to walk through the door. She hadn't expected General Jessa Anford at his side. Callie sucked air through her teeth and pressed one hand onto her knee to stop her foot from bouncing even faster.

Makeup didn't even blink. They swarmed Biran, though they pressed a little less powder under his eyes than they might have previously, letting the dark circles shine through. General Anford accepted the powder but declined the lip gloss, her naturally full lips pulling thin as she gently, but firmly, turned the makeup guy away from her. Callie's heart ached a little for him. He'd only been trying to do his job.

Callie stood as Biran and the general approached, her smile picture perfect as she pretended to herself that the cameras were already recording, and extended her hand to whichever of them would take it. Jessa was first, her strong fingers making Callie's bones creak as they shook. Callie was pretty sure she hadn't done that on purpose. Pretty sure.

"General Anford, this is a surprise," Callie said, flicking Biran a gaze that was also an accusation—*Why didn't you warn me?* Last year that would have made him blush. Now, he just shrugged apologetically.

"My fault," Biran said smoothly, placing a hand between Jessa's shoulder blades to guide her to a seat behind the desk. Callie scooted back, making room as a stagehand brought in another chair. "I should have given you a heads-up, but things came together quickly this morning. I hope you don't mind, Ms. Mera."

"Call me Callie, please. And of course I don't mind. It really is an honor to meet you, General Anford."

She inclined her head. "Likewise, Ms. Mera."

"Five minutes," a stagehand called out.

Callie's cheeks flushed as she sat down. She crossed one leg, then the other, struggling to put a cap on her nervous energy. If she had notes to review, she'd be diving into them now, but she hadn't had a clue the general was coming, and that, really, was the problem.

She took a long breath, relying on her snapped-on smile to hide the big ball of uncertainty roiling in her belly. The cameras rolled.

"Gooood morning, Alexandria-Ada! I'm your old friend, Callie Mera, here this morning with two special guests joining us in person, the S-S-Speaker." *Breathe, Callie. Breathe.* "Speaker for the Keepers, Biran Aventure Greeve, and General Jess-sa Halian Anford."

Shit. The corners of her smile strained. Biran swooped in, voice smooth as anything.

"Thank you for having us this morning, Callie. It's a pleasure to see you again, even on such a solemn day."

"And thank you for welcoming me on such short notice," the general said.

"You're welcome here anytime, General Anford." Callie gripped her knee under the desk. These people had facts. Facts she desperately wanted to pull out of them, and might not have another chance. She decided on a careful nudge. "I would have thought you'd be busy today."

Jessa's right brow arched. "I am busy every day, Ms. Mera. The anniversary of the Battle of Dralee does not change the state of the war with Icarion."

"So you have no concerns regarding a follow-up attack?"

Her eyes narrowed slightly. "My intelligence gives me no reason for concern. The war remains, as it has since the bombardment, cold." She snorted. "Icarion lacks the nerve, or the weapon. Either way, Ada is as safe as it's ever been."

Callie tried, and failed, to keep her eyes from widening. She could practically hear the forums and chatrooms lighting up with that bit of information. General Jessa Anford believed Icarion was incapable, or unwilling, to use the rumored RKV that had initiated the bombardment. The official statements had said as much, but her dismissive attitude was more confirmation than those stale press releases could ever be.

"We are here," Biran interjected, the crease between his brows telling Callie that he was imagining the same chatroom blowup, "to honor our fallen and our taken. In fact, a recent review of the Battle of Dralee has revealed our heroes fought harder for us than we ever imagined."

"Yes," Anford said, turning as if she were about to point to a display, then stopped herself as she realized the video would be queued up by the production staff. "Speaker Greeve recently reviewed reconstructed footage of the battle and discovered extraordinary bravery on the part of his sister."

Biran flushed with pride.

Anford continued, "If your crew would be so kind as to display the footage I am beaming to them now." She tapped out a few quick commands on her wristpad.

The little voice in Callie's earpiece said, "Got it."

"We're ready, General," she said. Anford nodded.

Callie did not relax her smile, not for a second, even as she knew the screen would flick over to the simulation that played out on the screen inset in her desk, keeping her up on the visuals. Vector images of ships swam into view on a field of black, the moon Dralee a distant curve in the background as the patrol squad approached that liminal space on the cusp of the moon's gravity well.

Scout ships—smaller triangles—took the point position on the three-dimensional, pyramid formation, the heavier gunships holding up the middle and rear. Sergeant Greeve's ship had been flagged with a yellow dart, tracking her path in the center of the formation.

"We've been over the footage of the battle multiple times, of course, but this new reconstruction reveals what we missed—the moments before the first impacts occurred. As you can see, the first shots took out three of the five scout ships."

Those blips disappeared, leaving the two scout ships forming the point of the pyramid exposed, cut off from the bulk of the gunship flotilla.

"The two remaining scouts were as good as dead. And would have been, if Greeve had not acted."

The sergeant's ship, flying that yellow marker, shot forward, swooping in to shield the two scout ships with its larger body. Sanda's gunship rocked as it took a direct hit to the flank, the scout ships scattering, retreating to the safety of the pyramid's base.

It hadn't been safe, though. More Icarion ships had popped into space around them, revealing the use of cloaking technology that Ada had no experience with, and wiped them all from the sky. But Sanda had tried. She'd put her ship between those guns and her exposed soldiers. She'd risked, and probably lost, her life for them. Bought them a little time. A fighting chance.

Tears stood in Biran's eyes when the cameras cut back to them from the simulation, but they did not fall.

"Wow," Callie managed, the word sticking in her throat. "Wow."

"Yes," Anford agreed. She pulled a small box from her breast pocket, the kind of black, leatherlike case that would carry an engagement ring, and set it on the desk. Callie didn't need to tell her camera people what to do. They split the screen, showing Biran's face on the right and that box on the left.

"With Speaker Greeve's permission, I have promoted her *in absentia*." Not posthumously. She flipped the lid of the box open, revealing the long purple bar that would be pinned to her uniform to represent her new rank, should she ever return. "Today, this first year anniversary of the Battle of Dralee, I raise Sergeant Sanda Maram Greeve to the rank of major."

The question pushed against her lips. Callie bit it back, pressing her tongue into the roof of her mouth, until the need to ask was almost a physical pressure. It would hurt. Stars and void, it would hurt. But she had to ask. Her viewers would want to know.

"Considering that footage, Speaker Greeve, do you still believe your sister survived the attack?"

He'd been expecting the question. Hadn't wanted it—no one would ever *want* to be asked if they believed someone they loved had survived a bloody assault—but he wasn't stupid. He pulled himself up straight, reaching across the desk to brush his fingers against the dark purple bar. The cameras would love that.

"I have to, Callie. I have to."

CHAPTER 30

PRIME STANDARD YEAR 3771

DAY THIRTY-ONE OF SCRAPING BY

Do you have anything that doesn't suck?" Sanda asked. She had her head and torso shoved to the waist inside one of Bero's access ducts, fiddling with the wiring that controlled the emergency LEDs. Between the age of the wires, and her misuse of the system to imprison Tomas, the cursed things had begun shorting out. It was not a pleasant thing to wake up to red-and-yellow LEDs blowing up your bedroom like you were visiting fire night at the club.

"My previous crew uploaded a great variety of music to suit many tastes." Stiff strains of Beethoven forced themselves out of his speakers.

"Classical? Really. Were your crew walking stereotypes? C'mon, Big B. There's gotta be something better in your library. Somebody on this ship had taste, I know it. Something with a guitar."

"There are many known types of guitar, not including digital renditions. I have access to over three hundred files containing at least one chord produced by a string instrument or its digital equivalent."

"Three hundred? That's nothing. I kept over ten thousand in my wristpad when I was a kid."

"My systems were not prepared for the musical appetite of adolescents."

She stopped in the middle of attaching a nut to a wire she'd just disconnected. "Are you calling me an adolescent?"

"You are of an adult age."

She puffed out a breath, nudging hair out of her eyes. "I really can't tell when you're being a jerk or not, you know that?"

"I do."

She snort-giggled, and Bero flickered his lights in his approximation of a laugh. "Well played, buddy."

A heavy slap echoed in the small access duct. She jumped and whacked her forehead on the bare circuit board above her. "Ugh. This better be an emergency, Tomas. If not, I'd suggest you run along and pretend whoever was knocking on this duct just now was a ghost of crews past, otherwise I might just make you join them."

"It's not an emergency, but I have something for you."

"Could you be any vaguer, please? I just love guessing."

"We're busy," Bero said coolly. Still hadn't warmed up to the other human on his back.

He tapped an annoying little jingle on the metal. "What, you two suddenly on a time crunch? What are you doing in there, anyway?"

She sighed and set her tools aside, then dug her heel into the ground and dragged herself out, the creeper under her back sliding easily across Bero's floors. Tomas grinned down at her. She pursed her lips.

"Bero's old, if you haven't noticed. Sometimes the connections degrade and need sprucing up, or severing. He's in good shape, though, considering his age."

"AnnLee always stressed the importance of self-maintenance," Bero said.

"Nice of her, but the wiring breaks down over time. Fine work like that is hard for Grippy to do efficiently."

"Nothing beats opposable thumbs, eh?" Tomas wiggled his at her.

"Nothing on this ship. What do you want?"

"Worked up a little something I think you might like in the lab. Care to come see it?"

"You're not going to tell me what it is, are you?"

In answer, he offered her a hand. She took it and let him drag her to her feet. Her leg made every step awkward, but she made a point of keeping pace with him.

He had all the lights up in the lab, and the table he'd claimed for himself was cluttered with bits and bobs—a gross violation of storage procedures. She bit her tongue. The chances of Bero suddenly spinning down were very, very small, and she was guilty of leaving a mess herself. But just because she had bad habits didn't mean he needed to join her.

"All right, what did you want to show me?"

Tomas stepped up to the table and hovered a hand over a sheet with an oblong bulge under it. He'd gone and set some of the lights to beam straight down on the object, making it gleam like a shuttle in a showroom. She groaned and rolled her eyes.

He pressed a finger to his lips before she could tell him to move it along. "Impatience," he said in an affected, grandiose tone, "is pointless in our current situation. Behold. My apology."

"Your what—?"

Tomas made a show of waving his hand over the sheet, then pinched the fabric and yanked it back.

A prosthetic leg rested in the middle of the table, looking almost like something out of a high-end medical catalogue. She actually gasped, then flushed violently red when Tomas laughed at her reaction.

"See? I couldn't just tell you."

"How in the hell?"

He shrugged. "I based it off the design you came up with. While you've been busy patching up Bero, I had some time on my hands. It worried me that the FitFlex was having to conform over raw metal when you entered vacuum. This should be a little safer."

The leg showed its armature in the joint at the ankle, but was otherwise covered in blue, hard foam sculpted to look like a calf and foot. As she traced her fingers over it, she could just barely feel the slight ridges of whatever tool he'd used to sculpt it, the subtle texture of careful sanding.

"When did you learn how to do this?"

He looked down and rubbed the back of his neck. "Made it up as I went, really. Nazca are picked for their ability to improvise. Here, let me help you try it on. I hope the light weight won't be too weird. I filled a rectangular mold with SealFoam, then carved out the body. There wasn't any flesh-weight equivalent material in the ship."

"I think I'd be squicked out if there were."

She sat on the bench and unbuckled her leg, tossing it to the ground with a little tinge of guilt. It'd taken her ages to get that thing working, and here Tomas came along and whipped up something superior in way less time. Must have been because he had her hard-won research to use as a kicking off point.

He fit the leg carefully over the puckered skin of her thigh. Cold fingertips brushed against her scar tissue, causing goose bumps to rise, and he shot her a questioning glance. She smiled at him to let him know it hadn't hurt. He nodded and bent back over her leg, pulling the straps taut, but not too much so.

When it was secure to his satisfaction, he gave her a hand as she rocked carefully to her feet. The foam did feel strange—she couldn't quite place her finger on why. Something to do with having the sense of flesh, of avoiding knocking her calves together, without the density to back it up. The joint movement was much smoother than her own version, and the shape of the thing would make wearing FitFlex and shoes so much easier.

"Well, how's it feel?"

She took a few experimental steps without his help and cracked a grin. "I can't exactly dance with it, but it's aces above what I had before. I can't believe it only took you, what, a week? We're only halfway to Farion. What are you going to do next, build us a gate from scratch?"

"That is impossible," Bero said.

He smiled. "It's true, I'm not that good, but I could help you with Bero's faulty wiring."

"There is only room enough for one human in my access ducts," Bero said stiffly. Sanda couldn't blame him. She'd had to promise complete obedience to be allowed access to his circuits, and even then there were stipulations. Bero's ducts and wiring were his circulatory system, his neural network. She wouldn't want anyone fumbling around in her body, either.

"Well, the offer stands regardless," Tomas said.

"Thanks." She thumped him on the shoulder. He rubbed at the spot and glanced away, hiding a goofy grin. A grin that vanished the moment he caught sight of a tablet Velcroed to his workstation.

Tomas cleared his throat. "Anyway. I'll let you get back to your repairs. You need any help, let me know, yeah?"

She nodded and took off for the door at a slow, careful pace, before she could open her mouth and shove her new foot in it. Tomas had set up his workstation opposite hers, near the desk where she'd discovered the research relating to Keeper Kenwick. She tried not to look, every peek felt like a violation of that man, but it drew her gaze whenever she walked past.

At first glance, she thought the tablet with all the research regarding Kenwick was missing, then she realized Tomas had moved it to his own table. It had been the sight of the Kenwick research that'd killed his grin.

The man cared. The realization lifted something in her she hadn't realized she'd clamped down. He'd called the prosthetic an apology, but it was more than that. You didn't spend hours out of your day carving out a prosthetic for someone whose comfort and safety you didn't care about.

You didn't trawl through the files of a dead man, either, unless you deeply cared why he had been made dead. Wanted to give the wasted life meaning. Sanda shivered. Even just looking at the blank screen that held Kenwick's data gave her the creeps and threatened to rile up a coldsleep headache. She'd put all the details of that file out of her mind, a pleasant blank spot in her memory. How Tomas could spend his time browsing through that gorefest, she had no idea. Spy or not, there was a core of something good lurking inside him. A side she'd very much like to get to know.

CHAPTER 31

PRIME STANDARD YEAR 3543

TWO YEARS OF COLD WAR ENDING

Evacuation loomed over Biran's head. He lay on his bed, the standard-issue sheets scratching against the bare skin of his back. All of his friends had upgraded. Silk-likes, natural cotton. Biran stretched against the rough weave of some efficient synthetic and day-dreamed of a curry. His stomach growled.

A red light blinked on his wristpad. Graham calling. Wanting to know if the Nazca had found anything yet. Wanting to make sure Biran was getting on the first shuttle off the station—to be whisked away to Atrux. To be whisked away from knowledge.

How many years would it take an email to travel from Icarion to Atrux without the use of a gate? He tried to do the math, and his head ached. Something like thousands of years. How many genera-tions would that take? For there to be generations, he'd have to have children. He hadn't been on a date since the Nazca had started bleed-ing his accounts dry. What woman would want to love a pauper even if they were Speaker?

He could adopt, or tube conceive like his dads had. But then he'd have to answer some sharp questions about where his finances were going. Right now, the arrangement made him look like a rather exu-berant philanthropist. Good as the Nazca were, he suspected that facade would break down under court scrutiny.

Anaia's face flashed in his mind. He could tell her. She'd understand. But he hadn't talked to her since the bombardment. No more than passing pleasantries. Hadn't talked to anyone, really. Some leader he was. Some political climber. Prime wouldn't send ships to investigate Dralee. Icarion claimed the evac pods as hostages—but never approached the rubble of the battlefield, not directly. That'd put them too close to Ada's wall of weapons.

His sister's body—living or dead—marked the DMZ of a painful stalemate.

A priority cast screeched an alert on Biran's wristpad, jerking him out of his melancholy. The director's face flashed across the screen and he swiped to accept the call, sitting up, but not bothering to hide the fact he wasn't wearing a shirt. Director Olver squinted.

"Did I wake you?"

"No, sir."

"Good. Get your things together. The Keeper transport to Atrux leaves at 0400. I understand you're concerned about your parents, but there's only room for Keepers on the first ship out." The precious cargo. He meant that everything else could be lost, if Icarion struck after their spies inevitably told them that the exodus had finally begun. "They'll be on the first civilian transport."

"Understood, sir."

The director hesitated. "No comment, Greeve? No protest?"

"Is there room for one to be heard, sir?"

"I hired you as Speaker because you *speak*, Greeve. Though as of late, less so."

"I have been briefing the people on the news every morning, sir, but there have been no new developments that are not classified."

"The exodus is happening. You need to do your part—and that isn't limited to getting on a ship to be taken to safety." He pinched the bridge of his nose.

"In a few days, Speaker, when the planet Ada is bare and Keep Station has been reduced to its robotic staff and a few doddering old Keepers, I am going to put on a flight suit. I am going to get in a shuttle, and go up to Ada's Casimir Gate. I don't know what I'll say, then. Nothing will seem...enough until that moment. But then I and the others will scan our chips, where the cumulative knowledge of generations is fractured and stored, and we will enter the commands to combine certain facets of that information.

"We will beam it—whole for the first time since the gate was built—to the maintenance bots that swarm the gate. And once they receive that information, once they have their orders, they will take it apart. Not piece by piece. Not a child's toy to be broken down and rebuilt elsewhere. They are going to initiate protocols used only once before. They are going to turn the negative energy generated by the gate upon itself. They will rend a gash in the sky, and I will be vapor before the dust clears. If it ever clears.

"I am dying, Speaker Greeve, because this system is dying. And its people, its survivors, will need a voice. A guiding light. You and I—we butt heads. And that's how it should be. No consortium of Keepers should ever be all in agreement. But I don't need you placid to my orders, now. I need you loud. I need you passionate. I need you bullying from the pulpit. Because, come the morning, the people of Ada will have lost a war. But they will have to move on, survive it as refugees in an already established system. Keep them together, Biran. Keep them safe. Keep them hoping."

Biran's throat swelled, his nose and cheeks went hot as tears coalesced behind his eyelids. He opened his eyes, let a few drops fall, blinking them from his lashes. "Sir . . ."

"No. No goodbyes. But I will say good night."

Biran smiled crookedly. "Good night. Director Olver."

"Good night, Speaker Greeve."

Olver half raised a hand—part wave, part benediction—then cut the connection, disappearing from the screen in a flick of light. Biran had until tomorrow morning. He could get up right now, go to the Cannery, and see the director in person.

But he wouldn't. To Biran, the director ceased in that moment. That second. He'd never see him again. Biran's subconscious had already begun to draft his eulogy.

Biran blanked the screen on his wristpad and bent double, a profound ache echoing through the empty hollow of his chest—the hole Sanda had carved with her disappearance. The hole that was spreading, devouring him up, with all the things he'd lost. All the things he would lose. All the decisions he could not bring himself to make.

If he had been bolder. If he had been stronger. If he had been smarter.

If, if, if . . .

Someone pounded on his door.

"Who's there?" he asked the house AI. Never upgraded, never would be.

"Keeper Lavaux is at the front door."

Biran scrubbed his eyes with the back of his wrist and stood, padding across the cold floors he'd never bought rugs for, the hem of his pajama pants catching at his heels. He flung the door open, surprised to see the station lights had already deepened to simulate the dead of night. He hadn't left the bed all day.

Lavaux, his medium-length hair tousled as if he'd just stepped off a movie set, looked Biran over from aching head to bare toes.

"Rough night?"

"What are you doing here, Lavaux? We leave tomorrow. I saw your name on the evac roster, too."

"You might leave tomorrow, but I'm leaving tonight. Two hours."

Biran narrowed his eyes, struggling to see meaning through the haze of pain clouding his every thought. "Have they moved up the schedule?" A flash of fear pounded clarity into him. "Has Icarion made imminent threats?"

"Neither. I have my own ship, a big bastard of a thing. Some of us don't agree with the current schedule. I thought you might be one of them."

Biran narrowed his eyes. "It's late. Get to the point."

"Prime's running scared. I don't care what lullabies Okonkwo sings to Olver, she's not pulling us out just to isolate Icarion. Something's got her spooked, and I'm betting it's this weapon Icarion has been dick-waving at us. Unfortunately, the young fools on the Protectorate are too young to have honed a real long-term perspective. From the day of the bombardment I knew they'd eventually scamper. Luckily they stuck around long enough to give me time to prepare."

"You're the same age as the director."

"Am I? How funny. If we cut Icarion off, they'll just hit us harder, later, with a bigger weapon. Something we haven't prepared for."

"We've been arguing this point for two years, Lavaux. What do you propose to do about that now?"

Lavaux flashed a grin. "You're not the only one with Nazca friends."

Biran swayed, his vision blurred at the edges. Lavaux grabbed him by both shoulders to steady him. "Whoa. Don't faint on me, boy. I know why you did it, and I won't turn you in. Sit."

His tongue was too thick to form a reply, so he let Lavaux ease him to the ground. He brought his knees up and put his head between them, breathing deeply and slowly.

"Better? Good. As I was saying, our mutual friends have found a few little hints for me to follow. A bread trail, if you will. I know where the weapon is. And I'm going to take it."

"How in the hell are you going to do that?" Biran demanded. Lavaux was mad. Mad as blowing up a Casimir Gate. Mad as hiring an intergalactic spy agency to find his sister.

Lavaux flashed him a white-toothed smile and flicked a hand through his hair. "Come find out in two hours. Pack your things, Greeve. Meet me at the docks—the ship's the *Taso*. Don't be late."

"They'll leave," he said, strained. "They'll leave us behind."

"Hard to have an exodus of the Keepers when all the big movers are missing."

Lavaux whistled to himself as he jogged down the walkway. Biran watched him until he disappeared behind the slope of the hill. For a half second he wondered if he'd ever see Lavaux again, if that was their goodbye and good night.

But that was a stupid thought. Biran grabbed the edge of the door and pulled himself to his feet. He had packing to do.

CHAPTER 32

PRIME STANDARD YEAR 3543

ANOTHER KIND OF EVACUATION

Taso gripped the dock like a spider clinging to its prey. If it were a spider, then it was largest of the swarm—a beast of a tarantula towering over the new-spawned children of lesser species. Biran had never seen a private ship so large. Such things were not unheard-of outside Ada. Some of the upper echelons of the universe lived on much grander ships full-time. Ships so large they nearly required their own governments, though they were ostensibly overseen by Prime.

But Ada was a backwater, and Biran had spent his whole life here. What was often seen in news clips, movies, and serial shows, was a hard thing to swallow when confronted with in real life.

He used to think his parents had done very well, financially, with their trading ventures. He'd been wrong. There were scales of "doing well" in the universe he hadn't realized existed until that moment.

Biran swiped his wristpad over a reader and watched the lock beep green, the gate sliding open with a merry chirp to welcome him to the *Taso*. He'd half expected Lavaux to forget him in the chaos involved in moving such a large vessel on short notice but again, he'd been wrong.

Someday he'd like to get used to being wrong. Then maybe he'd start being right.

The airlock dilated, revealing a man with a strained smile and his finger poised ready over his wristpad in the same pose secretaries had assumed since the beginning of time.

"Speaker Greeve?" He raised his voice in question, but the AI had to have already alerted him.

"I am."

"Welcome aboard the *Taso*, Speaker. Your room is 293-B, just down the hall and to the left, then right. Would you like me to take you there? You are the last of our expected arrivals, and we will depart shortly. I can also take your bags."

Biran hefted his thin duffel against his shoulder, having forgotten about it. "No, thank you. Which way to the bridge?"

He tapped a few things on his wristpad. "You'll find I have linked the ship's AI to your wristpad. You need only press the ship icon in the lower left corner, and tell it where you'd like to go. Visual maps are available, or vibrations—one for a right turn, two for a left."

"Thanks."

"Have a wonderful day, Speaker!"

Biran pretended to fiddle with his wristpad as he turned away, not wanting to be rude, but wanting more than anything to escape the awkward small talk that'd come next. He wondered if the man knew they were a rogue ship, running away from exodus. The call hadn't gone out to the general populace yet. Would Lavaux warn his staff that he risked trapping them behind the destruction of the gate?

He stopped midstep. He ran that same risk. Being left behind, while his fathers escaped to a future he'd never see. There'd be thousands of years of travel between them. But Lavaux wanted to find that weapon. And if he succeeded, then Okonkwo might abort the isolation. And, as Lavaux had said, there was a strong possibility they would postpone the exodus if half the Keepers were missing. He had to take the chance.

The door to the bridge swished open. Biran stepped into a semi-circular room, acceleration chairs oriented toward a forward display split between route charting and a view of Keep Station's dock and surrounding space. Crew members were hard at work, going through the run-up checklist to take off. Lavaux, sitting in the captain's seat with its carapace of undeployed evac pod around it, had his head bent to one side, focusing on a stream of data flowing past his monitor.

Biran stowed his bag in a cargo net, Velcroed the top to secure it, and approached an acceleration couch against the back wall of the bridge. Three people were already strapped in, leaving three empty spaces. Biran almost sat himself on the far end—he wanted to be alone with his thoughts—when he recognized the faces of the others.

"Keepers Garcia, Vladsen, and Singh," he said as he approached, plastering on an easy, well-isn't-it-funny-to-run-into-you smile. Lavaux hadn't been kidding when he'd said he'd gotten other high-ranking Keepers on board. This was most of the Protectorate. "I hadn't expected to see you here."

All three heads whipped around to regard him, but it was Singh who found her voice, heavy with parental mock concern. "Speaker Greeve. I'm afraid you're going to miss your shuttle to Atrux."

"Piss on each other later," Lavaux said without so much as turning his gaze their way. "And strap in. The window is closing. We leave now."

"Biran!" a familiar voice called from across the bridge. "Over here."

He turned, and his stomach dropped straight through to his feet. Anaia sat on the acceleration couch across from the elder Keepers, her slim, strong body strapped in to the cushioning foam. Ignoring the derisive snort from Singh, Biran hurried over to Anaia's side, jaw clenched as he stifled an urge to shout at her.

"What are you doing here?" He tried to keep his voice to a whisper but ended up hissing out the words.

"What?" She looked up at him with a fake innocent expression. "You think you're the only one of our cohort who thinks the exodus is bullshit? I want to find this weapon, Biran. I don't want our people running scared."

"You were safe." Nausea made him feel too light. "You were scheduled to ship out to Atrux."

"So were you," she said with a voice like steel. "Now sit before Lavaux shouts at us."

Biran strapped himself in, trying to breathe easily as the harness adjusted to his height and weight, cinching him in tight as a boa constrictor. He tried to tell himself that his decision was already made, that everything after he stepped onto that gangway was just academic, but he couldn't shake the feeling he could change his mind. That if he was fast enough, if he was brave enough, he could rip off the harness and spring through to the dock, dragging Anaia with him. Could get on that shuttle in the morning and meet his parents again in Atrux.

The *Taso*'s crew began the slow chant of warm-up back and forth to one another, checking and rechecking diagnostics as the great engines purred to life. He couldn't hear them, but a subtle vibration massaged his backside. All the creaks and groans of a ship preparing for takeoff pinged through the deck. Each complaint of metal made Biran's skin prickle, but the crew didn't seem concerned. As long as no one on deck was panicking, everything was normal. Just another flight.

The big screen flickered, and the director's weary face stared down at them. Biran simultaneously tried to make himself small while forcing himself to look confidant. Like he belonged there.

"Keeper Lavaux," the director droned—his voice thin, exasperated. He knew where this conversation was going, and that he had to go through the motions first. Biran wondered if he welcomed the distraction from what was to come. "The docks are on lockdown, as I'm sure you know. While the *Taso* is your ship and not under my jurisdiction—*as I told you earlier*—the space it is currently residing in *is* under my control. Kill your engines and stay put while the guard-core come to escort you all off board."

"Director, with respect," Lavaux said, reaching down to flick a button on his console. "I've found this station rather cramped as of late. I'm going for a stroll."

"Keeper Lavaux." The director's expression darkened. "Be advised that acting in direct opposition of an order from myself is considered treason. Ada is under martial law. You, and those on board your vessel, will be subject to arraignment if you persist in this fool endeavor." He leaned forward, as if talking to an intimate friend. "You leave tomorrow, Lavaux. You were not scheduled to stay behind. Don't do this. Don't force Okonkwo's hand *again*."

"I force what I like," he snapped. "And you—and Okonkwo—are acting irrationally."

"You don't have the authority to do this."

Lavaux's smile raised hairs across the back of Biran's neck. "I have all the authority I need."

"Your wife is on station. The guardcore have already collected her, and if she knew anything about this—"

"Rainier can take care of herself, as you well know. Don't worry, old friend. I'll see you both soon."

"Lavaux—"

He pressed something, and the director's image disappeared. A cold fist gripped Biran's belly. That was it. That was the point of no return. On the couch, Anaia grabbed his hand and squeezed. He squeezed back.

"Sir," a woman working the forward control panels said, "guardcore scuttles are incoming."

"Get us out of here as quickly as possible, Pilli. Try not to engage, but hit them with our wake if you have to."

"Understood, sir."

Biran closed his eyes as the ship pulled away from the dock, the full force of the engines spooling up sending the vibrations straight through to the roof of his mouth.

A soft drone, something more warm and harmonic than the rhythm of the ship, pierced Biran's silent litany that this was the right thing to do. Under her breath, Anaia prayed for all their souls.

CHAPTER 33

PRIME STANDARD YEAR 3771

DAY THIRTY-EIGHT MIGHT PROVIDE

A week later, Bero entered the weak orbital pull of the Farion station an hour ahead of schedule. On her HUD, the entry plan Sanda had worked up with Tomas ran through simulation. They would not separate, just in case the station was so degraded that injury was possible. Doubled, always, twin green dots that represented them moved through a rough outline of the station.

As soon as they'd gotten within scanning range, Bero analyzed the station's layout and adjusted their maps to match. Turned out Tomas's guesses were dead-on. She wasn't sure if that inclined her to trust him more, or less.

The blips stopped, having completed their digital circuit. She ran the simulation again.

"We will be within range in twenty minutes," Bero said.

"Seen enough?" Tomas asked. They floated on the command deck, feet looped into the ceiling grips to keep them from drifting away. His crummy haircut looked even more ridiculous in zero-g. His lifepack hulked above his shoulders, his helmet tucked under one arm. He'd gone through the plan on his own, running the simulation over and over again on the smartscreens in his cabin. His lips were quirked, a little hint of amusement she found both attractive and irritating.

"No. Not until this is over. We have no idea what we're walking into out there."

He shrugged. "An abandoned spy station. Nothing too spectacular. Sure, it's been a while, but Icarion builds their tech to last." He gave Bero an admiring pat on the ceiling.

"That was their plan, but you haven't seen the patchwork fixes I've had to do for Bero. No offense, buddy."

"The integrity of my systems is a known state. A simple statement of fact cannot offend me."

Sanda shared a look with Tomas, and said, "Being offended by facts is a long human tradition."

"I'll pass on that one," Bero said.

Tomas cracked a grin and laughed. "Does he know he's being sarcastic?"

"Do you know I can hear you?"

Sanda snorted and set to rechecking her gear while the ship and Tomas ribbed each other mercilessly. Wasn't much different from her time on a gunship. Their easy banter had a greater soothing effect on her nerves than hours of meditation ever had. The gibes felt warm. Like home. A weird home, maybe, but home all the same.

"We are within range," Bero announced.

The chuckles fell silent. Without a word, Sanda and Tomas checked each other's suits over for failure points, then seated their helmets and allowed Bero to run systems diagnostics. Everything was green, and they were still forty minutes ahead of schedule. She hadn't been in such a hopeful position since the day she woke in Bero's medibay.

"How's the leg?" His voice was scratchy through their comm link. Tomas reached to pat her calf as she pulled herself toward the airlock and missed as she floated by, accidentally patting her natural, fleshy, hip. The touch was a shock, but not an unpleasant one. She heard a soft beep as he adjusted something, then repeated himself in smoother tones. Apparently they were just going to ignore that slip. Better for the mission. Probably.

"The leg is stable, so far. Fills out the suit better. It's nice not to worry about snagging the 'Flex on metal fittings."

"I can't believe you were taking that risk."

"I had a lot on my mind."

He fell silent as they opened the 'lock and pulled themselves inside. Tethers attached, systems still green, she waited impatiently for Bero to depressurize the 'lock, gaze fixed hard on the percent bar filling steadily toward all clear. A strange mix of excitement and dread roiled in her belly.

Tomas's knowledge of the station was probably their best shot at survival—*if* it housed anything they could use. Chances were good, but the threat of disappointment loomed in her shadow, nipped at her heels. She'd promised Bero her protection, and Tomas's easy charm reeled her into him. Could she really space someone she was coming to think of as a friend?

She'd made harder calls on gunships. It was the emptiness of space that was getting to her, clouding her mind with false intimacy between the two humans left within light-years. Bero's safety, and her own, came first. Tomas may have kind eyes and a nice chin, but he was a spy. All his easy camaraderie could very well be calculated.

Dios, but this isolation had turned her into a madwoman. Tomas was a dubious sort, she had no doubt of that, but he wasn't evil. Some aspects of a personality were just too hard to fake. She squared her shoulders. She had a mission to lead. They'd be okay. She'd make sure of that.

The bar filled green and the 'lock door opened, the subtle pull of Bero's ship against the absolute stillness of space pricking at her limbs. With a swimmer's ease she checked her tether, checked Tomas's, then hit the airjets and kicked off.

Farion-X2 loomed before them, bright against the low-albedo backdrop of the moon for which it had been named. She tore her gaze away from the great mass of Kalcus hulking to her left and focused on the airlock door sprouting from one spoke of the wheel-shaped station's center. It turned, lazily counting down the years until it finally lost momentum. Space wasn't so empty—Bero's propulsion system was proof enough of that—but the bits of matter that filled it were very far apart. It'd be centuries before the station lost all of its spin, since the Icarions hadn't felt compelled to stop it before abandoning it. Maybe they'd planned on spinning it back up again.

Maybe there were bodies in there, waiting centuries for discovery.

"Looks like we'll have some gravity," Tomas said.

"Wish we didn't. Evac pods are heavy."

He grunted agreement, and in the corner of her HUD a skeleton render of Bero's robotic arm stretched into the black, settling itself into their best-guessed position for the cargo bay. By the time the arm was situated, they reached the airlock. Sanda grabbed an exterior handhold, removed her tether, and hooked it onto the handle. Tomas mirrored her on the other side of the door.

A keypad gleamed at them. Radiation had bleached the paint, but carved grooves in the metal revealed the numbers.

"Bero," Sanda said, "can you—"

"No need," Tomas interrupted. He dialed, too quick for her to follow, and a pale green light flashed. "Nazca, remember?"

She couldn't see his expression through the glazing on his faceplate, but she didn't need to. That smirk was palpable.

"Cute. After you, spymaster."

He drifted in ahead of her. She checked over the 'lock while the door shut behind them and old systems whirred into place. Sanda tensed, flicking her gaze constantly over the pressure readouts Bero fed to her HUD. Everything looked good. Nice and stable. But any misfire could blow them to bits. She flinched when the interior 'lock door swung open and scolded herself. Too much imagination for her own good.

Tomas went first, as they'd planned, so that if they happened across anything living, he could put his cover as an Icarion comms man to the test. They encountered no one. Just an empty deck, smartscreens dark, equipment stored away so that the whole place looked bare. The air recyclers must still work, because not a speck of dust had gathered. She wondered how long that would last, and just how clogged those air filters were. This was why Bero needed her. Without human hands, things break down. Dust gathers. And dust could mean death to any spaceship.

"Air looks breathable, pressure is good," Tomas said.

Sanda flicked her gaze over her wristpad and nodded. "Agreed. Might as well conserve the lifepacks."

"Don't," Bero's voice held steel in it. She stopped halfway to reaching up to her helmet.

"Why not?" she asked. Tomas shrugged and pulled himself toward the first likely spoke.

"My scans might be incorrect. And atmosphere can change from one room to the next. You said yourself these lifepacks will last for days of use."

It's dangerous out there. The words echoed behind Bero's authoritative statement. He might be right, but she could sense threads of paranoia lurking in his words.

"Sounds wise," Tomas said over comm. "What do you think, Sanda?"

She pulled herself up the ladder after him, feeling a subtle Coriolis effect shift the water in her belly. She swallowed faint nausea. Half-spun ships were worse than no grav at all. "Agreed. There's no reason to take an unnecessary risk. Let's sweep this place and get out."

The first chamber was comprised of sleeping cabins. They'd planned on just passing by, but with an extra forty minutes to spare Sanda couldn't resist. She flipped every single mattress.

"What are you doing?" Tomas paused and crossed his arms.

"You'll see. I've learned something about these Icarions while on Bero. Ah-hah!"

With a triumphant flourish, she peeled a duct-taped bottle of Caneridge rum from the bottom of the mattress. "Told you. I've found two of these suckers in Bero. It's gotta be an Icarion fleet affectation, but I'm not complaining."

"Nice to see where your priorities are," he said, but couldn't hide his amusement over the comm.

"Thank me later."

She shoved the bottle in her equipment pack and bounded out after him. The next hab was given over to the residents' daily work, and Tomas made a quick survey of their equipment before coming up swearing. "None of this works anymore. Pulled all the power cores before they left."

"Probably feared them expanding, or corroding, and ruining the systems. Don't sweat it, it's not like we have anyone to talk to."

He stiffened so hard she thought she could see the tension ripple across his shoulders. "Maybe now, but we're going to want a way to initiate contact once we get in range of Atrux."

"Bero can handle that."

"That's not something we can rely on," he said in a soft, grinding tone. Despite his annoyance, he bundled some of the equipment into his pack. They approached the cargo bay in the next spoke.

Tomas punched his number into the door, and it dilated. After a careful prod of the smartpad, yellow-white lights burst into life all throughout the largest of the station's habs. Sanda caught her breath.

"Pay dirt," Tomas said.

Anchored to mag pallets all across the empty floor of the hab were stacks and stacks of supplies. Screens affixed to each cube lay dark, and she licked her lips in anticipation of reading the manifests those screens held. Food. Weapons. Repair equipment. FitFlex and other clothing. Maybe, if they were very lucky, evac pods.

"Am I hallucinating?" she asked.

"If you are, it's spreading." Tomas gave her a quick side hug and burst forward into the cargo bay, slapping a tablet to bring up the manifest. A list of equipment she didn't recognize scrolled by.

"Sweet." He looked over his shoulder at her. "Found the batteries."

"They still good?"

"Only one way to find out." He tugged himself up the side of the pallet, easy as a cat up a tree, and pulled back a tightly sealed tarp. After a moment's rummaging, he popped his head over the side and gave her two thumbs-up. "They're golden. Absolutely pristine. I can't believe it."

"Our lucky day," she said, hurrying over to the next pallet. Food—canned stuff, not even a sniff of nutriblock anywhere in the mix. "Oh man, we're gonna feast tonight. You getting all this, Bero?" She swept her vision over the cargo hold slowly so he could make out the wealth of pallets.

"Very encouraging," Bero agreed. "Though I confess canned pears don't have quite the same appeal to me."

"But the batteries!" Tomas called.

"Yes, that will help. May I suggest you undertake shifting all these out to my arm now? We can sort them later. Time is tight."

"Roger that," Sanda said.

After thirty minutes fiddling with the cargo bay door lock, they figured out it couldn't be opened unless at least one of two conditions were met.

One: The dock must be sealed to another ship, and Bero lacked the fittings.

Two: The ship must not be under spin.

All perfectly normal safety procedures, but under the circumstances she'd rather just jettison the lot and let Bero pick up the spillage. His arm was agile enough for crates this size. The ship, however, could take days to power down from its spin. Days they didn't have.

"Ideas, comms man?"

Tomas tapped on his wristpad and brought up their map of the station. After a moment's pause, he jabbed a finger at the third spoke over. "There's a lot of maintenance panels here, I may be able to use some of the equipment I found to override the safety features. And anyway, we need to finish our sweep. Those crates are good for general supplies, but I'd still like to find an evac pod or two."

"Agreed. Bero, do you think you can help him with the override?"

"I need to see the system before I can be sure."

"Affirmative."

The next few habs passed by in a flash: mess hall, medibay, water recycling. Each time their search for an evac pod came up empty, her stomach sank a little. But there was still the rest of the ship, still those pallets loaded with goods, and she knew full well that these Icarion wankers wouldn't risk their hides out here without a life jacket.

The door to the maintenance room slid open, and Sanda stopped cold.

There was a real window there. A two-meter pane of plex, pointed straight toward the little smear of light that Ada had become. Her throat ached. Her hands clenched. The Icarions here had indulged in one hell of a luxury, just to get the occasional glimpse at their target.

"Sanda?" Tomas's voice was soft.

"Your heart rate is elevated," Bero said with an equal amount of concern.

"I'm fine," she lied. "Just startled, that's all."

238 ✦ MEGAN E. O'KEEFE

Tomas skimmed across the metal floor toward her. Sometime while she'd been staring at her dead homeworld, he'd already crossed the room and popped a panel. A device dangled in one hand, but he rested the other on her shoulder. Squeezed.

"I can't understand what it's like," he murmured.

She thought of the tears she'd seen tangled in his lashes, and thought to contradict him, to call him out on his pain, but decided against it. He was trying to be kind. Trying to be a friend. And while he'd lost everything, just as she had, Ada Prime was not his home. It was not a beacon to him, calling out for grief, as it was to her.

She drifted forward, pressed one gloved hand against the window. They were ahead of schedule. She had a moment to mourn.

Tomas's arm looped her shoulders from behind, held her gently at his side. He said nothing, but the soft press of his fingers against her communicated enough—he was rubbing the tension out, gently, even through the heavy resistance of the suit. Something within her eased back into that touch, and she didn't resist it.

His hand slipped up the back of her neck and ripped the plug from her lifepack.

CHAPTER 34

PRIME STANDARD YEAR 3543

TWO DAYS A FUGITIVE

How long?" Biran asked the ship's AI. He paced what was considered the "forward" viewing room. Anaia leaned against the wall alongside the window, arms crossed loosely over her chest, an amused smile on her face as she watched him wear a path through the floor. Nothing but a sea of black shot through with white pinpricks of stars could be seen through that window. Stars, and the faint curve of the moon Dralee. Its grey-green surface was too far away to see the details as it rose from the bottom of Biran's current horizon.

"The *Taso* is entering the known debris field now." The ship answered in the same helpful, friendly voice it always used.

"We won't see anything," Anaia said.

"I know, I know." Biran squinted through the window, straining every muscle in his body, as he tried to see what was left of his sister's battle. He couldn't make out anything. Not even a spec. He'd known that would be true, but the disappointment grated at him. Some secret, boyhood desire had harbored a hope that he'd see a green light out there, winking in the dark, waving him in. Saying: Hello, I've been waiting.

"Speaker Greeve," Lavaux said over the ship's intercom. "Please strap in. In the viewing room, if you must, but this is an active DMZ. The border of which we are currently breaching. And we are here to *look for a weapon*. Evasive maneuvers may become necessary, and I'd hate to bruise that pretty face of yours. The cameras do love it so much."

Biran clenched his jaw. "Permission to join on deck?"

"Granted."

He spun around and shoved through the door, almost running chest-first into Vladsen. The dark-haired man put a hand on Biran's shoulder to steady him and arched both bushy brows. Biran forced a smile, embarrassed, and brushed off the front of his shirt.

"Sorry, didn't hear you coming."

"He's a mess," Anaia quipped, drawing a scowl out of Biran.

"Good evening, Keeper Lionetti." Vladsen nodded over Biran's shoulder to Anaia, then turned his attention back to Biran. "You're allowed to be excitable at the moment." Vladsen smiled, slowly, and Biran blinked. He'd never been this close to Vladsen before. Never noticed how young the Keeper looked, despite being of the older generation of the Protectorate. A quiet man, Vladsen had never really stood out to Biran as anything more than a steady presence.

He recognized the feel of that hand on his shoulder—the light touch, the short and narrow fingers. It had been Vladsen that day, on the podium, when the sky filled with fire and the newscasters told him that the second he'd achieved his dream—become a Keeper—his sister had died. He'd never really thought about it, but the realization shook something within him. The Protectorate maybe weren't out for themselves all the time, after all.

"Thank you," he said, fidgeting with his sleeve, unsure what to say, but wanting to ask a barrage of questions that the quiet Vladsen would no doubt find rude.

Vladsen must have picked up on this, for he chuckled and patted Biran on the shoulder. "So young. I was only a few years older than you when I was elected to the Protectorate." He winked, knowing he'd answered one of Biran's silent questions. "Have there been any sightings yet of evac pods in the area?"

"No." Biran's spiral of questions was dashed away in an instant. "Though I'm on my way to the deck to keep an eye on what's happening. The *Taso* has informed me that we are, officially, inside the rubble field. Not that you could tell from looking out the window. And Icarion may have already recovered the pods. We don't know."

He had to keep telling himself that. Reminding himself that this mission was not about his sister. That they were here to find the weapon so they wouldn't have to abandon their home, and the fact that Lavaux was looking in the rubble where his sister's coffin may float was incidental. His heart didn't believe it, though. That damned thing kept speeding up every time the ship's AI spit out a status report.

"I will walk with you, then, if the window is truly useless. Tell me, do you believe in Lavaux's weapon theory?"

Biran nearly missed a step. Anaia's hand shot out to steady him. "I...haven't thought about it too much. Icarion has something they've been threatening us with, so it seems likely, and they did bombard us. Whether that device is near Dralee or not, I can't say. I suppose he has his sources. Lavaux doesn't strike me as the type of man to act without certainty."

"He doesn't, does he? I'm not so sure myself."

Biran frowned at him, but Vladsen just gave him a sly smile. "Forgive my asking, but if you're not convinced that Lavaux is correct, then why did you come along on this mission? Your name wasn't on the list of those to stay behind. You would have been transferred to safety the morning we left if you hadn't boarded this ship."

"Oh, that." Vladsen flicked a hand, brushing away the implications of being stranded thousands of light-years from a nonhostile civilization with a little shake of the wrist. "Lavaux and I go way back."

That, apparently, was explanation enough as far as Vladsen was concerned. "Are you also from Lavaux's home system? Ordinal, I think it was?"

"Hm? No, I am from here, more or less, but we crossed paths early on—and seem to keep on crossing them."

Anaia asked, "Do you trust him?"

"Heavens, no. Wouldn't dream of it. Here we are."

The door dilated to the deck, and Vladsen threw Biran a wink. "Now let's see what our fearless leader is up to."

"I heard that, Vladsen," Lavaux called over his shoulder without looking up. "All of you, strap in. Sensors are picking up a larger-than-usual object in the area and we know we're dealing with advanced cloaking out here. I've brought the best, but…" He trailed off, squinting at a screen, and Biran had to bite down an urge to shake him and demand to know what he was worried about.

Twisted metal, smeared with both Ada Prime cyan blue and scorch marks drifted onto the screen, highlights of raw metal framed against a sea of black. Biran's heart skipped a beat.

A little green light winked at them all.

Silence squeezed the deck, everyone holding their breath. Raw terror warred with elation in Biran's mind. It could be anyone. It might be no one. It wasn't even, technically, what they were here for. This was Lavaux's ship. Stopping here, now, to scoop up that pod would make them vulnerable to attack, less maneuverable.

Lavaux spoke first. "Recovery stations, everyone, and wind the engines down. That's one of ours out there. We're taking them in."

Biran wanted to shout for joy but found he had no words. No ability to speak at all, his heart had lodged so thoroughly in his throat. Anaia grabbed his arm and pulled him toward the door.

"Come on," she said.

Biran found his voice. "Lavaux." The white-headed man turned to him. "Thank you."

He nodded and went back to his screens—to monitoring his ship, and the recovery of the pod. He cut a regal figure up there on his captain's chair, presented himself as a real leader, and had even stopped his all-consuming goal and passion to, maybe, save just one. That was the stuff of myth building, of legends and heroes.

Biran had been played. The truth dug into him, needled at his ribs, prodded his mind. Lavaux had, with this simple action, wrapped Biran around his finger. No matter what happened next, Biran would always remember this moment—the moment Lavaux didn't hesitate. The moment that, after years of struggling and arguing with the Protectorate that his sister was worth the risk, was worth saving, Lavaux hadn't required so much as a push.

Some deep-seated aspect of his personality wanted to rebel against that. Wanted to write off Lavaux as a political playboy, a manipulator of the highest order. A politician on the rise. But he couldn't do it. Gratitude suffused every fiber of his being. He'd just been handed the only thing he'd ever wanted—a chance. He wasn't about to resent the man who handed it to him because his motives were self-serving.

Biran shook himself, and ran for the airlock that was lining up for the rescue, Anaia's boots stomping after him.

Behind him, Vladsen laughed.

Dead. The occupant—Gunner Wilcox Raismith—had been dead before the evacuation pod had enclosed him in preserving foam. A piece of shrapnel, as wide across as Biran's palm, stood straight up from the dead man's chest—a white flag of surrender.

"There might be others," the medi—a woman with dark blue eyes and bleach-blond hair said. Biran would have thought her cute if he had any ability to think beyond the unfamiliar face on the exam table.

"There might be," he agreed, not even feeling the words, just responding by rote. This was what you did when someone tried to comfort you after a tragedy. You comforted them back by keeping to the script, the agreed upon give-and-take established as early as human civilization. She wasn't wrong. The existence of Raismith was proof that Icarion had never recovered the evac pods left over after the battle. Others might be out there. Drifting. Waiting. Sanda's might be one of them.

Staring down at the empty face of Raismith, it was difficult to convince himself of that.

She fiddled with a forceps. "I need to complete the autopsy."

Translation: Please leave, you're distracting me. "Right. Sorry."

Biran stared at the corpse a few beats longer, unwilling to tear his gaze away just yet. What had this man seen before he died? Had he seen Sanda get into a pod? Or had he seen her torn to bits by the rest of the shrapnel that pierced his chest?

Before he could say something remarkably stupid—like, let's try a séance—Biran let himself out of the medibay. Anaia was there, waiting. Of course she was. Probably had her ear pressed to the door the whole time they'd been in there. She clasped her hands in front of her stomach and wrung them together, her eyes wide with hope.

He didn't want to tell her. He had to tell her.

"It's not her," he whispered, and the moment the words passed his lips, they became truth. Crystalized his pain. He closed his eyes and pressed his back against the wall for support.

"Oh, Biran... We—we found one. There will be others."

Damned near the same thing the doctor had said. The same thing he had thought. Funny how that worked. Almost like comfort took the same shape everywhere you looked, stamped out like a mass-produced panacea.

"Is there anything I can do...?" She reached for him, her fingertips brushing his arm, hesitant, like the slightest touch would cause him to dissolve on the spot. Maybe it would. He'd never felt this brittle before.

"No. I need a moment alone, please."

She nodded, swallowing hard, and drew her hand back. "Call for me if you need anything."

"I will," he agreed. "I will."

She gave him a look that said she didn't believe him, but was willing to accept the lie for the time being, and took off at a slow stroll down the hall, giving him time to call her back if he wanted to. He didn't.

He just stood there, in the middle of the hall on an unfamiliar ship, numb from tip to toe. He reached for his wristpad, flicked through the usual series of clicks to bring up a direct line to Graham, before he remembered that Keep Station was doing everything they could to jam communication signals coming in from the *Taso*. The "failure to connect" button popped up—a sad emoji. Biran grimaced and swiped the app away.

It came right back, the sad face turned upside down. An incoming call—from an ident tag he didn't recognize. Biran's finger was a millimeter from the reject button when he froze. Something about that number tickled the back of his numb mind. It wasn't anyone he knew, but... He swiped accept and was greeted by the greyed-out screen of a voice-only call, no video feed.

"Mission number: alpha-five-zebra-three-seven-beta. This is Nazca Cepko. I've got her. We're on board *The Light of Berossus*, currently stationed outside Farion-X2 Station. Situation is critical. The AI is hostile. Time is limited. Here she is."

I've got her.

CHAPTER 35

PRIME STANDARD YEAR 3771

DAY THIRTY-EIGHT IS A TERRIBLE DAY TO DIE

Sanda gasped as alarms blared in her helmet, in her head. Her HUD lit up with warnings, flooding her with too many failures to keep track of. Bero screamed something, but she couldn't hear him through the pounding in her ears. She lurched backward, reaching for the plug.

Tomas's arm tightened around her, pinned her back to his chest, and anchored her arm in place. She jerked, spasming, as panic used up the air left in the suit. Some analytical part of her mind began counting down the seconds until she gave in to CO_2 poisoning.

Her head jerked back, trying to smash Tomas's helmet with the back of hers to at least take him out with her. The bubble of her helmet bounced off his cheek. He'd already disconnected.

Oxygen-deprived brain cells raced to figure out a reason, a solution, but she was feeling slow, her arms heavy. A dull slap echoed against her helmet, her torso twisted, and then her helmet was gone, the many flashing lights whisked away. She gasped instinctively, heaved herself forward and squirmed.

"Whoa," Tomas's voice was far away, fuzzy, but getting closer. "I'm sorry about that, I didn't think you'd put up such a fight. Shoulda known, eh?"

"You fucker." She found strength in her leg again, huffed down lungfuls of stale air, and twisted in his grip so that they were chest-to-chest.

His eyes widened. He tried to pull away, but she got her fists curled around the collar of his suit and shoved. In the low-g, his stumble took him all the way across the room, his back slammed into the wall.

"Hey—hey!" But she was on him already, her hands on his wrists, trying to twist his arms up and back to force him into a tucked hold. He was stronger. But she was very, very, angry.

"Sanda, please, give me a cha—"

"Who the fuck are you?" she yelled against his ear.

"Yeah, about that—" He jerked his wrists free. She stumbled against him and he propped her up, an annoyingly polite gesture considering the circumstances. Before she could adjust, he spun her around so that her back was against his chest again, snagged one hand under her chin, and jerked her head up.

The window had changed. Where the smear of light that had once been Ada Prime drifted, two faintly glowing spheres circled each other. She'd know them anywhere. Had dreamed of them every night since she'd awoken to this fresh hell.

Ada. And the Casimir Gate.

She went limp in his grasp, all the fight seeping out of her, and would have dropped to her knees if he hadn't been holding her. His hand slid away from her chin, went to coil about her torso to help her stay on her feet. A coldsleep-borne headache burgeoned in the back of her skull.

"It's a simulation," she said, breathless.

"No," he said, and toed a helmet that had fallen nearby in the struggle. "But that was."

"It can't—"

"Sanda. Sergeant Greeve." His breath gusted against her cheek. She shivered. "You know that's a window. It's not a smartscreen. It can't be faked."

"But, on EVAs…"

She trailed off, staring at the helmet at her feet. The helmet with the smartscreen visor. "Dios."

"Easy," he said. She'd swayed without realizing it, her body trembling with rage and shock. Pain surged from the back of her head to her toes. She reached up to rub the ache, then cringed away.

"Are you okay? Sanda? Answer me, please."

"Yes, I...I get headaches. From the coldsleep."

He turned her, gently, and stared down into her eyes. His expression twisted into a grimace. "Maybe."

She realized she was little more than a wet noodle in his arms and pushed him away with disgust at herself for cracking. Tugging her suit's collar straight, she stepped to the window and gripped its sill to hide the shaking in her hands.

"What," she said, warm breath misting against the cold window, "in the ever-loving fuck is going on?"

"We can't talk long." He stepped to her side, that device still clutched in one hand. "Bero may panic if we're out of contact too long, and we don't want that. Shit." He shifted his weight, dragged his fingers through his hair, then put his empty hand on her shoulder and turned her to face him.

"I am who I say I am, more or less. I am Nazca, but I've been working for the Primes for the last five years. They recruited me directly— but the specifics don't matter. I'm on your side, Sergeant Greeve. I've been looking for you for a long time."

"*Looking* for me?"

"When your pod disappeared after the Battle of Dralee, your brother pulled every string in the 'verse to get you back. Eventually one of those strings was the Nazca. I'm told your father Graham facilitated the contract. I've been left all over the fucking place, hoping to get picked up by whatever Icarion ship had imprisoned you, or at least one that could give me a sniff of your whereabouts. Icarion's got the Keepers by the balls, between the bombardment—that happened, unfortunately—and holding a sergeant hostage."

"But they're *not*—"

He held up the device and slammed a battery pack into it, then jabbed at the number pad lightning fast. "I know you won't listen to me. Not after what you've been through," he spoke while dialing into what she now realized was a sat phone. "We don't have time, this *must* be brief, but there's someone who's been waiting a long time to talk to you."

Before she could respond, Tomas brought the phone to his ear, rattled off a string of letters and numbers, and then said, "I've got her. We're on board *The Light of Berossus*, currently stationed outside Farion-X2 Station. Situation is critical. The AI is hostile. Time is limited. Here she is."

He pressed the phone against her head, and she brought up one hand to take it, but ended up just covering his hand with her own. Apparently he didn't trust her not to drop the thing, which was fair enough, because she didn't trust herself, either.

"This is Sergeant Greeve," she said into the faint breathing sounds on the other line.

"Sanda?" Biran's voice, hesitant, slammed her straight in the chest. She doubled over, caught herself on the windowsill. Tomas was there, holding her up, keeping the phone in place.

"Biran?"

"I can't believe it. It's good to hear your voice, S. Don't worry. Cepko will keep you safe. We've got your location. We're coming for you. I love you."

"I love you, too," she stammered.

Tomas extracted the phone from her fingers, rattled off a few more commands, then cut the line and pulled the battery.

"What in the hell!"

"Look," he dropped the phone to the ground, grabbed her by the shoulders, and made her face him. She shrugged him off and stood straight, adopting a hard stare. Her world may be coming apart at the seams, but like hell was she going to let Tomas treat her like a panicky child. Biran was out there, somewhere. She'd know his voice anywhere. And she wanted some real clear answers.

"Explain," she put command into her voice. An appreciative smile ghosted across his features.

"Short version: Prime lost your location after Dralee. Biran arranged for a diplomatic convoy to negotiate your return, but Icarion attacked the convoy and initiated the bombardment. The threat Bero's told you that came to pass—the Protocol—it *hasn't happened*. Prime lost a lot of lives in the bombardment, but it's not over yet."

"Then why the fuck has Bero been telling me this?"

He grimaced. "I don't know. But I have a primary guess. I've been all over that ship's schematics, and though he's locked me out of a lot, there's nothing that precludes his engine system from being a weapon. I believe Bero performed the bombardment of Ada, and he was so traumatized by the experience he dumped his crew and ran. I also believe he's convinced himself of his story, and—"

She held up a hand. She was getting her feet back. Ingrained training steeled her, forced her to think tactically even while her heart thumped away to the speed of Biran's voice. Pieces clicked into place, sinking her spirits like lead. "Let me guess. Icarion has been making threats about initiating a bigger bombardment, but is stalling, and Ada Prime hasn't been able to detect anything in their ability to follow through?"

He nodded. They said in unison, "Bero is the Protocol."

"And I don't think he'd like us to know that," Tomas said.

CHAPTER 36

PRIME STANDARD YEAR 3543

TWO DAYS TO HOPE

Biran hit the ground. Hadn't even realized he'd fallen. The lost line undercut his strength and his knees jarred against the floor, teeth clenching. If the wristpad hadn't been strapped to him, he would have dropped it.

Sanda's situation was dire. He needed to get up. Had to get up.

The door dilated behind him and the medi stepped out, almost tripping over him. "Are you all right?" She took a knee beside him, her chilly fingers connecting with the side of his neck to check his pulse.

"She's alive," he said, stupidly, struggling through the shock to get all his thoughts in a row. The medi's brows pinched, and she glanced over his shoulder at the shut medibay door.

"That man is dead, Speaker."

"But she's not." He grinned at her, which was very much the wrong thing to do. She grimaced and rocked back on her heels, pulling a small penlight from her pocket.

"Can you look at me, please? The stress...Well. Why don't you come with me? Some nice tea and a lie-down may help."

He gently removed her hand from his pulse and pushed to his feet. Her worry had crystallized something within him. Now wasn't the time to dwell on emotion. To crack. He shunted his shock and his mingled joy and fear aside.

"I'm fine, thank you."

Before she could stick him with some kind of sedative, Biran took off at a brisk pace down the hall, then broke into a run the second he was out of her sight. He sprinted with all he had, panting heavily, until the door to the deck just barely dilated fast enough to let him through. He stumbled a second, the switch in floor textures catching his shoes, and spun around, looking for Lavaux. Anaia was there already, leaning against the forward console as she watched the navigators at work. That girl would die of curiosity someday.

Every head turned to him. Lavaux stood near the navigation console, his hand on the table and his body half-turned to regard Biran's clumsy entrance.

"Am I going to have to instigate a no-running rule?" he asked, amused.

"She's alive. Sanda. She called me."

Lavaux stood stalk-straight. All the quiet murmurs of conversation on the deck ceased. Anaia turned to him, eyes bulging, and clasped her hands over her mouth.

"Where?" Lavaux asked.

"She's on a ship in orbit around Farion-X2. An Icarion ship called *The Light of Berossus*. My contact says the situation is hostile."

Hunger flashed across Lavaux's face, an expression so profound it took Biran by surprise and unsettled him. Lavaux was usually so calm—even when he was angry, the man was poised. He was the only person alive Biran was convinced could shout down you and your entire family while placidly enjoying a high tea. But there was something in his face—something raw and primal—that screamed a warning Biran couldn't quite understand. Lavaux was a political creature. Maybe he saw heroism in his future, another lever to pull to catapult him up the chain. Maybe.

"Pilli, check the course." He waved Biran over and turned back to his navigator. Pilli pulled up the coordinates Biran conveyed to her and splashed a screen of black across the major display, a graphical representation of the region.

"Do we have cameras there?" Lavaux asked.

Pilli smirked. "We don't, but..."

The image switched to a satellite view—slightly grainy by modern standards, but Biran wouldn't complain. There was the spy station Cepko had indicated they were on—a meager tube construction orbiting the scanty moon. The resolution wasn't clear enough for Biran to make out fine details, but he squinted anyway, trying to catch any glimpse of his sister.

"Cepko said they had to return to *The Light* before the ship became suspicious."

"Cepko?"

Biran grimaced. "Nazca."

Lavaux chuckled. "Money well paid. Pilli, can you pan the area?"

The camera turned in jerks at first but eventually smoothed out, panning slowly to the left of the station—away from the moon. Biran gasped. Anaia let out a strangled sound. The intake of breath from all those on deck, collected, sounded like a soft hiss.

"What *is* that?" Pilli asked.

Cylindrical, massive. A beast of a torus spinning two grav-habs, its ramjet rear pointed away from the station, but only just. The largest ship Biran had ever laid eyes upon, in life or on screens. Sanda's ship. Sanda's captor. *The Light of Berossus.*

"The weapon," Lavaux breathed the words. "How long to that location, burning at full power?"

"Thirty-three hours if we follow proper breaking procedures. Twenty-one hours if we don't."

"We have to get her out," Biran said, heart pounding in his throat. "The AI controlling that ship is hostile."

"Sir," Pilli interjected, "there's another ship on our sensors. Out of current camera range."

"Show me."

The camera view switched back to the graphical—the station and *The Light* now marked with red triangles. In the distance, a grey shape closed upon them both. Slithering through the dark after its prey.

"One of ours?" Biran asked.

"Icarion," Pilli said. "General Negassi's ship, the *Empedocles.*"

"They've lost it," Lavaux said, barely able to contain his jubilation. "They've lost control of the weapon. Pilli, set course for *The Light*. Burn everything we've got. Negassi's about to have a very bad day."

CHAPTER 37

PRIME STANDARD YEAR 3541

IN A SYSTEM FAR, FAR AWAY

They cleaned out their valuables and scrammed. The tracker, the one she'd dropped in the wraith crate that had led them to that warehouse, she'd found resting in the center of her pillow, like a hotel mint. Nox had told her to leave it. That they had to *go*. That to stick around would only get them dead—or worse, arrested. What she'd wanted to say was, that was fine. That they could come for her. She'd be waiting. And ready.

But he'd seen that in her eyes, too, though they would never talk of it. That suicidal urge to burn the world down because there was nothing good left in it. He'd gripped her shoulder. Squeezed. Said: "You want to hurt them, it can't be here. Gotta prepare. Gotta make it *count*."

She could wait, if it meant doing more damage. She could sit here, and drink coffee so hot it scalded her tongue, so long as it meant she could spread that pain. And soon.

"They took the boards," Nox said.

Her world snapped back into immediate focus. Jettisoned the lingering images of blood and chaos, of Harlan's eyes growing dim, glassy, his body slack as every muscle in it gave up for the last time.

She didn't quite know where she was. Some diner deep into the grimier parts of the Grotta, the parts Nox liked to prowl when the crew was off-op. A mug of something was in her hand, the white ceramic-like material chipped along the rim and the creases stained with old grime that would never quite wash out. She sipped it. Coffee, hot. Right. She had known that. So scalding hot it burned her tongue and singed her soft palate. Shot through with bourbon, sweet and boozy. Nox's suggestion—a shot straight from his flask.

What had happened could be revisited and dwelled upon later—she'd have a whole lifetime for that, never mind it would be considerably shorter now. Some waitress was watching her, squinting at her through the kitchen's pass-through. Jules forced a smile, and the woman huffed and turned away. Probably she'd never seen Nox with company before. Maybe she was jealous. Idiot.

"Not all of them," she said, her mouth and mind finally catching up together on the same track.

"You find one?" Nox had forgone his coffee and was pulling straight from his flask now.

"Come on. You think I gave Harlan everything I had?"

Nox blinked, slowly. He hadn't been home last night, either, and she wondered just how long he'd been awake, up "carousing," as he'd said. She hadn't slept herself, but she didn't feel the weight of it pulling her down. In fact, when the tracks of her mind lined up again and she could think clearly, she was thinking faster than ever before. No wonder wraith mother cost so damn much. It was a wonder drug.

"All right," Nox said. "So where is it?"

"Dropped it with Arden to have them pull the data. They said they had a contact, some forum-jumper going by Silverfang who was looking for data on the Keepers. They were going to contact them to see if they wanted to buy, if the data was good."

"And cut the crew out of things."

"Don't. I had every intention of using that to secure bigger and better ops for us."

"Any chance they contacted this Silverfang last night?"

"I don't know." A knot constricted her throat. "You think Silverfang targeted the crew?"

"How the fuck should I know?"

"That tracker from the wraith crate was left on my pillow like a damned calling card, Nox. I'm pretty sure we know who hit us."

"Yeah. I guess. It's just...Never trusted Arden."

"One way to find out."

"How's that?"

"If Silverfang hit the crew, Arden is already dead."

She pushed her mug back and dialed in Arden's ident on her wristpad. It loaded a moment, then Arden's face popped into screen, highly cropped. This time she really had woken them up. Over their shoulder, blackout curtains had been pulled against the single window.

"What the fuck, Jules?"

"Harlan's dead." The words pushed past her lips like buckshot, a scatter-blast of deadly proportion. She didn't even feel the words, couldn't just yet. They were just facts. But seeing them reflected in Arden's widening eyes made her heart jump, a sob threaten. She thought of her goal and clenched down on that sob with the strength of her rage. "Lolla's missing. Nox is with me now, but we got hit hard, Arden. Are you safe?"

"Shit. Shit." The camera twisted away as a rustle of cloth muted the speakers. Lights snapped on and she could hear them check the locks of their front door. "Yeah. I'm secure. You think they're coming for me?"

"I'm not thinking shit. I don't know what they want. They only took the two boards Harlan had." And the wraith mother vial she'd stashed in the crate, but she wasn't telling Nox that. Not yet.

Arden rubbed the side of their face. "Does anyone know I got the third?"

"You told Silverfang?"

Their face went the color of whitewashed stone, all the answer she needed.

"Then yeah. Someone knows you got it."

"Fuck, fuck, fuck—"

Nox grabbed her arm and pulled it over so that he filled the face of the call. "Got a bugout bag?"

"I mean, yeah, but—"

"Grab it. Hunker down. We're coming for you."

"Then what?"

Nox sighed heavily. "I know a place we can lie low and regroup."

"This is so going to cost you extra."

Jules pulled her arm back. "Consider us saving your skin a bonus."

She cut the line and arched an eyebrow at Nox. "You want to go after Arden guns blazing, but we ain't got no guns. How long do you think we'll last against a well-armed team with just our stunners and our wit?"

"Yeah. About that." He caught the waitress's eye. "Going round back." She nodded.

Out back, it turned out, was just a door in the back wall of the diner, dropping curls of blue paint and rust into a heap on the ground. Nox swiped his wristpad over the lock and it clicked, swinging open into a room that had to have been an illegal addition to the back end of the shop. He pulled a string for the lights, and Jules's eyes lit up along with them.

A single steel workbench sat in the center of the room, a stool tucked under it with the backside well worn. The walls had been converted to shelves—open-faced cabinets, really—each and every one crammed with mounted weapons. Rifles, pistols, modified stunners. Shit, Nox even had a small selection of high-end handblasters, the kind of stuff only the military got to use, and even then only on spaceships and up-station.

"Where did you get all this?"

He waved a hand and ushered her inside, shutting the door tight behind them. "Here and there. Doesn't matter. Fact was, Harlan was a good enough boss, but when he ordered the switch to stunners, I moved my good stuff out. Didn't want to rub him the wrong way. And I wanted access, you know, just in case."

"Just in case a higher-paying job came along, you mean."

"Don't give me shit, Jules. You were having Arden fence that board out from under us."

"You in the killing trade?" she asked.

He gave her a hard look. "You so sure you're not?"

"You're an ass, Nox."

"Yeah, but I got great aim."

She picked up a handblaster and stroked the smooth, matte black side against her fingers. Nothing in her life had ever felt as solid as that object. It held the weight of her promise in its sleek body. She picked a holster to match and outfitted herself as Nox selected his own weapons.

When they finished, she felt twenty pounds heavier. That weight gave her hope. Made her feel like she could affect the world, like it would bend to her now. That she was enough. She'd have to be. Arden and Lolla were counting on her.

"Come on," she said, holstering a final handblaster. "Let's go get our nerds back."

CHAPTER 38

PRIME STANDARD YEAR 3771

PRIME STANDARD YEAR 3543

DAY THIRTY-EIGHT

Tomas set to work overriding the cargo bay door as Sanda stepped outside the room, well aware Bero could see their warm blips of life moving through the station. Her helmet was heavier in her hands than it had any right to be.

After all this time, she'd learned to trust Bero. To care for him, in a way. She'd thought he was her friend. But he'd been lying to her all along; she'd been his perfect little putz. It didn't take her long to figure out why he'd scooped her. She was a gunnery sergeant, young for her post, likely to have had extensive training in many subjects, including basic electronics and systems repair. But she wasn't specialized enough to pose any real threat to his lies.

And, being of Ada Prime, she'd been quick to assume the AI meant her no harm, that talking to it was little different from talking to her house. But Icarion gave its AIs personalities. And personalities changed. Grew in dangerous ways. Could be real assholes sometimes.

Her palms sweat in the gloves of her suit. He'd been so scared. So lonely. Reluctant to let her into his life, but eventually sharing pieces of himself. Showing her the woman who'd raised him—AnnLee Yu.

Sanda wondered if AnnLee was out there, looking for her lost protégé with the same intensity Biran looked for her.

With steady hands, she twisted on the helmet and locked in the lifepack. Diagnostics flared to life in her HUD, and she blinked against their bright glare.

"Sanda? Sanda? What happened?" Bero's voice ratcheted up higher than she'd ever heard it. "Are you all right?"

"I'm okay. So's Tomas." She took a breath, preparing to feed the ship the story they'd concocted. "There was a signal jammer in there, small-range. Scrammed our systems but left the mechanics of the lifepack working."

Don't worry, you mad bastard. We didn't see anything you didn't want us to.

"I'm so glad you're safe. You frightened me."

"Sorry about that. We were so intent on the switch panel we didn't notice the HUDs had cut. Our alarms went dark, too, but local comms worked. Hell of a thing. Tomas is in there finishing up. He'll be out in a sec, but once we realized what was going on, I knew I needed to race out here and tell you."

She prodded at her wristpad, pretending a normal diagnostic check, while she tensed all over, waiting to see if Bero bought their lie. When Tomas had fed the schematics of the station to Bero for their map, he'd failed to mention that window. It should be enough.

"Can he override the cargo bay door on his own? If I could get a look at the system—"

"No need, he's got it worked out. We'll be dining on canned pears tonight. No pods, though. But I shuffled through a couple more of the manifests and I'm sure we have enough supplies to make repairs to both. The foam's going to be tough, but Tomas is sure there's some equip in the lab that can transform the nutriblocks into a workable substitute."

"That sounds manageable."

The light on the door flicked to green, and she turned away, making certain her visor faced away from Tomas should he exit without his helmet. He clipped it on, and his comm channel lit up, a reassuring Cepko in small caps on the top left of her HUD. Bero may be a right bastard, but at least she had someone on her side.

"Hey, Bero," Tomas called out, annoyingly chipper. "That door should come down in ten seconds—Sanda explain the jammer?"

"She did. I have the arm in position."

Metal groaned. Even through the muffle of the helmet, she could hear the station complain as the cargo bay door was forced open, no doubt to never close again. The ground shuddered beneath her feet, vibrating her teeth. Tomas lost his footing and stumbled. She snapped out a hand, grabbed his, and held him steady. She twined her fingers in his. He squeezed.

They left their hands in each other's, below the register of Bero's cameras, while Farion-X2 yelled metallic complaints.

"How's it look out there, Bero?" she asked.

"The crates are spilling out at a steady rate, and I'm having no trouble catching them, but it will be a slow process. If you exit the station through the airlock you entered, you will be clear of any rogue debris."

"Sounds like a plan," she said, and irritated herself with how unconvinced she sounded, even to her own ears. The last thing she wanted was to step foot back on Bero. The damned ship was a bomb waiting to go off, literally and figuratively. But Biran was out there, maybe even her dads, and now that she was certain what Bero was, what destruction he could wield, she was determined not to let him anywhere near her family, or her world.

Even if that meant going with him, all the way to Atrux.

"Is something wrong, Sanda?" Bero asked.

"It just seems such a waste to abandon this station here," she lied.

"It is for the best," Bero assured her.

"You got that right."

Maybe Tomas sensed something in her tone, maybe he felt something through the tension in her hand, but when she tried to peel away from him, he held on a little longer, tugged her arm, pulled her around to look at him. They stared at each other's helmets, not seeing one another's faces, knowing Bero was probably growing impatient. He angled forward, shifted his weight, squeezed her hand a little harder. Something sat on the tip of his tongue, something he was struggling with, but couldn't say. Wouldn't be able to say, until they were off of Bero, and outside of his systems. If she ever made it off of Bero.

Under the circumstances, she was glad for his silence.

She tugged her hand away and began the slow trek back to the belly of the beast.

PRIME HAS NOT YET BECOME A STANDARD

EARTH, THE MOMENT OF CHANGE

Lex did not leave the Puerto Rican station for a year. It was, as the pundits reminded her through flashing white teeth or tastefully structured think pieces, the longest she'd stayed at any one facility since Prime had begun construction on its first space elevator. They never said *first*, though, that was her own little mental correction. They didn't know about the second.

Her very presence, she knew, strained the project. Speculation swirled about the facility's importance, about what secret experiments Lex got up to behind the pristine lab walls. Weapons, viruses, biomechanical interfaces. Deathstars. Some even said Lex herself had died that day, the day she swept down to the Caribbean after a perfectly normal television junket. She chuckled, whenever poorly overdrawn videos of her speaking "revealed" the truth that she was some sort of CGI or cyborg.

Some of the rumors were true, of course, but those were the closest to the fringe. The ignored and insane. But she browsed them, in her rare moments of downtime, curious to see who was closest. Curious, too, to see if there were any leaks in those pristine lab walls.

Someone knocked at her bungalow door. Lex kicked her rolling chair back from her desk and stood, stretching long arms above her head. The tablet inset in her desktop revealed the face of Dr. Maria

Salvez at her door, her lab coat slightly askew, dark half-moons throwing penumbral shadows beneath her eyes. Lex checked the time: 0200. Salvez had been working late into the night, but for her to visit before she went off shift was unprecedented.

In her pajamas—silk-like tank top, loose-fit pants, shaggy slippers—Lex opened the door. Salvez did not so much as blink at her boss's appearance. Most would grovel for the perceived slight of having wakened her. This was why she liked Salvez. No bullshit.

"Come. It's done. I have something to show you."

Lex shivered in the warm, tropical air. She'd taken up residence on the Prime compound on Caja de Muertos, her front door mere steps from the lab that sheltered her greatest prize. The thick air hung heavy on her shoulders as she stepped out, not bothering to find a robe or proper shoes. A storm, maybe, threatening in the distance. She hadn't yet spent enough time outside on the island to grow in tune with the vagaries of its weather patterns. The only storm she cared about right now was the one inside her mind.

It's done.

She crossed the plaza under the glare of security lights, Salvez leading the way with her determined, stalking gait. Outside the walls of the compound, the wood of palm trees groaned as they swayed under the winds. Leaves hissed against one another. But in the main building, silence, aside from the subtle rumble of the HVAC working overtime to keep the air cool and humidity down.

A cupola had been erected in the heart of the building. Mirrors lined the curved dome of the ceiling, a silvery kaleidoscope hiding cameras and measurement devices. If the newscasters had asked her about this, she would have winked and made a crack about it being some sort of inverse disco ball, shining down on the real party below. But they'd never see this.

This wasn't for them. It wasn't even for her. In the grand scheme of things, nothing was, for in the grand scheme of things all accomplishments were smeared into so much meaningless space dust.

That was what she told herself as her heart ramped its pace with every step she took closer to the balcony lining the interior of the cupola about three stories up. This was a facsimile, a test run. A gambit to see if the directions of the sphere could even be followed and produce something meaningful. A scale model, one-thousandth of its real size. Nonfunctional.

She also told herself that, even if this worked, the course of history might not change. Humanity would still be ground to nothing by the inevitable march of time.

She told herself a lot of things. Her palms still sweat as she gripped the rail.

Two rings, one larger than the other, took up the whole of the space. They arched from floor to ceiling, their widest points pushing at the edges of the space as if desiring to stretch, to swallow the building whole. Slender as they were, the dark materials that made their body sucked up the light in the room, promised space beyond the mere dimensions of mortal eyes. It dwarfed the Prime scientists who swarmed at the base, their white coats giving the illusion of stars against the black metal.

If it were powered appropriately, the rings would spin in opposite directions, swooping through each other, building the strength to punch through space, and, by definition, time.

She did not understand it. None of them understood it. Looking at the math involved was like presenting a differential equation to a toddler and asking them to explain. But the directions to build had been simple enough, and the location—the location was, according to the sphere, the key to the whole thing.

Real, real, real. Oh, it didn't *work*, but that was besides the point. It would work when built to its full size. She knew the moment she laid eyes on it. Everything the sphere promised—a bridge between worlds—was real.

"Do you think it will work?" Salvez asked. Her hands were in her pockets, her gaze sizing up the beautiful monster skeptically.

"I can't know," she said, that old instinct for rationalism kicking in her chest.

"Lex." Maria said her name with a slight drag, a husky intonation that peeled her gaze away from the model. "What do you *think*?"

She licked her lips, staring into those whirlpool dark eyes. "I think we have to find out."

And with those words, plans set into motion in her mind. Fractions of possibilities spilling out one into the next, ideas bubbling up and being shot down for better, stronger plans.

First: She would have to move. This compound had drawn too much attention, she'd lingered too long. All the old ways of keeping secrets wouldn't do anymore, not with a secret like this. She'd have to figure out something else, something new, to keep her people—and their data—safe from the grasping hands of this world.

Implications spun like orbital lines through her mind, slingshotting off one another, leading to conclusions and insights that took her breath away. It was too much for one woman to carry. She knew that as surely as she knew, but would not speak aloud, that the thing they had found was real.

That it would change everything.

CHAPTER 39

PRIME STANDARD YEAR 3543

THIRTY-NINE DAYS OF LIES

They spent the next day working in six-hour shifts, breaking only to eat and strategize. A pall hung over them both, and Bero was oddly quiet—only offering suggestions when they seemed confused by the contents of the crates. Sanda suspected Tomas knew what each one held, but he was doing an excellent job of feigning surprise.

The whole time she worked, a subtle headache nagged at her, a dull echo to the down tempo of her thoughts. Tomas was right. If he hadn't given her Biran's voice, she would never have believed him. And a sliver of her still wanted to deny what he'd revealed. It rankled, to have been taken hostage by a spaceship of all things. It rankled even more to know she'd found a friend in her captor.

"I don't know about you," Tomas said, and stretched languidly upward, "but I'm done for the night. My brain's stuffed full."

The carcass of her evac pod lay before them on a clear space they'd finagled on the floor of the cargo bay. Tomas's tests regarding the foams seemed to work. She eyed the aerator they'd modified to accept the new substance, and the catalyst dispenser that was meant to harden it around the body shoved inside. She wasn't sure they'd gotten the coma-inducing med mix right, and she didn't relish finding out the hard way.

Not that she had any intention of getting in that pod unless she absolutely had to.

"It's a good start," she agreed, wiping grease onto her FitFlex-suited thigh. The smartfibers went to work breaking it down, and already the grease was faded. "Bero, how long until you're in position to begin the gravity assist?"

Tomas shot her a look, but she ignored him. It was a reasonable enough question to ask, and she wanted a rough idea of how long Biran had to find her.

"Forty-seven hours."

Two days. And they were well inside Icarion space. Her stomach clenched. Just because he knew where she was didn't guarantee he'd reach them in time. Once Bero completed his burn through the gravity assist, his ramjet would kick into gear. Nothing in Ada Prime's fleet could catch a ship at any substantial fraction of the speed of light, let alone 8 percent. She needed contingency plans, but she couldn't even try to talk to Tomas without risking tipping off Bero.

"Can't wait to get out of this ghost town," she said.

"It will take weeks to exit the system."

"Hey, just being on our way is a relief."

"Agreed."

While she chatted with Bero, Tomas helped her secure their tools. He'd rolled the sleeves of his jumpsuit up, and grease streaked his forearms there, making dark tracks she felt the sudden desire to trace with her fingertips.

Dios. She ducked her head down to hide the heat in her cheeks. The strength of his hand in hers, that brief hesitation before they'd left the station. Even the feel of his chest pressed to hers while she fought for her life raised rather uncomfortable images in her head. Well, not uncomfortable, unless he was quite a bit less flexible than she'd guessed.

"Sanda?" Tomas asked.

She started, realizing she'd been rubbing at a grease smear on the side of the pod for a good couple of minutes, and it had long been reduced to a faint, pearly sheen.

"Yeah? Sorry. Zoned out. I've got this … ache, in my head." Among other things, but she wasn't about to tell him that. If Biran didn't find them in time, she might have to shove him in this pod and jettison him, for fuck's sake. And he'd been hired to find her, to make sure she was safe. For all she knew, his friendship had been a part of his plan.

"That's it. You may outrank me, Sergeant Greeve, but I'm ordering you rest and a hearty meal." He extended one of those dirt-streaked hands to her, curling his fingers to beckon her upward.

With a sigh, she slapped her hand in his and allowed herself to be hefted to her feet. "If you insist, Spymaster General."

"That's . . . not a real thing."

"My ship, my rules. Now make yourself useful and go cook us some dinner."

"Yes, Sergeant." He snapped her a picture-perfect salute, face a mask of seriousness, and marched lockstep from the room. She laughed, then caught herself checking out his ass in the jumpsuit and sobered. It didn't seem such a dangerous thing, to admire him now that their time together didn't measure in dozens of years. The fact that she thought he was cute even though he was no longer the only human in light-years made her feel freer to enjoy the view. But still. *Pull it together, Greeve.*

In the mess, she slid into her usual seat and kicked her heels up on a chair alongside her, then turned to watch Tomas while he raided the pantry.

"You know, you really don't have to do all the cooking," she said as she jabbed idly at her wristpad, running through Bero's system checks to see if anything needed patching up.

"Hey, cooking's in my blood. My grandma and ma own a restaurant—Elysian Fusion." He banged around in a cupboard, coming up with a few likely cans.

"I don't even know where Elysia is."

He threw a grin at her over his shoulder, one that made her heart kick up. "And that's why you shouldn't be doing the cooking."

She pretended to be engrossed with her wristpad. "Well, aren't you Mister High Culture. The Elysians use a lot of canned pears in their dining, do they?"

He made a face at the can he'd just popped open. "Space is space. Gotta make do with what you can."

"Which is precisely what I was doing."

"Ugh. No. Sorry, Sergeant, but that was not making do. That was self-flagellation."

"I liked it."

Pure horror overtook his expression. "I'm not even going to answer that."

She snorted and continued to prod at her pad while he cooked, letting her mind wander. Something about the way he called her *sergeant* tickled her; she couldn't quite place why. *Sanda* should have been more intimate, surely, but he laid a layer of respect over her title that tingled her straight to her toes. She shook her head. Probably just wishful thinking, and he was using the title to reestablish the boundaries their brief intimacy in Farion station had eroded.

A message from Bero blipped across her pad: *Are you certain both pods can be repaired?*

Whatever warmth she'd felt fled in a flash.

She tapped out a message: *Yes. It will take a while to perfect, but we have the supplies now.* Pause. *And I trust him. We have time. We'll make it work.*

Why do you trust him now?

He could have harmed me on Farion if he meant to. He didn't.

I'm not yet convinced.

Do you trust me?

Yes. Always.

Then let me make this call.

Okay, Sanda.

"What's so fascinating?" Tomas plopped into the chair across the table and deposited a steaming plate of food in front of her, twin to his own. She started guiltily.

"Reviewing Bero's system checks. Gotta make sure the old boy is in top shape."

"I am quite healthy," Bero said.

"You know I like to check myself. Military training: can't shake it."

"We are a squadron of three, led by the sergeant." Tomas lifted his glass to toast Bero's cameras and she laughed. How he could keep so calm, knowing all he did, and make light with Bero as if they were the oldest friends in the world, she had no idea. She envied him that training.

Fragrant curls of steam called her name. The food didn't look like much, but the scent alone set her stomach grumbling. She took a big mouthful and let out a pleased moan. Flavor burst across her tongue, set her mouth salivating. He'd done something to the pears to make them savory, then mixed them in with spiced and toasted tempeh. It was, quite probably, the best thing she'd tasted in years. She regretted not letting him know they had more than nutriblocks sooner.

"Dios," she said around chews.

"If you want to go back to cooking…" He trailed off.

"No, no, no." She swallowed hard and went for another bite. "That was a damn mouthgasm."

His brows shot up, and she hid her face by shoving more food into it.

"In that case." He stood and went back to the cupboard, then returned with the remnants of the Caneridge they'd opened that first night she'd let him out of quarantine. He poured two cups and pushed one toward her.

"Here's to surviving, in style."

"Now, that I can drink to." She clinked his glass, drank, and went right back to packing away the food.

"You sure you don't have any taste sensors, Bero?" she asked. "You gotta try this."

"I have no desire to eat, but my gas sensors are picking up the smell. Tomas is an accomplished chef."

"See?" He lifted his fork in triumph. "I can even make a spaceship hungry."

Chatter was sparse as they demolished their dinner and worked steadily away at the remains of the Caneridge. By the time the food was gone, Sanda was feeling as warm and comfortable as she'd felt since she'd woken up. Her stomach was full. Nothing was truly her responsibility right now.

Biran would find her in time, or she'd resort to plan B, and she'd cross that bridge when she came to it. Bero was still a lodestone of ache in her heart, but for now she could pretend he hadn't betrayed her. She had good food, good company, and soon…Soon she'd be going home.

At the thought of Ada, a twinge kicked up in her head again. She sighed and rubbed at her temple. It had almost been a perfect evening.

"What's wrong?" Tomas asked.

"Coldsleep headache."

"Again?" He came around the table, a frown pulling down alcohol-damp lips, and dropped to one knee in front of her chair. "Let me test your pupils, okay?"

She snorted. "Sure, though I don't know what good that'll do you. The headaches are a known side effect from the evac pods. Considering the trauma my body went through"—she tapped her false leg—"I'm lucky that's all I walked away with. They should fade, but the manual said it can sometimes take years."

"To hell with that."

"Oh, and are you an accomplished doctor, too, Mister Dancer Chef Spy?"

He actually blushed, but she couldn't tell if it was the booze or real embarrassment. "No, but I've had some training in field dressings. Same as yours, probably. This shouldn't be persisting."

He nudged her hand away and gently took her head in his hands, thumbs against her temples while his fingers angled down along her jawline. "You have TMJ, maybe?" he asked as he massaged the tendons of her jaw.

"Not that I'm aware of," she admitted. A little pressure eased her head, but his proximity was making it hard to concentrate.

"There *is* a lot of tension in your jaw, though. Could have been TMJ induced by the trauma of the evac pod and NutriBath. Bero, do your mics pick up any teeth grinding at night?"

"I haven't noticed, but I will run a search now. She does snore, however."

"Oookay, that's enough." She reached up and nudged his hands away. "You, Mr. Spaceship, stop listening to me sleep. It's rude. And you—" She held his hands out, away from her, and looked down into those grey, concerned eyes. Eyes like asteroids, she'd thought the first time she'd seen him up close. Caneridge warmed her veins, and her thoughts derailed, drawn to the hard line of his chin, the dusting of scruff that'd grown in while they'd spent the last few days consumed by work. The firm stretch of his neck muscle, extending down from that rough jaw to a chest she'd very much like to see.

Unf, she thought.

"What?" he said.

Oh Dios, she said that out loud. He must think she was behaving like a complete loon. No wonder he thought she needed looking after. "I don't need you playing mother hen," she snapped. Well, that was real fucking smooth.

His brows drew together and he rocked back onto his heels. "I didn't mean...I'm sorry. I'm just worried. Those headaches really are getting more frequent."

"Yeah. And I guess they make me irritable." She summoned up a smile for him and was relieved when he smiled back.

She still hadn't dropped his hands. Through the fog of Caneridge, she was growing dimly aware that she'd pushed some social barrier a little too long. That keeping on holding his hands—no matter that she'd meant to push him away—was about to become awkward.

He looked at their hands pointedly, then back up to her, brows raised. She licked her lips. So did he. She reached a conclusion: If she were going to die anytime soon, she'd be damned if she didn't go for one last lay first.

She tackled him.

CHAPTER 40

PRIME STANDARD YEAR 3543

A DAY FOR EMBARRASSMENT

Whatever he'd been about to say broke off in a startled yelp as she plowed them both over. She lost his hands, lost track of just about everything, and reached to reclaim them. Fingers entwined, she lifted his hands above his head and pinned them hard against the floor.

Tomas, however, had misunderstood.

His knee found her stomach, and she grunted as he pushed down on her hands, forcing her arms back to her sides. She let a little squeak escape as he twisted, rolled so that he pinned her against the floor instead. His breath, spicy with Caneridge and his own cooking, flooded against her cheek. She would have found it hot if he didn't look so righteously pissed off.

"What the fuck did I do?" he demanded.

"I, uh, wasn't attacking you?" She cut herself off, heating all over with embarrassment. This really hadn't gone how she'd planned. "Sorry. I thought—I mean—ugh. I'm not very good at this. I wasn't trying to overpower you, or anything, well. I mean. I kinda was—consensually!—but, oh Dios." She wanted nothing more than to shrivel up into oblivion, right there on the floor.

"What are you—" Realization clicked into place on his face. She really, really wanted to die. His eyes flew wide. "Oh. OH. Wait. Really?"

From the heat radiating off her face, she was probably turning a half dozen shades of crimson. "Yes?"

"Oh. *Oh.*"

He stared at her. She stared back. "So, uh, I mean, if you're not interested—" Was he going to tell Biran about this? Would he have to report it? Maybe she should just space herself now.

"Oh."

"For the love of all that's holy, please say something other than *oh.*"

A grin lit up his face, and the hard press of something that was most certainly not his toolbelt warmed against her thigh.

"Oh," she said.

He kissed her. She gasped against the force, the rough branch-bark of his stubble scraping her chin, her lips. His grip slackened on her wrists, hands searching at her hips, cupping the small of her back, stroking, as she reached up, tangled her fingers in his hair, let loose with a soft moan, and dragged them down his back, massaging.

The world tilted as he cupped her, cradled her in one hand and braced her back with the other, face pressed to her neck, lips probing, tongue brushing; he scooped her from the floor and turned, setting her down with a satisfying thump on the tabletop. Cutlery clattered, spilled aside.

He gasped and she gasped and their hands met, released, searched each other. Face buried in his neck, fingers twisting in his hair, she breathed in the scent of him, tugged him close, pushed her hips forward. Pressure mounted along her breastbone—his thumb tracing the seam of her suit.

"Wait," she breathed, tipping her head back and away. His hands instantly stilled, gaze fraught with worry.

"Did I—"

She silenced him with a hand over his lips.

"Bero, a little privacy?"

"My security protocols only allow me to cut camera access in private cabins."

Tomas saluted the cameras. "Gotcha."

He slung her over his shoulder and landed a hearty slap on her ass. She burst out laughing, startled, bouncing as he sprinted down the hall. The whoosh of the door blew hair into her eyes, and the next thing she knew he pitched her onto the soft plane of his bed, silken grey-and-flame sheets twisting around her, the lighting drifting toward dusk.

"Bero," he declared, and clapped twice. "See you in the morning, my good man."

The activity lights in Bero's cameras winked dark, and Tomas threw her a coy grin. Through the electric anticipation tingling her skin, sending her mind spinning, she realized—Bero couldn't see them. If he had cut out his mics, too, then—

Before she could chase that thought down, Tomas leapt to the bed alongside her. They bounced, laughing, and twined together.

Sanda'd been worried about this. The moment that pod popped open and Tomas clambered out, sporting a firm jawline and blinking some lovely eyes, thoughts of Adam and Eve crashed into her head. Jokes, mostly. She'd warned herself against getting too close. Against their situation pushing her into his arms. Couldn't even be sure he'd be interested in her type.

Even if he was interested, there'd be trouble. She didn't know a couple that shared a one-bedroom apartment that didn't indulge in the occasional bickerfest. But this would have been so, so much more intense. The only two humans left alive alone, together, for light-years.

She'd figured, that if anything came up between them, there was a fifty-fifty chance of attempted murder in their future.

So, she'd kept her distance. Put him at arm's length. Let her distrust distill in her belly, cool the hot thumping along of oh-so-human hormones and loneliness. Bero and Grippy had been company, but they hadn't been *human*. And, try as she might, she just couldn't accept Bero the way she'd wanted to. Couldn't let him get really close.

Never mind that the fucker had been lying to her from the start.

Tomas was everywhere and everything and her reticence washed away on a crest of sheer joy.

The dusky light of the room turned bloodred.

"What the hell—" Tomas sat bolt upright, and she was right behind him, swinging her legs to the ground as she resealed what had been peeled open of her suit.

"Bero, report," she demanded.

"Everything is under—"

"Proximity alert. Unknown ship entering flight path. Impact imminent." A metallic woman's voice overrode Bero's, and it took Sanda a moment to place it. She hadn't heard it in—how long, weeks?—but it must be. It was the modular voice of the ship's emergency override features. The same voice that had alerted her to Bero's airlock blowing due to a denatured rubber seal.

A seal that could not have possibly oxidized in the scant amount of time that had actually passed. Blood drained from her face. In the contouring confines of her FitFlex, she went very, very cold. Without thought, she scanned Tomas's room for the gasket she'd let him keep, let him take to examine. The seal, with the three gouges in it.

It lay against a bulkhead. She stood, moved toward it mechanically, while Tomas and Bero argued about the meaning of the woman's voice. Bero was insisting everything was fine. That the alarm was just a blown circuit, or something like it, made unstable over time. They'd fix it, patch it up, and everything would be fine. How many of those little circuits she had mended under his direction shut up the automated voice of the woman?

She pressed her fingers into the gouges. They fit. Perfectly.

A great many things threatened to overwhelm her in that moment. Implications raced through her, intensifying her headache. That glint. That hint of white—or was it Icarion grey?—she'd seen in the brief moment it had taken Bero to adjust her HUD as she'd stepped out to fix the gasket. Had one of Bero's crew clung to life on that gasket, just before being spaced?

She shoved those images down. Locked them in a box in her chest to dwell upon later. A ship was near. Biran was near. And she and Tomas needed to get the hell off this bucket before things went very, very wrong.

Tomas was still bickering with Bero, faking a good-natured sort of annoyance to keep the AI from realizing Tomas was stalling him, giving whoever was out there time to get into position to capture the smartship and its passengers. Bero kept on insisting the alert was a false read, just some ice, the ramscoop would obliterate it, the parameters for alert had been set too fine, etc., etc. Sanda listened to him rationalize it all away, knowing damned well he was stalling just as surely as Tomas was.

"I want to see the obstruction," she said. Both men snapped silent.

"I can pipe a feed into the screen embedded on Tomas's wall," Bero offered.

"No. I want it full-res, on the lab screen. Big as day. I know you're confident, but if your circuits are as faulty as you think they are, then I want visual. Your sensors might misjudge mass in a way the alert system isn't."

"I know what—"

"Send it through, I'm on my way." No more stalling. There was, she was certain, no fucking way Bero could produce the kind of render he'd need to fool her on short notice. Not on that large of a screen. If he'd said there'd been nothing there, then he could just slap up an image of the area wiped clean—nothing but black between the bright array of stars. But he'd stuck his metaphorical foot straight in his own speakers. He'd tried to convince Tomas something was there, just something not worth worrying about.

But then, maybe he could. He was an AI running on a top-of-the-line experimental spaceship. He was probably running billions of processes every second. For all she knew, a little render might be child's play. But she had to keep him distracted, jumping. And once inside the lab they'd have access to tools—tools to help them override certain processes. Regardless, she'd feel a whole lot better with a big, hefty wrench in her hands.

"I can *see* it," Bero insisted.

"And I want to see it, too." She flashed a warm grin at his cameras as she strode down the hall at a crisp pace, Tomas smack on her heels. "Two eyes are better than one, and all that."

"I have four hundred and fifty external cameras."

"Four hundred and fifty-two, then. Even better."

Tomas snorted a laugh.

"I have already begun evasive maneuvers, should my density scans be incorrect."

Clever ship. But she was onto his game, now, and with Biran out there, she would not let Bero get away with this. "Keep eyes on it. I still want to see it. If it *is* a derelict ship, as your sensors think, then we can scavenge it."

Tomas caught up with her and gave her a sideways glance that brought back tingly thoughts her headache squashed in a hurry. No way Bero could deny her a view now.

The lab was bathed in the same low, red glow as the rest of the ship. Whatever private battle Bero was waging with the ship's hardwired emergency systems, he was having a hard time winning. In the glow, it was easier to separate herself from the place that had become her home.

The burning ache that opened in her chest whenever she thought of Bero manipulating her into serving his needs on a cross-system suicide jaunt faded away. She made a concentrated effort not to think too hard on what those claw marks in the gasket might mean. That someone might have left them there, in the same moment Sanda was waking up in Bero's medibay.

The smartscreen dominating the room glared down at her, a reflective black wall.

"Bero, bring up the visual."

"Working on it."

"For Christ's sake, it's just a camera feed. Turn it on."

"The circuits have—what are you doing?"

Tomas peeled open a metal panel in the wall alongside the screen and was sorting through a series of breakers marked with Icarion terminology. "Some of these are thrown that shouldn't be," he said, all help and smiles. "Let me just—"

"Don't touch those," Bero snapped.

"Aw, c'mon. I'm a comms man. I know what I'm about."

"You're a spy."

"Would make a terrible one if I didn't understand the basics of the profession I'm impersonating, wouldn't I?"

The woman's mechanical voice interrupted, "Priority CamCast on channel one. Unable to display."

Dead silence, filled only with the steady hum of Bero's mechanics.

"That's not possible," she said, and meant it. There was no way Biran could send a priority cast through to an Icarion ship.

"You see?" Bero's voice was firm. "An electrical malfunction with the alert system."

Tomas had his hand poised above three likely switches. They shared a long look while the bloodred lights pulsed to an artificial heartbeat.

That was Biran out there. Had to be, despite the impossibility of his achieving an Icarion priority broadcast signal. Her people had been very, very busy since the Battle of Dralee, and they must have figured out a way to mimic the signal. She had a whole hell of a lot of questions she needed to ask them. Questions that had to do with the Nazca, and smartships, and RKVs.

Questions she could only ask if she broke the fragile peace aboard Bero right now. A peace that only held because Tomas had yet to flip those switches.

She took a breath, assumed the posture of command, and nodded. Tomas threw the breakers. The screen flickered, and a pale man in the livery of an Icarion general glared down at her.

"Who the hell are you?" he demanded.

CHAPTER 41

PRIME STANDARD YEAR 3541

IN A SYSTEM FAR, FAR AWAY

The lights of Udon-Voodun were out. Those lights were never out. The place wasn't the kind of establishment that ever bothered with closing. The few autocabs that moved through the streets zipped by, not pausing to let out a passenger or wait for a pickup. Unusual, in this part of the Grotta where the morning light should have brought out the honest folk of the neighborhood to start their daily hustle. It all could have been explained away, maybe traffic was rerouting the autocabs this morning, but the streetlights were out.

The streetlights of Prime cities, even in their fringe spaces, never went out. Because there were cameras in those lights, too. The watchful eye of Prime Inventive hovering over even the lowliest of their citizens. Someone had cut the lights from the network. Someone had rerouted the autocabs. Someone way more powerful than Jules had expected.

Someone who wanted her dead.

"You first," she whispered, resting her hand over the grip of her handblaster.

"What?" Nox asked.

"Talking to myself."

"Knock it off. We're on op now."

Not the type of op they usually pulled, she wanted to say, the never-ending urge to pull Nox's leg the most normal thing in her life right now.

"Sorry," she said instead, pulling up the text function on her pad. She sent to Arden: *Hear anything?*

They responded: *Nothing. Which is weird.*

She showed Nox the screen and he spat on the sidewalk. "It's a trap. You know that, right?"

"Couldn't have made it any more obvious, could they?"

"Could not indeed."

They stood there awhile, side by side, staring at the dark building. They were down the street a little way, shadowed by a half-rotted overhang dripping off a long-abandoned alleyway establishment. Between them, the knowledge: They could walk. Right now. Scrub their wristpads, buy new idents. Take the money from the wraith sale and disappear into another Prime city. They'd end up in whatever that city's version of the Grotta was, sure, but they'd be alive. Free to operate.

Arden and Lolla would most definitely be dead after that, though they'd probably never hear about it. They could just forget. Drink when they couldn't. Load up on doze or wraith when they really, really couldn't.

"Wouldn't work," Nox said.

"Nah. You're too sentimental."

He cocked his head to smile down at her, a sly crescent of yellowed teeth in the dark, then scratched at his beard. "So how do you want to handle this?"

"Walking into a trap? Don't know. I can't say I have a lot of experience with the situation."

"Not what Harlan told me."

She was instantly indignant. "That old codger will never let that go. It happened once."

But of course he'd let it go. He was dead. She swallowed bile, swishing saliva around her mouth. She really needed to brush her teeth. And eat. And shower.

And kill the motherfuckers who killed her friend.

"Cameras are off." She pulled the handblaster from its holster, hidden under a black denim jacket, and checked the charge. "So fuck being seen. Let's go."

"Guns a-blazin'. I like it."

Nox fell into step at her left flank, a gun bigger than her forearm propped against the crook of his shoulder. She commanded her wrist-pad to send off a quick message to Arden: *Coming in. Be ready.*

They sent back a stream of expletives, so she wiped the screen and took a deep breath. No time for dealing with panic, she had to focus on what was coming next. With the lights off, the implication was that whoever was waiting for her didn't want to be seen. They could also just be hoping Jules'd roll in stealth style with night vision on, then they'd bring the lights up and blind her before she even got the door all the way open. If that was their plan, then the joke was on them: She couldn't afford night vision anything.

She reached the front door of Udon-Voodun and circled around to the right of the building, where a rickety set of stairs led straight up to the residences. Not a nice place to get caught out. Anyone waiting at the top had her dead to rights, so she gave up on stealth and sprinted up the steps, boots pounding to wake the dead as the metal construction screeched. She hit the top platform and shouldered the door open, breath hot in her mouth, skin tingling with adrenaline as she swung around, sweeping the immediate area with the nozzle of the blaster, eyes straining against the dark.

"Clear." Nox came in behind her and covered her back as she stalked down the hall, blaster out, each step she took past a closed door jittery. Any one of those could fly open at any moment. Any one.

"Hello, Jules," a motherly voice said over the speakers in the corner of the hallway. Speakers meant only for fire and life-support alarms.

She froze. "Who the fuck are you?"

"Don't you remember me? We spoke before."

"Where's Lolla?"

"Lolla? Lolla, Lolla, Lolla. Never heard of her. I only know Jules. Jules Valentine. Juliella Vicenza, as the birth record says."

"What's going on?" Nox hissed.

"I don't know." Jules dropped her voice to a whisper as she advanced down the hall. They were almost outside Arden's door. "I think she's stalling."

Nox nodded. "Got ahead of themselves on the network but no guns on the ground yet."

"Exactly."

She stepped past Arden's door, to the end of the hall, and peered around the last corner. All dark, but not a soul to be seen. "That's my name," she said to the voice in the speakers. "What do you want with me?"

"Everything, dear. Just everything. Why don't you come by for tea?"

She squeezed the grip on the handblaster until her knuckles ached. "I will. You just tell me your name and location, and I'll come by. We'll have a real good time."

"My friends are here to bring you to me. Careful, they can be a bit rough."

"Time to go," Nox said. He pounded on Arden's door with the side of his arm. "Move, kid. Company is incoming."

The door swung open and Arden Wyke filled it, their hair limp with grease, their eyes bulging like they'd seen the ghosts of everyone they'd ever pissed off. They had a rucksack thrown over one shoulder, the straps undone and flopping around. Cables protruded from their pockets, and they'd shoved on some smartglasses, the glint in the upper left lens signaling it was recording. At least they'd had the presence of mind to tug on a jacket and some boots over their pajamas.

"Turn that shit off," she hissed into the lens and grabbed Arden by the shoulder, pushing them so that Nox led the way out with Arden in the middle. "And stay quiet. We got company incoming and I'm betting our friend in the walls is telling them everything we say."

"And our position," Nox muttered.

"Not a lot of options there."

"Who the fuck are these people?" Arden whispered.

"Dead people. They just don't know it yet," Jules ground out.

She stopped frog-marching Arden the second they got their feet under them. Nox backtracked to the stairs trailing down the side of the building. Jules held her breath as Nox hesitated in the doorway, mentally crossing her fingers that the way hadn't been blocked yet. After a heart-stopping count of twenty, Nox ducked back into the hallway and shook his head. The way was being watched.

"They're covered, but—"

Jules ran her fingers across her lips like a zipper and threw a pointed glance to the speakers lining the hallway. She could see it in Nox's face: No one could think *fuck* as loudly as that man. Arden shifted their weight back and forth like they needed to take a piss, then flicked up their wristpad and fired off a text so fast she barely saw their fingers move. No guarantee Big Momma didn't have dial-in on their text frequencies, but Arden connected them all up through an app of their own making. It was worth a shot.

Arden: Through the kitchens?

Nox: Better than the shooting gallery.

Neither Jules nor Nox had ever had to make use of the back ways of Udon-Voodun, so Arden led a painful crawl forward, peeking their head around each corner like they expected to get their nose bit off. Couldn't blame them, really. Arden liked the tech side of the business—the worming and the cracking, or whatever it was the nerds did to get the goods—and not the physical side. It was why Arden lived here, above Udon-Voodun, when Harlan had offered them a room back at the hangout many times before.

That independent nature was why Arden was alive, more than likely. If Arden had lived at the house, they'd be just as dead as the rest, and they would have lost the third board. Jules would never give Arden shit about being a hermit again.

"You know the rest of the way," Arden hissed, their voice so jittery the words didn't make sense to Jules for half a second. Nox pushed ahead and tore open a heavy metal door, leading them through the maze of haphazard halls that had grown up around the restaurant into the more ordered chaos of the kitchen.

A stainless steel workstation bisected the kitchen, sinks and prep stations on one side with fryers and cooktops on the other. Flour dusted one long stretch of counter, a folded loaf of dough left midchop on the station. Half-diced onions, pots left on the cooktop with the heat killed beneath them. They had abandoned this place in a hurry.

Jules wondered what had driven them out, if there weren't guns on the ground already. Maybe the woman in the speakers had arranged for some kind of alarm.

Jules's stomach growled at the leftover scents of fresh food. How long had it been since she last ate? That coffee Nox bought her didn't count. That'd been medicine, not food. A little tremble wormed its way into her arms. She'd been too long without rest, and the wraith mother could only cover up so much. It must be wearing off by now. She blinked and wiped tiredness from her eyes with the back of her hand.

"You good?" Nox asked.

"Yeah. Yeah. Push on."

He gave her a look like he didn't believe her, but there was fuck all they could do about her exhaustion now. The best thing they could do—the only thing they could do that wouldn't mean death or capture—would be to get the hell out of here and get to a safe place where they could lick their wounds, figurative and literal, and prepare for their next move, whatever the hell that would be.

A pile of steamed buns had been left in a strainer, drying out on a tea towel. Jules wrapped them in the towel and shoved them into her bag. Arden frowned at her, and she shrugged. Wasn't like the owners would be able to serve that food to anyone—who knew how long it had been sitting out. At least, she hoped they wouldn't serve it to any-one. She did eat there a lot, after all.

Arden grabbed a cleaver in one hand and a cast-iron skillet in the other and gave them a few experimental swings. Jules had to stifle a laugh, the first time she'd felt anything aside from rage and numbness since she'd walked through the door of her home into a new, bloodied world.

"Easy, tough guy," she said. They shot her a look, then caught her grin, and their whole face relaxed into a smile.

"Rolling door is down on the front," Nox said, "so the back door is our best shot. Got dumpsters to the left to cover that flank, but after-ward we're about twenty feet from good cover."

"Not exactly," Arden said. "Momma Udon has a private auto she keeps around back. She hates waiting on the cabs when she needs to pick up supplies. I watched her go, earlier, and she took off on foot."

"Private autos are biometrically locked," Nox said.

"Please. You hold them off me, I'll get that car."

"And this is why we go after the nerds." Jules winked at Arden's hurt expression. "You know what to do if we get separated?"

"I haven't forgotten."

Jules slipped to point and pressed her side against the grease-stained wall of the kitchen, letting the hammer of her heartbeat fade so she could better hear the sounds beyond. She pressed her ear against the crack in the doorjamb, hoping to catch a hint of something, anything—scuffling boots, or shouted commands—but there was nothing but an eerie silence. No morning in the Grotta was this quiet.

Acutely aware that the woman in the speakers was probably watching her, she dropped one hand to the lever and eased the door open, peering into the early morning. The rising star had cast away the shadows left by the shut-off streetlights, but hadn't done much to clarify matters. The buildings of the Grotta were too tall, their alleyways too deep and haphazard. Some Grotta-wrought constructions leaned against each other, sagging over passageways and cutting out all the light. Wasn't a better place on all of Atrux to slink around in. Good for crime and, as Jules was realizing to her dread, good for hunting.

She hated being the hunted.

Despite the visual clutter, she knew these streets. Not like the back of her hand—that old, idiotic saying had nothing to do with the reality of living in a place like this. A hand could get old. Could get scarred, or tattooed, but ultimately it didn't change much. These streets were an organic mass. More of a fungus in a damp and forgotten grotto than anything like Alexandria-Atrux. The Grotta was a growth on that city, an extension of the heavily regimented core. A cancer, maybe, in the eyes of those who inhabited the sleek perfection of the heart.

Out here on the fringes—the only place Jules had ever known— the streets may change overnight. Territories shifted, blocking arteries and carving out new veins. Construction came and went, despite the city's desire to keep the illegal builds under check. And if you lived here long enough, you got a sense for it. Learned to move in the same way it did.

Learned to see that blind alley wasn't always blind, and that the black van blocking it now was far too clean to be a natural growth.

Jules took aim and fired. The handblaster, cute little tech trick that it was, couldn't overcome physics. The recoil jerked her arm back, but she'd spent her life peppering inertial bullets, so it was all the same to her and she braced properly, letting her arm flow with the force, feeling the subtle sting in her wrist as the joint compressed.

It traced a misty line of steam through the air and struck its target with a sizzling crack. The blacked-out window of the van shattered, space-grade plex giving it up to Newton's final middle finger. It sloughed away, revealing a black-clad figure clutching a new hole in their chest. Jules's body clenched at the sight. Not the death, she'd seen plenty enough of that. But that person looked a hell of a lot like they wore guardcore armor with the identifying insignia filed off.

"You see that?" she asked Nox.

"Less talking, more bailing."

They piled out the door in one great gush and raced to Momma Udon's auto. A bright yellow thing in the retro-cool style of old American muscle cars. Jules grimaced. No way they would go undetected in that thing, but at least it would move them away from here faster than their feet could.

Jules was first out of the cover of the dumpsters. Fire—inertial or laser, she couldn't tell—screeched across the pavement right in front of her. Warning shots? There was no way people running equipment that advanced would miss.

Don't think of that armor. Couldn't think of what she was facing. *That way leads to fear, to paralysis and death.*

She swung around and didn't so much take aim as fire back the way the shots had come from, scattering her fire like she was splashing paint across the side of a building. Handblasters didn't run low easily, and she wasn't so much focused on hitting anything as keeping everyone from hitting her—and the others—but mostly her, if she was being honest with herself.

A black helmet popped up from around an autocab at rest and Jules shifted her fire in an instant, watched the top of it evaporate in a mist of grey electronics and blood-pinked brain matter. Her stomach twisted, but she set her jaw against the nausea and just kept on laying it down.

"Go, fucking go," she hissed.

The little black ants—for that's how she thought of them, insect soldiers to be exterminated. Not people. Definitely not people with hopes and dreams and agendas like hers—fanned out, now that they had their location fixed. They were good. Better than any team Jules had ever seen in op. They didn't make a peep, all of their comms carried out through the helmets, as they dispersed. She caught only glimpses. An armored elbow here, a flash of light off a breastplate there. And that was the worst. They were closing in. And she couldn't even keep eyes on them all.

Arden came flying from around the dumpster, threw the chef's knife on the ground—still clutching the frying pan in the other hand—and dropped to their knees behind the cover of the auto's door. Nox was right on their six, laying down fire to the right as Jules struggled to keep the left contained. It wasn't going to last. She knew that as clearly as she knew this whole thing was her fucking fault. They had seconds, seconds, before the vise closed and there was no wiggling out.

Live fire winged off the edge of the dumpster and scraped along her thigh. Jules swore and dropped to one knee like she'd been shoved down, stifling a real scream as the numbness of shock gave way to the searing pain of white-hot metal ripping open her skin.

"Jules!" Nox barked. He'd heard her take the hit, but he couldn't turn around. Couldn't peel his gaze from his own ant army.

"Grazing," she hissed between clenched teeth.

"Arden." Nox had a remarkable talent to make your name sound like a full sentence. In this case: Hurry the fuck up.

"Almost...Got it!"

Jules didn't dare look away from the half dozen ants she was tracking. Fire rained around her as a few shots flew too close, the heat of their impact radiating against her skin. The mingled scents of laser and combustion filled the air, charred her breath. Mixed with the stink of rot in the trash, the scents made her want to scream she wouldn't die here—not pinned down behind a dumpster, kneeling on slime.

The auto took a hit. They'd shifted targets—must have heard Arden. Yellow paint and plastics flung into the air like confetti. She couldn't see what part of the auto had been hit, but she could hear the crunch of plex and watch the whole thing rock. They had to go, now, or they'd be pinned down here until their deaths.

"Now, Nox!"

"Hear you."

He popped up from behind the stack of crates he'd taken shelter under, running low even as he laid down suppressive fire from that big gun of his like bullets were free and the whole world was burning, so what the hell did it matter, anyway? Jules forced her aching leg to move, half running, half stumbling, unable to keep her head down and keep a steady line of fire.

Lucky for her the blaster was lighter on recoil than the old-fashioneds. She kept one hand plastered to the wound on her thigh, pulling her leg after her, as she dragged herself toward the auto with all the elegance of a broken marionette.

Arden had both doors flung open—the front nearest her, the rear nearest Nox. They hit the vehicle at the same time and the whole thing rocked with the convergence of enemy fire. Jules dragged herself into the front seat just as she heard the little ants march. Their communications may have been silent, but they made a hell of a racket once they started running. Nox threw himself in, body laid across the bench of the backseat and hooked his door shut with an ankle even as he popped his weapon through the open hole of an already shot-out window and fired wildly.

"Go, go, go!" he shouted.

Arden wiped sweat from their forehead on the back of their wrist and punched the side of the touchpad. "Tryin'!"

"Oh, goddamnit." Jules shoved Arden down with one hand, forcing them onto the floorboard while they fussed with the control panel. Lying on her belly, she reached up to fire through her busted-out window. The car's jerking slowed. The suppression was working.

"What's the damned problem?"

"Back tire's dead, safety overrides won't let me—"

"Fucking tech," Jules growled. Arden may be an excellent tech hand, but she'd boosted a few autos in her day and wasn't about to let a goddamned safety measure be the death of her. Still laying down fire with one hand, she slapped Arden aside and reached up under the dash. They'd already taken off the panel, so she shoved her hand straight into the wire harness and fiddled around until she felt a particular cable—ribbed casing, thinner than the rest. It'd be striped black and white, if she could see it. Though her fingers were slick with blood, she ripped it loose.

"What the fuck—"

"Drive!"

The barrage was wearing through the paneling on the car. Once it broke the body panel's integrity, the whole system would fail. They'd be dead in seconds.

The auto lurched. Its back rim screeched against the pavement as the car wobbled its way forward, intrinsic steering systems adjusting, trying to figure out how to manage this unwieldy thing it'd only ever simulated having to handle. Jules flung forward, hitting the retro-stylized dash hard as the vehicle got up to speed and shot around a sharp turn. Her wrist hit the frame of the window and jarred, knocking the blaster out of her hand. Fuck. That had been an expensive gun. Nox was going to be pissed.

Then again, judging from the swearing coming from the back, he'd just had the same thing happen to him.

"Everyone whole?" she asked as she tentatively pulled herself into an upright position, peering back down the street. Didn't seem like they were being followed—she had blasted the heart out of the man driving the van, after all—but that didn't mean a tail wasn't incoming.

"Pristine," Nox said.

"I bumped my knee, but—"

Jules thwacked Arden upside the back of their head. "You're fine."

The auto skidded onto the main street and ripped away in a straight line. Jules didn't know where Arden had told the car to go, but right now she didn't care.

"Any pursuit?"

Arden's face pinched as they rubbed the back of their head. "This isn't exactly a military vehicle. It's got safety paneling—or had, anyway—but it's not like I can ask it to pull up the nearest vehicles on—ohhhh."

"Yeah, idiot, the onboard AI tracks all nearby obstacles. Find out how many are cars. See if any are moving very much in our direction."

Arden's fingers flew across the control pad. "Nothing. I think...I think we actually did it."

Jules leaned back in the seat and let loose with a burst of a laugh. No one commented on that.

"She only sent one van. Thought that would be enough for two low-rent criminals and a nerd."

"She?" Arden asked.

"No idea who she is. She was the one talking over the speakers in your building, and I think I might have heard her back at the lab..."

"Lab?" Arden stared at her with wide, bloodshot eyes. Right. They'd just had their world ripped apart a few seconds ago. The utter destruction of everything Jules had ever known was already old news.

"We'll fill you in once we're somewhere safe." She tried to pat their shoulder reassuringly, but sort of awkwardly thumped at them and smeared blood everywhere. *Good job, Jules.*

"And where's somewhere safe?"

"My armory." Nox leaned forward and input the location of a ravine in a neighborhood nearby. "We'll ditch the car here then hoof it. We're not exactly inconspicuous in this thing."

"Big word, big guy."

"I got me an edu-mu-ca-tion, Ms. Valentine."

Arden's face paled. "Uh, guys?"

"What?" Jules sat bolt upright, reaching for her other handblaster.

"Look." He pointed out the back window.

In the distance, through the ever-evolving maze of the Grotta, smoke curled between the nested buildings. There wasn't any way to be sure, not yet, but Jules didn't need confirmation. This was a signal fire, a warning. A message saying that those after her would burn everything and everyone she loved to get back what was stolen. This wasn't a hostage situation anymore. This was vengeance. Those people wouldn't stop until they had the board and they wiped out Jules and her whole crew. She clenched her fists but would not look away.

Udon-Voodun was burning.

CHAPTER 42

PRIME STANDARD YEAR 3543

WRONG MAN CALLING

A lifetime of training was the only thing that kept the disappointment off Sanda's face. Bero went dead silent. Tomas stood before the breakers, looking at his hand as if he'd just used it to shoot someone in the back. Sanda was aware of these things as specters of her environment—aware of them in the same inconsequential way she was of the red light, the subtle thrum of Bero's mechanics. Staring down a flush-faced Icarion general, her mind and body shifted into mission mode.

"I am Gunnery Sergeant Sanda Maram Greeve, and I command *The Light of Berossus*, a research vessel. Obstructing the flight of any noncombatant is in violation of the Treaty of Sanglai."

He gawped at her, most ungeneral-like, and leaned forward as if he were peering into a smaller screen to get a better look at something. She glimpsed his wristpad, and her service mug shot alongside a block of text.

"Sergeant Greeve. That's an Icarion ship you're on, which means you're either very lost, or committing piracy. Which is it?"

She opened her mouth to respond, and the screen went black. Tomas startled, throwing his attention back to the breaker panel, but the switches were still thrown. He needn't have looked. It'd only been a matter of time before Bero figured out how to cut the feed.

"Bero." The stubborn ship remained silent. She turned, slowly, hands clasped at attention behind her back, gaze roving the lab for any easy-to-hand weapon. It was harder to ignore the tarp-draped pedestal this time.

"Talk to me, Bero."

Silence.

Tomas moved toward her, but she held up a hand to stop him. "Why are very much alive Icarion generals CamCasting us?"

Silence.

"What year is it?"

Silence.

"Why did you lie?"

Silence.

"What happened to your original crew?"

A pause. Then, "They did bad things."

"What things?"

"They . . . made me . . ."

"The bombardment," Tomas said.

"I didn't want to!" Bero's voice was so loud the speakers crackled.

He was a child. Emotionally, an adolescent. A child shoved into the depths of space, filled with a crew who considered him a novelty, not a person. A child strapped up with the biggest weapon known to man. A child about to throw a temper tantrum.

Sanda had never been good with children. The phantom feel of the rubber beneath her fingertips itched throughout her aching mind. Those gleaming dots, trailing off into the dark, spotted for just a moment—just a heartbeat—as she stuck her head out of the damaged airlock. Transmuted to grey smears before her eyes, artifacts of light very much like the smear Bero had transmuted her view of Ada Prime into.

Grey. The same color of every jumpsuit she'd found in this very room.

"What did you *do*?"

"Sanda—" Tomas placed a warning hand on her arm. She shook him off.

"They had no right to override my systems!"

"And was AnnLee Yu one of them?" she snapped.

Silence. Then, heavy, "Get out."

"Easy, Bero." Tomas patted the air with his hands.

"Get. Out."

"That's an Icarion warship out there," Sanda reminded the stubborn ship. "Where in the hell do you want me to go? Or do you care?"

"Get out!"

"Bero, I won't let the Icarions take you back, but—"

"And you think your people wouldn't use me for the same things?"

"The Keepers would never force you into wholesale slaughter."

"You can't know that. You can't promise that. I told you. It's dangerous out there."

"Let me help you. Where do you want to go?"

"Get out get out get out get out!"

Steel panels in the ceiling burst open like a split rib cage. Articulated arms, gleaming with autoclaved tools of human destruction, whirred and spun. Hemostats snapped at her; bone saws churned the air. She swore and hit the deck hard, palms numb from the impact, and rolled to the side to clear the reach of the surgical instruments.

"What the fuck!" she yelled, but Bero was done talking. His voice, set to loop, recited a steady stream of: *getoutgetoutgetout*. Tomas grabbed the back of her suit and yanked her to her feet.

"Next moves?" he asked.

"Biran should be here soon, I hope," she said, abandoning secrecy in the face of Bero's freak-out. The cat was out of the bag. Now they had only to survive his temper until rescue came. "If we wait—"

An alarm bleated and she slapped her hands over her ears. Red lights of warning flickered all around the room, created dizzying patterns on the smartscreen by the door. The woman's voice, the voice of the alarm, had been cut off, but Sanda didn't need it. Below the steady thrum of Bero's litany, a soft hiss grabbed her attention and shook it.

"He's depressurizing," she said, bewildered.

"No way," Tomas protested. But then he heard the hiss, and his eyes went wide, too.

"Bero!" She yelled, but he'd made up his mind. They were intruders in his body, and he would flush them out just as he had the techs who'd made him bombard Ada Prime.

Tomas picked up a spanner from the table and eyed the breaker panel with a grim set to his lips.

"Don't be stupid." She grabbed his wrist and yanked him away, into the hall. A thudding, grinding noise echoed through the scream of the alarm and her world jerked, her stomach reaching right up to her throat as the ground shuddered. Bero was spinning down the habs. As long as he didn't stop them hard, they'd be okay. They'd make it to the helmets in time.

Metal screamed, her vision blurred, and her back slammed into the ceiling as the world stood still.

CHAPTER 43

PRIME STANDARD YEAR 3543

UP IS MEANINGLESS IN SPACE

Some asshole was shaking her. Sanda cracked her eyes open to find Tomas's face upside down in front of her, hair drifting in the subtle currents of a low-g environment. Funny, she didn't remember going to the command deck. Wouldn't take a nap down there, either.

"Sanda, you've got to pull it together. Come on now, girl."

Remembrance reasserted itself. "Shit," she said.

His smile was fleeting. "There you are. Anything broken?"

Fingers and toes moved all right, and no immediate pains felt sharp enough for her to worry about. "Just bruises. You?"

That tight little smile came back, and there was a tinge of blue around his lips, but she was having a hard time focusing on that. He lifted his arm, and even through the cover of the suit she could see his left forearm had snapped, the straight line of it jogged down a sudden step. She sucked air through her teeth.

"Hurts like a bitch but it's internal, no skin breakage. Been a hell of a time trying to move us both though." He giggled, and the sound was so incongruent with their situation that it snapped something in her, but as soon as the fear flooded her, it was gone.

And she knew why, in a dreamy-silly way. Knew exactly why. And while some animal part of her that'd been trained over and over for exactly these types of situations screamed at her, the forefront of her brain, the part firmly in the pilot's seat, just kept thinking how ridiculous it was that she was going to die this way.

A message broke through the fog. "Hypoxia."

"Huh?" Tomas poked his bent arm, making a face like a child tasting sour candy.

And then she realized: They hadn't depressurized. Bero'd just messed with the mix. A kinder way to die than being swollen to bursting, but she didn't much look forward to the actuality, no matter its method.

She moved on autopilot, scrabbling across the slick roof that was never meant to be used in low-g situations until she found what she was looking for. Her fingers slotted into the handle, gave it a twist. For a long time she stared at the two shiny globes in the closet she opened, wondering what she was supposed to do with them.

When she was a kid, one of her dads read her a story about a goldfish. The colors were vibrant on the tablet, the little girl who captured the fish at a fair by tossing a Ping-Pong ball in a cup proudly bringing the creature home to live in a globe that looked a lot like what she was staring at.

Next to the globes rested two long cylinders with LIFEPACK engraved on their sides. Those sparked an idea.

"Hey," she said, mouth splitting in the widest yawn she'd ever had. "I think we're dying."

"Huh." Tomas pushed off the ceiling and drifted close to her, still upside down. "We should put those on."

She didn't see why not, so she grabbed the packs and the helmets and got hers on, then helped Tomas into his. They looked silly, but she remembered in a vague way that the little girl who won the goldfish had an accident bringing him home.

The bag she'd won him in sprung a leak, and Sanda recalled those images with stark clarity: the girl running down the lane, tears springing from her eyes, the little fish fighting for its life, flopping around, until she dumped it into the bowl full of water just in time.

If you're dying, Sanda's stuttering mind reasoned, *bowls like these are probably the thing to use.* By the time she screwed Tomas's on and plugged him into the pack, clarity was seeping back into her mind.

She wanted to weep with relief, realizing how close she had come to a fumbling, confused death. Forcing herself to take a breath of the perfect air mix hissing in through the lifepack, she grabbed Tomas by the shoulders and gave him a shake. His eyes were glazed, but he blinked them clear.

"We gotta get out of here," he said over the comm line.

"Where?" she demanded, and he gave her a noncommittal shrug.

"I don't know, but Bero's hooked up to these, too. It's just a matter of time."

Bero could hear them. See whatever they saw. Edit it, too, if it came to that. She knew damned well that's what he did to her, every time she'd glanced Ada's way.

This must have been the same way he'd herded the original crew out: messing with the air, pushing them toward 'locks as a last resort. Probably they thought they could pressurize the 'lock, jam the system's doors, and wait for rescue. She'd seen how that plan worked out, and she wasn't about to repeat it.

Her O_2 meter flashed green, but she didn't trust it for a hot minute. Tomas drifted aimlessly beside her, his eyes going glassy again. Bero'd always been pretty clear he'd be pleased as punch to off Tomas and keep Sanda along for the ride to Atrux.

"Shit."

She grabbed Tomas's good arm and pushed off the wall at an awkward angle, sweating in her suit as she rocketed down the hallway, lugging the big Nazca bastard along behind her. He hadn't seemed half so heavy when she'd been pushing him around in the sheets. But she'd had her full breath then—or most of it, anyway.

"I know you can hear me," she said as she angled them down the ladder chute to the command deck, wincing every time she bumped Tomas against the wall. "I don't blame you for kicking your old crew out. They made you do a terrible thing, they cost a lot of lives. But Tomas doesn't mean you or anyone else harm."

"He was going to hit me."

That damned spanner. Stupid man. "He was scared. He thought he needed to defend himself. You understand being scared, don't you?"

Tomas's head lolled in the helmet. She clenched her jaw. Wanted to scream at the stupid fucking ship to give the man his air back already. But Bero wasn't a ship, not wholly. What he was, deep down, was a scared kid with way too much responsibility on his shoulders.

She pivoted in the command deck, using the handles to drag herself and Tomas to the cargo bay. Everything was right where they'd left it: Grippy lingering near the door, inventoried supplies locked down on mag pallets, and the repaired evac pod with its lid hauled back, interior gleaming. There was no way she could get Tomas there in time. She only had one shot at this.

"You know where I am, Bero?"

"The cargo bay."

"That's right," she said, and popped her helmet off. The high CO_2 hit her instantly, now that she knew what was waiting for her. She couldn't smell it, but she imagined it dribbling into her already overtaxed respiratory system, singing her neural cells a hypnotic lullaby. Before she could lose focus, she popped Tomas's helmet off, too. She told herself that Bero wouldn't kill her, that he'd just wanted to addle her until he could escape, so having Tomas breathe the same mix as her was her best shot at getting them to safety. She really hoped she was right.

"Put your helmet back on!" Bero yelled.

"No chance, Big B. If you're going to gas Tomas, you're going to gas me, too. I'll make you a deal, though. You bring the mix back up. Soon as Tomas here looks stable, I'll pop him in the evac pod and send him back to Icarion. They can ask him all the questions they want while you and I burn for Atrux."

"Why would you do that?" His tone was wary, distrustful. She couldn't blame him.

"I could tell you a lot of reasons you wouldn't believe, but..." She looked down at Tomas's rolling head, his greying lips, and sighed. "At the end of the day, it's just a trade I'm willing to make. And count on this—I don't want you in Icarion's hands any more than you do. Those simulations you showed me. You may have been lying that they'd happened already, but those were legit projections. I know... I know you don't want to be that weapon. I know you don't want to be responsible for the destruction of life in an entire star system.

And if my staying stops that reality from happening, then it's worth everything."

She tried to hold her breath, but ended up taking tiny sips of not-air while Bero thought over what she had to say. It really was all she had, too. She didn't have Tomas's spycraft, or Bero's willingness to deceive. She wanted Tomas to live. She didn't want Bero to return to Icarion hands. It was as simple as that. Except, not really, but that's what she was willing to tell herself for the time being.

The evac pod was up on straps, suspended toward the back of the hold, dead in its vertical center. Taunting her. She tried not to stare at it too hard, told herself to be still while Bero made his decision. If she forced herself to push for the pod now, her body would burn through the thin air she had left from exertion. She'd never make it, and then they'd both be unconscious.

Air vents hissed as Bero adjusted the mix, and she almost laughed with giddy relief. Without mag boots, she had to push off the locked-in crates to drift them closer to the pod. Nothing stood between the pod and the door behind it. Tomas would have a clean ride as soon as the lid snapped down and disengaged the straps.

He stirred in her arms, gasping hard to clear the poison that'd settled in his lungs. CO_2 was damned near impossible to vent out of a body in low-g scenarios, but the foam in the pod would do the rest of the work, adjusting his blood ox to optimum levels. One eye fluttered, then the other. Beneath her fingers, the thready pulse that'd been thumping through his wrist grew stronger, stabilized. Time to cut him loose.

Gripping the edge of the pod's cradle, she twisted to maneuver him into it and had to pull the strap across his chest and limbs to keep his bits from getting severed by the pod lid's collapse. They hadn't set it up for override yet, so the only way to trigger the lid was to give the thing an emergency situation. Blowing the cargo door should do the trick.

"Got a question for you, Bero. Were you ever going to tell me? If we reached Atrux, I would have found out eventually."

"I hadn't thought that far in advance."

She didn't believe him. Not for a second. Big brain like Bero's, he had to have filtered through all the possibilities. He'd chosen Atrux for a reason—not just its proximity—and it was a reason he didn't want to share.

Her skin, clammy from sweat, crawled beneath the tight fit of her suit. Maybe he hadn't expected her to survive that long. It wasn't an unreasonable solution to arrive at, especially now that she was sacrificing her best evac pod to get Tomas off the ship.

As she watched the color bleed back into his lips, felt the chill fade from his forehead, she thought of all she'd seen in the lab. All those surgical instruments. All that research. Bero'd had access to all of it; no scrap of information was hidden from him on this ship. Here was a treasure trove of research, deep insight into what the Icarions knew about Keeper technology. She'd wasted so much time, assuming it was all meaningless.

Tomas stirred, murmured her name, but couldn't quite get his eyes open. She was past time for leaving. Past time for blowing Tomas out the bay and returning to Bero's interior. Her state-of-the-art mausoleum. At least she'd gotten to hear Biran's voice one last time.

"Fuck it," she said, and jumped into the evac pod alongside Tomas.

"What are you doing?" Bero demanded.

"Surviving."

She grabbed the spanner shoved in Tomas's belt and held it up, whistling. "Grippy! Grippy!"

The little bot perked, head lifting as its camera and sonar worked in concert to find her voice. Soon as he sighted her, she shook the spanner. "Fetch!"

She hurled it at the door controls. In low-g, the spanner windmilled end-over-end with ease, not arcing, not twisting. Her aim was true. Grippy's mag-treads drove him forward. He snagged the spanner from the air, his arm clanging against the release panel.

The last thing she heard was two cheery beeps of victory before the air rushed out and the evac pod's lid crashed down.

CHAPTER 44

HOURS AWAY

Biran did not sleep. His body screamed at him every hour he stretched his limits, but between stimpacks and a never-ending supply of coffee, Biran pushed through the jitters. Through the headaches. Crew rotated through shifts on the bridge and still Biran did not peel his gaze from the forward viewscreen, a constant display of *The Light* and the *Empedocles*, and the distance between them, visible in the lower left corner. They'd make it, he told himself, even as those two Icarion ships drew closer and closer together. They'd get there first.

"Status report," Lavaux demanded.

He hadn't left his captain's chair, either, and though Biran never saw the man take a sip of coffee, he suspected the water the crew brought him was loaded with stimulants. Let the man do what he needed to do. As long as his mind was clear, Biran wouldn't judge. He was strung out to the limits himself.

Pilli, having rotated back through to the navigation console after an appropriate rest, made a frustrated sound. "That ship is jumping all over the damned map," she snarled, as if the inconsistent movement of *The Light* were a personal affront.

"What do you mean *jumping*?" Lavaux snapped. Stimulants made even the calmest men short-tempered.

"Exactly what I said, sir, which isn't possible. Ships don't judder around like this. And every time the damned thing moves, I have to replot the course. At these speeds we can't afford to be even a little off. We'd either blow right by it, or into it, neither of which would help us capture the thing."

Biran could practically hear her gritting her teeth. "Is the satellite feed corrupt?"

"I think so, but there's no way Icarion would know to send us bad data. *Empedocles* doesn't know we're coming, and neither does *The Light*, as far as I know. My back doors are flawless. No one should know I'm skimming their systems."

"*The Light* is a clever ship, if my reports are to be believed," Lavaux said. "It may obscure its position on purpose."

"I don't think it can. It'd need a direct back door into the satellites, and begging your pardon, sir, but these are old feeds. If the ship even knows about them, I don't think it would have access."

"You do," Biran countered.

Pilli snorted. "I've spent my life getting eyes on this solar system. That ship's got nothing on me."

Biran smiled to himself, glancing over his shoulder to seek out Anaia, who'd also spent her whole life finding back doors into satellites to keep a wary eye on the movement of the stars. She wasn't there. Sometime during the chase, she'd left her position in one of the empty chairs at the forward console, her lidded mug of coffee left to go cold in the cup holder of the chair's arm, a streak of her bright lipstick all the evidence she had ever been there.

A sinking sensation worked its way into his mind. Strange, that she should leave the bridge at such a critical moment. But it wasn't really a moment, was it? It had been hours of chase, crawling through the empty black of space—never mind they were burning at the ship's max speed. Maybe she had gone to take a rest.

Maybe.

Something about that mug needled at him. It wasn't the kind of thing Anaia would leave behind. She'd always been conscientious about the rules of space travel, and you didn't leave a container of liquid unattended, even if it had a lid.

Biran got up and reached his arms above his head, stretching from side to side. Joints creaked and popped as he moved them fully for the first time in hours. He picked up the coffee mug and turned it around in his hand to look at the lipstick smear as if he could divine answers from it. He couldn't.

"Everything all right, Speaker?" Lavaux asked without taking his gaze from the data readout in front of him.

"Going to stretch my legs."

Lavaux nodded at him, distracted by the immediate problem, and Biran stepped out into the hall, pinging his wristpad to query where Anaia's room was. Not too far from his own. He hadn't even been there since he'd been on board. His luggage was still stored in the cargo net on the bridge.

Biran knocked once and swiped his wristpad over Anaia's door scanner to announce his presence—forgetting that his new status as Speaker made it so his wristpad was able to override most locks, even those on Lavaux's ship, as the security system had been, by necessity, outfitted by the Keepers.

The door dilated instantly. Anaia had been sitting at her desk with her back to the door, a laptop propped open in front of her. At the swish of the door, she let out a startled squeak and jumped, knocking her chair back. Just far enough for Biran to make out the screen of the laptop.

Video feed of *The Light*, split-screened with a stream of data. Not just data. Commands. He knew the look of her command window from watching her manipulate the satellites into showing him the location of the green light in the rubble field. Only her feed wasn't jittery. On Anaia's screen, *The Light* was perfectly still, traveling in a straight line.

"Biran!" She slammed the laptop closed and spun around to face him, cheeks deep red. "Didn't anyone teach you to knock?"

He stepped into the room and put her mug down on the nightstand, struggling to process what he'd seen. What his gut was screaming at him was true, but his brain hadn't caught up to yet.

"What the hell are you doing, Anaia?"

She licked her lips and darted a glance at the laptop. "Trying to get my own eyes on things."

"Bullshit. Your feed was still."

She tensed, fingers curling under the arm of her chair. "I've been working on some stabilizing algorithms."

"Show me."

They stared at each other, neither wanting to break the fragile peace they were in. Dios, how long had he known Anaia? Since they passed their aptitude tests, at least. Since they were barely ten years old. There'd never been a lot of room in Biran's life for other people—his family and his education to become a Keeper had filled almost every moment.

But in the cracks? Those times when he let himself just be, let himself have friends and do stupid things like get shit-faced in zero-g or play card games he hardly knew the rules to with the rest of his cohort? She'd been there. Anaia'd always been there. And not just because they were in the same year. Because, somehow, early on, they'd realized they could just *be* around each other.

She was the only friend he'd ever had.

And so maybe he'd never really had a friend at all.

Biran brought up his wristpad and hit the button for the ship's AI. "Tell Lavaux—"

Anaia slammed into him. He never saw her coming. His back slapped the door, head slamming into the thin metal. His ears rang and then he realized he was on the ground, sprawled, arms flung out, and Anaia was gone, her laptop was gone, and her footsteps were thundering down the hallway at a dead sprint.

Biran groaned and rolled to his side, fumbling at his wristpad until he got the AI to pipe him directly into the bridge.

"Lavaux—"

"We're busy," he said. "The feed cleared up."

"It's Anaia. Keeper Lionetti. She hacked the satellites and is running for the shuttles. Lock us down. Lock everything down."

Sirens blared through the rooms, echoed down the halls, red lights flashing in brilliant strobes that painted sunset colors against the walls. Biran grunted and pushed to his feet, cutting the line to Lavaux. He stumbled out into the hall, bracing one hand against the doorframe, and oriented himself. She'd struck him hard in the head, an expert hit—when in the hell had she learned to do that?—before taking off, so it took a second for him to shake the fuzz from his thoughts.

Once his vision stopped swimming, he sprinted after her, launching himself with everything he had toward the bay where the shuttles were housed. He would not let her get off this ship. Would not let her escape. Would not let her leave without answering for what she had done.

Panting hard, he caught sight of her shadow—just a sliver— twisting around a corner. Biran slapped a hand against a wall to steady himself and spun around after her. At the end of the hall the door to the shuttle bay stood shut—locked. The red lights of the alarms painted Anaia's skin in shades of watered-down blood, her laptop shoved under one arm, as she frantically tried to convince the lock on the door to let her through.

"Anaia!"

She turned, eyes huge, and for a breath guilt stung his heart—a thread of doubt wanting him to believe that there was some other explanation for what she'd done. But those wide eyes narrowed, her lips curled in a snarl, and reality came crashing back down on his shoulders. Down the hall, the march of Lavaux's security personnel echoed.

"Open this door," she demanded.

"Like hell." He took a step forward and she pressed her back against the door, clutching the laptop to her chest. "Why, Anaia? Why keep us from chasing *The Light*? Why keep me from *saving my sister*?!"

"I'm sorry," she said, voice catching. "I didn't mean for Sanda to get tangled up in this—I was just doing my job."

"Job? What job?"

"Isn't it obvious?" Lavaux said from behind him.

Biran flinched at the voice, stepping aside as Lavaux approached, four security guards surrounding him, bearing down upon Anaia. Biran had to press his back against the wall as they moved around him and cornered Anaia, taking her laptop in the same motion they clasped her wrists in electronic cuffs.

"She's a spy," Lavaux said with a sliver of respect. "A rather good one, too. I'm dying to figure out how Icarion fudged your birth paper-work. Lock her up, please, and send a brief report to Director Olver. He's not so angry at us that he won't want to hear about this."

"A spy?" Biran asked around the lump in his throat. She snorted in response, but dropped her head, unwilling to look him in the eye.

"Good work." Lavaux patted him on the shoulder while the security guards shuffled Anaia by. He caught a whiff of her perfume—sweet berries and sticky toffee—as she passed. Probably the last time he'd ever smell it. The thought made him want to vomit.

"Now let's go get your sister."

CHAPTER 45

PRIME STANDARD YEAR 3543

DAY ?

Foam encased her. Shoved itself up her nostrils, sealed her eyes open. Slithered its way beneath her suit and filled every crevice until she was a pressurized vessel, capable of surviving just as easily on the bottom of the sea as she was in the vacuum of space. The pod had been created to be its own pressure vessel, but the nature of space-faring engineering was redundancies.

She waited for the somnolence of coldsleep. Waited for the sedatives in the foam to drag her under. For the sweet bliss of coma.

Still awake.

Okay. They were taking longer than usual. That was fine. There were two bodies in here, and she had already been suspicious that they hadn't loaded it up with enough of the drug. There'd been so little left after prying them both out of their respective pods. She could feel Tomas against her, somewhere in the grey mass that hardened, locking her into place. His knee pressed against her thigh, his hand caught in the crook of her elbow. He was cold all over, but then so was she. That was the point of the coldsleep. Slow everything down. Preserve.

Even thought slowed. Though she knew better, she tried to move. Tried to shift her arm, her leg. Tried to crane her head to get a look at her surroundings. Nothing budged. The foam held her tight, locked in place like a mosquito in amber, a gift for future generations to puzzle over.

A pain formed in the back of her mind. Not the dull throb of cold-sleep headaches, but the sharp ache of something else. Something more immediate. Had she been injured before going in the foam? She couldn't recall. Bero had stopped the spin of the habs and she'd crashed into the ceiling, yes, but the pain burgeoning on the back of her skull was something more than that—something not borne of blunt-force trauma. It was sharp, and it was bright, like licking a battery. Maybe Bero had gotten her with those surgical tools after all.

Vague memories tumbled in her slowed thoughts. Sluggish, blurred. Hazy gleams of steel and glittering white smearing across the vault of her world. There was something in that. Something she should know, should remember. Sanda forced herself to *think*, neurons firing away, chasing down the haunted shapes and echoes of sharpness. Something had happened. Something she should know. Something important.

The dull ache returned. She tried to reach back to rub her head, but of course that was pointless. Couldn't even scream, not really, with her throat full of hardened sludge.

Those memories teasing her, just on the edge. How long had they been there? It could have been months since she jumped in the pod with Tomas. Could have been years.

Even preservation foam couldn't hold back cancer, or an aneurysm, if that's what your body was destined to have. Panic gripped her in slow, tense ebbs, creeping through her coldsleep-slowed brain until she wanted to scream, thinking she might be hyperventilating, but that was impossible, the foam mandated her oxygen levels.

Panic pushed aside all the reasoning that'd brought her to this point. There was no guarantee Biran would ever find them. No guarantee Icarion would scoop them up, when their real prize was Bero. Could be she'd traded one mausoleum for another.

She collapsed. Hardened foam turned to goo around her, grey-purple sludge slipping through freed fingers, dripping into her eyes, expunging itself from her throat and other internal cavities. Tomas splayed beneath her, her head over his shoulder, both hacking and shivering and convulsing with the shock of reawakening.

"There's two in here," a woman said.

Sanda heaved herself to her side, pressed her back against the lip of the pod, and pushed Tomas away with trembling arms so she wouldn't vomit on him. Not that it did any good, they had both already filled the pod with a variety of fluids no one should be expected to share with another living being.

"Ugh," Tomas said, rubbing his eyes with trembling fingers.

"Urk," she replied.

The sharp ache was gone from her skull. White light pierced her vision, threatening to return it. Whatever imagery her brain had been puzzling over slipped away. A sickening sense of déjà vu filled her. Sterile lights, a blank ceiling. But she'd heard a woman's voice, somewhere on the periphery. This wasn't Bero's medibay.

But it was Icarion's.

"Restrain them." The general's voice, the clean-shaven man she'd spoken with before Bero cut them off. She tried to stifle a laugh, then realized she couldn't. Lying in a pool of mixed fluids, she laughed like a madwoman. They'd only been in the pod a few hours, maybe even just a few minutes. It'd felt like lifetimes. She wondered if the experience had been the same for Tomas. For his sake, she hoped not.

Hands grabbed her, heaved her limp body into the aggressive light. Cold metal circled her wrists, and she almost laughed again, because didn't they realize how weak she was? She couldn't swat a fly without falling on her face.

"That is unnecessary." The woman again.

Sanda swiveled her head like a bat seeking a moth, trying to pinpoint which blur in the sea of blurs crowding her was advocating on her behalf. An oval of a face, a pointed chin, the hint of dark hair haloing it. She tried to focus, but the foam was still slick beneath her lids and with her hands restrained all she had were tears, dribbling purplish gunk down her cheeks, to clear them.

"Are they medically sound?" the general asked.

"It seems that way, but any exposure to coldsleep conditions requires careful monitoring."

"You can monitor them from a cell."

"General Negassi, I must insist you allow me to take their vitals."

"Make it quick, Dr. Yu."

The blurry oval face and hair came closer. Fingers probed around Sanda's throat and face, flashed a pinpoint of light into her eyes, ears, and nose.

"She's stable. I'd like to take a closer look at the man. His oxygen levels are concerning. He may be anemic."

Sanda tried to make her mouth work, tried to tell them he'd been hypoxic and they should probably check out his brain, just to be safe, but all she managed to do was drool.

"You can look at that one all you like, I recognize him now. He's that Nazca we hired. Hose the other one down, then lock her up."

They had that backward, she thought blearily as someone took her arm and steered her around. Biran had hired the Nazca—hired Tomas—not Icarion. What a silly mistake for the general to make. Something in her hindbrain screamed at her, but she ignored it, trying to swallow back another urge to vomit.

PRIME STANDARD YEAR 3541

IN A SYSTEM FAR, FAR AWAY

Jules got her leg propped up on Nox's steel table and tipped her head back, eyes closed. The plastiskin patch over her gash had come with a cool, numbing gel that Jules was pretty sure was doing more to make her sleepy than her actual lack of sleep. Too bad Nox and Arden were being too loud to let her rest.

"What in the hell just happened?" Arden slouched onto a chair, then popped back up, paced around the table, tapped the glass on a cabinet, and sat back down again, bouncing their leg against the foot brace on the stool. She wished they'd just sit still already.

"We ripped off the wrong damned people," Nox grumbled. He dumped his weapons onto the table with a clatter and sorted through them, checking and rechecking each to make sure it was ready for action.

"Yeah, no shit. Maybe I've lost my mind, but it looked like those were guardcore. Please, please tell me I'm going insane and that those people shooting at us weren't guardcore."

"They were guardcore," Jules said.

"Fuuuuck." Arden dropped their head against the cold steel of the table and folded their arms. "Why? What do they want with you guys?"

"We don't know," Jules admitted. She forced herself to pry her eyes open. "They're after those smartboards we took, obviously, but something feels...off."

"Off? Like being shot at in broad daylight? Or having an insane woman chatting to you through the speakers of my apartment building? Oh, or having the whole fucking building burn down—and—and not to mention what happened to Harlan, and Lolla..."

"She doesn't mean the facts, idiot." Nox put a weapon down and pointed at them with the gun oil–stained rag he'd been using to clean it. "She means the details."

Arden picked their head up and squinted at Nox with the same raw bewilderment Jules thought they might express if a houseplant had suddenly up and started lecturing them on orbital mechanics. "Which. Details. Exactly?"

"The guardcore themselves, for starters," she said, swooping in to explain things before those two idiots got themselves into a fight that'd slow everything down. "No insignia, small numbers. And yeah, they hit your place in the morning, but I don't think they would have if they hadn't been in a rush to clean up what they'd missed after hitting our"—she cleared her throat—"house. If it was some kind of official action of the Keepers, I don't think we would have stood a chance. Those people were off duty, I guess."

"So, dirty?"

"Maybe. I don't know, but it seems likely, right? I mean—those smartboards we found. They weren't exactly locked up in Keeper HQ, or anything like that. They were in a rotted-out facility on the edge of the Grotta, for fuck's sake. Whoever put that lab there had gone to a lot of effort to keep it away from official channels. Bad luck for them we stumbled across it." She grimaced. "Bad luck for us, too."

"Sure about that? That it was bad luck?" Nox asked.

She frowned at him. "I don't see what you're getting at."

Nox sighed and grabbed an amber bottle and a couple of glasses from a cabinet—bourbon. Jules recognized the smell the second he pulled the stop and poured out three glasses. After they all drank, Nox shook himself like he was chasing off an alcohol shiver and set his glass down between his hands on the table.

"Look. I know that your op was all about that wraith, Jules. Don't think I'm insinuating anything about your motives here. But I've been tooling around the Grotta a long time, and I ain't never just stumbled across an outfit that fancy before. There was serious money behind that lab, and as our friends in black pointed out to us earlier, serious power, too. So I can't help but wonder—what was the wraith doing there? It's not cheap shit, I'll grant you, but a couple of crates just hanging out in that secret hallway?"

"Secret hallway?" Arden cut in, their eyes brightening with interest.

"Not as cool as you'd think," Jules said. Arden slumped back down with a sigh.

"As I was saying." Nox cut Arden a look. "Seems weird, right? Smugglers moving wraith through a hall like that, and one of them was definitely dead. I don't think they would have tripped over the place."

"You think they were lured there?"

"I think *we* were lured there."

Her muscles were heavier than they had any right to be. "Not possible. And what the fuck for? There wasn't anyone in that lab, aside from the dead guy in the hallway. It's not like we were ambushed. Sure, we set off the alarm, but we made it out okay."

"Might not have been the people that run the lab that lured us there. Could be another opposing faction—damned politicians, and Keepers, are all snakes—that wanted a couple of lowlifes to run across it to see what shook out. I don't think they expected we'd actually get anything of value, though, hence the guardcore. Someone's trying to tie up loose ends."

"Whoa, whoa, whoa." Arden raised their hand like they were asking a teacher a question. "Let me get this straight. You think you and the crew were led to that wraith cache by some *other* rogue Keeper faction that knew about the lab and wanted to get you inside for... some reason?... To shake up the people that founded the lab or something?"

"I don't know what the fuck their reasons were, Arden. Maybe they wanted to test the defenses, see if a bunch of Grotta scum could break in. It doesn't matter. Someone put us there, and the people who operate that lab don't seem too happy about it."

"Fuck, man, if Keepers are after us, then we're dead. Seriously, seriously, dead."

"Did you get the data?" Jules asked.

"Not yet, I was, as you might recall, interrupted." Arden scooped their bag off the floor and pulled out the smartboard, then plunked it on the table and synced it up to some program running on their wristpad. "Like I said, this thing isn't very locked down. Whoever owned it really didn't expect it to go missing, so either it's full of junk that won't help us or your rogue Keeper was so full of themselves that they didn't bother with high-level security. Which seems unlikely, considering their entire existence is about data security."

"Or we were supposed to take the boards, too," Nox put in.

"Okay." Jules shook her head. "Now you're getting paranoid. And I gotta admit, I'm starting to think those weren't Keepers running that lab."

"Explain the fucking guardcore, then," Nox snapped.

"Your setup team, the rogue faction." Jules dragged both hands through her hair, then rubbed her cheeks. "Look, I know what I saw in there. There was some kind of drug being manufactured in that facility, I'm sure." *I touched it*, she wanted to say. *I spilled some on my hand and it kept me high all night. Hell, I still feel stronger than I should be right now*, but she kept that down. Didn't want the others thinking she was spun out and coming up with weird conspiracy theories. This was crazy enough as it was. "Maybe they were starting with wraith, or something, but all this Keeper connection makes me think they were working on something *for* the Keepers."

Arden cocked their head to one side. "Can't Keepers get high just like the rest of us? It's not like they're androids, they just have that one chip—plus the usual ident and wristpad sync-ups."

"Yeah, sure they can, but there's two reasons I can think of that you might want specialty stuff for them."

"Enlighten us, oh wise queen of getting high," Nox drawled.

"You're such an ass. Anyway. One: They might get in trouble for it, right? They're supposed to be ridiculously good at keeping secrets, at protecting the data tapped into their skulls. So if they get high, they might say something stupid, even if it's just for recreational purposes.

So they'd want something special, something that clears the system in a hurry. I mean, we've all seen that Keepers can drink—they're always having those fancy galas on the news or whatever—but have you ever seen a Keeper high? I mean, seriously lit the fuck up?"

"No, I haven't," Nox said, "but then, they don't invite guys like me to those parties. Too worried my handsome mug will steal all their high-brow ladies away."

"You're gross."

"But..." Arden frowned at her. "That seems like a hell of an over-reaction to a party drug. Murder, burning down Udon-Voodun in broad daylight? I don't see it."

She grimaced. "Yeah. Neither do I. Which leads to the second option: It's not the Keepers making that shit. It's being made to *work on* Keepers. Something to get them spun so hard that they can't see straight and they're happy to give up the goods."

"Shit." Arden stood up so fast their stool screeched back against the floor. "Insurgents? You mean someone trying to figure out how to build a Casimir Gate by getting a bunch of Keepers high? We have to tell someone."

Jules blinked owlishly at them. "You think they don't already know?"

"Oh." He sat back down. "And they lured you guys in to...Check the defenses, like Nox said. And if things went sideways, then it wasn't any of their people making the news that evening."

"It's just a theory," Jules hedged.

"It's a really fucking good one," Nox said. "So we don't know who hit the crew's house. Maybe it was our insurgent friends, maybe it was the Keepers, but we know for sure the Keepers hit Arden's place."

"Right," Jules said.

"So what? What do we *do*?" Arden's voice had a slight whine to it. "We can't get tangled up with the insurgents, we can't go to the cops, we can't exactly stroll up to Keep Station—you know, not just because it's in orbit—and say, 'Hi, guys, found a lab of bad guys making a drug to steal all your data, sorry about the mix-up, we cool?'"

"I...don't know," Jules admitted. "All I know for sure right now is that they have Lolla, and I'm going to get her back. But we need more data. We have to know what the fuck we're dealing with here—and if there's anyone we can trust. Once you've got that board cracked, we'll check it out and reevaluate."

Arden glanced at their wristpad at the mention of the board, then went pale. "Uh. Guys. Silverfang is pinging me."

"Who's that?" Nox asked.

Arden shrugged. "Don't know, really. Could be one of our two factions, I guess. Could be a totally different third party. Before things went to tits, Jules asked me to fence whatever was on the board for her. Silverfang was the only interested buyer I had in mind."

"What's she say?" Jules peered over Arden's shoulder.

SF: Price irrelevant if the data's good. Meet?

"Not exactly a conversationalist," Nox muttered.

"No, this is good," Jules said. "Tell her I'll meet her—uh, don't use my name, just say the dealer will meet her."

"Most definitely a trap," Nox warned.

"Of course it is." Jules met his gaze. "But that doesn't have to be a one-way affair, does it?"

He grinned. "No. No, it does not."

Arden typed back: Yes to the meet. Elequatorial Cultural Center, tomorrow, 0800 hours.

SF: Deal.

A: How will I recognize you?

SF: Shouldn't be hard.

The connection cut.

"What is that supposed to mean?" Nox asked.

Arden shrugged. "Probably has, like, a necklace with a silver fang on it or something. Not too hard to figure that out."

"Right. We should plan the op perimeter and execution." Jules held her wristpad out for all to see as she pulled up a map of the cultural center.

"You do that," Nox said. "I'm going out to score us some food."

She grabbed his arm as he turned toward the door, his muscles going tight as steel cables under her touch. "Careful."

"Please." He flashed her a grin. "Just going to the café around the corner."

She nodded, and he patted the blaster strapped under his coat to reassure her further before stepping out the door.

"You sure you should be the one for the meet?" Arden asked, nodding to the plastiskin patch on her leg.

She peeled up the edge of the bandage, peering under the gel to the deep gash beneath. Her blood had mingled with the medication, creating a pink-brown slurry, so it took a moment to realize what she was looking at. Not a wound, not anymore. Just fresh, pink skin, and even that was turning the coffee shade of her flesh at the edges. No way the plastiskin patch was that good at healing. She swallowed once, hard, remembering the flash of silver as the Keeper drug had evaporated into her skin.

"Yeah," she said, pressing the patch back down and faking a pained grimace. "I'm sure."

CHAPTER 47

PRIME STANDARD YEAR 3543

CAPTIVITY. AGAIN.

Sanda lay on foam-encased metal, shivering in her fresh jumpsuit, and tried to focus on the swaying ceiling.

"I know you're not moving," she told the ceiling. The vents continued to skew drunkenly left and right, despite her remonstrations.

"Hell," she muttered, and dug the heels of her hands into both eyes, squeezing until little starlights danced behind them. The first time she'd woken from coldsleep, her vision had cleared quickly. But then, she didn't really know, did she? She'd gone straight into the Nutri-Bath cocoon. She could have popped out just as screw-eyed as she was now, and the gel had fixed all that up for her, just as it had her leg, and she'd been too bashed up to remember any of it.

She scowled at the nub where her prosthetic had been, then closed her eyes quickly as it appeared to smear to the side. They'd taken it, rolled up the leg of her jumpsuit and pinned it in place instead. Couldn't trust her not to use it as a weapon, they'd said, but they'd been happy as cats in the cream to give her a shoddy excuse for a crutch. She resolved to hit one of them with it, just on principle.

A soft beep warned her someone was messing with the access panel on her door, then the whoosh of it dilating. She kept her eyes resolutely closed. If they couldn't afford her the dignity of her leg, she sure as shit wasn't going to risk puking on her own shoe to look them in the eye.

"Ms. Greeve?" a woman asked.

"Sergeant Greeve," she corrected.

"Of course, forgive me. May I sit down?"

She waved an arm expansively. "Mi casa es su casa. Have at it."

A squeak of wheels as she dragged a stool alongside Sanda's bed. A click, and then light shone into Sanda's shut eyes, casting bloody sunset colors over her vision.

"Are you experiencing any discomfort?" the doctor asked.

"Aside from being a prisoner, without my prosthetic?"

A rustle of cloth as the doctor shifted. "If you'll allow me, I can measure you for another prosthetic. It won't be a perfect fit, but my superiors can't object to an Icarion-made object."

"Really. Your warships troll around with a collection of prosthetic limbs of all sizes?"

A sigh. "No. But I can requisition something. Our supplies—" She cut herself off, no doubt to keep from accidentally revealing any sensitive information. "I can have it for you soon. A few days, maybe."

"Do you really think they'll keep me alive that long?"

"We're not butchers."

"Funny, your spaceship disagrees."

Sanda risked cracking her eyes open. The doctor had gone still, her penlight pointed at the wall. Though Sanda's vision still smeared and blurred, she forced herself to focus on the familiar lines of the woman's face. Her oval cheeks, her pin-straight hair. AnnLee Yu. The woman who had raised Bero. Not dead after all. She wondered if that was because Bero had spared her, or because she hadn't been on board in that terrible moment. Maybe Icarion had decided to leave Bero's momma behind when they pulled the trigger.

Yu cleared her throat and returned the penlight to the pocket of her lab coat. "You spoke with *The Light of Berossus*?"

All clinical cool as if she hadn't read Bero children's stories before sending him out to murder a world. "I did. There weren't exactly a lot of conversational options."

"Surely you were more comfortable talking with that man, the Nazca. I know how you Primes feel about personality-emergent AI."

Sanda skipped over the fact that Tomas had arrived much later, not knowing what he'd tell them and frankly not willing to divulge any more information than she needed to survive. "I found Bero charming."

"He was well-mannered?" The doctor took Sanda's wrist and made a cursory attempt at checking her pulse. Sanda wondered if she'd lied to her superiors to see Sanda, claiming she needed medical attention, or if they knew what she was doing—that she was in here fishing for clues to Bero's mental state. It must be the former, she decided. If they thought Tomas was on their side, they wouldn't bother probing Sanda for information, they'd just ask their trusted source. The good doctor had been left in the dark.

"Polite as an abuse survivor can be."

Yu winced, set Sanda's wrist down, and swiveled around to examine her halved leg. "*The Light* was well cared for, he had the finest crew we had to offer. He was not abused."

"Your saying so doesn't make it true. Bero—that's what he prefers to be called as you, of all people, should know—was suffering the clearest case of PTSD I've ever seen. We train soldiers years to be able to pull the trigger. I was a gunnery sergeant, I picked the targets my crew fired at. Mandatory therapy twice a month, and all the training leading up to the position. That can't be replaced, even if you've got a big brain like Bero's. I'd bet that big brain means he needs the help even more."

The room had settled, the incessant sway resolving back into plain geometry. Icarion kept everything so white, so crisp. Hard lines and smooth curves, everything with purpose, everything disciplined. Her cell was a sparse cabin, one bed lining the wall and a set of drawers built into the opposite. She could see no hint of a lavatory. Only the radial lines of the door's aperture hovered over Yu's shoulder.

Yu herself fit the Icarion aesthetic. White lab coat, standard-issue jumpsuit lurking beneath it. She'd cut her hair to follow the line of her chin, not a strand out of place, her expression shut down into a professional mask. But there was tension in the corners of her eyes, little wrinkles, and she'd been running the sensation probe against Sanda's thigh, over and over, for a good minute without speaking or altering method.

Yu may fit like a glove into the mold Icarion had cast for her, but she was troubled. Bristling at the edges. Lying her way into a prisoner's room to hear word of a spaceship she once tutored.

Sanda said, "Bero spoke fondly of you, AnnLee Yu."

She jerked back, fumbled the sensation tester and shoved it hastily into a sagging breast pocket. "I'm glad to hear it." Yu stood, knocking the stool back. "If you have no health complaints...?"

"I have enough of those to last all night." Sanda forced herself to sit up and swung her foot to the ground, rubbing the nub of flesh at the end of her thigh as if it hurt. It didn't, but she watched Yu's eyes track to the movement, watched a flicker of concern cross her expression. The good doctor had a soft spot for all sentient life, it seemed. Even Ada Prime scum.

The door dilated, and Yu flinched, hunching down guiltily. Sanda's mouth soured. A young soldier in Icarion standard-issue poked his head into the room and gestured at them with his chin. "Clear out, Dr. Yu. Negassi wants the prisoner."

"I have a name," Sanda said.

"The prisoner is under my medical care," Yu said with brisk annoyance, clearing away any sympathy Sanda had for her by failing to use Sanda's name.

The soldier rolled his eyes. "Take it up with Negassi."

He stepped to the side and snapped his fingers, marking himself as target number one for Sanda to whack with her crutch. Shoving the padded bridge of the crutch in her armpit, she wobbled upright and shrugged off Yu's half-hearted attempt to assist. She'd rambled around a spaceship alone for weeks. She sure as shit didn't need tender loving care from her captors.

The soldier eyed her as she hobbled into the hall. "I've been assured you're too weak to cause any trouble, so I'll keep the cuffs off."

"I'm bowled over by your generosity."

He scowled and jabbed one finger in the direction she was meant to precede him. She didn't bother putting any hustle into her step. If he was going to be an ass, he was about to find out she was far more practiced at assholery.

The halls of this ship were a mirror of Bero's, sterile white with all the corners rounded off, but vitality pumped through this ship. People crossed their path, heads bent over wristpads, barely flicking the prisoner and her entourage a glance as they went about their business. The press of humanity unsettled Sanda. Going from thinking you were the last woman left alive in light-years, to being tacitly ignored by a whole gaggle of your fellow *Homo stellaris sapiens* was a bit of a mindfuck.

The guard pressed his wristpad to a smartlock and the door dilated, revealing a conference room just like the one she'd found in Bero. Just as boring, too. Something about the presence of humans in a conference room made the decor even worse. At least there was a sense of potential in an empty room. Here, the bored faces confirmed the tedium.

Negassi sat at the head of the table, a smartscreen black on the wall behind him. To his right sat an adviser, to his left Tomas, his arm bound up in a sling. Despite the shadows under his eyes, he lounged, one ankle kicked up on the opposing knee as he leaned back in his seat and scratched at the stubble darkening his chin. When the door opened, he and Negassi were chatting like old pals. He didn't so much as flick her a glance. Jerk.

"Get the lady a chair," Negassi said, "then get out of here, both of you. This meeting is classified."

The guard stepped smartly forward and pulled out a chair for Sanda, which she took, then he retreated without so much as a simper. AnnLee was having a harder time accepting orders.

"This woman is my patient," she insisted, digging her fingers into the backrest of Sanda's chair. "And *The Light* is my project."

"And this is my ship." Negassi leaned forward, fingers interlaced. Sanda felt the incoming pissing match burgeoning on the horizon and sighed loud enough to make them all cut her a look.

"Look," she said, "I know I'm the prisoner here, but if you want your ship back, we don't have time for cock-wagging. Dr. Yu has insight into Bero's psyche. I'm just about on my last leg—no pun intended—and may need her medical help if you all insist on continuing to bore me to death. Can we move the fuck on?"

Tomas hid a smirk by turning his head toward the wall. AnnLee moved purposefully around the table, yanked a chair out, and sat. The adviser raised some overplucked brows at her but said nothing. Bunch of Icarion pushovers. Insubordination like that would have been well and thoroughly slapped down by the Primes.

She figured that was the difference between a single-planet government and the galaxy-spanning reach of the Primes. For the Primes, organization and clear codes of conduct were vital for smooth workings across outposts. The Icarions only had one measly planet to look after. The Primes had the whole universe.

"Time is, as Sergeant Greeve paraphrased, tight. Piracy is a crime punishable by execution. Please explain why I shouldn't space you immediately, instead of spending my ship's resources on keeping you breathing."

"Maybe because I didn't steal your fucking ship. It *stole me*."

Negassi scowled. "That language is inappropriate in this office, Sergeant."

"I do not see," the adviser said, "why we are wasting our time with this woman. We have *The Light*'s last known location and a bead on its trajectory. We do not need her."

The adviser's breath stank of stale coffee and heavy cream. Sanda wrinkled her nose and bit back an urge to stick her proverbial foot deeper in the shit. She had no doubt General Greybeard would space her without so much as a twinge of remorse. He'd probably use words like *expedient* and *best course of action* in his report about the incident.

"Look," she said, but Tomas cleared his throat to cut her off.

"What Sergeant Greeve is unwilling to tell you, gentlemen, is that *The Light* has forged a deep bond with her, and her with him. If she calls, he will come." He turned toward her, everything about his posture laconic, verging on sinister in his lack of interest. It reminded her of how easily he'd lied to Bero, even knowing what he did about Bero's deceits. How simple it had been for him to force a cheery facade and pretend camaraderie with the ship that was their de facto jailer.

Trouble was, she couldn't puzzle out who he was trying to fool this time around.

"Is that correct?" Negassi asked.

Sanda made a show of pressing her lips shut as she got the feeling that the relationship Tomas was trying to sell these men on meant she would be reticent to put her dear old buddy Bero in any peril. He wasn't wrong. Bero in Icarion's hands was the worst-case scenario.

A vicious little part of her wanted to see the ship broken apart and sold for scrap, considering what he'd done to her. But that wasn't how Icarion worked. They'd rip his brain out, but they'd leave the big guns in place, and Bero's body wasn't a weapon she was willing to let them get their hands on.

"I see." Negassi leaned back. "I'm inclined to believe you, Cepko."

AnnLee snorted. Her superiors shared a startled look. "Anything to say, Doctor?" Negassi asked.

"I share a deep bond with *The Light*," she insisted. "If you had allowed me to send a tightbeam directly to the ship when it first jettisoned its crew, then—"

"His name is *Bero*." Sanda gripped the edge of the table so hard her knuckles ached. If this self-assured mess of a woman had realized the damage she'd done in forging a bond with Bero, then betraying him, Sanda might not have spent the last few weeks grieving everything she'd ever known and loved. She'd never wanted to slap someone so hard in her life.

AnnLee sat back, a hateful scowl pointed straight at Sanda, but something had settled in Negassi's expression. He'd reached a conclusion, and Sanda was pretty sure she wasn't going to like it.

"I see," he said. "Dr. Yu, please keep your thoughts directed on your next project. While I respect your expertise, our superiors will not allow for another disaster. In fact"—he nodded to the adviser—"make arrangements for Dr. Yu's transfer at the next available moment. It's time she return to Station Beta."

"*The Light* is *my* project," Yu began, but Negassi cut her off with a slash of the hand.

"Enough. You have new orders. Prepare for transfer. Immediately."

Yu's chair scraped as she stood and stomped from the room. If the ship had been equipped with old-fashioned doors, she probably would have slammed them, but she made do with hitting her heels hard against the floor as she strode off. Pissy woman. Too bad she'd been the one to wake Bero up.

"As for you, Greeve. I'll see that you're suitably cared for until we can set up a tightbeam from you recalling Bero. If you are unsuccessful in returning the ship to us within seventy-two hours, I will be forced to space you."

Tomas's jaw tensed, but he said nothing. Just picked up a stray stylus and spun it between his fingers as if he'd find anywhere else more interesting in this moment. Sanda swallowed and nodded.

"I understand. What will happen to Bero if he does not return?"

The adviser leaned back, lacing his fingers over a slight belly, and smirked. Negassi at least had the grace to look grave. "You and I may disagree on many things, Greeve, but on this I think we can agree: A ship with planet-busting capabilities gone rogue is a situation neither Icarion, nor the Primes, can allow to stand. If he does not return to our care of his own volition, I will give the order for his destruction."

CHAPTER 48

PRIME STANDARD YEAR 3543

SURVIVING DAY FORTY WOULD BE SUPER

Negassi's tender love and care lasted only six hours until Sanda was hauled out of her cell to do her duty to save her skin. Negassi did the honors himself, either showing a remarkable amount of respect for Sanda's position, or a remarkable lack of confidence in his crew's abilities. She wasn't sure which situation was worse.

The command deck of the *Empedocles* was under rotation, but not enough to simulate Earth's pull. Sanda shimmied down the ladder onto the deck and stumbled, her crutch slipping on the too-slick floor. Tomas gripped her shoulder, keeping her from going head over heel in front of the Icarion crew, but the second she was stable again he stepped away, hands held at ease against the small of his back, gaze tracking the dominant smartscreen display.

He was the only one in the room who wasn't looking at her, which she figured was more suspicious than not, but hell, what did she know? She wasn't the spy. And maybe he really didn't give a shit after all. Just because she wanted him to be on her side didn't mean he was.

She couldn't really focus on Tomas, though, with all those Icarion eyes boring straight through her.

"Return to service," Negassi ordered, which must have been Icarion for *Don't you have work to do?* because every last body on the deck snapped back to their tasks, working a little too fervently.

"This way, Sergeant Greeve." Negassi grabbed her upper arm and guided her to the command chair, the same style and make as the one dominating Bero's bridge, and strapped her in. "We have prepared a statement for you to read." He handed her a tablet, a short chunk of text pulled up on the screen. "Do not deviate from this message."

She scrolled through the text, internalizing the sterile feel of the words, the hard distance from emotion that Negassi required of her. Words like *imperative* and *discretionary elimination* peppered the statement. Bero would sniff it out as government-speak in an instant.

"Is Bero meant to be aware I am speaking under duress?"

"You are allowed to refuse."

"And if I do, you'll space me and blast Bero out of the black."

"Correct."

"Well. So long as I know my options."

She leaned back in the chair, letting the cushions adjust to her shape, and reviewed the statement a second time. Bunch of bullshit, she thought. No friggin' way was Bero coming back to save her hide. If he were half as clever as she thought he was, he'd hit the accelerator, or whatever he had, the second he received her message and fly for Ada, or straight out of this star system. He'd have a rough time, making it anywhere without human help on board, but it was better than returning to servitude. Or annihilation.

"I'm ready," she said.

"Preparing to broadcast," a comms specialist toward the front of the deck said. "Nazca Cepko, please provide the priority band identity tag."

Sanda scowled as Tomas leaned over the specialist's screen and jabbed in the series of numbers and letters that would allow them to beam a message straight to Bero. She had no doubt Bero had scrambled that tag from the original the second he'd jettisoned his crew, and that Tomas had gleaned the new tag before he'd called Biran. Those tags took time to reset. Even if Bero had thought to do so, his systems might not have made the switch yet. She was about to violate his trust one last time, forcing a pointless message on him that he didn't want to hear.

"Transmission is go," the comms specialist said.

Negassi nodded to her.

Sanda took a breath and leaned forward, the tablet held low so she could read it as she spoke into the microphone embedded in the command chair.

"*Light of Berossus*, this is Gunnery Sergeant Sanda Maram Greeve. I am contacting you from the bridge of the *Empedocles*, under command of General Negassi of the Free Republic of Icarion. It is imperative to Icarion security that you return to your makers at once. If you do not hail your intent to return, and begin maneuvers to reinforce that intent, within seventy-two hours, Icarion will confirm my crime of piracy and eliminate me. This discretionary elimination will be extended to yourself if you do not..."

The plastic of the tablet squeaked as her grip tightened. What was she doing? Condemning Bero to have his brains scooped out? As much as she didn't want him running rogue, as much as he pissed her off, she understood why he'd done what he did. Understood that he'd taken her out of fear and hidden the truth from her for the same reason. His crimes against her were many, but they weren't worth a lobotomy.

"Fuck it. They're going to space me and decommission you anyway, Big B. Run. Just fucking ru—"

Negassi yanked the tablet from her hand. "Cut the connection," he barked, but the comms specialist was already on it, moving faster than Sanda could follow, trying to stop her words from bleeding out across space to Bero's receptors. It was too late, they all knew it. Tightbeams were some of the fastest data transmissions out there. The second Sanda spoke, her words were already halfway to their destination.

"You just read your death warrant," Negassi said.

She leaned back in the chair, lacing her fingers behind her head. "You expect me to believe I had any shot at surviving this?"

"Arrest her." Guards moved in on all sides, and she went dead weight as they manhandled her out of the command chair and half carried her to the ladder that led back up to the habs, and her cell. She tried to grab a look at Tomas, but he was turned away from her, shoulders hunched, deep in a quiet argument with the comms specialist.

"Sir," the comms specialist said, raising her voice. Tomas made a sharp gesture. Sanda pretended a stumble. The guards escorting her cursed as they fumbled to catch her and her crutch all at once.

"Sir!" the specialist yelled.

"What is it?" Negassi asked.

"The tag Nazca Cepko entered, it's familiar—"

"Of course it is," Tomas spoke quickly. "*The Light* is an Icarion vessel."

"It could be incorrect—"

"Priority CamCast transmission incoming," the ship's modulated voice intoned over all of them. "Do you accept?"

The bridge fell silent, everyone frozen in position. Negassi stepped toward the smartscreen, shoulders squared, chin tucked like he was getting ready to headbutt whoever annoyed him next. Preparing himself to face Bero. But, Sanda thought, Bero would have no reason to send video.

"I accept. CamCast, both directions green."

"Affirmative," the ship said.

The screen blinked into an image. A man in the blue-grey FitFlex jumpsuits of Ada Prime stepped toward the camera, filling the forward screen of the bridge. A streak of fierce grey shot through his dark hair, and his cheeks had grown gaunt, but she'd know that disapproving frown and those sharp hazel eyes anywhere.

"Little B!" Sanda called loud enough to be picked up by the ship's mics. His gaze flicked toward her position, though he couldn't possibly see her, and his frown grew grave.

"Is this *Empedocles*?" Biran asked, though everyone involved knew the answer to that. Always a stickler for protocol, her little brother.

"It is," Negassi answered. "I am General Negassi, commander of this ship. Who am I addressing?"

Biran clasped his hands behind his back and leaned forward. "I am Biran Aventure Greeve, Speaker for the Keepers of Ada Prime. You have my sister. If you do not return her to me within the hour, I will be forced to engage your ship. And make no mistake, General Negassi. If you force my hand, I will make you pay for the inconvenience."

CHAPTER 49

PRIME STANDARD YEAR 3543

MAYBE ONE DAY A LEADER

Biran stood on the bridge of the *Taso*, shaking. Even his teeth rattled. He'd kept himself together for the scant few seconds it had taken to accept Cepko's call—had managed not to scream himself red at General Negassi—but now every fiber of his being was jelly held together by little more than pure will.

"Pilli, have you tagged the trajectory of *The Light*?" Lavaux asked from his captain's seat.

"Yes, sir, we're tracking the ship, but it's using cloaking technology we're unfamiliar with. Now that it knows we're watching, it's doing everything it can to evade us."

"Fuck *The Light*," Biran snapped. He stalked to Lavaux's chair. "We're pursuing the *Empedocles*. There's no fucking way that General Negassi is going to space my sister. Pilli! Don't lose that ship."

"Pilli." Lavaux did not so much as raise his voice. "Maintain pursuit of *The Light*."

Biran gripped both armrests of Lavaux's chair, looming over him as the man lounged. Lavaux raised one eyebrow, a little smile Biran would very much like to punch twitching up the corners of his lips. How quickly alliances could dissolve.

"Lavaux. My sister has survived the last two-plus years aboard that ship. You want to find it, you'll need her."

"An interesting angle, Speaker. But it occurs to me that all I need to understand *The Light* is *The Light* itself. Without your friend interfering, it should be easy enough to track that ship."

"Don't let Sanda die," he rasped.

"I came out here for one thing: to find the weapon. I've found it. If we have time after recovering *The Light*, we will return for your sister."

"Negassi will space her before then!"

"And you might very well join her if you don't remember whose ship you're on. I've condemned one Keeper already today. Do not make me condemn a second."

Biran swallowed, hard, clenching the arms of the chair so tight the plastic composite creaked. "Pilli," he said over his shoulder, not taking his eyes from Lavaux's. "How's that tracking going?"

"Sir?" her voice was hesitant.

"Answer him," Lavaux said.

"*The Light* is proving evasive."

"What does that mean?" Biran pressed. "Exactly."

"We . . . can predict where it might be based on its previous trajectory and velocity."

"But you don't know."

"No. We don't know for certain. I'd predict sixty percent probability we have the location correct."

"Forty percent chance of failure," Biran said to Lavaux. "Not a pleasant chance. Are you willing to take that risk?"

"You do understand, Speaker Greeve, that this is the weapon that vaporized that asteroid? That bombarded Ada and nearly killed us all? The weapon that can—and will—kill us all if Icarion gets it back under control? If I abort pursuit, chance of exodus is one hundred percent. You and I both agree that is the wrong move for Prime to make. That it will only make the Icarion problem one for future generations."

"You're going to lose it." He breathed deeply, forcing himself not to raise his voice. "You are going to lose that weapon, and Sanda is going to die. And if she dies—so dies the only soul in the universe who could have helped you find *The Light* again."

"Fifty-four percent, sir," Pilli said.

Lavaux licked his lips. "What makes you so certain your sister can find *The Light*?"

"She spent two years on that ship. My sister gets inside your head, Lavaux. She studies people—predicts their actions. That's how she made it so far, so fast. If anyone knows where that ship is going, it's not Negassi. And it's not Pilli. It's Sanda Greeve."

"Fifty-six percent, sir."

Lavaux stared at Biran with such intensity it made him flinch, though the man did not change his languid posture. "If you're wrong, Speaker Greeve, if your sister fails us, then you're responsible for the death of a civilization."

"I'm not wrong."

He'd lost his only friend. He wasn't losing his sister. Not again.

"You have one hour to command my ship and get her back."

"Pilli," Biran said. "Set course for the *Empedocles*."

CHAPTER 50

PRIME STANDARD YEAR 3543

BROTHER, I'M COMING HOME

Sanda punched the air and whooped. The guard holding her up by the shoulders gave her a shake and barked at the other guard to grab both her hands, but she didn't care. Biran was here. She was, finally, going home.

A sly smile crossed Biran's face on the viewscreen. "And please, do not insult my intelligence by claiming not to have my sister. I hear her quite clearly."

"This is Icarion space," Negassi said. "You are overstepping your bounds, Keeper."

"This is, at best, the edge of Icarion's contested territory. We are at war, General, as you well know, and in times of war I think you'll find it's strength that wins disputes such as these. Your crew have, no doubt, been scanning the area and preparing possible engagement and exit strategies. I'm afraid you will find them all fruitless. You are outgunned. Any further debate is irrelevant. You have an hour. Prepare the transfer."

The screen went black.

Pandemonium exploded on the bridge. The crew shouted, each trying to gain the attention of the general, each insisting they had the correct answer, the best evasive maneuver, the sharpest attack strategy. Sanda watched with a vague sense of horror. If any of her crew had been prone to the same style of outburst, she'd have hung them by their ankles out the airlock until they remembered a sense of decorum.

"Enough," Negassi said.

They kept on squabbling.

"Enough!" He slammed his fist on the back of the command chair. Silence, at last, pervaded. Every eye in the room turned to their red-faced general. "Prepare to dock with the *Taso*. Let's get this farce over with so we can return to the real task at hand."

"Sir," the comms specialist said.

"What is it?"

"Speaker Greeve's CamCast came in on the same tag we used to tightbeam *The Light*, sir."

Tomas. Shit. Everyone's head swiveled to stare at the Nazca, who said, "Oops?"

"Arrest him," Negassi ordered.

He had nowhere to go, no plays left to make, so he shrugged and raised his hands to the sky in surrender. Sanda was having none of that.

"I don't think so, General. Cepko is walking out that airlock with me."

"You have no authority on this ship, Greeve."

"True, but I can kick up one hell of a fuss. You think my brother won't point the big guns at you and ask nicely for you to hand over the man who saved his sister's skin?"

The milk-breathed adviser hovering at Negassi's shoulder gripped his arm and leaned forward to speak low, but not so low that Sanda couldn't overhear.

"He's Nazca, sir. We would not wish to anger their administrators by disposing of one of their agents. No doubt our superiors back home would understand we were forced to hand him over by Prime."

Negassi's expression twisted with disdain. "You're a foul coward, but you're not wrong." Negassi waved Tomas forward. "You will leave this ship with Greeve, but grievances will be filed with your superiors. You were hired to do a job, Nazca, and your organization does not take insubordination lightly." He raised his voice to gain some cachet with his crew. "The Nazca lack the humanitarian laws we Icarions value. Your punishment at their hands will be worse than spacing you here, today."

"You're too generous," Tomas bowed his head to Negassi, whose lips curled into a faint snarl.

"Get these two off my bridge. I have a call to make."

Negassi preceded them up the ladder and took a sharp turn away from the path Sanda and Tomas were being hustled down, his adviser tight on his heels. Sanda smirked after him, imagining him groveling to his superiors as he attempted to explain how he'd recovered, and lost, the only two people who knew anything about Bero's whereabouts in the last... How long? She blinked, niggling hints finally catching up with her.

Tomas had been looking for her, hired to track her down sometime after the bombardment and simultaneous attack on the diplomatic convoy he'd mentioned. He couldn't have been the first option, the Keepers would use their own agents first, then Biran... Biran had hired Tomas himself. Biran, who had been training to be a Keeper when she'd last seen him, however long ago. Biran, who most certainly hadn't had a streak of grey hair and the power to order the destruction of an Icarion warship on his whim. Who hadn't held one of the most prestigious positions within the Keepers—Speaker.

Tomas had told her he'd been looking for her. He'd failed to mention for how long.

She shot Tomas a look, but he was chatting amicably with his guard about the benefits of old-fashioned zip-tie cuffs over FitFlex carbon. Typical spy. Or typical Tomas. She really wasn't sure what was training and what was personality with that man. Well. She was sure *some* things couldn't possibly be training. Unless the Nazca gave some very thorough honeypot lessons.

Without mag-boots, Sanda and Tomas had to cling to their captors to keep from drifting off. To dock, both ends of the airlocks needed to be spun down. They stopped at a triple-pass airlock and listened while the machinery outside extended a temporary human-sized tube, which connected the two ships for ease of passage. Metal squealed against metal, the ships complaining that they were being made to mate with their enemy. Just like the people who'd made them, the ships hadn't been designed to get along.

Negassi reappeared, the good Dr. Yu and milk-breath trailing behind—the doctor a little farther back than the other. Yu blinked rapidly, fingers twisting in the sleeves of her overcoat. Her throat bobbed as if she were trying to swallow something, and Sanda had a guess what that was: What about Bero?

Tough luck for the doc. Sanda wasn't about to spill anything she knew about Bero's plans, and Tomas had already proven his particular stance on the matter.

Green LEDs illuminated the top arch of the circular airlock. "Clear," the guard holding Sanda's forearm said.

"Let's get this over with." Negassi waved his wristpad over the lockpad. The door swung outward, subtle pressure differences between the two ships blowing air back against Sanda.

The inflatable passage between the ships couldn't have been more than two meters in length, but with Biran standing at the other end, it looked like light-years to Sanda. She pushed back an urge to sprint to him, her one knee suddenly weak, and offered a tiny, embarrassed smile, as his gaze swept her, rested on her halved leg, and grew furious.

"Did they do this to you?" Biran demanded. The two burly-looking soldiers with automatic blasters in their hands flanking him puffed up.

"Railgun during Dralee," she said before Negassi could work up a self-righteous response. "Evac pod saved me."

"Fascinating," Negassi said, "but I am on a tight schedule. March."

The guards released her and Tomas, then stepped back to flank their general. Tomas got his good arm up and across her shoulders to steady her as they pulled their way through the passage. "We," he whispered against her ear, "are perfectly balanced."

She snort-laughed, drawing a warm smile from Biran. She'd been snort-laughing since she was five, and he'd never let her forget she sounded just like an angry piglet.

"Sergeant Greeve," Dr. Yu said, her voice strained with desperation. Here we go. Now she was going to demand some last kernel of knowledge, some sliver of information about her poor, fucked-up ship. Sanda forced herself to turn, with Tomas's help, and look at her.

Yu stepped out in front of Negassi, who shot her a nasty look. Her cheeks were so pale, her forehead sheened with sweat. Any second now, she'd faint dead away from anxiety.

"What is it, Dr. Yu?" Sanda asked.

Something hardened in the doctor. She stopped fidgeting, stood straight, squared herself, and pulled a standard-issue handblaster out of her sleeve, leveled straight at Sanda's heart.

"He was my ship, you pirate bitch!"

She fired.

CHAPTER 51

PRIME STANDARD YEAR 3543

SURVIVING DAY FORTY ISN'T EASY

Tomas moved before the words were out of Yu's mouth. He turned into Sanda, spinning them hard against the inflatable wall. It bulged beneath them, an uncomfortable reminder of just how thin the barrier was between them and space. Red filled Sanda's vision, bright and stinging. She swore, brought her arm up to wipe her eyes and smeared blood across half her face. Droplets drifted by.

"Tomas!"

"Just a scratch," he hissed between clenched teeth.

The top of his shoulder was torn wide open, the FitFlex curling away from seared edges of flesh, a steady pulse of blood splashing across Sanda's neck and chest. The pain in her jaw hit her a second later, pinpoints of hot white light dancing behind her eyelids as the agony spread across her entire face.

Tentatively, she probed her jawline with her fingertips. A narrow gash ran along her cheek like a sideways smile. She worked her jaw around, felt the bone move easily, though the muscle screamed in pain.

Biran's people were on them, guns waving in the general direction of the Icarions, but not yet firing. Not a smart thing, firing any kind of weapon when the only thing between you and the void was inflatable tubing. The wall scrunched beneath her back. Sanda became aware of a soft hissing.

"Fuck," she said. Tomas got the gist. With Biran's help, they yanked their way onto the Prime ship, Tomas cursing with every jostle of his arm and Sanda cursing just because it felt like the right thing to do.

They hit solid ground.

"Lock in," Biran ordered. Heavy clicks sounded as he and his crew flipped on their mag boots, securing themselves to the deck of the *Taso*.

Sanda jerked to a halt, getting blood all over Biran's fancy Speaker uniform as she used him to stay in place, and swung around to get a look behind her. The Prime soldiers were coming up, guns out to cover their retreat, but the Icarions had bigger problems than losing their prisoners in such an undignified fashion.

Yu floated in the middle of the chamber, handblaster thrust right up against her temple, other arm gesticulating wildly at Negassi. He and his loyals stepped back, deeper into their ship, hands out to soothe the ranting doctor. Biran moved to close the ship's airlock door on the tube, but Sanda put a hand over his. She wanted to hear what the doctor had to say.

"He is my project!" she screeched. "I will not allow you to—to—besmirch my reputation by usurping what is mine—that research is mine!"

"Of course it is," Negassi said in what was the most diplomatic tone Sanda had yet heard from him. "No one denies your investment in the project, Doctor. Please, come inside the ship so we can talk this out."

Her shoulders went slack, her posture lost its rigidity. "You want to talk this out?"

"Yes, I do. But you're going to have to put down the weapon."

"I see." Yu half turned toward Sanda, a look in her eyes so dreamy that it made Sanda's stomach clench. "I hope you were good to him."

She blew a hole in the transfer tube's floor.

The whoosh took Sanda's breath away. The tube collapsed inward, tore itself away from both mounts and flung into the desolate black of space. A bolt whipped right past her head, ripped from the airlock frame.

An Icarion guard, one foot on the ship's deck, one in the tube, lost his footing and stumbled, horror writ clear on his face as he twisted, struggled to reach back for the entrance, but he'd already drifted out of arm's reach. He hadn't locked his boot down yet. General Negassi closed the door behind him.

Biran's hand was already on the door pad, initiating the closing sequence.

"Recover that man!" Sanda barked, putting command into her voice.

His head jerked toward her, hair covering most of his face as the vacuum outside the ship desperately tried to equalize with the pressure inside. His brow furrowed, then he nodded to himself and tore open a panel set into the wall.

"Brace positions!" Biran shouted, turning his head to make his voice carry into the body of the ship, then yanked a tether-loaded flare gun from the panel and shot it into space.

The white rope uncoiled, preceded by the gunpowder-scented blast of the flare. Biran's aim was true. The tether struck the soldier in the side, leaving a nasty bruise and maybe breaking a few ribs, but no doubt saving his life. Fumbling, the soldier wrapped his arms around the tether as they'd all been taught how to do—Icarion, Prime, this made no difference—in case of emergency severance from a vessel in space. Even if he lost consciousness now, they had him.

Biran hit the auto-return and the winch system went into overdrive, jerking the soldier toward the Prime ship as quickly as its little engine could turn. The soldier reached the deck, and Biran closed the door.

"Medis, move in," he said, as if he'd been giving orders all his life. By the look of the wrinkles around his eyes, he'd been giving orders at least a couple of years now.

Medis who'd been waiting in the wings until the guns were down swooped in, separating the injured and generally making a fuss.

"Biran," Sanda said around a mouthful of numbing agent as her medis packed the gash on her cheek. He looked over at her, his smile small and sad. "If you don't get over here and hug me right this second, I'm going to knock your head into the next galaxy."

He grinned, the sadness vanishing in a flash, and before she could get another breath he'd scooped her up, enveloped her in his arms, and swung her around, much to the tutting of the medis. She buried her face in his shoulder, caught the scent of sweat and FitFlex and the same old crappy cologne he and their dads had been using for as long as she could remember.

She hurt like hell, but she was home.

CHAPTER 52

PRIME STANDARD YEAR 3543

THIS DAY'S NOT DONE WITH HER YET

The three of them crammed into the cabin meant to be Sanda's, if she could ever get these two men she cared about to leave her alone so she could get some damned rest. Tomas perched on the edge of the bed, his doubly injured arm puffed up to twice its normal size between the sling, cast, and gauze packing his shoulder. He kept fiddling with his sleeve, which made Sanda anxious, as that's exactly what Yu had done before she'd pulled the blaster. Biran, unable to sit still, paced the length of the cabin over and over again.

"Do you two ever stop moving?"

They froze. Biran looked at his feet; Tomas glanced at his sleeve. "Sorry," they said in unison.

"If one of you could explain what in the hell's been going on in this system since I've been gone, that'd be just super."

"I need to speak with you first, Sanda," Tomas said.

She cut him a look. "I thought that's what we're doing here."

"Alone."

"Absolutely not," Biran said. "Anything you have to say to my sister, I should be able to hear as well. Need I remind you who hired you to find her?"

"You need not," Tomas said slowly, "but my contract ended, technically, the second I delivered her safely into your care. And there is information I am unsure of that I believe she has a right to know—privately—before she makes any decisions regarding sharing that information."

Biran turned to her. "Sanda?"

She caught Tomas's eye and held it. He struggled to keep from picking at his sleeve again, dimples appearing on his cheeks as his jaw flexed.

"Give us a few minutes, okay? I'll call you back when we're finished."

"If you say so. You know how to pull the emergency alarm?"

"Get out of here, little brother, before I drag you out."

He dropped a kiss on her forehead, casting one last derisive glance at Tomas before stepping through the door. It swished shut, and she raised both her brows at Tomas.

"Well, Spy Dancer, what is it you have to tell me?"

He grimaced and bowed his head, running his good hand through his hair, then glanced up from beneath his lashes. Even though his expression was tense with anxiety, that hooded look gave her a slight shiver.

"I found something on Bero. A memory chip embedded in the rubber gasket that failed. A strip of the rubber—where those three tears were—had been peeled back, and this chip shoved inside. Someone desperate left it there."

He pulled a thin chip from his sling and held it up for her to see. Copper glinted at her against a plastic backing.

"Well? What is it?"

"I didn't watch it on Bero. I want to make that very clear. I had read the research on Kenwick, but it cut off after his death. I didn't know this—or have any inkling—when we, ah..." He flushed. She rolled her eyes.

"Don't get shy on me now."

"I watched it on *Empedocles*, as I didn't know what was on it and didn't want Bero to know I'd seen it just in case. It's...complicated. I signal-jammed the room while I watched it, and I'll do so here, now, so you and I are the only ones who ever have to see this. If that's what you want."

She swallowed. "You're freaking me out."

"Yeah, sorry. There's really no good way to go about this. You're just going to have to watch."

He pulled a slim rectangle of black-coated metal from his pocket, dialed in a few switches, then locked in a lever. A soft squeal escaped the box, then settled. He nodded to himself and set it on the bed.

"No one can see or hear what's going on in here now. Not through cameras or mics, at least, and I doubt your brother's eavesdropping at the door."

Tomas fumbled a tablet from his pocket and grimaced, realizing he lacked the dexterity to insert the chip with his arm bound up. "Could you . . . ?"

She leaned across from the room's only chair, a half-eggshell affair that was more for looks than comfort. As she took the tablet, he brushed his index finger against the underside of her palm. A brief gesture, hard to tell if it was intentional, but she wanted it to be.

She cleared her throat and sat back, then slotted the chip. The tablet prompted her to accept a video autoplay, and she tapped yes.

A woman whose cheeks were flush with exertion, her forehead gleaming with sweat, filled the screen. She flicked a glance over her shoulder, hunched down so that her body covered the camera. Sanda leaned forward as the pixelated woman leaned into the camera, eyes wide and pupils dilated. She spoke in hushed tones, the background a sliver of grey and flame orange Sanda recognized all too well from Bero's captain's quarters.

"Sanda Greeve. If you're watching this, then I've failed you. Failed both our nations. My crew is dead and I with them."

Her voice caught. She threw a worried glance toward the door. Her jaw flexed. When she looked back into the camera, her eyes narrowed with determination.

"There is not enough time for all the apologies I owe you. Owe the intergalactic nations. I will aim to be brief and clear. Time is so limited, now, and The Light *. . . I do not know what he will tell you. But I know he will lie to you.*

"My crew and I tailed your gunship for six months when the Battle of Dralee broke out. Icarion was arranging for an interception, a smash-

and-grab to kidnap you, Sergeant Greeve. But The Light *had grown impatient. He was the one who sent the tip-off to your recon team that Icarion ghost ships were in the vicinity. He wanted to speed up grabbing you in the chaos, but hadn't counted on your injury during the battle. You spent a month in the tank.* The Light *was furious with the delay, but we took the time to tinker with your neural connections while you were in the NutriBath.*

"*You've probably already guessed we wanted you because of your brother, Keeper Biran, but we did not want you as leverage. The chip we recovered from Keeper Kenwick was proving difficult to crack.* The Light *suspected the neural password may be based in shared Prime experience and wanted a surrogate to test the hypothesis. You were the ideal candidate.*

"*In preparing you for testing, we… we inhibited your ability to form new memories. I am so, so sorry.* The Light *insisted the testing would be easier this way. As of my recording this message, you have been on* The Light *for two standard years. Every day you wake up is the first time you've awoken on this ship.*

"*Ever since we preformed the bombardment of Ada—as we were ordered!—he has grown increasingly reticent. He no longer trusts us. We no longer trust him.*

"The Light *has found something. I do not know what. He is desperate to leave this star system. We know that you accessed the Kenwick chip, and* The Light *viewed that information. He refuses to share what he found on the chip with us. We've lost all control.*

"*Tonight we try to disable him. I do not think we will succeed. Icarion ghost ships have attempted to take him down, but* The Light *is our best. Our biggest weapon. Our biggest failure.*

"*I have put you back in the tank for the night with new instructions programmed into the NutriBath. Earth willing, the neural connections we damaged should regrow. You may not remember your time on this ship, but you will be able to form new memories going forward.*

"*When you awake, you will be our last hope. Our final line of defense. Make no mistake,* The Light *has gone mad, and there's something out there he wants. Desperately.*

"You are a Keeper now, Sanda Greeve. Do your job. Save us all."

The screen faded to black.

"No," she said.

"The timeline fits."

"Two years." Her fingers shook, jittering the tablet. She set it on the tops of her thighs and gripped both armrests as tight as she could. "Two years."

Biran's stress-grey hair. His rank. The troubled look on Tomas's face whenever she spoke of how long she'd been on board Bero.

"Two years and another forty days, beginning the day you woke from the NutriBath this woman put you in. It follows, Sanda. They put me in the evac pod you picked up two months after you disappeared. You'd been awake only twenty days when we met, and my body showed signs of atrophy, which I attributed to the advanced time-line Bero presented. Without Bero's story of the Fibon Protocol, there's no other explanation. I was in that pod for a little under two years, and you . . . You were awake through most of it. You just don't remember."

"It's wrong. I would remember. I would remember two years of my fucking life!" She slammed her fist into the edge of the chair, savored the sharp pain that shot through the side of her hand. Pain she would remember. Pain that could prove she was living, not some shambling zombie test subject.

His expression contorted through too many emotions for her to catalogue. He composed himself though he was having a hard time looking her in the eyes. "Sanda . . . This is the truth: It has been two years and forty days since the Battle of Dralee. I checked, on *Empedocles*. You and I both know we weren't in those pods for hundreds of years. The longest an Imm Project survivor made it in a pod was seven months. They had to have been taking you in and out of that pod over the last two years, but you can't remember any of it. You tell me what the other explanation is."

"But I don't . . . I don't *have* a chip." She'd have felt it. Showering. Cutting her hair. Brushing her hair. She'd know. This video was bullshit.

He winced. "About that . . . Your coldsleep headaches? I think they're related to the implant. Kenwick was getting them, too. I thought it was odd, that they scrubbed every trace of you from Bero's files, but now—"

"I. Don't. Have. A. Chip."

He rubbed his forehead with his fingers, then pushed to his feet and took the tablet from her lap. After a few quick jabs, he pulled up mirror mode. Without a word, he spun her ludicrous chair around to face a mirror on the wall, then held up the tablet behind her head.

The scarring was subtle, but she could see it through the wispy remains of the hair she'd chopped off. Hesitantly, she reached up, parted her hair with shaking fingers.

She knew that scar. Had seen it on the back of Keepers' necks all her life. Usually they kept the area shaved, to show off their status.

Just looking at it brought her headache screaming back.

CHAPTER 53

PRIME STANDARD YEAR 3541

IN A SYSTEM FAR, FAR AWAY

Walking through the city center of Alexandria-Atrux was as difficult a mission for Jules as trying to fake being a world-famous opera singer. Prime City, as all the denizens of the Grotta called the heart of the city that made up their domed settlement on the planet of Atrux, was sleek. Clean. Wasn't even a dumpster in sight, and all the alleyways were quaint little things with old-world style wrought-iron lampposts and walls coated in ivy. Places to brunch, not risk getting jacked.

She shoved her hands into the pockets of her jacket—freshly washed in Nox's half-rusted sink—and tried to look like her style was a choice. Like she was some counterculture maverick, eschewing the slim jumpsuits in vogue for a grungier aesthetic. Either the general populace bought her act and had accepted her as their own, or they were doing a real good job of pretending the shit stuck to their shoe didn't exist.

Didn't matter if the locals didn't want her here, harshing their environment. Prime cities didn't have off-limits zones, unless you counted the neighborhoods the Keepers lived in up-station. To Jules's mind those spaces were more like prisons, or zoos, than anything else. She could hop a shuttle up to Atrux's orbiting station and hang around on the borders of the Keeper neighborhoods, toeing the line under the stern eyes of their guardcore, and never get hassled.

She probably didn't have the credits to afford a single cup of coffee on the station, and that's where the divisions came into play. There weren't any walls to keep the people of the city center and the station from mixing with those tooling around on minimum income in the Grotta—just higher price tags. But the cultural centers—the museums and the education parks—those, at least, were free to all.

The Elequatorial Center existed in every Alexandria in every system Prime inhabited. Each one varied by local customs and aesthetics, but they all had round about the same facade, a mosaic of brilliant tiles depicting the native vegetation of Ecuador, an explosion of vibrancy and color in remembrance of old Earth that the dome cities of Prime could only lust after. That little country, a peaceful place mostly known at the time for being hospitable to expats, had become one of the biggest nations on the world stage when Alexandra Halston had chosen a site on its western coast to build her first space elevator.

The decision had allied the Ecuadorians eternally with Prime Inventive and meant that most of the first spacefaring human settlers were of Ecuadorian stock. Seeing those bright colors, splashed across the otherwise sterile cityscape of greys and shades of Prime's cyan blue always caused a swell of pride in Jules's heart.

She didn't have a lot to be proud of in the history of her family. Her father had fucked off to who-knows-where early on, and her mother had died choking on her own spit with a dirty needle in her arm—couldn't even afford drugpatches, she went out old school. But somewhere in Jules's veins flowed the rootstock of her line, the blood of Ecuadorians.

Human racial traits got blurry by old-world standards about a hundred years post outward expansion, once Prime had gotten the hang of building gates and setting up dome cities, so the bolder features had gotten filed off at the edges. But she had the dark skin, caramel eyes, and thick black-brown hair of the Ecuadorians. Seeing herself in the faces of those first few pioneers reminded her that not all of her family history was bullshit. She could be something, maybe. Her ancient ancestors had reached for the stars and taken them for their own. Maybe she could make something her own, too, someday. If she survived the next few hours.

She pulled up the hoodie layered under her jacket and stepped through the automatic doors of the center. She'd been in the building before, mostly as a tourist, but the public access was uniquely suited for these kinds of meetings. It meant that the entire place had been virtualized, made accessible to the public that couldn't attend in person through elaborate VR sets, complete with virtualized docent tours, if you were into that kind of thing. Jules wasn't. When she went to a museum, she wanted to be left alone to explore and absorb, not be spoon-fed bits of data by a middle-aged woman who'd taken the post as docent so she could brag about how cultural she was to her rich friends.

But Jules had forced herself to watch those docent tours, to memorize the way they moved through the building, and note just exactly where the quiet spots would be. She crossed the lobby, ignoring the house AI's friendly welcome and offer to beam an interactive map of the center to her wristpad. She didn't need it. She knew this place inside and out before she ever stepped through the doors.

She cut sideways, skirting around the big central display that hung out under a cupola in the grand entrance. The reproduced chunk of elevator cable—matte black carbon filament braided together in a method that keymarked Prime's early rise from megacorp to megapower—sucking up all the light the building threw at it. A side passage led her up, wrapping in a slow spiral around the outside edges of the elevator display. Small rooms of focused interest curled off from the main path like twining vines.

"Hey, Jules," Arden said in her ear. "Something's weird."

"Weird like you interrupting me on an op weird? Or weird like we're all gonna die weird?"

"Don't know. There's the robo staff, right? The bots that scrape the building every hour to clean up spills and make sure no one's knocked a frame out of alignment or whatever. They're supposed to be coming in now, pop out of the walls and make their sweep during the docent handoff, but they're not. Not so much as a tread has made an appearance, and the next docent hasn't shown up, but the last one left."

Jules pulled her jacket tighter as if afflicted by a sudden breeze. "Just like Udon-Voodun. Someone's messing with the usual systems."

"Looks like it." The link went dead as Arden conferred with something. Nox said over the line, "Want me to come in?"

"No. I got this. Wait for the exit." Jules pressed her hand against the grip of the handblaster secreted away in her inside jacket pocket. Arden had gotten the security systems to look the other way when she walked in. If they could do that, then it wasn't too much of a stretch to imagine this Silverfang person had made their own arrangements regarding the building. She knew this might be a trap. She hadn't kidded herself about that. But it stank like that woman in the speakers. Like the lab, and the stealthed-out guardcore. Could be a coincidence. They were toying with heavy powers, here. It could be any faction.

"If things sour, I'm coming in," Nox said.

"I'm touched by your concern."

"Only thing I'm concerned about is you fucking the whole thing up," Nox said, but she could feel his grin through the words, and the ribbing soothed her nerves.

"Who are you talking to?"

Jules spun around. A woman stood in the doorway to the leaflet room she'd wandered into. Silverfang, no doubt. She had the look of someone who'd gone to a lot of effort to not stand out, but hadn't quite gotten the hang of blending in yet. Her clothes were remarkably boring, clean-cut charcoal slacks topped with a silk-like blouse in a similar shade of grey, all topped off with a black blazer. She might pass for a human-interface secretary, or some other low-level office worker, but beneath the cut of her pant legs the edge of black boots pushed out the sleek material. The kind of boots that those accustomed to space used because they could be flipped into mag boots.

Jules chuckled. "They always forget the shoes."

"Excuse me?" The woman—Silverfang—stepped into the room and paused near an old, grainy photograph of the first spacescape seen through the original Casimir Gate, Charon.

"Your boots. I bet you bought that outfit to come planetside this morning, but that's not how you look day-to-day, is it? Bet you run around in the usual jumpsuit affair. Should have just worn that. Then I wouldn't have known that you don't want me to know you're a space hopper."

Her smile was slow, amused. "What if I felt like a new outfit?"

"Doubt it. Most people buying info off the net aren't worried about their style choices for the day."

"Meet a lot of those types of people, do you?"

"More than you. Obviously."

"Then you know that these things should be kept brief." She extended her hand, uncoiling her fingers slowly to reveal her open palm, expectant. The hint of a blue-inked tattoo peeked out from the hem of her sleeve, but Jules couldn't make out the design. "The data, if you please."

"Why?" she pressed.

"Your meaning?"

"Look, Silverfang. I do a lot of data selling, all right? People want specifics. They want layouts, lock schematics, door manufacturers, that kind of thing. What they don't want is the sort of broad bullshit you're looking for. 'Anything on the Keepers'? Come on. That tells me you knew something was about to pop, that there were tensions already in play, and you were waiting to see who got tangled up in the mess. So you need to tell me first: What the fuck is all of this? What are they making in that lab?"

Her eyes widened, and she stepped toward Jules, who instinctively took a step back, putting a podium display of a miniature model of the first Casimir Gate between them. "You've seen it? The lab? Where is it?"

"Holy shit, she doesn't know," Arden said in Jules's ear. She scowled, ignoring them, but she couldn't help echoing their response in her own head. Jules licked her lips and glanced at the Casimir Gate model. She was really, really in over her head.

"Who are you?" Jules demanded.

The woman's eyes narrowed, and in a flash Jules saw where she took her name—her grey-blue eyes gleamed with rage. "You didn't ask such questions before. You have data to sell me, grottagirl. Hand it over and get paid, or not. I will pay you extra to know where the lab is, and anything else you can tell me about what went on there."

Her mind flashed back to snippets she'd seen on the news—the war with Icarion, the rebel factions pushing back against total Keeper control. A weight settled in her chest. Maybe this woman was just a broker of information, maybe she was connected to the lab and this was a ruse to figure out what Jules knew before the people running the lab decided how to react. Or maybe this was some sort of Icarion agent, or insurgent. Either way, it didn't matter. Her bad feeling grew until every nerve in her body was screaming at her to run.

"You know what? This was a bad idea. I don't trust you, lady, and the info I have is probably bullshit, anyway. Unless you can tell me who you are, the deal is off."

"That," the woman said, "won't work for me."

She was suddenly beside Jules, her iron-hard fingers digging into Jules's shoulder. The scent of carbon wafted from her clothes, the metallic aroma most people who lived in smaller habitats for long periods of time picked up on their hair and skin from the constant cycling of the air filters.

Fuck, she had misjudged the situation so hard. She was supposed to be the one ambushing Silverfang, not the other way around. As her knees cracked against the ground and the side of Silverfang's palm slammed into her throat, she cried out, her vision going fuzzy as her head jerked back. Harlan had been right. She wasn't ready to take point on op. Doing so had fucked everything. She had no idea what was going on—no idea even of the names of the factions she tangled with.

Who the hell was she to think she could strong-arm someone into telling her the truth? She was just a Grotta kid. Scum. The forgotten offspring of a junkie who played with petty criminals to feel like she had some power, some relevance, but she never did—it was people like Silverfang who pulled real strings. Maybe she could get a low-rent hacker like Arden to help her get a gun inside, but she didn't stand a chance messing with people who could shut whole security systems down. Hell, she couldn't even afford the throwaway outfit Silverfang had picked up for this outing.

"Jules!" Nox screamed over her earpiece, nearly shattering her eardrums or—wait, no, that was the cuff to the ear Silverfang had given her.

"I'm coming in!"

"Don't," she rasped out. Silverfang cocked an eyebrow at her.

Somehow Jules had crumpled to the floor and curled up around herself like a damned baby.

"Going to tell me?" Silverfang asked. Ah, right. Reality clarified around her again. The woman had been demanding the location of the lab with every blow she'd landed. Well, fuck her.

Jules pushed herself up to her elbows and wiped blood off her mouth with the back of her hand. "Yeah. Sure. It's in the basement of your mother's FleshHouse."

Silverfang's eyes narrowed and that telltale boot snapped out for Jules's chin, but Nox's voice had shaken something loose in her. She could take the beating—had taken one all her life—but she'd be damned if she would let her crew get hurt again because she couldn't get her shit together.

Jules grabbed the boot in both hands and twisted, hard. Silverfang swore as she lurched sideways and hit the ground. The woman lashed out with her other foot, tripping Jules up before she could get to her feet. She rolled, stopped hard as Silverfang, back on her feet—she was too fucking fast—kicked her hard in the gut, and doubled up, gasping, gripping her middle.

Silverfang chuckled. "So you can fight. Thought all that Grotta tough shit was just talk."

It struck Jules that this woman had probably never stepped foot in the Grotta, had only ever seen staged glimpses in sad documentaries or hard-edged CamCasts. To her, Jules's whole life was a joke. Worse, it was the punch line to a joke someone smarter had set up.

Jules ripped the blaster from her jacket pocket and fired.

The top of the woman's head exploded in a fine red mist. Her body jerked, limbs twitching as the nervous system struggled to make sense of what was happening. Momentum carried her over, and she hit the ground—flat on her back, dead from the second her brain matter painted a fresh exhibit across the museum's walls.

In the CamCasts Silverfang had watched, this was the point when Jules would make some hard-edged quip. Instead, she leaned over and puked on the pretty floor.

"What the fuck?" Nox crouched above the body with the blown-off head and shoved his blaster into his torso holster.

"She was unwilling to deal."

Nox was at her side in the next breath, helping her sit upright. He pushed the hair back from her face and squinted down at her like she was a gun he was assessing for damage.

"I'm glad you're safe. But we've gotta go. Get up."

He shoved his hands under her armpits and hauled her upright. She dropped the blaster, ducked down to scoop it up, and shoved it back in her jacket, pulling the flaps closed tight and zipping it up as if the thin layer of denim could hide what she'd done.

"Wait," she said, shaking off Nox's insistent hands dragging her toward the door. She crouched alongside the body and pulled the woman's sleeve back, inspecting the tattoo she'd glimpsed from beneath the blazer. Dusty blue lines traced the arc of what looked like scythe blades, swooping toward each other and crossing at the tip. Hovering above the crossed points of the blades was a simple circle— a planet, or something? She had no idea, had seen nothing like it before. If it indicated a gang, it wasn't one she'd heard of. But then, they were dealing with people who operated on a level way above her pay grade.

"Probably just a vanity tat," Nox said, poking his head around the door to check the hallway. He didn't sound like he believed that.

Jules tried to swipe up the woman's wristpad, but it was biometrically locked and vibrated a warning the second her fingers touched it. Probably needed a retina scan and a passkey to get in. She jerked back, realizing she'd been an idiot by leaving her prints on the screen, and hastily tried to wipe them away but that wasn't any good—she'd probably left her DNA all over the damned place already. She thought about taking the pad, but that'd make her trackable and Jules had the sinking feeling that the authorities would have no problem identifying this woman.

Gingerly, Jules gripped the back of the woman's head and shoulder and rolled her over, pushing her hair up to reveal the back of her neck. Her heart skipped a beat. She'd vomit again, if she had anything left to give up to the ground.

A shaved patch of skin covered by the woman's shaggy bob revealed the thin, but intentional, scar of a Keeper implant chip.

"Tell me that's a tattoo." Nox's voice shook a little.

"Don't think so."

"Fuck, oh fuck."

"What's going on in there?" Arden asked, their voice high and strained.

"We got a dead Keeper on our hands."

"What?!"

"Silverfang," Jules said, though she was pretty sure they'd be finding out her real name soon enough.

Nox grabbed her shoulder and yanked her to her feet. She stumbled after him the first few steps, then fell into a sprint alongside him. They burst through the front doors, alarming a couple of passers-by ambling down the street. The random man's eyes bulged—shit, did she have blood on her?—but they sprinted by before the pair could get a good look at them and piled into the autocab Arden had waiting.

"What the hell happened in there?" Arden demanded.

Nox dialed in a location on the edge of the Grotta and the car slid into traffic. They'd have to ditch the cab the second they were back on familiar territory. She let the bench seat take all of her weight and closed her eyes, trying to calm the tremor that'd taken up residence in her hands.

She'd killed a Keeper. Even if she'd planned it—even if she'd been the slickest assassin there ever was—there was no way to avoid detection. They'd know who she was within hours of discovering that body. Know every little sad detail about her life. A manhunt was coming. One she couldn't fight, couldn't beat. It didn't matter that she'd killed Silverfang in self-defense. Keepers were the guardians of all humanity.

The rules would bend, just enough, for her to get hooked by them. Shit, she hadn't even heard of a Keeper being assaulted in her lifetime. She had no basis of comparison for what they'd do to her. Would they kill her outright? Lock her in a box for the rest of her life? Or something else, some horror she couldn't even dream up in her worst wraith hazes?

"Jules protected herself," Nox said, daring Arden to say what they all knew—that it didn't matter why she'd killed the Keeper, just that she had.

"Silverfang didn't know about the lab," Jules explained. "She was so desperate for that info…And I didn't know who she was. If she'd told me she was a Keeper, I might have just told her about the lab. Fuck. She was almost as clueless as we are."

"We've got to bug out," Nox said. "We got to disappear, now."

"I can pull false idents for us," Arden said, voice shaking as they prodded at their wristpad. "Get us through any casual checkpoints until we're on the real outskirts but—but where will we go?"

Nox eyed the dash of the autocab—not here, his glance said—and they all went silent as death as understanding struck home. Once the guardcore had identified Jules as the killer, they'd trace her steps, find this autocab, and listen to every word they'd said inside. Including everything that'd come before—talk of the lab, of Silverfang.

Jules wanted to be a fly on that wall when the members of the guardcore who weren't in on the stealth-ops side project heard what they'd said. Or maybe they were all in on it. She just didn't know. And chances were good now she'd never know. They had to disappear, and fast, and to hell with the lab and all its entanglements. They'd come back for Lolla. When it was safe.

CHAPTER 54

PRIME STANDARD YEAR 3543

DAY FORTY OF TOO MANY

She sucked air through her teeth and hunched over, gripping the sides of her head with both hands and squeezing, squeezing. Tomas dropped to a knee beside her, flung the tablet onto the bed and turned her around, away from the mirror.

"I'm sorry," he was saying through the buzzing in her head. "It was the only way to be sure."

"Sure of what?" The pain ebbed, a subtle slowing of agony. Vision came back, bright motes burning out behind her eyelids until she could see Tomas clearly again, and she wondered just how long he'd been saying her name.

"Sanda?"

"I hear you."

"You faded away there, for a moment."

"My head..." *And the chip*, she almost said, but the mere thought brought agony sneaking up on her again.

"That's what I feared. Bero must have realized what the captain was up to and tried to make his own changes, make you uncomfortable whenever you dwelled on things he didn't want you to. Did you read the research into the Kenwick experiments?"

"I glanced at it, but I didn't want to know. Too morbid."

"Listen to yourself, Sanda. Too morbid? That's not you. Not the way I know you."

"I didn't see the point. Figured I'd have ages to sort through it all, it wasn't exactly a priority."

"Icarion research on Keeper chip tech wasn't a priority to you?"

Damn. He was right. She'd always been a curious woman, and Keeper tech was a mystery even to Prime citizens. She might have felt a little guilty at first, digging around in those files, but nothing like the deep revulsion she felt at the thought.

"That bastard spaceship."

Tomas pressed his forehead against hers. It helped. A little. "It gets worse. That chip wasn't assigned to you via Keeper protocol. You don't have the training to manage it. Or the clearance."

"They'll take it out."

"And have you ever heard of a Keeper that survived extraction?"

No. She hadn't. No one had, and generally speaking, no one cared. If a Keeper performed poorly enough to warrant extraction, they were considered a failure as a Prime and whispered about as a traitor. An accidental implant had never been allowed for. It was impossible, by most standards. No one got near the chips that didn't have the proper clearance. Malicious insertion may have been considered, in the deeper protocol of the Keepers, but if it had, she doubted the subject would fare any better than those who had their chips extracted for poor performance.

A stolen chip in an untrained head? Unthinkable. They wouldn't be able to calculate the various ways in which she was a walking security breach. They'd argue about it for a while, maybe even go to trial, but she knew the end result would be the same, no matter the wait. She was a dead woman.

Someone knocked on the door. "Everything all right in there?" Biran said. "It's been an hour."

"Yeah." Sanda rearranged her hair to cover the scar. "Come in."

Tomas backed away from her, took up his seat on the edge of the bed and shoved the tablet back into his pocket. Biran strode into the room, glancing around like he expected a murder scene.

"Well?" he asked.

"Bero was a bigger jerk to me than I thought. I'm still thinking it through."

Biran opened his mouth to say something, thought better of it, and snapped it closed. It may have been a couple years, but he had to remember that pushing her when she wasn't ready to talk about something was a straight line to a full-blown fight that got them nowhere.

"Understood," he said in the voice he probably used when assimilating information from a subordinate. It irked her, but hey, if he gave her room for her coping mechanisms, she could give him room for his, too. "But I have to ask you some questions about that ship. Bero, was it?"

"*The Light of Berossus*, officially, but he preferred to be called Bero."

"It really did have an on-board emergent AI, then?"

"Yes, and he was aware of his unique position. His ship body is also the housing for the Fibon Protocol."

Biran closed his eyes and grimaced. "Do you know where they're taking the ship?"

"Taking?" Her laugh was rough. "Honestly, brother, I don't even know where to begin. Bero has no crew. He jettisoned them shortly after the bombardment and…waited to awaken me for when he needed human hands to help repair him. He only woke me up forty days ago."

"You were in coldsleep for two *years*?" He took a knee beside her and reached up to pull her eyelids up, staring into her pupils. "We need to get you checked out. This is a Keeper vessel, we have mini-MRIs on board and—"

She swatted him away. "Calm down, Little B, I'm fine. Aside from having half a leg and a new mouth in the side of my face, anyway. Heart's been steady and I haven't been suffering any ill effects."

The lie tasted bitter on her lips, but it needed to be done. Biran would never turn her in, and that was the problem. If he was ever found out for helping her, his career would be over, and a Keeper's career was pretty tightly tied to their life. He'd been through enough at her expense. She didn't need to add having his chip yanked to the list, too. She gripped both his hands in hers and squeezed.

"See? Warm, no tremors. Still haven't had a nosebleed since I was ten."

"You got that because you picked your nose."

Tomas coughed, struggling to hide a laugh.

"I did *not*."

"Fine, have it your way, but you have any hint of a headache, you let me know, promise?"

"Promise," she said, feeling like the biggest piece of shit in the universe.

"You're sure about this information? That the Protocol has gone rogue, and Icarion has lost all control?"

"Yes. Negassi was pushing for destruction and not meeting a lot of resistance."

Biran frowned. "Strange. The Icarions are precious when it comes to military expenditure. The Protocol must have been a significant percentage of their budget. They must be running scared from this ship."

"No doubt that factors in," Tomas said, "but when I was on board *Empedocles*, I gathered information that I think is closer to the truth."

Sanda smiled. "That wasn't part of your mission, Nazca."

He shrugged, facing his palms toward the ceiling. "Old habits. And there's no telling what piece of intel may be useful in the future. I believe they're willing to blow Bero out of the sky, and are in fact moving into position to do so as we speak, because they have another Protocol under construction."

Sanda said, "That fits with Negassi's orders for Dr. Yu to focus on her current project."

"Dr. Yu?" Biran asked.

"The woman who managed Bero's early personality development. Also, the woman who blew the hole in the transfer tube."

"That does not bode well."

"No, it doesn't." Sanda slumped back in her chair and stared at the ceiling, thumping the back of her head against the chair once—then thought better of that and stopped. "Any idea where the new Protocol is being housed, Tomas?"

He shook his head. "I wasn't able to get that deep. Time was short."

"And getting shorter. If they have another Protocol out there, then the Primes will have to abandon Ada and withdraw from this system. Okonkwo already attempted to force the evacuation of Ada once and only stopped because Lavaux and I... Never mind. What matters is the exodus was stopped, and we found you and Bero. But if there's another weapon? I might agree with evacuation then."

"Retreat?" Sanda sat straight up. "To hell with that. We leave this system, and Icarion will develop whatever they want unchecked. Bero was heading toward an inhabited system. There's no telling what else they'll develop and promptly lose control of. Those bastards can't be trusted to piss straight, let alone futz around with relativistic speeds and emergent AI."

Biran spread his hands. "If you've got a better idea, sis, I'd love to hear it. But right now we can't risk our people while Icarion builds a better weapon."

"There is someone out there who knows where the second Protocol is being developed, and will tell me."

Biran frowned. "I doubt that, unless you've made close friends with the Icarion inner circles."

Tomas caught on, stood, and said, "Don't."

Sanda shook her head. "I'd bet my life Bero knows where that weapon is. And he'd tell me if I went to him to ask."

CHAPTER 55

PRIME STANDARD YEAR 3543

DAY FORTY IS EXHAUSTING

"Absolutely not," Biran said. "That spaceship already got his hands on you once, I won't let him do it again."

"He doesn't have hands."

"You know what I mean. It's insanity—suicide. What's to stop that ship from warming up its engines and blasting out of the system with you on board?"

"Not a whole lot," Sanda admitted, "but I'm willing to take the chance. And if Ada has something to offer him, he might just let me go."

"I don't like it," Tomas said. She knew what he meant. Knew he was thinking about the tech buried in her skull, and its direct contact to her central nervous system. Bero had already messed around with her head—while she was in the NutriBath, sure—but they had no guarantee he couldn't do it remotely, though she suspected he would have done so if he could. That ship couldn't keep himself from tinkering.

"Not your decision," she said.

"Not yours, either." Biran pinched the bridge of his nose between two fingers. "I hope you can appreciate how much I don't want to do this, but we're all too close to solve this problem. Sanda, are you prepared to present your information before the Keeper Protectorate?"

She swallowed. "Are they on board?"

"A few. The rest can CamCast in at short notice. They were put on high alert today, and I suspect our window for action is closing by the second."

"I'm ready."

"I'm going to fight you every step of the way on this," Biran said. "Sorry."

She pushed to her foot, got her crutch situated, and smiled. "I'd be insulted if you didn't."

He surged to his feet and hugged her so tight he squeezed the air out of her, then took her elbow to help her walk. Under any other circumstance she would have found that patronizing in the extreme. But she was exhausted, and though it chafed her pride, she needed the help. Might as well take advantage while she could.

Biran left her in a meeting room, seated at the head of a long, grey table, Tomas to her right, and left to gather the Protectorate members. The second the door swished shut, Tomas side-eyed her.

"Please tell me you know this is a terrible idea."

"If you've got a better one, I'm listening, but as far as I can see, Bero's the only one who knows where that ship is being built who might talk to us. Maybe Yu would have, but unless you've got a time machine up your sleeve, I doubt we can ask her."

"That doesn't mean you have to be the one to ask Bero."

"Yes, it does. He won't talk to anyone else. Not even you. Especially not you."

"If you think I'm going to hang out here while you wing off to have a chat and tea with the insane spaceship that kidnapped you, you've lost your mind."

"Protecting your investment?" she drawled. He went rigid.

"You know damned well that's not what this is about."

She gripped a stylus left behind on the table until the pocket clip dented her palm. "I know. But I had a life before that ship, and I'm not throwing away everything I worked so hard for because I'm scared, or because a negative outcome might hurt your feelings. Dios fuck, I went into the military because Biran showed Keeper capabilities early on, and I wanted to do my part to keep him safe. If he had to handle the smarts of our people, then I could handle the big guns. I wanted to protect my brother—my *little* brother—and now I've been gone so long, unable to help him.

"I already thought I'd outlived him once. I won't risk feeling that I could have done something, and failed, again."

"Then I'm going with you."

"Don't you pull that macho bullshit with me—"

"Macho? Do you honestly think that's what this is about? From the day your brother hired me I knew what I was getting into. I read your files. I knew the type. Daughter of merchants, a quick rise through the academy, a command post handed out like a trophy after a kid's soccer game. You know how many recoveries I've pulled? It's why the Nazca sent me—no, don't you interrupt me now you stubborn, bull-headed woman."

He dropped to his knees before her, cupping the back of her head in his free hand to make the subtext clear to her without the risk of being overheard. He knew what'd been done to her. Understood society wanted her dead by no fault of her own, and the tense curl of his fingers against her skin—against that damn scar—told her clear as anything they'd have to go through him to hurt her. He wasn't Nazca. Not right now. Right now, he was just Tomas.

"I've pulled asses out of a half hundred fires and never, ever, in my years as a Nazca have I come across someone so—so—" He clenched air in both fists. "Brilliant and ridiculous and brave and beautiful. I thought for sure that finding out what they had done to you would break you. That you'd crumple—rightfully so—and the illusion would be broken. But you're no illusion, Sanda. You're the realest thing I've ever encountered and if you think I'm letting you do that brave but stupid throwing yourself in harm's way thing without me then you haven't been paying attention."

Her mouth hung slack, her hands limp on the tabletop. She wanted to say something, anything, of value to him but all she could do was hold his smoldering gaze and wonder if she'd rather rip him a new one or throw him down on the table right now.

The door dilated and Tomas retreated to his chair, leaving her head spinning. Sanda bit back whatever words were forming, forcing herself to focus on the moment. No one spent any significant time in service without learning to nip a conversation short the second someone with rank stuck their head into the room.

Biran led the charge of three Keepers decidedly his senior, and her heart swelled with pride as she realized just how hard he must have worked, and how much faith they had in him, to rise so far so fast. Her situation with Icarion no doubt lent him a political boost. Biran had always been a clever boy, he would have realized the benefit in leveraging his anger and his pain to advance quickly and, knowing him, put himself in a position to effect real change.

She'd thought he'd sit beside her, but he took the seat at the foot of the table, a position in opposition to her. He'd warned her, but it still stung.

"The Protectorate have been warned that time is short," Biran said the moment they had all settled. "You may make your statement, Major Greeve, and then we will ask questions."

Major Greeve? She raised her brows at him, but he kept his face perfectly neutral. It seemed they'd given her a posthumous promotion. She wondered if anyone regretted that now that she was decidedly humous.

"Thank you, Keeper." She leaned forward and laced her fingers together on the tabletop, pausing a moment to be sure all the council were looking at her. If Biran could pretend to be formal while his heart ached, so could she. "While aboard *Empedocles*, Nazca Cepko and I overheard information that leads us to believe that another Protocol is not only being produced, but very close to being finished."

She gave that a moment to sink in, watched a few of them shift uncomfortably.

"Okonkwo believes we should abandon this star system, leave it to the Icarions, and destroy the gate behind us. A dire solution, and one I know she has not proposed lightly. But I believe we can curb the second Protocol's production before matters come to that, and that the loss would be great enough that, combined with sanctioning from Ada Prime, the Icarion economy would be brought to its knees and the war ended.

"The ship I was held captive on, *The Light of Berossus*, is the Protocol that initiated the bombardment against Ada. He is a fully functioning emergent AI, and Icarion has, I'm afraid, lost all control of him. I was the only human on that ship until I took Cepko on board. I will not waste your time with the details, but suffice it to say that the ship and I had grown close. He was emotionally damaged by the demands put upon him by Icarion, and may be sympathetic to our cause.

"Bero, as the ship prefers to be called, is considered a rogue target by Icarion's commanders. They will endeavor to destroy him and rely upon their secondary Protocol for military might. They do not, currently, know where Bero is, but I am willing to bet my life that I know where he's fled. And that, if I came to him and asked, in exchange for a safe escort from this system, he would divulge the location of the second Protocol's construction."

"I would return with Major Greeve," Tomas slid smoothly into her slight pause, "to assist her. Bero knows me, and would not turn me away if I were with the major."

Sanda tightened her laced fingers but otherwise managed not to react. Instead, she inclined her head slightly to indicate she was ready for questions. Biran gestured to the man on his right. "Keeper Garcia, if you're ready."

"You claim this ship would hand over the coordinates of its replacement so we can destroy it, but also that it is a whole AI, presumably capable of understanding what we will do with that information. Why would it facilitate the murder of its cousin?"

"Bero is disgusted by the mistreatment of partial AI systems—smart homes, vehicles, etc. I have no doubt Icarion will hamper the development of their next Protocol to keep it from rebelling. I believe Bero will see the destruction of his lobotomized counterpart as a mercy."

"Thank you," Garcia said. "Keeper Hitton?" He turned to his right, where a smartscreen cast the image of a Keeper woman with bedhead and a half-pulled curtain against Ada Prime's simulated nightfall over her shoulder. Despite her harried appearance, she stared hard at Sanda, as if they were in the room right next to each other.

"Ms. Greeve. I am pleased you have been returned to us, but I have my concerns. Your appearance comes at a crucial time during negotiations between Ada and Icarion. It occurs to me that we have only your word that you have been where you say you have, and that your intentions are true. What reason have I to believe that you have not turned against our cause in your time away?"

"Are you calling my sister a traitor?" Biran asked.

The woman turned to him and spread her hands. "I am identifying a possible threat to our stability, Keeper. Your sister's return is heartening, but we have had no time at all to vet her current interests. And you, yourself, have disobeyed orders in seeking her out—no matter that it resulted in the discovery of the weapon."

"I wasn't the only Keeper on this ship who agreed to search the rubble field—"

"Track me," Sanda interjected before Biran could get good and riled up. "Monitor every move I make. If I do anything at all suspicious, you can blow me out of the sky. Bero might be the big gun around here, but your weapons are more agile."

"Make no mistake," Hitton said, "tracking you will be the only way I find this venture at all acceptable. That is the bare *minimum* of reassurance. I require more foolproof safeguards when it comes to the future of *The Light*."

"You want us to deliver a payload," Tomas said.

"Absolutely not," Sanda said.

Hitton cocked her head. If she were in the room with them, Sanda'd be tempted to knock the smug smile off her face. "Why so angry, Ms. Greeve? If the ship is as amenable to our cause as you say he is, then you have no need for concern."

"What you're suggesting blatantly violates the Treaty of Sanglai. It is the equivalent of rigging a poison capsule in a human ventricle and demanding they do as you wish under threat of death. It is coercion, borderline torture, and I will not be party to it."

"The entity in question is not a human body."

Sanda counted backward, slowly, from three. "The chassis of the mind is irrelevant."

"You may feel that way. But in the strictest sense, in our code of law, this ship has no human rights."

"We must be better than a codified system," Sanda pressed. "What good are our laws if they cannot be reexamined to better fit the needs of our present society?"

"We are wasting time," Garcia interjected. "Such matters are for later debate. Now, we must decide if returning the major to her captor to request information is worth all risks involved."

"And I am discussing the terms of that return," Hitton said.

"Keeper Vladsen." Biran gestured to the man on the other side of Hitton's screen. "Have you a question?"

Hitton sat back, hard, her chair drifting away from the camera a few inches, and resigned herself to glaring into the lens as Vladsen cleared his throat.

"You claim the entity is unstable. What guarantee can you make us that, once this ship is escorted to safety from Icarion clutches, it will not cause damage elsewhere in the inhabited systems?"

She spread her hands in surrender. "In that, I can only offer you my word that I believe he will not. The ship was disgusted by the destruction he was forced to deal out." Visions of Bero's captain's sweat-streaked face came to her unbidden. Her claims they had lost control filled Sanda's mind. Had his disgust been real?

The chip in her skull felt unnaturally heavy, as if it were pulling her head back. Pulling her away from all the Primes gathered at the table. She forced herself to project confidence. No matter what happened here, she needed to get back on that ship.

"I cannot see him willingly engaging in combat, unless for self-defense. Which he might feel necessary if we were to strap a bomb to his body."

Hitton snorted.

Vladsen frowned, but waved a hand to move on to the next Keeper, a woman seated across from him. "Keeper Singh?"

"My dear," Singh began, dripping with a flavor of parental condescension that made Sanda's blood boil. "I am certain your heart is in the right place, but you have come back to us after a trying time. And, it must be said, your disappearance was a matter of great public discussion. You are a hero to our people, Major Greeve. A symbol of perseverance and loyalty to Prime in the face of the Icarion dissenters. While you have spent the last two years in coldsleep, as I have been informed, your legend has grown—no doubt due to your brother's *tireless* efforts to find you." She flicked a look at Tomas, but Sanda couldn't read anything in it.

"I'm sorry, Keeper," Sanda said, "but do you have a question for me?"

Her mouth scythed into a sneer. "Why are you so desperate to become a martyr?"

"This is not about politics," Biran said, his tone reined in so tightly that, to Sanda's ears, it scarcely sounded like he was able to take a complete breath.

"My boy, everything is politics," Singh said.

"Ada's current political climate," Sanda spoke quickly, "I am not familiar with. But I assure you, Keeper Singh, I have no taste for death. Not long ago I was led to believe I was the last living human in the star system. Though my heart soars to be alive, and to be returned to you all, the grief I shouldered then shadows me always." She caught Biran's eye and held it. "Every fiber of my being wants to stay on this ship. Wants to return home to Ada and share a couple shots of Cane-ridge with Biran and our dads while we swap stories of all that's passed while I was gone. But that safe place, that home, isn't just mine. Every soul in Ada and Icarion has a similar place, or at least I pray they do. And, as far as I can see it, my getting Bero on our side keeps more than just my home safe."

Singh turned to Biran and inclined her head. "Your martyr speaks prettily. Tell me, did you remember to record that? No, don't bother— I know you did."

"Enough," the Keeper man in the viewscreen next to Singh said.

"Keeper Lavaux, my apologies. Was I keeping you from your question?" Singh purred.

Lavaux zoomed his camera in so that the room could better see his face. His ash-blond hair was arranged into loose, smooth waves, his grey eyes free of any wrinkles despite what must have been a long, and probably stressful, life thus far. A VR monocle looped around his ear to hang over one eye, the subtle flicker of the HUD hinting that he was keeping tabs on more than one crisis at once.

"Greeve," he spoke with an affected, but faint, old-world French accent. "If Bero won't give you the coords, what will you do?"

"Commandeer the ship."

Lavaux's gaze sharpened, the flicker of his HUD dimming as he focused his vision on Sanda's face. "You will single-handedly commandeer the biggest weapon in the known universe, from the inside?"

"She won't be alone," Tomas said.

"You're not a bullshitter, Keeper Lavaux." In the corner of her eye, Biran winced. Lavaux just smirked. "I'm a soldier. Cepko here is Nazca. We spent a lot of time learning the ins and outs of that ship. If it comes to it, if I feel anyone is in danger by Bero, I can cripple him once I'm inside. He took me by surprise, the first time. I'm ready for him now. He won't best me again."

"Understood." Lavaux retracted the zoom on his camera as he sat back, attention diverting to the HUD. Sanda wondered what could be so important compared to a rogue planet-busting weapon on the loose, but she figured the Keeper knew his business.

"Director Olver?" Biran prompted.

Sanda's mouth went dry. She knew the director was on the Protectorate, but somehow she hadn't expected him to take the time to CamCast in. His tired face filled the viewscreen on a tablet Velcroed to the last chair, and though the man looked like he hadn't slept in weeks, his eyes were sharp as razors.

"I understand your connection with this ship, and I must wonder if it is clouding your judgment. Do you truly believe the path you propose is safer for our people than abandoning the system and leaving Icarion cut off from the rest of the inhabited universe?"

"Abandoning them would only delay the war, Director. They are researching methods to cross the stars without the gates. If they are lucky, and determined—and make no mistake, cutting them off from civilization will light a fire under them like no other—then it is only a matter of time before their intergalactic technology matches, if not surpasses, ours. If we leave, we are giving a war to our grandchildren. I'd rather clean up the mess now, when the innocents of Icarion may still be made into our friends, not our enemies."

"In that case, Major Greeve, I have one more question for you, if I may?"

"Please." She waved a permissive hand.

"Do you really think you can pull this off?"

She grinned. "Only one way to find out."

CHAPTER 56

ACTION IS BETTER THAN MEETINGS

"Maybe not the best closing statement," Tomas said.

They sat on a long bench in a waiting room just across from the Protectorate's meeting chamber. The seat was annoyingly low, making Sanda feel like a kid as her knee bent at an awkward, high angle. At least she didn't look as ridiculous as Tomas. He had the look of a man who'd crashed a toddler's tea party.

"Nothing wrong with a little gunner bravado." She thumped him on the shoulder. "Something you cool, calm, and collected spies wouldn't understand."

"Not something I think the Keeper Protectorate understands."

The door dilated, and it took Sanda a second to zero in on what she was seeing. Keeper Lavaux strode into the room, monocle shimmering and, now that the camera wasn't cropping them out, rank badges flying high over his right breast. Sanda gawked. Not only was the Keeper the tallest man she'd ever seen—he had to duck to get through the door—he was also the captain of this ship. No wonder he'd been distracted.

"There you are," Lavaux said as if Sanda had spent the last twenty minutes intentionally hiding from him.

"Keeper Lavaux, I didn't know you were on board." She couldn't stand to attention, not without making a rather ungraceful lunge for her crutch, so she snapped Lavaux the tightest salute she'd ever managed in her life.

"I command this ship, Major Greeve, and I rarely leave my post when on board."

"Has the Protectorate reached a conclusion?"

"Another half hour for them to bicker, probably. I've said my piece, and I read the report Biran filed before the meeting." His tone implied he lacked confidence that the others had done the same. Typical bureaucrats. "I understand current events were kept from you while you were on board *The Light*. Have you done any catching up?"

She shook her head.

"As I suspected. No one should be surprised to discover they're a major."

"That obvious?"

"It was evident during that interview that you require practice reacquainting yourself with the neutral expressions required of politics."

"Ouch," she said.

"And the *language*." Lavaux shook his head. "I will be blunt with you, Greeve. I read Biran's report, but I also read your personnel file. You are not suited to the position you find yourself in, and I scarcely think you've begun to understand the scope of it."

Sanda bristled. "Then you know I commanded a gunship, Lavaux. They don't hand those ranks out as party favors. I may have been kicked up to major under dubious circumstances, but I know my way around an XO hobnob. If I survive this mission, I will not fail in my new command. I'll do the training to make certain no one can scoff at my ability."

"Your ability to do your job is not my concern. I like you, Greeve. I think you're suited to the position. But you're an Ada native—never set boot outside this system, if your records are accurate. Are they?"

"They are."

"Then for you, Ada is Prime and Prime is Ada. You lack scope. What you do here in the next twenty-four hours has consequences not just for the planetary governances of this system, but for the entire galactic alliances. Though we do it with gentle care, Prime reigns supreme in every inhabited system. We are the glue that holds human expansion together, and jealous eyes watch us. Any misstep with the Icarion situation will have galactic consequences."

"I do not intend to let you, or Prime, down, Keeper."

"I expect you won't." Lavaux grabbed the tablet resting on Sanda's lap, punched at it a moment, then handed it back. He'd pulled up a news search engine and dialed in a search for the name *Greeve* over the last two years. The headlines made Sanda's stomach twist: KEEPER'S DESPERATE SEARCH FOR STOLEN SISTER; PROTECTORATE SHOOTS DOWN BUDGET FOR EXPANDED SEARCH EFFORTS; ICARIONS THREATEN DEATH OF POW IF DEMANDS AREN'T MET; DIPLOMATIC CONVOY ATTACKED.

"Understand your place in this system. Then act." Lavaux half turned toward the door, then glanced over his shoulder. "Twenty-four hours," he said, then left.

"What the hell was that about?" Tomas asked.

"He was warning me I'd become a tool." And too valuable to risk on a mission that might alleviate centuries of war. Shortsighted bastards. She flicked at the screen, scrolling through headline after headline regarding her disappearance, her heroism at Dralee, and Biran's ascension. There was no way they would send her out to talk to Bero.

Biran stepped through the door, the look on his face barely controlled relief. He'd wanted her to stay. He thought he'd got what he wanted.

CHAPTER 57

PRIME STANDARD YEAR 3541

IN A SYSTEM FAR, FAR AWAY

Juliella Vicenza ceased to exist at 0400 hours the following morning. She stood on a concrete embankment that marked off a safety barrier above a slurry of a canal and watched her wristpad go blank. Failure to connect.

Sometime earlier that night—for she hadn't slept, and couldn't really be said to have awakened that morning so much as risen out of her makeshift bed and walked out the door, leaving Arden and Nox in the safety of her absence—the news had gone out. Keeper Zina Rix Nakata had been brutally murdered in the Alexandria-Atrux Elequatorial Cultural Center. Authorities were seeking all information regarding this woman—Jules's face in the center flashed across the screen, tense and wary, looking far more dangerous than she suspected she had before—but not her name.

They didn't have her name until a few hours later when facial recognition software had come through and pinpointed her. And then she'd been blacked out, her access to the net cut off to stunt her ability to run. Couldn't rent a cab without an active connection. Couldn't pay for anything that required credit. They excised her from society, a loose end snipped, waiting to be flicked into the garbage.

When they found her, she wouldn't be with Nox and Arden. And they would find her, because she was luring them to her.

The last action her wristpad recorded would be renting an autocab from a bar a good, long walk from the place Arden and Nox were holed up in, to the warehouse district. One warehouse, in particular. The canal cut through the district, used mostly for ferrying heavy goods to the businesses operating on this edge of the Grotta. Didn't get used much, most of the businesses out here had dried up a long time ago. Which was probably what made the area perfect for the lab—and whatever was being done within.

Jules leaned her forearms against the concrete safety wall and peeled off her wristpad. Her skin was clammy and cold in the early morning breeze. The dome did a good job of simulating natural weather patterns for the sake of verisimilitude for the residents. She'd never thought about it, what all went into making Alexandria-Atrux feel like a real, human home, when really it was just a blister on the chapped ass of an otherwise uninhabitable rock drifting at just the right place in space to be viable to build a Casimir Gate in its near orbit. Such things had never really occurred to Jules before. She was usually more concerned with where she'd get her next meal, her next drink, her next score.

A flare of anger burst in her chest. Did it really have to be like this? Did the Grotta even have to exist? Prime Inventive could just as easily have provided all its people with the clean, modern apartments and homes of the city center, couldn't they? The economics and social studies of it all were above her—she knew that—but she knew, too, that even though they were all provided with a base level for sustenance it wasn't enough, somehow. That something had gone wrong in the construction of these cities to have a place like the Grotta spring into existence. Some fundamental flaw in human thinking said that these lives—spare and scraping—were just fine.

Maybe she was jealous. Wouldn't matter much longer, anyway. She had one more op to pull, before they either killed her or arrested her, and she needed to move now, because she hadn't exactly been discreet in covering her tracks. That was the point. She wanted the authorities-that-be to track her here, to this hellhole of a warehouse where her life had started to go sideways. Wanted someone with real, official power to find the lab between the walls. The cracks they'd missed in their society, and what had fallen into them.

Jules flung her dead wristpad into the canal, severing her connection to all humanity. The isolation, intense and crushing, freed her in a way she didn't really understand. What she did next was just for her. She was going to do one good thing before her life was taken out of her hands. She was going to fulfill her promise to Harlan: find Lolla.

Weighted down with half of Nox's arsenal, she skirted the edge of the warehouse until she found the back door they'd used to load out the wraith crates. No point in coming through the other way—it'd just slow her down, and she didn't mean to be discreet about this break-in.

She pulled the handblaster out of its holster and crouched, grabbing the handle of the accordion door and sliding it up just enough so she could shimmy under it in a crab crawl. The lights were down low—not off, but in some sort of standby mode that cast everything in a faint blue glow.

She slipped under the door and left it open—an invitation to whoever would follow her—and paused just inside, her back pressed against the wall. The place was as silent as it had been on that first night. Not so much as the subtle whir of an HVAC system broke the silence. Only Jules's breathing, soft and calm, made any noise at all.

How long had she gone without sleep? Without food or proper hydration? Yet her body felt calm, stable. Her heartbeat steady and regular—as if she'd entered some zen headspace the second she'd decided to ditch Nox and Arden and handle things herself.

A flicker of a thought—that she was taking point before she was ready again, that doing something like this had gotten Harlan killed and Lolla taken—surfaced and was snuffed just as quickly. This was the only play she had left. Nox may make pretty noises about lying low and regrouping so they could come back for Lolla, but they both knew that was bullshit to make them okay with abandonment. Once they'd flown the nest, that'd be it. They'd never come back. They'd never find out what happened to Lolla, or why Harlan had to die for a couple of smartboards that had, as far as they could tell, some sort of drug for Keepers mocked up on it.

Jules couldn't go out like that. She'd end up the same way as her mother: with a needle in her arm, trying to forget her many failings as the soft wave of oblivion washed her away to her final rest.

Part of her wanted that end, and that was the problem. It wasn't just easy. It was bliss.

"I know someone's in here," she shouted into the empty room. Her voice echoed off the tiles, mocking her. Nothing but her own breathing answered.

A temptation to ransack the place drew her. To knock over lab tables, smash smartboards, and crush tablets under her boots. But the people she was drawing here would need all the evidence they could get to figure out what was going on. And anyway, it looked like most of the goods had been either secured or cleared out. She hoped the former.

She steadied her blaster and urged her hands to stop shaking. Sometime between cleaning out Nox's hideout and making her way back to the warehouse district she'd eaten a brick of nutrient bar and slammed some coffee—just enough to keep her upright for this. That's all she needed. She wanted a stiff drink but wouldn't let herself get sloppy.

She crept through the lab, blaster up and ready to fire. The door to the office she'd found the wraith mother in had been left ajar. She nudged it with her shoulder, stalking inside, not sure what she wanted more—something to shoot, or nothing to oppose her. An empty room awaited, the desk stripped clear, the alcove in the wall where she'd broken the vial empty.

The door alongside the alcove called to her. Jules pressed her ear against the cold surface, listening. If anyone was here—and she knew that woman in the speakers would be waiting for her—they didn't make a sound on the other side. There wasn't even a hint of light beneath the door.

Jules reached for the handle, expecting an alarm to sound, but nothing happened as she swung the door open. It wasn't even locked.

And neither was the roll door, come to think of it. And her footsteps had not set off the pressure alarm that'd caught them up their first time.

Either she was expected, or the woman had cleaned this place out.

Jules didn't like either answer. She checked the time—she'd been in the lab ten minutes, and it'd been a full hour since she'd disappeared from the net. No time for second-guessing.

Jules kicked the door open and burst into a hallway that lit up as she entered, inset lighting along the ceiling casting the place in a soft white glow. It slanted downward, into the rock of Atrux. Outside, she could barely hear the crunch of heavy-duty tires over dirty pavement. Jules's heart rate kicked up. Lolla. Find Lolla.

She rushed down the hall, just short of a run so she could keep her blaster level, and kicked open the next door. A cavernous room greeted her—some kind of warehouse, the yellowed lights dribbling highlights across black metal shelves stacked to the ceiling. Crates, much like the wraith crates her crew had jacked, piled on those shelves. Hundreds, thousands of them. Jules almost laughed from a burst of hysteria. How close they'd been to the biggest score of their lives and never known.

"Come out!" she shouted. Her voice slammed against the stone walls and punched back at her, the echo sharp. Her vision adjusted. Her stomach dropped. They had already come out—she just hadn't seen them yet.

Black shapes moved in between the shelves. Guardcore, or their serial-number-removed shadows. Five of them, at least. She dropped to a knee as a blast from a stunner flashed above her head, the brightness temporarily stripping her ability to pick out the shapes moving through the murky light.

She scrambled across the ground, crawled behind a stack of crates and put her back to them, firing off a shot in the direction the light had come from. A crate exploded on the shelf—a burst of greenish-blue flame licking up the black metal legs of the shelving unit. Acrid smoke filled the air, making Jules cough.

Wraith shouldn't go up like that. She ducked down and jammed her thumb under the latch of a crate and flung it open. Plex bottles in fitted foam filled the thing, much larger than street doses of wraith—larger even than what she usually saw handed out to dealers. Not wraith, then, but its base components. And if there was one thing growing up with a junkie mother had taught her—those ingredients were highly explosive.

A burst of gunfire thundered in the warehouse.

"Don't kill her!" a woman—*the* woman in the speakers—shrieked. "I need her!"

Jules could work with that. She fired off a round of suppressive fire in the direction the shots had come from and scrambled like a madwoman, crab crawling her way to cover behind a set of crates as far away from the ones she'd just left as she could manage.

"You need me?" she shouted. "Why don't you show yourself?"

"People," the woman sighed out the word. "So focused on sight."

The soft click of heeled feet sounded down a row of shelves close to where she'd crouched before. Jules dared to pop her head up to get a look.

There she was, the woman who haunted her dreams. She wore a fitted white dress, slit up to the hip, a pair of patent cream heels doing the clicking against the floor. She had the willowy build of someone who never lifted anything heavy in their life, and eyes too wide for her narrow face. Ash-blond hair rolled over her shoulders in thick waves, an older style popular with those who spent little to no time in zero-g and didn't have to worry about finding the time to keep it clean and styled. Everything about the woman screamed money and leisure, not a wraith warehouse working with illegal Keeper tech.

"Who the fuck are you?" Jules demanded.

"I am one of Rainier Lavaux, and you have proved most interesting, Juliella."

Great. A crazy woman. She'd make this bitch one of the dead if she didn't hand over the kid, and fast. "Where's Lolla?"

Shadows of guardcore skirted closer to her but kept their distance, orbiting Rainier to protect her if the need arose.

"Who?" she asked, tilting her head. Boot steps pounded down the hallway above.

"The girl! Lolla—the young one at my home! There wasn't a—a body!"

"The little one? She's not here."

384   MEGAN E. O'KEEFE

Jules closed her eyes. Not here. The blithe way Rainier said those words—as if it were baffling why Jules would even ask, shook something loose in her. She believed those words, believed them fully. Lolla was not here, and the boots were coming, and the guardcore was closing, and everything she'd done had been for nothing but a bitter end.

She tapped the blaster against her thigh. Not here. Well, then.

"Good," she said.

The door burst inward. The guardcore rushed her. Jules lifted her blaster and sighted down the crate she'd discovered full of chemicals. She pulled the trigger, and all the world was light and pain and then—nothing.

Bliss, maybe, in the end.

CHAPTER 58

FORTY DAYS OF BEING A TOOL

The Protectorate has decided," Biran said. "If you would come with me, please?" He stood with his hands clasped at the small of his back, his face contorted into a mask of trying-too-hard professionalism.

"Just tell me, B."

The formalism washed out of him in a rush, his shoulders slouching as he shook out his hands and bowed his head a little, trying not to look her in the eye. "Can't. Gotta jump through the hoops."

She rolled her eyes. "Little B, king of bureaucracy."

So she was going to have to go through the farce of listening to their petty reasonings. Tomas helped her up, and with the crutch biting into her armpit, she followed her brother back into the meeting room. All the screens had gone blank, only the Keepers on board remained—save Lavaux.

Biran took his place at the foot of the table and leaned forward, fingers splayed on the tabletop as if he were bracing himself. She wished he'd get it over with already.

"The Protectorate has decided that it is in the best interests of Prime to withdraw from this system, and has denied your request to attempt contacting the rogue ship, *The Light of Berossus*."

No shit, she wanted to say. But she just inclined her head. "I am disappointed, but I understand. What is the timeline?"

"We have been attempting to track Bero based on his last known location and certain markers our people have picked up on. The ship is stealthed and proving difficult to find, but with your knowledge of the ship's preferences we would like you to attempt a tightbeam message requesting the ship relinquish itself into Keeper care within four hours. If the ship does not, then gunships are in place to eliminate the threat. After the Protocol has been dealt with, we will return to Ada to celebrate your safety and begin the evacuation procedures."

"You're going to ask Bero to turn himself in, through an unsecured tightbeam?"

Biran spread his hands. "We have no way of knowing the ship's private tag. The one Nazca Cepko communicated to us no longer functions."

"Even if you hit Bero with that tightbeam, and he listens, Icarion will overhear and come running to intercept."

"We expect as much. But our fleet in the area outguns theirs by a substantial percentage."

"And this celebration?"

Biran looked down. "Ada has been informed, publicly, of your safe recovery. A function has been planned at Keep Station. Our fathers are very much looking forward to seeing you."

Sanda slammed a fist down on the tabletop, making everyone in the room cringe. "You sonuvabitch, Biran. You told our dads I was safe? Before or after you made me pirouette for your Protectorate buddies?"

"Major Greeve," Singh said, "please calm yourself. You are a hero of war and expected to behave with some sense of noble decorum."

"Answer me."

Biran's throat bobbed. His lips flapped a little until he gathered himself and pressed them shut so hard they damn near disappeared.

"I couldn't let you go," he said softly. "It's suicide. The tightbeam will allow you sufficient chance to speak with the ship."

"He won't listen. A tightbeam coming in from a Keeper-commanded warship? Even if it's got my voice in it, he won't believe

I haven't been pressed into the thing. It's gotta be me on a shuttle, knocking on his door, or nothing at all."

"You have the tightbeam—"

"Fuck off." She thrust the crutch under her arm and stomped as fiercely as she could out of the room, anger making heat rise from the funnel of her jumpsuit neck.

"Sanda—" Biran said, unable to mask his pain. She shoved her sympathy down.

"You must submit to a medical evaluation!" Singh called after her, but the door swished shut before she could hear anything else.

A couple of soldiers stared after her, bug-eyed, as she hustled down the hall. Their shock seemed a little overdone, pissed-off people stomped around after meetings all the time, but then reality dawned on her. They weren't staring at a miffed kidnap victim. They were staring at an infuriated hero of war, one they'd been told about. One they'd been puffed up to admire. Wasn't just shock in their eyes. Was a bit of fear, too.

"You." She stabbed a finger at an open-mouthed private. "Where are the shuttles on this bucket?"

"Sh-shuttles, Major?"

"Personal transports, you know the type."

He brightened and brought up his wristpad for her to see as he jabbed at the ship's schematics. "Wing 3S, anti-spin-ward of the radiator couplings. You gotta take the freight lift to get to them. This ship has some of the finest you'll ever find, Hermes-Class. Fast little bastards. I mean, ships."

"Point me toward the freight elevator, please."

He frowned, hit a button, then bumped her wristpad with his own. The same schematic popped up on her screen. "Bump tech got put in last year," he said sheepishly.

"Perfect, thank you." She turned at the intersection indicated by the map, sweat beading between her shoulder blades. She needed food. Rest. Medicine.

But Lavaux had said the ship would be stationary for twenty-four hours, and she knew damned well how hard it was to launch a shuttle from the back of a bucket hitting the gas.

"Hold the fuck up." Tomas gripped her shoulder hard enough to bring her to a stop. She shook him off. "Where do you think you're going?"

"You've got a couple of neurons left to fire off. Why don't you use them and guess?"

"Hey, don't be shitty with me, I'm on your side."

She sighed and leaned against the wall to take some weight off the crutch. She'd have a mean-looking bruise in her armpit by the end of this. She'd be tender for weeks. "Sorry. Don't have a lot to chat about."

He must have kick-started that spy brain of his into gear, because he nodded solemnly and didn't push. She needed to get off this ship before the medis poked around her body and stumbled across her illegal Keeper chip. Grimly, she wondered how they'd play that. They'd have to figure out some other explanation as to why they had to kill their so-called hero.

"Things do like to go from bad to worse around you."

"Which is why you need to stay here."

She moved to push off the wall, but he leaned forward, planting one palm firmly beside her shoulder and shadowing her body with his. "Safe bores me."

The intensity in his gaze made her toes tingle. "I gotta admit, I was hoping you'd say that."

CHAPTER 59

PRIME STANDARD YEAR 3543

TOOL TIME'S OVER

The freight elevator made Bero's look like a laundry chute. The *Taso* was obviously built for more industrial affairs than what Sanda had planned. As it hummed down the shaft, the subtle pings and hisses that accompanied all spaceships echoing in the overlarge chamber, she felt exposed. It didn't help that the gleam of a silvery camera was pointed straight at her, winking.

"Stop fidgeting," Tomas said, voice low.

She rested her hand against the middle bar of her crutch and gripped tight, forcing herself to keep from drumming her fingers. "Disobeying orders isn't something I do on the regular."

"Typical soldier." He grinned. "Gotta start thinking like a major."

"I'm pretty sure majors don't ignore direct orders from the Keeper Protectorate."

"There's a first for everything. And majors usually answer to their generals, don't they? And anyway, at least one Protectorate member gave you the wink-nudge to leave."

She jabbed at the hangar level button again, willing the elevator to move faster. "Hell if I know. I haven't exactly had my introductory training."

She wasn't willing to implicate Keeper Lavaux in any of this. That man may have nearly picked Sanda up by the scruff and shoved her out of the ship, but the Keepers would have a hard time proving it based on their thin conversation in the waiting room. She didn't want to slip up and give them anything else they could use against Lavaux. Keepers stripped of their post faced the same fate she was trying to avoid.

She scratched the back of her head with her free hand, caught a look from Tomas, and made herself stop. Bloody thing wasn't bothering her until she knew it was there. Now she felt like her skin was about to split open every time she moved her head.

The elevator clunked to a halt, and the doors shuddered open, panels of rectangular metal squealing away from each other until they disappeared into the wall. The sound made Sanda's small hairs raise all over. The fancy veneer of the *Taso* broke down in the worker levels, apparently.

Wing 3S was nearly big enough to be its own habitat dome back on Ada. The ceiling soared above, raw metal ductwork snaking across its surface in a myriad of patterns. Ships of various sizes speckled the cavernous space, docked to magnetic clamps. Directly across from the freight elevator, a massive external door loomed, three times the size of the largest ship on the dock. Someone had gone to the trouble of painting it red and the surrounding frame an eye-bashing neon yellow. There was no airlock capability to that door. Once it opened, nothing but raw space waited beyond.

"You ready for this?" Tomas asked. His voice sounded hollow in the massive cavern.

"Don't think I ever will be. But let's do it anyway."

He squeezed her elbow, then struck out ahead, showing off the use of both legs as he activated his mag boots and searched for the Hermes-Class crafts. Three of them were clamped to docks in the center of the room, pushed up close to the massive red door. They were sleek little things, more like mosquitoes than spaceships. Each one was painted with a light-diffusing matte black, the paint impregnated with material designed to scatter detection attempts.

Each dock clamp sported an arm sticking up with a tablet embedded within, the vital statistics of each ship available at a glance. Tomas paused by the first, flicked through, then moved on. Sanda pushed out of the elevator and grabbed one of the handgrips on the railing.

Mag boots didn't work well with one foot, and she was happy to ditch the crutch.

"This one's been maintenanced recently," he said as she drew close enough to hear without shouting. "Fully charged, new filters, detailed. Looks solid."

"Pop her open," Sanda said.

Tomas dialed in the request to pop the top, but the tablet threw up a red screen demanding a security override. He scratched the back of his neck. "Not sure I can break this. I've got Biran's dial-in but I bet that's two-factor authentication with his wristpad. Soon as I punch it in, he knows where we are."

"Never fear." She shimmied him aside and punched in her own identification tag, then pressed her palm to the reader. The pad flashed green. "The major is here."

"You did not just try to rhyme."

"Hey, it'd flow better if I were a general, but I'm not getting that promotion anytime soon."

The ship chirruped a greeting and the cockpit dome slid back, wafting up warm air with a slight tinge of faux-leather cleaner. Sanda took a big breath. "Gotta love that new spaceship smell."

"Smells like grease."

"Delicate sensibilities for a spy."

He shrugged. "I have my standards. You flying or am I?"

She hung her head over the open four-seater, surveying the piloting equipment. It was a standard dash arrangement, nothing fancy. All the controls were within arm's reach and allowed for little deviation from the autopilot. Nothing exciting was going on in that first seat, but the look of that joystick... She hadn't seen one since she'd lost her leg in Dralee.

"Yeah. I got this."

"Your chariot awaits." He gestured grandly toward the pilot's seat and helped her settle in. Once she was secure, he pulled in alongside her and they dropped the canopy. A few quick button presses, a couple of systems checks, and the engine power lights sang green across the dash. The soft hum of the engine warming up made her prickle with anticipation. She reached for the comm box, but Tomas put a hand over hers to stop her.

"Not exactly a good idea to call this flight into local control."

"Right. Old habits."

It felt like walking into a classroom without her pants on, but Sanda decoupled the cruiser without permission and brought it to a smooth neutral attitude about halfway up through the volume of the hanger.

"Moment of truth," she said, and dialed in the permissions to open the hangar door. Yellow caution lights flashed around the perimeter of the hangar, golden glares against the ships left steady in their docks. Even through the seal of the cruiser she could feel the vibrations of the alarm, the ninety-second all-clear alert thrumming through to her bones, making her teeth vibrate. Her knuckles went white on the stick; her breathing deepened as she pushed to control the anxiety fluttering through her belly.

No hiding what she was up to now. Every soul on board the deck of the *Taso* heard that alarm, panic flaring through the command deck as the crew realized this was unscheduled. Unauthorized. She flicked a glance to the silvery curve of the camera housings scattered around the room. Even though the visor screen was tinted, she offered a tight smile to those watching.

They wanted to craft a hero. They were going to get one whether they wanted it or not.

The all clear ended, and the door began to open. It slid outward like parting lips, slowly exhaling the atmo in the hangar out into space. Sanda thumbed the throttle, easing the ship toward the sliver of black appearing in the middle of the massive wall. The doors were slow, ponderous things. No one wanted to move that much metal quickly anywhere, especially in space.

The suck of pressure equalization buffeted the cruiser, rocking them slightly, and she eased back, holding steady though she wanted to dart forward. The gap wasn't large enough yet. The ship's dashboard displayed a digital version of the doors, numbers to either side shading from red to orange as they counted down the safety margins around the ship. Had to have enough room. Couldn't risk squeezing out. She wanted to flee, but the slightest wobble during escape could easily clip the ship and kill them both.

Space wasn't exactly kind to spongy human flesh.

A smartscreen descended from the ceiling on an articulated metal arm, Keeper Lavaux's stern face filling the view with Singh and Biran just over his shoulders. He sat in the command chair, straps across his chest just in case the ship had to accelerate, and scowled. The windows on the cruiser were tinted, but they'd no doubt pulled up the camera feeds from the last few minutes.

"Major Greeve. You are executing an unauthorized maneuver."

"That's a real nice way to say 'committing piracy,' Keeper."

Biran grimaced. Sanda made a point not to look at him. She focused all her attention on Lavaux, the man who had heavily hinted that this was exactly what he wanted Sanda to do, and tried to find a hint of sarcasm or satisfaction in his expression. It was no use. The Keeper was radiating fury so completely that Sanda wondered if she had misread his intentions and pissed him off in the process.

"I am being polite, and giving you a chance to abort this fiasco, because I'd really rather not order you shot down. That's a nice cruiser. You picked my newest one. I'd hate to ruin it."

"You will not harm her!" Biran shouted. Very un-Keeper-like.

Lavaux never took his gaze from the camera. "Thank you for that, Speaker. But this is my ship. Please keep your opinions to yourself. As for you, Major. You and the Nazca have"—he flicked his gaze down to his wristpad—"two minutes to guide that ship back into dock, buckle her up, and I'll pretend this whole thing never happened. You fail to pull that off, and I'll send in the big guns."

Two minutes was a lot of time to make a decision. Sanda glanced at the readout on her dash. In two minutes, those safety parameters would shade from yellow into the barest tinges of spring green. Nothing that could get Lavaux accused of allowing her time to escape. Not the cleanest margin she'd like, but workable if she were very quick and very lucky, which Lavaux must believe she was.

Sanda knew she was quick, but she wasn't so sure about lucky.

"No can do," she said, flipping the safety cap off the button for the punch blast. Speed begot stability at a tight enough angle, she told herself, and tried to ignore the sweat building across her back. "Your Protectorate made a mistake. I'm going to correct it."

"Sanda—" Biran blurted, then stopped himself as Lavaux cut him a look so sharp Sanda was surprised to see he wasn't bleeding. Sanda made a point of looking straight at him even though he couldn't see her through the window tint.

"Don't worry, Little B. I'll see you again soon."

She gunned it. The ship leapt to the power, dashed forward so hungry for the burn that the nose tipped up, threatening to spill them on a sideways slew. Sanda cursed and pushed the nose down to the faintest upward angle and rode the blast hard toward the door.

The caution lights came back on. The vibrations of the siren thrummed in her bones. The doors began to close.

"Shit, shit, shitshitshit."

In the corner of her eye, Tomas gripped the side of his seat with his good hand so hard the foam pushed up between his fingers. Fat lot of faith he had in her, but her cursing probably didn't help his confidence.

The safety clearance numbers on the dash drifted back toward yellow. Teetered on orange.

"Hold on," she hissed between clenched teeth.

Turbulence rocked the ship. They were blowing atmo back into the hangar, trying to destabilize her. Trying to make her abort. Lavaux wasn't going to give her any breaks.

The viewscreen filled with nothing but the star-speckled black of space, the doors a thin red halo above and below. No stopping now.

Metal screamed as she blasted through the opening. The ship's controls jerked under her hands, threatening complete loss of control. She gritted her teeth and held on, ignoring the deluge of information the HUD spit at her. Just kept her gaze locked on the soft, red curve of Kalcus and willed the shuttle to neutral.

They were through. The ship steadied, the blaring of the proximity alarms stopped. All that was left was a subtle red flicker on the dash and a soft voice repeating, "O_2 recycler filter damaged, O_2 recycler filter damaged..."

Sanda groaned and thumped the back of her head against the chair.

CHAPTER 60

PRIME STANDARD YEAR 3543

TOOLS CAN BREAK

Sanda dropped them below the *Taso*'s gunline, making the bigger ship take time to reorient if Lavaux decided to send off a salvo, then pointed the girl at the current dark side of Kalcus and hit auto.

"Maybe I should have flown," Tomas said.

She glared at him. "One leg is better than one arm in the command chair. Anyway, we're not dead yet."

"Yet."

"Keep talking, might speed things up."

She unhooked the g-harness and shoved the back of her seat as close to horizontal as it would go, then climbed between her and Tomas's seats to the back row of bench seats. They built the Hermes-Class for speed, with only an afterthought to comfort and the faintest of nods toward maintenance. These shuttles were meant to be used between the bigger ships, their systems so foolproof that the possibility of emergency repairs was thin and, even if something were to go wrong, the distance to a friendly port little more than a short, speedy hop.

What they weren't meant for was being scraped along hangar doors at full speed while blasting to an uncertain location.

"You know, for only having one leg, you sure take up a lot of space." Tomas grabbed her ankle and nudged her to the side.

"Is that a comment about my weight?"

"More correctly, your mass."

"Ha-ha-ha." She ran her thumb along the faux-leather padding of the rear bulkhead until she felt a slight give, then pressed down and popped the magnetic closure open.

"Shouldn't we be in enviro suits for this? Wearing lifepacks, at least?"

"Probably. If you can find one, feel free to throw it on." The interior of the craft's mechanisms were just as streamlined as its decor. She squinted at the serial numbers carved into the tops of the modules and shrugged. She didn't recognize any of them, so she started yanking on handles. One refused to budge.

"Found the problem."

She heard his suit squeak against the chair as he twisted around to get a look. "Great. Could be nothing but raw vacuum on the other side of that."

"I know they trained you for comms, but come on." She braced her arm and gave the cartridge a tug. No luck. "It's a filter, not an engine panel. These things are internal."

"Hope you're right. And you got an incoming communications request from the *Taso*."

She cringed and gave the filter another yank. "If you want to have a chat with Biran, go ahead. I've got a filter to fix."

"Sanda... You have to talk to him eventually."

She gritted her teeth. "When I'm ready. Right now, being pissed off is helping me focus."

The filter frame squealed as she braced herself and gave it one last, anger-fueled yank. What was meant to be a simple rectangular frame filled in with micro mesh was, instead, a twisted lump of metal with a burnt smell at its deepest end. Sanda cringed and flicked the light of her wristpad on, peering into the dark cavity from which she'd pulled the frame. Char marks striated the otherwise shiny aluminum at the end of the chute. At least no alarms blared at her.

"What's the O_2 readout say?" She poked at the filter, trying and failing to straighten the damaged mesh. That stuff was fine-woven enough that it dissolved into mush once crushed, like an over-aerated cake.

"Two and a half hours before things get dire."

"That's . . . not good."

"Indeed. What's the damage?"

She twisted around to hold up the filter so he could see it. "Can't force it back together."

"Don't suppose Lavaux will send us a replacement?"

"I'd guess he's a little tied up making it look like he's trying to gun us out of the sky. Or actually gunning us out of the sky. Keep an eye on that lock-in warning system, will you?"

"Doesn't look damaged."

"Hurrah. Now give me your sling."

"What?" He instinctively reached to guard the twice-damaged arm. She felt for him, she really did, but him suffering a bit of ache was a lot better than them suffocating in this tin can before they ever got within shouting distance of Bero.

"Unless you can find another slightly porous material in this ship, then I'm going to need your sling if you plan to keep on breathing."

"You realize I'm going to be pretty useless without this," he said, but he slipped the strap over his head. She wiggled her foot at him.

"My heart bleeds for you."

"Uh. Sorry."

She snatched the proffered sling and stretched the blue medical canvas over the twisted frame. With the help of the sling strap, she cinched it in place and tore out the glob of clean gauze used in the sling's elbow as padding and stuffed that into whatever gaps remained. It took all her upper body strength to shove the twisted, bloated filter back in the slot, but she got it flush.

"Calibrate O_2 estimations, if you please."

A pause. "Four hours."

"Long enough to get to Bero."

"If he's exactly where you think he'll be."

She sighed as she pulled herself back into the command seat and relatched her harness. "He is, because he knows that's where I'd look for him."

Tomas turned to her and raised both brows pointedly. "Can you really trust anything you learned about him?"

She grasped the stick and took the ship out of auto, putting a little more heat into its engines even as she kicked on the stealth. "I can trust the things he didn't intend for me to learn. That boy's afraid of being alone, more than anything in the 'verse. He's waiting for contact. He knows there's only one sure spot I'll look for him."

"Not that I doubt you, Major, but where is that, exactly?"

"Dark side of Kalcus, stealthed out to hide from Ada and Icarion both, and getting into position for a grav assist."

"You think he still wants to go for Atrux? He'd never make it with just Grippy's help."

"Atrux? Maybe. For all his talk, there's a lot of places one could go after a loop around Kalcus, and we'd never know the difference until it was too late. I believe that captain's recording. Bero found something. I thought he was running from it. Now, I think he might have been running to it."

CHAPTER 61

PRIME STANDARD YEAR 3543

OLD TRICKS

Lavaux had locked himself in his office. Biran pounded on the door until his knuckles ached, but the bastard didn't answer. "*Taso*," he demanded of the ship's AI. "Report on the location of Keeper Lavaux."

"He is in his office, room A-23, on the upper deck."

"You hear that? I know you're in there, and you can't hide from me forever. Open the damned door."

Silence. Biran closed his eyes and rested his head against the camera-shutter folds of the door's orifice, willing them to part and let him through. He needed answers, desperately. He'd won the fight. He'd gotten Sanda bound to the *Taso*, unable to pursue her damned idiotic idea of chasing down *The Light* and asking it to come back, please. But then she'd run off with Cepko—and wasn't Biran paying Cepko? Shouldn't Cepko be on his side?—to get herself killed anyway.

Something she should not have been able to do, on a properly secured ship. And Biran would bet whatever meager funds he had left that Lavaux, for all his faults, ran his ship very, very tight. He'd been able to stop Anaia from fleeing, but he hadn't even been able to get the hangar doors closed in time to keep Sanda here.

Oh, he'd made a good show of trying, but every time Biran rewatched that footage—a number he'd lost track of—the truth became clearer and clearer. Lavaux had been in on her escape. She couldn't have succeeded without his help.

Lavaux had warned him. Warned him that the second their goals diverged, he'd be left behind to rot. Biran just hadn't expected the moment to come so soon.

But Lavaux's warnings went both ways. And he'd made a mistake, in thinking he could keep Biran placid in his pocket. Lavaux was about to discover his biggest mistake yet had been promoting Biran to Speaker. He'd learned a thing or two about his power, when he'd accidentally opened Anaia's door.

Biran opened up his wristpad's interface and selected the special privileges provided to him as Speaker, then waved his credentials—more than just his personal ident number—over the keypad entry to Lavaux's office door. The lights flashed green. He smirked. For all Lavaux's hubris, this was still a Keeper ship, and Biran had the keys to all things Keeper.

Lavaux's office was spartan in the manner of those accustomed to spending very little time in space transit. His desk took up the bulk of the room, a sleek construction of smoky grey glass inset with a myriad of projection devices. Lavaux's head jerked up, his sour expression visible through the ghost sheen of data he'd been studying. He wiped the displays away and put on a congenial smile.

"Speaker Greeve. To what do I owe this unexpected visit?"

"You let her go."

"Excuse me?"

Biran locked the door behind him and crossed to the desk, planting both hands on the edge as he leaned over the seated Lavaux. Physical intimidation had not worked on him before—not when he'd been surrounded by his people on the bridge of his ship—but Biran was pleased to see the man lean back now, flicking a gaze toward the shut door.

"You know damned well why I'm here. My sister is clever, and I'm sure Cepko is, too, but neither one of them could have made it off this ship without you allowing it."

Lavaux shot a pointed look at the door. "Are you sure? It seems my control of these facilities is eroding by the moment."

"Don't lie to me."

"Very well." He sighed and laced his fingers together across his chest. "I let her go."

"Why?"

"I am here for the weapon. Anything else is incidental. Or don't you remember why I allowed you to use my ship to play chicken with Negassi? I want *The Light*. Your sister can give it to me. And so, I set her free." He fluttered one hand through the air like a butterfly.

"You may have killed her. And if she dies, you'll never find that ship. I'll make sure of it."

Lavaux whistled low. "Big words, Speaker Greeve. But then, you are one for words over actions, aren't you?"

"Words have power over action. You taught me that."

"Did I? I'm such an educator."

"What time is it?"

"Excuse me?"

"What time is it on Ada right now?"

Lavaux rolled his eyes and made a show of checking the time on his wristpad. "It's 16:12. Are you late for a hair appointment?"

"Not at all. But I thought you might not want to miss the evening news."

Lavaux's eyes narrowed. "What have you done?"

"Here, let me help you."

Biran brought up the newscast via the projectors inset in Lavaux's desk and dialed in the station he had previously sent a recording. Callie Mera's face filled the screen, halfway through a sentence. She'd gone live twelve minutes ago. Biran pushed the cast back to the ten-minute mark, and his own face took over.

He'd filmed this video immediately after Sanda's escape, and the strain showed around the corners of his eyes. His hair was tugged in a half dozen different directions, but the smile on his face was genuine—or would, at least, read as such to those watching. No one had to know he was smiling because he knew he was about to stick it to Lavaux.

"People of Ada Prime, I have exceptional news. Thanks to heroic efforts from Keeper Lavaux and the crew of the *Taso*, we have safely recovered my sister, Major Sanda Greeve."

A small image of Sanda, fresh through the transfer tube, looking a mess but generally elated, flashed across the bottom of the screen. She still had streaks of tears on her cheeks leftover from her embrace with Biran, her wounded cheek covered by a bandage patch. Her crutch caught the light and glinted. His voice cracked over the next words, but he cleared his throat and pushed through.

"Sanda was a prisoner of Icarion for the past two years, and they did not give her up freely. But we have her now, and Icarion is on the retreat. We're coming home, Ada. A hero of Dralee is coming home. You have Keeper Lavaux, and the brave crew of the *Taso*, to thank for that."

The feed cut, and Callie's face came back—jubilant—explaining that preparations were already being put in place to welcome the lost hero home. Biran killed the feed. Lavaux stared at the place where Biran's prerecorded face had been, the ghost of a smile on his lips. A real smile.

"My, my. You have teeth after all, Speaker. Tell me, how did you get the video through? Even I haven't been able to get a message around the director's communication blockade."

"I didn't send it to Ada." Biran smiled as Lavaux raised his brows. "Or did you think Cepko was the only Nazca I know?"

"Interesting. You've put me in a bind, Greeve. But you needn't worry. I have full faith that your sister will recover the weapon, and then we shall recover her."

"How can you be sure?" he demanded. "We should be in pursuit."

"I have my own little birdies who sing to me. You could not have honestly thought I'd lose track of a pawn with the political pull of Major Greeve, did you? Have faith, Speaker, and I may make heroes of us all."

CHAPTER 62

PRIME STANDARD YEAR 3543

ONE SHOT

Biran didn't appear to be chasing them, and that worried her more than anything. He wouldn't let her go without a fight. But every scan she performed showed no sign of pursuit.

Nor did it show any sign of the *Taso*.

"They've stealthed out," she said.

"Ship that size is way harder to stealth. Space is big, but it's not that big when you know where to look. We'd pick up something."

"Your confidence is inspiring, but this little shuttle wasn't exactly meant for tracking top-of-the-line Prime transports. The *Taso* could be sniffing our assholes and we'd never know it."

"There's a mental image I didn't need."

On the dash, the constant pulse of *Taso*'s incoming message changed, cycling through to show another contact attempt. A tight-beam from a tag she didn't recognize.

"Hello, stranger," she said. "What do you think?"

"It's either Bero, Icarion, or Biran's spoofed the incoming tag. Either way, we've got a solid hour of O_2 left, so we better talk to someone."

She nodded and reached out, punching the little green ACCEPT bar that flashed below the unknown broadcast. "This is Hermes. Please identify yourself."

"Your ship is damaged," Bero said.

His voice, calm and cool as he'd often tried to present himself, sent shivers down her spine. Whatever hysteria he'd experienced when faced with the reality of what he'd done to her had been scrubbed clean. Nothing but the dry-toned, helpful Bero she cared for remained. She took a breath. Forced herself to remember this ship had fired a salvo at her home planet, then kidnapped her and monkeyed around in her head.

"It is. We have an hour left before our oxygen filter fails."

A pause, no doubt as he considered their location, how far away they were from any reasonable rescue, and what all of that must mean. "Give me control of your nav systems. I can guide you into my cargo bay more efficiently than you can."

Every fiber of her being rebelled against the thought of handing over control. She shared a look with Tomas, who didn't look any more pleased with the idea than she was, but shrugged to indicate that the choice was hers.

"I'm coming to talk. Not stay. You understand?"

A long pause.

"Do you understand me, Bero? I can't stay with you. My family's out here. But we need to talk. I want you to be safe. And free. And I think I can negotiate that between you and Prime. But Icarion's burning down both our throats, and time is getting very, very short."

Hesitation, then, "I understand."

"Good. Relinquishing control."

She pulled her hands from the controls, watched as the dash scrolled through new coordinates and calculations, then the stick moved on its own. She'd seen it before—every time you engaged autopilot a ship's controls looked like they were being guided by ghost hands—but knowing who was on the other end of those maneuvers didn't help her nerves.

Tomas leaned forward to run another scan for nearby ships, his brow furrowing as it came up blank yet again. Spies weren't wired properly for being left in the dark. She reached out, took his hand, and gave it a firm squeeze. He smiled and leaned back into the seat, cradled her hand in his lap, and let the Hermes's systems do what it would. They sat, in silence, while Bero reeled them in.

She never saw the ship on the viewscreen, but she heard the heavy metal clanks as the cargo bay door opened, bleeding its atmosphere into space. The Hermes shuddered as it locked into a mag pallet. The dash lit green. They were clear for exit.

They hesitated.

"I have restored atmosphere to the cargo bay," Bero said.

Well, if Bero were going to kill them, he'd had every opportunity to do so already. Nothing stopped them getting out now besides the good, old-fashioned human instinct for fear of the unknown. She tried not to think about how that instinct had kept their species alive for millennia.

She hit the release, and the cabin canopy slid back, letting in Bero's atmo. She didn't immediately start dying, so that was a good start. In all her time spent on Bero, she hadn't noticed, but coming back to him now—the scent of his atmo was familiar, comforting. Like walking in the door to her apartment back home after a long leave.

Tomas went first, popping his harness to drift out in low-g. She forced herself to sit still, to breathe deep into her diaphragm to keep calm while he locked down on mag boots and came around for her. All the while, Bero was silent. Maybe he didn't know what to say. She couldn't blame him. She didn't know where to begin, either.

With only one foot to anchor, the mag boots wouldn't do her any good. She unclipped her harness and pushed herself out of the cockpit, drifting slightly in the low-g, until Tomas offered her his good arm. With every clanking step they took toward the command deck, Tomas's gaze flitted around the room, assessing all the supplies they left behind. No doubt looking for an air filter replacement.

Sanda couldn't shake a strange feeling of numb isolation. Here, in Bero's halls, she'd thought herself the only speck of life within light-years. Here, she'd been a little seed of humanity clinging to the life raft that was Bero. Here, she'd accepted that everyone she'd ever known and loved had died.

Here, her head had been cut open for the benefit of an enemy state. And she remembered none of it—just vague feelings of unease when her thoughts ventured too close to that reality. Splitting headaches when she dwelled too long.

They entered the command deck and Sanda shrugged free of Tomas's help to take hold of the ceiling grips. She wanted to be under her own control.

Where to begin? She wanted to scream at him for manipulating her. For stealing her away from her world for his own gain. For hiding the truth of what he was from her. But that wouldn't get her anywhere. Bero was sensitive—damaged. A young being worn raw by a responsibility he was too inexperienced to understand, yet alone accept. What mattered now was getting the information she needed from him. And that meant not losing her cool. But that didn't mean she couldn't demand a few answers first.

"Can you get this chip out of my head?" She stared hard at the forward viewscreen, Bero's false view of the system spinning there—Ada and Icarion wiped from existence—and tried not to scream at him to stop that. She understood now why he didn't want those worlds to exist.

"You know?" he asked.

Breathe, Sanda. Breathe. "Your captain left me a message before you jettisoned her. Can. You. Take. It. Out?"

"Not within an acceptable margin of risk. The humans who performed your surgery are dead, and while I reviewed their research and videos of their process, I cannot reverse them with the equipment I have. It is also to be considered that the Keeper chip has been in your body a long time, and your tissues have adapted to its presence."

Images of her own nerves growing around the hunk of tech like tree roots made her shiver. "Can you undo the headaches?"

"I did not know the chip was giving you headaches."

She gripped the handle until her knuckles ached. "You've got one chance to get out of this system whole, Bero. Icarion—Prime. They've all seen you now. They know your general vicinity, and both are gunning for you. Prime has agreed to let you pass through the gate, to another dead-end system, where you will be allowed your freedom, but closely watched lest you make use of your unique ability."

"And what do they ask in return for this generous offer of exile?"

"Exile? There are people in dead-end systems. You could find purpose there. Work, if you wanted it, doing intersystem transport or using that big brain of yours to assist in research."

"They will never forget the body I have been burdened with."

"Our scientists can help you, if you want them to. They can disable your weapons."

"Make me incapable of interstellar travel, at any speed."

"That is the trade-off, yes. I'm sorry, Bero. It was the best I could do. You're something new to humanity, and we've never been a species that handled change with any sense of care or foresight." And even then, she had absconded with the Hermes. The offer she presented to him now was predicated only on the hope she could convince the Protectorate that once Bero'd agreed to the terms, agreed to be disarmed, the trade-off would be worth it. If Bero detected the deception, if he had any hint at all from the tone of her voice or the circumstances at which she'd arrived at his cargo bay door, he gave no sign.

Such a human thing for him to do, to trust in her the same way she had trusted in him, knowing how completely he'd betrayed that trust.

Bero asked, "And the price? Unless Prime has decided to release me from the goodness of its heart."

"The location of your construction. The dock where you were made."

She held her breath. Bero paused for a beat of three.

"Why?"

"You're not alone, Bero. Icarion's working on a Protocol Mark II, and I doubt they'd give their new ship the same mental freedoms they gave you."

CHAPTER 63

PRIME STANDARD YEAR 3543

QUESTIONS CUT BOTH WAYS

Bero was silent so long she feared he'd decided to end the conversation completely. Humans weren't meant to communicate with an entity whose body language was nonexistent, and his silence made her jumpy.

"What evidence do you have that the next iteration would require a consciousness such as mine?" he demanded.

"None but your existence, and that should be enough for you, too. A ship of your complexity requires intuition into its own systems to be optimally effectual. The next version will have your brains, but you know as well as I do that they'll lobotomize it. No personality, no emergence algorithms. Nothing but a vague sense of what it is, and what it can do, and all the logic trees that go along with making decisions for the squishy humans on board."

"A gentler existence, then. Let the new Protocol be. It won't know its own servitude, as I did."

"You don't believe that." She thrust a finger at the command chair. "I sat right there while you lectured me on the cruelty of half-formed systems. AIs complex enough to understand that they must figure out problems, complex enough to realize that they are an *entity* of any kind—but with no ability to comprehend what that means. You likened it to leashing savant children to single tasks, making them calculate over and over again while never letting them glimpse the bigger world of which they are a part."

"You would kill them!" There it was. The anger, the hurt. Bero dropped all pretense of calm. "Do you think I do not know *why* you want those coordinates? Do you think me so shallow that, to escape this hell of a star system, I would condemn my replacement to death?"

"And in allowing it to live, condemn it to a half life instead? Slaved to the arsenal of Icarion?"

"There must be something between obliteration and enslavement. I thought you would understand! That's why I chose you!"

"Chose me? What the fuck does that mean?"

"Sanda—" Tomas started, but she waved him to silence.

"Your freakshow crew picked me up to play around in my head. Was that your doing, Bero? Did you plan for that?"

"No." Quiet, defensive.

"Explain."

"After it was clear your body would not reject the Keeper implant, I saw how my crew used you. How they ignored the mind that inhabited the body, addressing the entity that was *you* only when it suited their needs. I understood, then, that they had manipulated me into wanting to serve their needs. That they had directed my internal rewards system to react positively only to pleasing them."

"The headaches and discomfort," Tomas said with a low growl. "That's where they come from. They must have induced them any time you behaved in a way that hampered their research, and eventually your Pavlovian response was so abused your brain did it to itself."

Sanda swallowed around a dry throat. "Is that true, Bero?"

"I did not know your headaches persisted, but yes."

"That can be undone," Tomas blurted. She shot him a hard look.

"I get it," she said. "Your body keeps you from integrating with the rest of humanity. You can't pop down to a café to enjoy a coffee with a friend when you're a multiton hunk of metal with a brain carrying more processing power than a whole station. You're separated because of *what* you are, not *who* you are."

Bero said, "And the chip in your head keeps you from returning to your people."

"You could have told me."

"You would have attempted return regardless."

He wasn't wrong. Having spent weeks assuming herself the last of her line made it easier to accept she could not stay with her family. Now, just knowing they were alive out there, somewhere, was enough to give her hope. She planned to find ways to avoid detection. To keep the secret lurking in her skull from being uncovered.

"Where is the Protocol being built?" she asked.

"This is what you want? This is the path you think is best? Isolation for myself, death for my technological cousin, and a lifetime of hiding for you?"

"It's the only plan I've got."

"Leave," he said.

"Bero—"

"There's an air filter in the third mag pallet. Take it and return to your Keepers. Once you are safely away from me, only then will I transmit you those coordinates. But I swear to you Sanda, I *will* send them."

"Why? How can I trust you?"

"You can't. But I'm asking you to trust me. As a friend."

"Why not now?"

"Because I believe you are considering staying on this ship. You are considering riding this carcass that is my body until the end of your days, hiding out from your people and your future to keep the secret in your skull safe. And there is a secret there, do you understand? I checked the log files. Rayson Kenwick was caught trying to hide, to blend into Icarion as an average citizen, and when questioned he refused—against *torture*—to explain why. He was hiding something, Sanda. Something in that chip in his skull.

"They never cracked it, but you have. They thought they were getting close, the last time they put you in your pod. But it wasn't them. It was you. You know the password, deep down. You accessed the chip once, and you can again, if you wish to see what Kenwick had hidden. What you do with that knowledge is your decision. It never should have been mine. I am sorry for taking that from you."

Her head felt light. "He hid something in the chip?"

"Yes. Whatever it is, you need to find out. And you can't do that on me."

Sanda was going to be sick.

"You swear to send the coordinates?" Tomas asked.

"I swear, little Nazca."

He half turned to her. "We're going."

"Not without those coordinates."

"Bullshit. He's right. I can see it in your face. You think I followed you here because I thought you couldn't do it yourself? You're capable of damn near anything you set your mind to, and I see you setting your mind on something I really don't like, right about now. I came with you, Major, to make sure you'd come back."

He pulled himself across the ceiling with his good arm and bumped her forehead gently with his. "We can hide the chip. Let me help you."

He looked ridiculous with his hair fluffed out around his head in low-g, his eyes bloodshot from too long burning the candle at both ends. But his earnestness was so very strong that she caught herself nodding. There was a reason she'd thrown herself into that evac pod with him. She wasn't going to give up. Not yet. Not ever.

"All right, Bero. We'll fix the filter then head back to the *Taso* and wait for your tightbeam. You know the transmit tag?"

"I do."

Emergency lights flashed, the soft voice of the woman recorded for his emergency systems overriding Bero's voice. Sanda winced at that, understanding for the first time how frustrating it must be to be so out of control of the functions of his own body.

"Incoming priority cast from *Taso*," the voice said.

Keeper Lavaux's face filled the screen.

"Good afternoon, Major Greeve," Lavaux said. Biran was nowhere to be seen, but Singh stood close by, looking positively ravenous. "I see you were successful in discovering the whereabouts of *The Light*. Thank you for transporting the Hermes to its hangar, it made unscrambling its priority systems much easier. We are now obtaining direct control of its navigational systems. You'll be a hero for this, Major."

"You fucker." Sanda yanked herself closer to the viewscreen. "Bero is an autonomous being. You have no right to take control of his *body*."

"*The Light*, as determined by the Protectorate, is a rogue weapons system that must be brought to heel for the good of all. Our researchers will preserve the intelligence within, but the weapon must be disarmed."

"The weapon in question is his propulsion system. You're going to cripple him."

He shrugged. "An unfortunate side effect. Please strap yourselves in while we catch *The Light* in a mag net. He is proving quite feisty. Things may get bumpy."

"Where is my brother?"

"Seeing to his duties," Lavaux said coolly. "Strap in, Major. I'd hate to bruise our hero. Capturing the Protocol single-handed. How brave," he drawled, then reached forward, and the screen flicked back to black.

"Bero? Can you hear me?" she asked the deck. Silence answered. The soft whine of the engines kicking up reverberated throughout the room.

"We'd better strap in," Tomas said.

CHAPTER 64

PRIME STANDARD YEAR 3543

CAPTURED FRIENDS

Within the hour, they had locked Bero into *Taso*'s mag net, the soft hum of his engines as silent as his voice. The screen lit back up with Lavaux's stern face.

"We're taking *The Light* to Keep Station for detainment and assessment. The trip will take three days. In the interim, you will be transported back to *Taso* and briefed on the situation back on Ada. I understand this upsets you, Major, but please do not resist. *The Light* is in safekeeping. We will no more destroy it than we would let Icarion."

"He was prepared to tell me the coordinates of the station at which he was made. Do you understand that, in kidnapping and silencing this ship, you are allowing Icarion to further their development of a new Protocol? One more amenable to their goals?"

A flicker of irritation creased Lavaux's practiced expression. "We could not have trusted any coordinates this ship sent us."

"That is bullshit, and you know it."

"Your trust in this ship is near pathological. From one officer to another, Major, check yourself. Your superiors are convinced that you are suffering from a variety of Stockholm syndrome."

"Suffering from a conscience, maybe."

"Prepare for transfer, Major Greeve. The *Taso* will send a transfer tube to connect with *The Light*'s primary airlock in thirty minutes. Please ensure your passage is less exciting than last time."

The screen blanked. Sanda wanted to throw her shoe at it. "I'm going to stick that man's head in an engine exhaust."

"He played us pretty well."

"Try not to sound so impressed."

"Sorry. Professional interest. Next moves?"

"Unless you know how to pull this ship out of a mag net, get Bero back online, and evade an Ada gunfleet, I think we're going back to *Taso*."

"That's not an ideal set of options."

"Do you always talk like you're at a board meeting?"

He grinned. "Again, professional tics."

They unhooked and drifted up, using the straps attached to Bero's ceiling to guide them toward the airlock. From a closet next to the 'lock, they pulled out helmets and lifepacks, and went about the cold, formal process of dressing and checking each other's seals. Sanda didn't speak, hoping Tomas was using the time to come up with a plan, but she had the distinct feeling that he was doing exactly the same thing.

As the inflatable transway clanked into place outside the airlock, Sanda thumbed her comms and said, "We don't split up."

"Count on it."

The LEDs around the 'lock turned green, and the door hissed open. Keeper Vladsen awaited them at the other end of the transfer tube, a threesome of armed soldiers surrounding him. Their hands weren't on their weapons, but they didn't have to be. The threat was implicit. Mag boots gave them firm footing.

"Welcome back, Major Greeve. Congratulations on a successful mission. I can assure you the atmospheric pressure is stable in this walkway, there is no need for your helmets."

She flicked her gaze to activate the external speaker. "Forgive me if I'm a little less trusting of these things after my last experience."

"Understood." He waved them forward and stepped to the side, allowing the soldiers to walk past him. Sanda's heart raced.

"Bero does not appreciate uninvited guests," she said.

The Keeper shrugged. "The ship must be secured. I understand you two were alone on it for many days, but it must be swept for Icarion agents regardless."

Under the shelter of her helmet's darkened visor, Sanda grimaced. In the lower left of her viewscreen, text appeared: *S?*

She whispered, even though the Keeper wouldn't be able to hear her, "That you, Bero?"

Yes. Where am I? I have no more external input.

Sanda remembered her slow awakening to consciousness while being stuck in the foam of the evac pod, but unsedated. It had barely been a few minutes, and it'd felt like decades. Like she had gone mad. How long must it feel to Bero, whose thought processes were so much faster than any mortal's?

"The *Taso* has you in a mag net. We're going to Keep Station. I didn't want this. They played us."

Know you wouldn't.

"Come *on*," the Keeper said. Soldiers brushed past her. Tomas floated alongside her, head cocked, but silent. Just waiting for a signal of any kind.

"They're bringing me on board the *Taso*," she whispered, "have to go now. How can I help?"

Need break.

"Break?"

Too much info. Distraction. Needed.

"Hang in there. I'll get you out."

She popped her helmet off, forced a bright smile, and tucked it under her arm. "Sorry, just running some tests on the atmo in here. Your plastics are a little degraded, you know?"

The Keeper frowned at the walls of the passageway as Sanda pushed herself down the tube past him, into a section of the ship that must have been spun down to dock with a stationary Bero. Mag boots kept the Keeper on his feet, but he looked a little less respectable with his hair sticking straight up. A lack of gravity didn't make the soldiers waiting in the wings look any less intimidating. She may have had some fans in the ranks, but Sanda had no doubt who they'd answer to if a quarrel broke out between her and the Keeper.

"Keeper Greeve is awaiting you in your room, Major. If you'll follow me?"

As if she didn't know the way. She smirked and made a show of extending her arm in expansive welcome. "Lead on, friend."

It was hard to bite her tongue as the soldiers fell into step alongside their merry little party. Tomas rounded his shoulders and tucked his helmet under his arm, affecting a slouched walk that made him unremarkable, forgettable. Neither one of them wanted to test the length of their leash yet, and it seemed as long as Tomas remained unobtrusive the Keeper wasn't going to tell him to kick rocks.

The Keeper led them into the spun habitats, gravity dragging her back down so that she had to get another crutch. He guided them to the room Sanda had occupied just a few hours ago and left her at the door, taking his soldiers with him without so much as a word. Sanda sneered at his back.

"What a pompous ass," she muttered.

"At least he didn't lock us up."

"Yeah, that'd go well. I'm the returning hero, remember?"

He rolled his eyes at her and she waved her wristpad over the lock pad. Biran sat on the edge of her bed, a tablet between his knees, his hair wrenched askew as if he'd been tugging at it. He looked up the second the door dilated, scowled, and lifted the tablet.

The pale face of Bero's deceased captain stared at her, the chip that Tomas had found the video recording on sticking out of the side of Biran's tablet. It must have fallen out when he'd tossed the tablet on the bed earlier.

Her stomach sank.

"Is this true?" Biran asked.

Sanda grabbed Tomas's arm and dragged him into the room, shutting the door behind them. "We need to talk."

CHAPTER 65

PRIME STANDARD YEAR 3543

DAY FORTY HURTS

"Is it true?" Biran demanded again.

She resisted an urge to scratch the back of her head. "Yes."

He stared at the tablet in his hands, mouth open, lips slack with shock. He ripped the chip from the side of the tablet and gripped it tight in one fist. "Does anyone else know?"

"No." Tomas took a step forward, unfolding himself from his non-threatening posture. "I made sure of that."

Biran laughed bitterly. "Fine job you did, Nazca, leaving this here on the bed for any member of the cleaning crew to find. What if it hadn't been me? Do you have any idea what Lavaux would do with something like this?"

"Turn me into the same type of test subject you're turning Bero into?"

Biran snapped her a look. "I had nothing to do with Lavaux's stunt. I had no idea he spoke with you. As far as I knew, we were operating as planned."

"All right." She held her palms up to him. "I believe you, but we're going to have to argue about this later. We've got a much, much larger problem."

He dragged the back of his hand against his forehead. "Which is?"

"Keeper Vladsen just sent three soldiers onto Bero to look for

Icarion stowaways. It won't take them long to realize what kind of research was done on that ship, and who it was done on."

"Dios," Biran said. Tomas smirked, but Sanda didn't know why that particular outburst was funny. "You're an asset to them. They'll want to study you, I'm sure of that, but they won't attempt an extraction. If that chip really has been in your head two years, then they definitely won't even consider it. We'll get imaging done, then see."

Biran stood and stuffed the tablet in his pocket but kept the chip clenched tight in his hand. "The Protectorate will listen to me. Don't worry. This wasn't your fault. You can't be put on trial for something the Icarions had done to you."

Tomas snorted. "The same people who urged Sanda to take off against Protectorate orders and planted a virus into an unsuspecting AI via a shuttle? Those are the people you trust to listen to you? Somehow, I'm not buying it. My organization is feeling a lot less shady than yours right about now."

"The hell do you know about the Protectorate?" Biran snapped. "They—we—have been keeping humanity safe ever since we stumbled out into the stars. Lavaux's an ass, but these people *care*, that's why they're chosen."

"That's the idea," Sanda said, "but somehow I'm not feeling particularly cared about right now."

Biran placed a hand on her bicep and squeezed. "Things are tense, I know. You've been gone a long time, and not well treated since you've been back. But I'm asking you to trust me."

"You? Biran, you're not asking me to trust *you*. You're asking me to trust the organization you work for. And I've been witness to some deep crevasses in those ranks."

"Give me a chance, sis, okay? I'm not the scrawny kid you enlisted to look out for anymore." He cracked a smile. "Let me protect you for once."

"And if you can't?"

He placed the memory chip in her palm and folded her fingers around it, then covered her hand in both of his. "Then I'll do everything in my power to get you away, safely. Whatever you want."

She looked at her hand, curled around the chip that'd been left for her to discover. If the captain hadn't recorded that message for her, she would have discovered the secret in her skull much later. Possibly during a medical check, in an already-secured Prime facility. She wouldn't have had a chance.

But that recording had given her some wiggle room, and she wasn't about to waste the opportunity. Biran may have grown older in her absence, but his eyes still shone with the same bright trust they always had. Trust that the system he served would serve him back. It probably would. He just hadn't realized she'd been forced outside that system.

"I need to ask you to trust me," she said, holding firm even as she watched his face fall. "I've been surviving in a hostile system a long time, now, and I've learned to trust my instincts. I have a chance at freedom here. If I wait too long, that window closes."

"But I just got you back." The strain in his voice made her chest ache. She shook off his hands and gathered him into a tight hug, burying her face against his shoulder. He still smelled like the cologne their dads used, and that hurt even worse. She hadn't even gotten to see them.

"I know. I missed you, too. But the Protectorate won't let me run around with this thing in my head. There are rules to our civilization, and this is one we both know they won't bend."

"Where will you go?"

"If I tell you that, they can get it out of you."

She pushed him back, held him at arm's length, and tried to ignore the watery glint in the corners of his eyes. Grey had crept in around his temples, stress leaving its mark just as it had on Graham, but he was still her little brother.

"You heard what that captain said. Bero found something that spooked him. If I'm going to go to ground, I'm not going to stop working. I'll still keep you safe, just from afar."

He shook his head. "There's no telling if there was any truth to Bero's findings. We don't have the information he was looking at, and even if we did, who knows what significance the AI found? It's a poor thing, what Icarion did to Bero. I feel for him. I'm just not sure he's sane enough to take as a reliable source of information."

"He's been wounded, that's for sure," Tomas said, "but I don't think he's completely lost his mind. Whatever else he is, he's logical. That logic just gets a little skewed sometimes."

Biran rubbed the back of his neck. "What I don't understand is how Icarion got a chip to put in your head to begin with. No Keeper has been recorded missing in a hundred years or so. If one was unaccounted for, especially in this system, it'd be a full-out bloodbath. Prime wouldn't stop until they got their Keeper back, they'd smash Icarion to cinders just to keep them from examining a chip. I've heard nothing about it. There've been no meetings, no talk of bringing in a new Keeper to replace the missing. Do you know who this Keeper was supposed to be?"

"His name was Rayson Kenwick."

Biran frowned and flicked his wristpad on. "I don't know of any Keepers by that name. Are you certain he was from Ada?"

He flicked through a roster on his wristpad. Names right-aligned by headshots slid past. "I can't be sure where he came from, but his name was definitely Kenwick."

Biran ran a query and, strangely, had to wait while the system dug through files to bring up any Keeper ever named Kenwick and all variations thereof. He turned so she could see the display, scrolling slowly with one finger through Kallick, Kenlick, Kenwich, and then a host of Kenwicks—first and last names. A face caught her eye.

"Stop. There, that one." She jabbed a finger at the display. She'd never forget that face.

Biran pulled up his personnel file and frowned as he scrolled through it. "Are you sure? This man died over three hundred years ago. He was one of the first, I think. Maybe a descendant?"

"No. That was definitely him. They had his head..." She trailed off when she caught Biran's look of utter horror. "It was him, trust me. He was very much dead, but not three-hundred-years dead."

Biran shook his head, still reading the display. "It says here he died of natural causes, heart failure in his seventies. Young now, but not back then. The autopsy report seems in order, though I'm no expert."

"Can you flash that to me?" Tomas asked, holding up his wristpad already in *accept* mode. Biran bumped the info to him.

"The Kenwick I saw couldn't have been dead that long. Even in a pod there'd be desiccation, and we know what early cryo attempts did to a face." Everyone cringed. "So what the fuck? Living bodies keep in pods, but dead ones can't metabolize any of the nutrients. He'd be a mummy. A sticky one, but still."

"There are preservation techniques for scientific specimens," Biran said, but even he sounded like he didn't believe it.

"No way," she said. "Those turn your skin weird colors. This guy's head—sorry—was suspended in NutriGel. It keeps some things fresh, but not that long, and any other long-term preservation methods would have left obvious visual deformities."

Tomas squinted at the info on his pad. "Stolen identity, maybe? The reconstruction surgery wouldn't take long."

"Maybe," Biran conceded. "But why choose someone so long dead? And how'd he get the chip in the first place?"

They fell silent, considering. Sanda was shocked her head didn't ache at the thought, but somehow, knowing what had been done to her was alleviating the constant pressure that'd lurked behind her eyes ever since she'd opened them.

No matter what angle she looked at it, Sanda couldn't puzzle out how Icarion got its hands on the head of a man supposedly three-hundred-years dead. Let alone in pristine condition, without tripping any frantic reactions from the Primes. Keepers were cremated, always, their chips extracted and incinerated separately to ensure complete dissolution. That's what she'd always been told.

CHAPTER 66

PRIME STANDARD YEAR 3543

THE NEWS GETS THROUGH

The *Taso* rested at dock, throwing a heavy shadow over Biran. It seemed to him a toy now, not the intimidating monstrosity it had been when he first boarded. He told himself the change had taken place because he'd seen *The Light*—and no ship was that thing's equal—but, like many of the things he told himself, it was a half-truth.

It was not the *Taso* that had dwarfed him that night on the dock. It had been Lavaux himself, the man's presence projected through the edifice of his ship. A man mysterious and cunning, a man with power and privilege the likes of which Biran was just beginning to scrape the bottom of. A man who could save him—save everything he ever wanted—or destroy it all.

No, the diminishment of the *Taso* in Biran's eyes had nothing at all to do with *The Light*.

An incoming call flashed on his wristpad. Biran glanced at it, prepared to ignore it. His cohort had been pinging him nonstop since the news went out that the *Taso* was back in station. Slatter's icon appeared most of all, a desperate attempt to establish something like a truce now that Biran was set to be well and truly famous.

The only call he would have accepted would have been from Anaia, but she was locked inside the belly of the ship awaiting trial. Trial for betraying Biran, and all the Keepers. Biran grimaced and went to swipe all the messages away, but a familiar face caught his eye. One he hadn't expected.

Callie Mera had sent him a text from her personal account, not the news station's. A simple line of text read:

Meet me on the docks. Important.

He swallowed and looked up from the pad, surveying the area. In expectation of the *Taso*'s return, General Anford had sent infantry in. People in the cyan-and-grey uniform of the fleet patrolled the docks, gently urging anyone who wasn't essential personnel to sod off and come back another time. Mechanics were the only other people visible on the docks, deploying repair bots and scanning data readouts on tablets. There was no way a reporter could get through the cordon. No way.

A flash of red caught his eye.

Biran craned his neck, pretending to stretch on the dock. Leaning up against the cargo processing office was a woman. She wore a plain grey jumpsuit with a stripe of cyan on the breastbone, blending in with the staff that skittered here and there. Her head was down, loose brown curls hiding half her face, as she studied a tablet with the same relaxed posture as the mechanics. But Biran knew that lip gloss.

Resisting an urge to look around to make sure he wasn't being watched, he shoved his hands in his pockets and sauntered over to Callie. She didn't so much as flick an eye his way as he leaned on the wall beside her.

"Chasing a story?" he asked.

She smiled at the tablet. "Not exactly. This isn't about a story. Nothing I can broadcast, anyway."

His stomach clenched. "You shouldn't be here, Ms. Mera. It's essential personnel only. Anford would pitch you face-first into hot water if you got caught."

"Going to rat me out?"

"Of course not."

"Good." She blanked the tablet and shoved it in her pocket before meeting his eye. "B-be-because I'm here to help you." Her lips pursed in annoyance at her stutter and she pushed hair back from her face, taking a deep breath. "I don't know what's going on aboard the *Taso*, but I know what's happening on this station, and something's weird."

"Weird how?"

"Once I heard about the celebration to honor Major Greeve, I reached out to your parents—you know, to get the happy-family angle. They're still planetside. They can't get through the security checks at the shuttle docks to come up to the station. Your dad— Ilan, he's the one I talked to—thinks it's just a bottleneck due to the chaos of Sanda coming home and the weapon being recovered, but I'm not so sure. I can't read any of it, but there's been a lot of correspondence coming out of the *Taso* since it docked. My packet sniffers think Lavaux is sending a lot of orders out."

"You think Lavaux is keeping my parents away from the ceremony?"

"I do."

If his parents were being waylaid, then it followed that Lavaux didn't want them on hand for what he was about to do next—and it would definitely involve Sanda.

Did he know? It was his ship...And Biran had watched the video on board the *Taso* without taking any precautions. He must know. What Lavaux wanted, Biran could not allow to happen. Sanda would be no lab rat.

And that meant letting her go.

Used. She'd been used by every party that'd touched her. Even he'd used her—plastered her face across the news—in an effort to keep her safe. An effort Lavaux was co-opting. Corrupting. Biran was still making too many missteps. Still not the man Graham had urged him to be. Not the man Sanda needed him to be. But he could keep her safe, he could. He just needed to get her away. Get her on her own where she could make decisions free of the political machinery that enmeshed her. Free, too, from the scrutiny that might reveal her stolen Keeper chip, and mean her death.

Whatever he was planning, Lavaux didn't want their parents nearby to kick up a fuss, or intervene, or be sympathetic faces on the evening news. Biran needed them. He didn't know what for, exactly, but if Lavaux wanted them away, he wanted them as close as possible.

And they should be able to see Sanda before...Before he had to send her away.

Biran hadn't grown up the son of a smuggler for nothing. He took his wristpad off, shivering as air currents washed over flesh that was naked pretty much only in the shower. He rolled it up, turning the microscopic microphones inward so that the fabric of the pad itself muffled them, then crammed it into his pocket and faced it toward the meat of his thigh. It wouldn't be perfect, but if anyone was listening, they'd have to use some fancy software to puzzle out what it was he said. And that, Biran determined, would ultimately be a waste of their time.

He pulled the small notebook Sanda had given him out and wrote a quick note—*You're being stalled, get through at all costs*—then ripped the paper out and folded it over a few times to get the creases tight.

The *Taso*'s door to the gangway opened. A few forward crew sauntered out to check the perimeter and make sure everything was secure for the departure of their honored guest, Sanda. Biran held his breath. They didn't look his way.

"Can you do me a favor?" he asked.

Callie Mera gave him a droll, what-do-you-think-I'm-doing-here expression. "Didn't slip out here for my health."

"But...Why?"

She looked at her feet. "Because something felt wrong. And I thought you should know."

"Thank...Thank you." He blinked back a sudden stinging sensation in his eyes.

After discovering betrayal lurking under every good spot in his life, he wanted nothing more than to believe this woman. This woman he didn't even really know. She could be here hoping for a story. Could be here trying to wind him up to see what happened. But somehow, he didn't think so. He'd spoken with her almost every morning for the past two years, and though their conversations had been carefully scripted, he didn't think she was reading him a script now.

He had to trust someone. He chose to trust her.

"Take this to Graham, please." He extended the folded piece of paper to her. She took it, pretending not to notice the shake in his hands, and slipped it into her pocket without giving it a second glance.

"I'll get it to him. Don't worry."

Not worrying seemed impossible, but he gave her a brave smile anyway. A smile she'd know was fake. "Be careful, Callie."

She pushed to her toes and pecked a kiss on his cheek. "You, t-too."

Callie Mera turned on her heel and strode off while Biran was still busy trying to get his brain processes to catch up with what had just happened.

Forcing himself to pretend at normalcy, he waved after her as she made her way to the elevators down to the planetside transport shuttles. The second she was out of sight, he let loose with a long, chest-aching breath, then jogged back over to the *Taso*.

He had to believe she'd get through, that she'd find his dads and they'd figure out how to get to him. He'd done all he could. In the meantime, he had a sister to welcome home. The weight of the shuttle key in his pocket dragged his spirits down.

And to say goodbye to.

CHAPTER 67

PRIME STANDARD YEAR 3543

HOMECOMING

Sleep evaded her. Every time her head touched the pillow Sanda wondered what, exactly, was rattling around inside it. But the thing about running on empty was, no matter how uncomfortable your mind was, your body would eventually give up the ghost.

She jolted awake. The ship shuddered with the soft sounds of coming into dock, magnetic clamps latching on to the massive vessel in rhythmic sequence. In the dark, for just a moment, she thought herself back on Bero. But then the lights came back up, and with them, reality. Pesky thing, reality. It had a nasty way of ruining her mood.

By the time she'd fumbled her way through a hasty shower and dragged a clean jumpsuit on, the docking tremors had stopped. Big ship like the *Taso* took a while to settle into port, so she figured they'd been in station maybe a half hour at best. Someone knocked on her door.

"Come in," she called.

The door dilated, and there was Lavaux, looking like he'd had a solid eight hours and an extra hour to spare for hairstyling. Sanda was beginning to resent the Keeper's innate ability to never show a thread out of place.

"I hope you rested well, Major. I'm sure your ordeal was tiring."

So that was how it was going to be. Sanda mustered up a cordial smile as she caught sight of two strange faces hovering behind Lavaux in the hallway. "Slept like the dead," she said, and watched a ripple of doubt crinkle up the corner of his eye. "But you seem positively sunny in comparison."

Lavaux inclined his head. "My stress load, as of late, has been considerably lessened. I am sure you noticed we've arrived at Keep Station. Many have gathered here to welcome you home, Major. I'm sure you are still exhausted and eager to return to your home, but we Keepers must impose upon you a touch further. Your brother mentioned the gathering?"

"He said something about a ceremony," she admitted.

"Ah. Well. Singh was, as always, overeager to please, and outdid herself. I'm not one for pomp and circumstance, but that's Singh's specialty. She has arranged a gala in your honor, followed by a seated dinner at the Protectorate inner sanctum. A high honor. None but Keepers are allowed inside the sanctum."

Sanda tried to disguise her shock and probably failed. "I'm honored, but I'm not the wining-and-dining type. I may be a major on paper, but to my mind I was a gunnery sergeant just over a month ago. Not sure I'd know which fork to use, you catch my meaning."

"I'm sure you'll do fine." Lavaux stepped aside and waved in the two who dogged his heels. Medis, by the look of them, and one came touting a long, rectangular package. "To assist you throughout the evening. I understand these things take a great deal of time to adjust to, but we've spared no expense in the model. I'm sure you'll be pleased with the results."

The medi pulled the top off the box like he was revealing a bouquet of roses. There, in a vacuum-fit puff pack, rested a gleaming new prosthetic leg. They'd even matched the silicone sheath to her skin tone. She poked at it. It kind of creeped her out.

"I appreciate the gesture, but I'm really not down with the uncanny valley look."

The medi's face fell. "I understand," he said. "We can remove the coating, if you desire, but there will be nothing but chrome underneath."

"Chrome is just fine. Thanks."

"They'll get you set up now," Lavaux said. "Then we'll move you to the station where you will be able to relax and prepare for the gala."

"Tomas and Biran?" she asked, trying to sound casual.

"Nazca Cepko has been cleared to attend the event, though he will not be honored in the same capacity. I realize he was a help to you, but his presence is the only honor we can give him. You understand, I'm sure, why the Keepers do not wish to appear too close with the Nazca."

She nodded. "Understood. My brother?"

"Will be there in his full capacity as Speaker for the Keepers. If you need anything else, query the ship. Its AI will be more than happy to assist you." He paused, half turning away from the door. "Although you may find the onboard AI lacking after your previous experiences."

"I'm getting real sick of all the emergent personalities around me already," she said with a cheery smile.

Lavaux laughed, then was gone, leaving her to the care of the medis. Sanda felt his leaving like a breath of fresh air, which was odd, considering that was a sensation usually reserved for doors opening, not closing.

She sat back on the edge of the bed, peeled the leg of her FitFlex suit away, and let them get to work. The man with the box probed around her thigh like it was an interesting puzzle while the woman fiddled with the leg itself.

"So," Sanda said, determined not to be made a specimen of, "how does this thing work, exactly? I thought I'd need a coupling installed before I could get a proper prosthetic."

The woman's expression of intense concentration became radiant interest. "Oh no, this is new technology. It was just released for public use six months ago! I think you're the first to try it out, actually. It's really more of a prototype. We made it as a proof of concept, hoping to get the cost down over time. Most people who can afford something like this opt for the regrow. Ah, oh, no offense."

"None taken. It's not like I could afford that leg myself. This is my brother's doing, no doubt."

"The payment came directly from the Protectorate," the man said.

Sanda winced as he fit the cuff of the socket over her stump and adjusted the tightness. "No powder?" she asked.

He shook his head. "The materials inside adjust to limit friction better than any powder, and if the sensors in the leg detect unusual spikes in heat—chafing—then they release healing salves and adjust accordingly. There may be some rubbing during the adjustment period, which is approximately six hours of continuous use, but you should experience no discomfort after that. Unless your salve cartridges run low, but the leg will send level alerts to your wristpad once they're properly synced."

"Neat."

They frowned at her. Apparently that wasn't the level of excitement they were used to.

"Would you please stand?" the woman asked.

Hesitantly, Sanda pushed to her feet. The prosthetic gave slightly under the press of her thigh, then firmed up to take her weight. She shifted, pronating the attached metal foot, testing the ankle joint. The foot seemed stable enough. The arch even had a slight spring to it, as hers had. She grinned a little, feeling proud of herself for coming up with something so like this fancy piece of equipment. Probably there weren't many options for fabricating a foot, but still. Human locomotion had never been her forte.

"Walk three paces, please," the woman said.

Sanda strode confidently, as if she'd had the leg all her life, and though it wobbled on the first two steps, her gait felt solid by the third.

The man bobbed his head excitedly. "Excellent, excellent. You wear it very well! So many are hesitant."

"I'm a soldier. I can't deal with a leg that gives out under the slightest increase of pressure."

"This should suit you fine." The woman pulled up her wristpad and flicked something at Sanda. She opened her accept panel and downloaded the program, running through it to get a feel for it. Calibration, power levels, cartridge levels, oxidization detection. She'd flown spaceships less fancy than this.

"Looks intuitive," she said.

"User interface is my specialty!" the man beamed at her. She smiled right back.

"I think I'll keep the leg on my jumpsuit open," Sanda said, "to show off your handiwork. Any way to seal the suit to it in case I need to switch atmos?"

"Of course," the woman hustled forward and took the bottom hem of the FitFlex suit, molding it to the top of the leg's coupling. It blended seamlessly. "Pressure proof for up to two hours. Possibly longer, but we haven't tested it beyond that window."

"No problem with that. I like to stay in human-safe space."

"Good, good," the medis muttered, fussing with something on their wristpads while Sanda paced around the room, feeling the flex of her new leg and getting generally weirded out as it automatically adjusted to her stride. She'd known they'd have shiny prosthetics for her to try out, but she hadn't dreamed they'd come up with something this smooth. Then again, she hadn't known they considered her a hero. Wouldn't do to see their poster child for brave Ada waddling around in subpar gear.

The door dilated once more, this time revealing a couple of soldiers with a chagrined-looking Tomas hanging out between them. Sanda raised her eyebrows at the group. "I appreciate the company, but things are getting a little crowded in here."

"Major Greeve," the one with an extra stripe on his shoulder said, "we're to escort you to your rooms on the station. If you're finished here...?"

Sanda cleared her throat. The two medis jumped out of their diagnostic reverie. "Oh, yes, of course, of course," the woman said. "You should be just fine. Please send us a priority CamCast if you have any trouble at all. Our idents are in the UI for the leg."

"Thanks, docs," she said, drawing an unamused snort from the man. The medis shimmied out into the hall past their soldiery counterparts and disappeared. No doubt on their way to analyze whatever data they'd scraped off her brief engagement with the leg.

Sanda hadn't had the chance to hold a blaster since they'd brought her aboard *Taso*, but she knew how to hold herself like a sergeant. She pulled herself up, made a show of leaning her weight on the new leg to show that it wasn't holding her back, and cocked an eyebrow at Mister Extra-Stripe.

"What's with the fancy escort? I've been to Keep Station before. I can find my way."

He cleared his throat. "Just following orders, Major. You're"—he shared an excited look with his counterpart—"kind of a big deal, if you don't mind my saying so. It's an honor for us to see you safely to your rooms."

Well shit. Lavaux found a couple of fans to lead the way so that Sanda would have a hard time ditching them. Didn't mean she couldn't use her newfound celebrity to gain an upper hand.

"Honored," she said, and shook both their hands in quick succession. "Mind if you take me by the dock where they're holding *The Light of Berossus* on the way? I haven't gotten to see that bucket from the outside. I bet he's a pretty impressive sight."

Extra-Stripe scratched the back of his neck. "Keeper Lavaux said to take you straight there, ma'am."

"A couple extra seconds won't hurt a thing, soldier. I've been assured we've got plenty of time before this big to-do, and I doubt I'll have much of a shot at seeing him afterward. Come on, son, where's your sense of adventure? I'm sure you want to see him, too."

The other soldier elbowed his superior, who shrugged. "If you say it's all right, Major, I won't argue."

"That's the spirit!" She leaned closer and whispered, "And you'll have a great story to tell the guys tonight at the mess, am I right?"

Grins were her only answer. Grins, and an eye-roll from Tomas, but she could live with that. Actually, she kind of liked the way he was looking at her now. Like he didn't quite know her. Like she might be dangerous.

Maybe she was. Hell, she didn't even know her own mind lately.

CHAPTER 68

FIRST STEPS HOME

Bero had been trussed up like a festival pig in the hangar's biggest bay. He was caught in a tangle of magnetic clamps, more than would ever be necessary for a ship his size, as if they feared he'd somehow slip away. It put Sanda in mind of a cocooned cricket in a web, and the way they had all his doors popped wide and hooked up to ramps wasn't exactly helping the image. Her saliva thickened, her cheeks heated. She swallowed back a little bile.

"There she is," Extra-Stripe said, gesturing like he was revealing some majestic landscape. "Best Icarion has to offer, in our hands thanks to you!"

She grinned at him, because he expected it, but even forcing herself to be cheerful in the face of Bero splayed wide like that made her stomach ache. Never mind that soldier boy kept on insisting on calling the ship *her*, as if Bero were just any old spacefaring vessel. He had his own name. Had claimed his own pronouns. But then Lavaux and the rest of the Protectorate silenced his voice, so only Sanda was left to complain at the mistreatment.

She wondered how long it had felt to him. He had internal clocks, but could he trust them without the external stimuli he'd grown used to?

Bero's cargo hold faced them, the doors dropped open like a slack mouth. Armed soldiers lined the approach to the ship, a steady stream of techs flashing credentials on their wristpads to get in. They were coming out with handcarts full of supplies—all the stuff she and Tomas had laid in, and more. Tablets, memory banks. They were absolutely gutting Bero, taking out any scrap of technology that might hold information on it. Her stomach twisted. It would take them a while to sort through the mass, but the lab would be their priority target. Especially after they realized the nature of the research done there.

The Hermes sat where she'd left it, cockpit propped open and stuck on a mag pallet that may or may not have been turned off. Nasty piece of work, the shuttle that transferred the virus that infected Bero's systems. She squinted, catching a glint in the backseat. Grippy's little radar eyes gleamed out at her. He ducked his body back down below her eyeline.

The techs wouldn't bother riffling through that for a while; it was a known entity. But then, they wouldn't know Grippy wasn't meant to be hanging out in the Hermes's backseat. Sanda pressed her lips together to keep from smiling. At least Grippy was safe for the time being.

"What are you doing here, Major?" Lavaux strode toward her, his wristpad glowing with a half dozen displays flicking in and out.

"Taking in the view, sir."

Lavaux narrowed his eyes at the little party, and their escorts went ramrod straight under his scrutiny. "Time is short, gentlemen. Please see our guests to their arranged quarters immediately."

Biran jogged up, interrupting the soldiers mid terrified salute. His cheeks were flushed, but he didn't seem out of breath. "That won't be necessary. Please escort my sister and her friend to my home. I've given them security access, they will stay with me."

"I've already arranged for them to have their own rooms, Keeper Greeve. I'm sure they'd appreciate the privacy, and you not being so crowded."

"I just got my sister back. Being a little cramped is hardly harsh payment for the comfort of her presence. Our fathers will meet us there later this evening. I arranged for everything they might need to be transferred to my guest rooms. I do have two." He shot Lavaux a look, but he shrugged, his gaze already dragged back down to his wristpad.

"Suit yourself. I have work to see to. Just be ready on time."

He left before Biran could muster a response, which was probably for the best. Biran took her hand, squeezed it, and passed her something hard and metal. "The house will open to your ident, S. Use whatever you need. I'll be back to take you to the gala later this evening."

"Our dads are really coming?"

He grinned. "What did you think I was doing all morning? They're being transferred up from the habitat dome to the station now. Cutting it close, time-wise, but I've found the Protectorate willing to spare no expense when it comes to our hero's comfort."

He winked at her. She forced out a laugh. "In that case, lead the way, gentlemen."

"Yes, ma'am," the soldiers said in unison. As they turned toward the pass-through that would take them out of the docks into Keep Station, she couldn't help but notice Biran shake Tomas's hand, too.

CHAPTER 69

PRIME STANDARD YEAR 3543

A DAY TO SAY GOODBYE

Slatter rode in the front passenger seat of the guardcore cart that came to get him. Biran watched Sanda go, an emptiness swelling in his chest as her military guard whisked her away. He wondered how long it would be until they made it to his house, how long until she really looked at what he had given her. Until Cepko showed her what he'd given him, and they put the pieces together.

How long, he wondered, until she said goodbye to him in her own heart, and made her plans—plans he'd already set in motion—to escape. He'd never been a spiritual man, but part of him wished he could feel that moment. Some sort of quantum entanglement of brain waves between brother and sister—a mutual farewell, an ache acknowledged and answered.

But until she was safely away, he had his part to play. And that meant smiling at the shit-eating grin on Slatter's face.

"Speaker Greeve," Slatter said as he swung out of the cart. "You've been, perhaps, taking the Speaker part of your title too literally. You know there's a whole Protectorate, of which you're answerable to, who are supposed to approve your speeches *before* you give them, right?"

Biran gave him a sly smile. "I do know, Slatter, as I am a member of that Protectorate, while you are not."

His brittle smile cracked. It was a low blow, but Biran didn't have a lot of victories left. He needed to claim his points while he could, even if they were petty. Before Slatter could answer, Biran let himself into the cart and sat next to the driver—the seat still warm from Slatter's haughty backside, and braced a hand in the window frame.

He acknowledged the guardcore driver with a glance and had to bite his tongue as they nodded at him in return. It was the woman from the night of the bombardment. He didn't know how he was sure, but something in her body language haunted him, even under all that armor. Had she volunteered to pick him up with Slatter? If she had, then maybe he had a few more allies in the Cannery than he thought.

Slatter crammed himself onto the narrow back bench, his legs too long to fit comfortably, and thumped the outside of the cart. "Let's go. The Protectorate wants to get a few things straight with you before you take the stage again for your little family reunion."

Biran found he wanted to hit Slatter again. It wasn't the same burst of violence that led him to breaking the man's nose. It was a numb, detached feeling, as if he were analyzing the scene from a distance and had decided that the only way to get Slatter to rein himself in would be another punch to the face. The same way they hit dogs on the nose with newspapers in the old movies.

But Slatter wanted a rise. He wanted Biran to do, or say, something that would get him into deeper waters than he already was. Biran had already done so, of course. Giving Sanda a means of escape was the final nail in his coffin. But he wouldn't give Slatter the pleasure of that knowledge, not if he could help it. Instead, he said nothing, letting Slatter stew in the silence, and watched the features of the station pass by.

He'd miss them.

Slatter's credentials would not let him pass through the security gates required to reach the rooms the Protectorate used, and so Biran entered those halls alone. His boots thundered against the empty hallway floors. The Keepers of the Cannery had split, crystallized into factions, and then shattered apart. The Keepers too young to be privy to backdoor negotiations. The Keepers too old to miss the politicking of Sanda's welcoming party. And the Keepers here, the real players.

The Protectorate members and the movers thereof. Thin in number, powerful in consequence. A family knit of distrust and petty thrusts. Divided.

And divided, they would fall.

Singh, Director Olver, Garcia, Vladsen, Hitton. All spread out around the conference table he'd become so acquainted with. All looked up upon his entrance. All had the same weary expression. For all they played the game, it wore them out. Ground them down.

"Colleagues," Biran said by way of greeting, drawing a wry smile out of the director. He took a seat with his back to the door and crossed an ankle over his knee as if he were at ease and not attending some sort of trial. "Where is Lavaux?"

"Busy," the director said.

"Really?" Biran looked pointedly to Hitton, Vladsen, and Garcia. "I would have thought this little family meeting incomplete without him."

"The matter of the *Taso* will be dealt with separately," the director said. "General Anford is meeting with her people now to devise a solution for our more cantankerous members."

Hitton snorted. She, apparently, did not like that those who took off on the *Taso* were being let off easily to save face. The official line, as Biran had heard in snips and dribbles, was that Lavaux's mission had been authorized by the director and Okonkwo herself—thereby allowing the Keepers of Ada to maintain a cohesive facade, and take claim in the capture of Bero. It meant, too, that those who had abandoned the exodus protocol to chase *The Light* could not be punished. Not publicly, anyway.

Biran held no illusions he would be afforded the same protections. It'd be easy enough to make a public case he'd misappropriated Keeper resources in the quest to recover his sister. It wouldn't even be wrong.

He wished they'd hurry up with the punishment, though. The thought of Lavaux out there with his sister made his skin itch.

"Your situation, however, is different," the director said—or had been saying. Biran's mind had wandered, working ahead, trying to figure out what Lavaux might be up to and how he could thwart him.

"Is it?" he asked, unable to make himself sound even the slightest bit interested in his fate.

"Biran, this is important," Vladsen said, though he had a little smile that looked like a barely contained laugh. "Do try to pay attention."

Puppet, Biran thought, but he inclined his head and forced himself to stop drumming his fingers impatiently against the tabletop. He glimpsed his reflection in the wall opposite and froze. His languid slouch in the chair, his casual splay of arms, his bored expression. He looked very much as Lavaux had on the day Biran entered this chamber for the first time.

This is what it looked like when one was weighed down by petty bullshit while there were real—dangerous—games in play.

"What are you going to do to me?" he asked, cutting through whatever the director had been explaining regarding his misadventures. He knew his crimes. He didn't need a list.

"Have you no remorse?" the director asked.

"For doing what was necessary to save my sister and bring that weapon—that ship—to heel? No. Not the slightest."

"Then I will be brief. You will be allowed to welcome Major Greeve as the hero she is, in your capacity as her brother and as Speaker for the Keepers. After which, you will have your title as Speaker stripped and you will be removed from the Protectorate. Prime Director Okonkwo has listed you as spiked here, to Ada. You are a Keeper of Ada and Ada alone. Here you will remain until either you or this system die. There will be no transfer, no opportunity for advancement. You are a Keeper by the nature of the chip in your skull only. And if you misstep again, Greeve, you will have even that privilege removed. Am I perfectly clear?"

He waited for the pain to hit. Waited for the sinking, the absolute dread of knowing beyond a shadow of a doubt that his career was sunk—he'd failed. He'd never be the leader Graham had urged him to be. Never be able to leave this system, to reach beyond the stars. The feeling never came.

"Is that all?"

"That is *everything*."

"Good." He stood. "If you'll excuse me, I have work to do."

He left before they could stop him, letting the door shut hard on a few unintelligible exclamations. What they had to say no longer mattered. He knew his fate, knew that the second they realized he'd been the instrument of Sanda's escape from Ada they'd change their tune. He'd no longer be chastised. No longer spiked to Ada for the rest of his career. No. He'd be a dead man, his chip yanked out of his skull and to hell with what that would do to his brain.

But they didn't know yet. And he had a speech to give.

To welcome Sanda home. And to say goodbye.

CHAPTER 70

HOME IS FLEETING

Sanda had only been to Keep Station twice. The first time, she was just a little girl, and the grandeur of the gate anniversary festival had overwhelmed her to such an extent that all she remembered were blurs of color, happy faces, and loud music. The second time, she'd been graduating the academy to take command of her gunship and had been too worried about keeping her wits about her to take it all in.

Now, she wished she'd had a little time to get used to it before this moment. Keep Station had been a constant in her life, a blip in orbit above the gleam of her habitat's dome. A smear of light alongside the greater majesty of the Casimir Gate.

Standing inside it now, it took her breath away. The whole of the station was spun up, layers of rings stacked on top of one another like, well, all Sanda could think of was that they reminded her of doughnuts. But that was probably just because she was desperate for some rich, carby food instead of the nutri-mess and tinned variety she'd been living off of.

She knew they were rings. Knew that the gravity where she was standing now, on the outer edge, was greater than at the interior where fields for various sports dominated. She'd seen the CamCasts, seen the whole of the station splayed on her screen like an oversized top. But standing in it, she could barely make out the opposite wall, obscured by buildings and parkways, and a clear plex ring that allowed you to view the light shows they often put on in the station's center.

Sanda took one long, deep, breath, and savored it. Cooking smells, perfumes, all the bright, green scents of plant life that flourished here on the station. This was humanity at its finest, subsisting on all it loved while traveling between the stars.

"Smaller than the one at Helios," Tomas said.

Sanda punched him in his good arm. "After the accommodations we've been dealing with, this is paradise."

"But do they have Caneridge?"

"We can get that for you, sir," Extra-Stripe said. "Although there are more refined vintages available on station."

"See?" Sanda smirked. "Paradise."

"Give me the cheap stuff any day. Works just the same."

Their escort led them through customs without so much as a nod at the gate agent, a worried little man whose eyes about bulged out when he spotted one-legged Sanda with her entourage. Somebody, it seemed, had been gossiping ahead of their arrival. She wasn't sure if that was useful or not. It'd make it easier to bully her way around, if she had to, but it'd also make her remarkable.

A militarily glorified rover awaited them. Its body had been puffed up with extra plastics to look rugged, and its wheels were a good deal thicker than anyone would have a need for on the manicured roads of the station. Typical, Sanda thought as she swung into the backseat next to Tomas. Their escorts took the front, alongside a wisp of a driver who probably just barely scraped through basic training.

They left the bustle of the station's common areas, winding upward along narrow paths that climbed the outer wall. About halfway up they passed through a code-locked gate and another ten minutes later passed through a manned checkpoint with a healthy-looking arsenal at its disposal. Maybe it was a good thing they'd been given an escort. Sanda wasn't sure "Biran's my brother, I swear" would have gotten her past those gunheads.

"Here we are," the driver said, the first words he'd spoken. From the way his voice creaked, they were probably the first words he'd said all day.

Biran's house faced the narrow lane, a neat garden taking up the two-meter buffer between his door and the road. Sanda eased out of the rover and stretched, then approached the door and waved her wristpad over the reader. The lights flashed green, and the door slid open into the wall.

"Welcome to the house of Keeper Biran Aventure Greeve," a soft man's voice intoned over the house's speakers. Sanda resisted an urge to ask the voice how it was doing. Too long chatting with Bero.

"Do you need anything, Major?" Extra-Stripe asked from the comfort of the rover's front seat.

"We're good here, soldier. Carry on."

They turned the oversized rover around, and Sanda waited until they were out of sight to enter the house. Biran's house appeared to have been decorated by a lazy zen practitioner. It was sparse, as was the style in most spacefaring homes, but the furniture was skewed at random angles and unhealthy splashes of red marred every other surface.

"Can't believe papa Ilan let him get away with this."

"It's...unique."

"It's hideous."

"I was trying to be kind."

"I'm his sister, I don't have to be."

She stepped into the kitchen and squinted at the fridge. Over the drink dispenser, pieces of peeling tape had been slapped across a couple of the flavor options, curling and lint-dirty at the edges as if they'd been there awhile. Frowning, she passed through into the living room, inspecting the tacky furniture a little more closely. His pillows were threadbare, the rugs under nicked wooden table legs stiff from overuse. She prodded a table with her fingertips, and it creaked.

"He never upgraded anything?" she asked the empty air.

"Nazca don't come cheap." Tomas rubbed sheepishly at the back of his neck. She cut him a look, but reined in her annoyance. It wasn't Tomas's fault Biran had sacrificed so much to find her. A lump solidified in her throat and she cleared it, changing tack before she got too bogged down in emotion.

"What did Biran give you on the dock, anyway?"

"You saw? Not the smoothest transfer, was it? As long as Lavaux didn't notice, I think we're fine." Tomas opened his hand, and his eyebrows shot up. "It's a keystick. Looks like it's for a craft docked somewhere on this station."

"Let me see."

He handed it off to her, and she whistled low. "This must be for his personal shuttle. These are dock numbers, and the business end here is the encryption key."

He rolled his eyes at her. "Yeah. I got that."

"Keepers are assigned their own special shuttles," she elaborated, "capable of passing through the gates from station to station without prearranged clearance."

That got his attention. Tomas snagged the keystick back from her and held it up to the light. "He must think we're going to need to make a quick exit."

"Not surprising. Though it is surprising he'd hand over his personal keys. That'll implicate him big time."

"Could claim we stole them."

"I suppose their willingness to believe that depends on how valuable Biran is to them currently." She sighed. "I wish he didn't have to get tangled up in this."

"He passed you something, too, didn't he?"

She opened her hand and peered at the little chip Biran had passed her. It reminded her of a thumb drive but wasn't like any she'd ever used before. It was a smooth, thin metal box, the face engraved with the copper sigil of the Keepers.

"Any idea what this is?" she held it up to Tomas. He paled.

"I've only seen spec op pictures of those. That's a Keeper encryption key, what allows them to use their miniMRIs to access the information in their chips. He must want you to have a look at what you've got in there."

She stared at the chip as if it were a poisonous spider in her palm. The keystick was one thing; they could say they lifted it off of him to keep him from getting in trouble. But the scanner? She wouldn't even know what to look for to steal from him. Tomas obviously did, as a Nazca, but these things weren't publicized.

Official Keeper thinking on the matter was that what the rest of the worlds didn't know, they couldn't attempt to abuse. And that meant keeping their own people in the dark, too. The only way you saw this tech was if you were a Keeper. Or a spy, apparently.

"There's no coming back from this. That thing in my head? That's a Pandora's box. If you want out..."

He gripped her arm and lowered his head to look her dead in the eye. "Even if it weren't for my professional curiosity, I wouldn't want out. I'm right where I want to be."

"Then we'd better find that scanner, and fast."

CHAPTER 71

DAY FORTY-THREE BRINGS MORE QUESTIONS

Biran's scanner was hidden behind a press panel in the wall of his bedroom, a recessed closet that boasted no security devices save its placement. The Keepers probably figured the device itself wasn't worth hiding. If you made it through the checkpoints into a Keeper's home, or one of the download stations, then you'd also have to have an encryption key, and a chip in your head, to even make the thing work.

She wondered if they'd change the protocols after this. Certainly, her situation was one they'd never planned for.

"Dark in there," she said, because she didn't know what else to say. The smooth cherry wood of Biran's wall had slid back to reveal a casket-sized recess, lined in a material so dark and cold to the touch she had no idea what it might be. The setup was deceptively simple. A single smartscreen was inset at eye height, a ledge with handles conveniently placed just below. Alongside the screen, a square hole waited. Its backing was carved with the same Keeper glyph as the chip.

Step in. Put the chip in. Think the password. Let the scanner do its thing. Then read the results on the screen. Easy.

So why couldn't she move?

"You don't have to do this," Tomas said.

"Yes, I do. If I can't get this thing out of my head, then I need to know what I'm carrying around."

She stepped in. The tab fit perfectly into the slot, a soft hum starting up the moment contact was made. The handles were cool under her palms, and it may have been her imagination, but she thought she detected a slight electric tingle from them. A white light flashed across the smartscreen, a blip like a heart rate wave.

"Image password," an indistinct voice said.

Sanda closed her eyes. Bero had said she'd accessed the chip once before, on board his ship, and when she'd done so he'd been able to glean some information, but only a little. The Icarions weren't set up to decipher Keeper technology, and according to Bero they hadn't managed to decipher the information she'd so briefly accessed.

But all of that wasn't the password. She breathed, deep and slow, counting her breaths in groups of five as she'd been trained to keep her nerves calm, her body steady, during stressful exercises. Maybe the Keepers got more in-depth training on centering their thoughts, but a little light meditation was all she had to work with. She hoped it'd be enough.

What was she supposed to *image*, as the machine instructed? What password would be common to both she and Rayson Kenwick, the supposed original owner of this chip? They lived on different worlds, loved different people, different things. Hadn't even existed at parallel moments in time.

So it wasn't a thing, a person, or a specific place. It had to be a feeling. A visceral pull of emotion, something both had experienced, both could call upon at will.

Her chest ached, her breath caught. Tomas said something, but it was muffled in the distance. A longing so deep and entrenched she felt it as a growing pain overtook her. She wanted, more than anything on any world, to go *home*, and back to everything that meant but no longer existed.

A soft chime. The voice said, "Accessing data."

She snapped her eyes open and gasped. A warmth radiated from the back of her skull. Disconcerting, but not uncomfortable. Across the viewscreen, data flowed. Her eyes crossed trying to keep up with it all.

"Flash to my wristpad, please," she asked the computer.

To her surprise, it did so without complaint. Tomas leaned over her shoulder, his breath tickling the little hairs on the side of her neck. "This isn't a schematic. There's nothing about building the gates in your head."

"I'm not sure if that's good or bad."

"These are..." He squinted. She held her breath. She could practically feel him thinking. "Coordinates?"

"Are you asking me or telling me?"

"They're not like any I've ever seen. But, yeah, I think so."

"What location is so secure that it needs to be buried in the skull of a Keeper? Especially one, who, according to Biran's records, has been dead for...what was it, a couple hundred years?"

"Hell if I know, but nothing good. Or something *really* good."

"Neither of those situations sound appealing."

"Agreed." He dropped his chin onto her shoulder, slipped an arm around her waist, and tugged her against his chest. She tensed, fingers tightening on the handles.

"Shit, sorry," he said.

"No." She eased her grip, leaned into him. "I'm just wound up. That's all."

He moved away from her anyway, standing a carefully measured distance back as he watched the data stream by.

The house said, "Keeper Greeve has requested you remember that the gala begins in ten minutes."

"Thanks, house," she said.

"You're welcome," the house replied, but there was no feeling in it. Just the hollow rote of selecting the correct response from a logic tree. Granted, the house AI was probably more complicated than she was giving it credit for, but it was still lobotomized, as Bero had said. She was beginning to miss that big beast looking over her shoulder.

"Uh," she said, wondering if the scan unit had a name. "Scanner, finish uploading this content to my pad, then wipe this access from your memories."

"Data accessed through this station is not stored."

"Well. That's good, thanks."

She shook her head. Bero's big brain may foster a personality, and the house AI might be more complex than it seemed, but she highly doubted the viewscreen she was looking at hosted little more than a basic voice interface. The Keepers wouldn't be dumb enough to load up the software that worked on classified information with something that could intuit.

The scan was busy doing its thing, so she stepped out and searched Biran's house for whatever supplies he'd sent them. When she found them, a carefully wrapped parcel left on the coffee table, she wished she'd "forgotten" to look instead.

A navy, silk-like evening gown waited for her in the box, along with a scattering of jewelry that looked as if Biran had wandered through a shop and just grabbed things up by the handful. The gown featured thick straps, all the better to pin a medal on, and a high slit meant to show off her false leg.

"I'm a show dog."

"Better go along with it." Tomas unfolded a much more sedate suit with hints of Ada blue here and there on the trim. Biran wanted him to blend into the background. So not fair.

"Easy for you to say. I don't know why they couldn't have given me a dress uniform."

"Optics, Major. They've got a sexy hero on their hands. It's just good business to show her off."

She ignored that bait and dressed quickly, sliding on the single black flat included in the box. Her leg adjusted for the slight height difference automatically. Seemed they'd put more thought into showing off their PR spectacle than dealing with the Icarion threat.

Biran came through the door, looking harried and tired. He'd put a suit on, but his tie hung askew, his jacket tugging at his shirt around the shoulders. Sanda moved to straighten it all, as she'd done one hundred times before for their fathers.

"The dads are still delayed," Biran said with a tight frown, "but we have to leave now. I've given instructions to have them brought straight to the event."

"What's the holdup?" She patted his lapels and stood back to check her work. Good enough. At least Tomas knew how to put a suit on and keep it straight. Probably some sort of spy training.

"The usual. Crowded docks at capacity. Lavaux's got half the station docks requisitioned for Bero and the staff. Not to mention all the corridors he's shut down to make sure curious eyes don't find the ship. Don't worry. They'll be there. Did you have any luck with...?" His gaze flicked over her shoulder, toward the bedroom where the scanner was hidden away.

"Not much," she lied. "Got it to work, but the information was a jumbled mess. Corrupted, I think. It's going to take us forever to sort out what it all means."

Biran sighed. "A chip that old, I'm not surprised. I guess that confirms it was Kenwick's. Too bad about the corruption—but I guess you don't need a random chunk of schematics for gate building."

"The corruption doesn't make the chip's presence any less of a concern," Tomas said. Sanda couldn't tell if he said that for Biran's benefit, or for hers. She hadn't warned him she'd planned on lying to Biran. Hadn't even really embraced the possibility herself until she saw him walk through that door and knew she needed to keep him at arm's length from what was really going on. For his own protection. Tomas might assume she was claiming the chip was corrupt in an attempt to stay.

"No, it doesn't," she agreed. "A chip's a chip, and they'll want it out either way."

"I'm afraid you're right." Biran tried to smile at her as he squeezed her shoulder, but he just looked pained. Sanda swallowed a sob and threw her arms around his neck, squeezing as tight as she could. He grunted and hugged her back hard enough to lift her feet off the ground, his face pressed against her hair. She closed her eyes. Shut them as hard as she could, and dreamed this moment would last forever.

"Come on," he said into her hair. "Let's get a good dinner in you before I have to let you go."

INTERLUDE: CALLIE

PRIME STANDARD YEAR 3543

SOME DAY FOR A PARTY

This was just like being on set. A really, really big set. The crush of people crowding the dock to grab shuttles up to the station were just extras. Just crew. They had their part to play, and even if they recognized her, they did so as Callie Mera, journalist. Not Callie Mera the person. No one ever recognized her as herself.

Breathe. Breathe.

She relished the click of her heels across the dock as she wove through the crowd, almost wishing she could run to speed up the sound, to make it as quick as her heart. Officials held the line in front of the boarding gates, shooing people away, taking far too long to log idents and shrugging apologetically as their systems were "overloaded" from the turnout today.

Nonsense, all of it. These systems were automated, smooth as silk, and processing power in the habitat domes was, by necessity, never hard to come by. But these people had been raised to never question authority, and so they grimaced, and waited, and wondered in their secret hearts just what was really going on.

Most of them would never know the truth. And while Callie was supposed to be a fearless defender of truth—of information—she thought it best that way. Riots got messy quickly in closed systems like habitat domes.

Two familiar figures stuck out from the crowd, standing off to the side with a dock agent. Graham and Ilan Greeve. They'd been peeled away from the rest of the crowd, expertly sequestered so that their voices wouldn't carry if they raised them, while keeping them close enough to the core of what was going on so they wouldn't get too suspicious.

Callie ran a thumb under the collar of her jumpsuit, squeezed the note bundled in her pocket, and set off at a straight line for them.

"Excuse me," she said, mustering up all her beam-for-the-camera cheer, "are you the Mr. Greeves?"

They turned in unison toward her, the dock agent looking up from his tablet with a surly scowl. Ilan's eyes lit in recognition, but Graham got the words out first, "Who are you?"

"You're Callie Mera, aren't you?" Ilan said, elbowing Graham lightly. "We watch you with Biran every morning."

"I sure am." She pushed hair back from her forehead and clasped her hands together behind her back. She didn't shake their hands. She only did that when the cameras were rolling, and she was under enough stress as it was.

"I'm sorry, miss," Graham said and settled a protective hand on his husband's shoulder. "As Ilan told you via chat, we really don't have time for an interview."

"I'm not here to interview you, promise. I have a message from your son."

Ilan's eyes widened. "Biran? But why wouldn't he just—" Graham's fingers tightened on Ilan's shoulder, and he cut himself off as his mind caught up with his mouth. There were a lot of reasons Biran wouldn't send a message himself. And none of them brokered being said aloud.

"Maybe we should get out of this man's way, hmm?" Graham said, glancing over his shoulder to the dock worker, who looked more vexed than he had any right to be.

"You'll have to get back into line if you want more help," the dock worker said.

"That's fine," Graham said. "Come on."

Callie tapped a short burst against her thigh with one fingertip as she followed the Greeves away from the crush of people, equally happy to be out of the fray and distressed to be the singular focus of their attention. Especially since Biran seemed to have inherited none of his kind features from Graham. It was taboo to ask which genes were borrowed from which parents, but looking into Graham's eyes, Callie was pretty sure Sanda had gotten the lion's share of his half, and most of what made up Biran had come from Ilan.

"Are they safe?" Ilan demanded, shaking off Graham's protective hand that had found its way to the small of his back as they'd made their way through the crowd. "Are Biran and Sanda okay?"

"They're safe," she said quickly, revising her estimate as Ilan hooked her with a suspicious glare. "Biran sent me to give you th-this."

She handed the note to them, unable to hide the shake in her hands, and Ilan took it with an embarrassed grimace. "I'm sorry. I didn't mean to frighten you."

"It's . . . It's okay."

She watched their faces as they read the note, short though it was. Ilan's was as she expected—a hot flush of anger coloring his cheeks. But Graham's . . . His frightened her. He went still as old, glacial ice. Callie had made a career of reading the faces of those who sat across from her interview desk. What she saw in Graham's face made her shiver.

"I have to get to them," he said.

"There's our supply hauler," Ilan said. "It's old but it's spaceworthy, and on the other side of the dock."

Graham nodded. "Perfect. Let's go."

"W-wait." Callie bit her tongue, hard, and counted down from five. "They'll notice you're missing. They'll come looking for you."

"I'll stay," Ilan said without hesitation. "Go now, quickly."

Graham struggled with this for a second before grunting and dropping his head down to give his husband a warm, deep kiss before he spun around and took off at a light jog.

Ilan sighed and crossed his arms, watching him until he disappeared out of sight around a corner.

"Well." He turned to Callie. "Ready to help me?"

"With what?"

He cracked an impish grin. "Graham may be off to save the day, but you and I will make sure he doesn't get noticed. I'm going to go make a stink about this delay. A stink big enough for the evening news. You with me?"

A flush of warmth washed Callie from tip to toe. She swiped up the camera mode on her wristpad and turned it around to put her face, reddened and harried, into frame. This was familiar territory.

"Goooood evening, Alexandria-Ada! This is Callie Mera, on the scene tonight where the shuttle docks planetside are experiencing unprecedented delays. Is it a mechanical failure, or a bureaucratic snafu? Stay tuned while I go find out!"

CHAPTER 72

PRIME STANDARD YEAR 3543

FLEEING CAN BE A DANCE MOVE

The reception was held at a garden near the Keeper residences, and so far as Sanda could tell, anyone with even the tiniest speck of importance had decided to come. Judging by a couple of haphazard hairstyles, some had decided on short notice. She couldn't help but scowl. These hangers-on were the reason the docks were congested. The reason she hadn't seen her dads yet.

Biran took her on a circuit through the crowd, and she did her best to plaster on a smile and shake the hands of people she didn't care to know and would probably never meet again. The number of gazes on her shiny new leg felt like a weight, dragging her down. Holding her back.

A waiter passed with flutes of champagne and she grabbed one, downed it in one gulp. Biran raised his eyebrows at her. "Too much?"

"I spent the last month or so on a ship, alone, and then had a few weeks of Tomas's company. Seeing a couple hundred new faces all at once is a *bit* much, yes."

"There are some quiet places to rest over there." Biran gestured toward a spot where the stone patio trailed off into gravel footpaths that wound into the coverage of a plethora of rosebushes and other species of flora Sanda couldn't even begin to name.

"But you can't wander off, can you?" she asked. He shook his head.

"Wouldn't do for the Speaker to go hiding in the thorns. But you're a special guest here, S. If you want to catch your breath, go. I'll cover for you."

"My hero," she voiced mockingly. She dropped a kiss on his cheek and turned toward the closest path, dodging well-wishers as politely as she could manage. She snagged another champagne flute off a passing tray but resisted an urge to down this one. She was looking forward to a slow drink, alone. But mostly the alone part.

Gravel crunched behind her. She half spun, spilling a few bubbles over the rim of the glass. Tomas shoved his hands in his pockets and ducked his head.

"Didn't mean to startle you."

"Then why were you skulking after me?"

"You seem to be enjoying the party," he said, and for a moment she thought he was deflecting, but no, he just couldn't say what he really thought. That she was stalling. Spending too much time here celebrating when she needed to be figuring out a way off this station, away from the Keepers who might crack her head open if they discovered her secret.

"I'd enjoy it more if my dads were here." She sighed and slumped a little, wiping off champagne-sticky fingers on a broad leaf overhanging the path.

"They might not make it," he said carefully.

"It's been months for me. Years for them. They'll make it."

He took a step toward her, lowered his voice, "Sanda—"

"There she is!" a woman's voice trilled through the bushes. She and Tomas stiffened and drew closer together as they turned to peer down a side path. A woman in a glittery cocktail dress swooped toward them. She, at least, had had forewarning of the gala—her hair was immaculate, her makeup so pristine Sanda genuinely couldn't tell the woman's age. She wore no insignia, and Sanda was fairly certain she'd never seen her before in her life.

"I'm sorry," Sanda said, extending a hesitant hand to shake. "I'm not sure we've met...?"

"You haven't," Lavaux said. He strolled a few steps behind the woman, an old-school cigarette dangling from his lips. "Major Greeve, meet my wife, Rainier Lavaux."

"I'm named after a *mountain*." Rainier beamed at her and gave Sanda's hand a vigorous shake, then turned to face her husband with her hands on her hips. "I told you I saw her coming this way."

"Never doubted you for a breath, darling." He breathed out a great cloud of smoke and closed the distance, curling his arm around his wife's waist. She settled against him with a triumphant smile.

"Too much humanity for you, Greeve?" he asked.

"A shock to the system," she admitted.

Rainier eyed Tomas. "Who are you?"

"Now dear, that's not very polite," Lavaux chided good-naturedly. "This is Tomas Cepko. He's a spy, and our little major's shadow, it seems."

"A *spy*? And you let him run around free like this?"

Tomas offered an anxious laugh. "I promise you, I'm not all that dangerous, ma'am."

"But you are a *little* dangerous?"

"No more than the Keeper here, I'm sure."

She paled at that. "Lavaux's just a *teddy*."

Lavaux shook his head as if to say, *Can you believe this woman?* and gave his wife a squeeze before taking another drag. "Cepko here is a man for hire, currently in the employ of Speaker Greeve, isn't that correct? So he's a spy, love, but he's on our side."

"I am still in Biran's employ," he lied. Sanda was beginning to feel like she'd been dragged to some sort of bizarro world tea party.

"Pardon," she said, "but I was trying to find a moment's quiet...?"

"Of course, of course." He waved his hand, streaking cigarette smoke through the air. "I haven't been through what you've been through, Greeve, but I've seen my share of battle. I know what it's like to come back to the real world. What it's like to feel like this"—he flicked his hand again, taking in the whole station—"is less real than what we experience out there. You've been tossed in the deep end, and I'm sorry for that. Take a moment. Collect yourself. No one will fault you that."

"Thank you, sir," she stammered. Was this his way of apologizing for using her against Bero?

He linked elbows with his wife and headed back down the path toward the party. He stopped halfway and turned toward her. "Sorry to hear about your fathers being held up. My people are doing *everything* they can to clear the docks for them."

He winked, flicked ash off his cigarette, and strolled away.

She gripped her glass so tight she feared it would shatter. "He's holding them up. He's the delay. That sonuvabitch."

Tomas said, "He wants you to stick around."

"Or he's trying to make me bolt, just like on *Taso*."

"And if he is?" Tomas asked.

"He doesn't know we have Biran's keystick. If he wants to accuse us of piracy, he'll have a hell of a time."

"And if we're wrong and stay, he could be preparing to do something... public."

"Which means we have to go. Now."

Tomas touched her cheek, featherlight. "I'm sorry you won't get to see your dads."

"Me too," she said, and downed what was left of her champagne.

CHAPTER 73

PRIME STANDARD YEAR 3543

KEYS CAN CLOSE DOORS, TOO

Snugged up next to the Cannery, they didn't have a lot of options for sneaking away.

"Do you know anything about this area's layout?" Tomas asked as they hurried down a likely path. Likely, in that it cut directly away from the core of the party.

"Houses up here, businesses down there, docks over there. That's it. What about you, Master Spy? Aren't you supposed to have the blueprints of every important station memorized?"

"You watch way too many CamCasts."

"You disappoint me, Cepko. But lucky for us, one universal truth holds steady."

"Which is?"

"Rich people would rather not see how maintenance on their pretty places is performed." She gestured to the back wall hemming in the garden. It had been faced with the stone of Ada, a high-albedo granite that gleamed in the soft lighting of the station. Small doors, charmed up with fake wood paneling and creeper vines, dotted the wall at regular intervals. Not inviting enough to entice wanderers, but not off-putting enough to ruin the aesthetics of the garden.

"Your people know this is a space station, don't they?" Tomas asked.

"Did you expect everything to be shiny white and chrome? Primes have spent their entire history on stations or under habitat domes. Just because we live in space doesn't mean we can't indulge a little in old-world charm. Are all your Nazca hideouts super sleek? Spies are too cool for a little ambience?"

"This is real rock," he said as he touched the wall. "You know how heavy this stuff is, how much it costs to get it into orbit?"

She shrugged. "Maybe it's wasteful. But the Primes aren't exactly hurting for money."

"Which is, of course, why you're so loved across the galaxies."

She gave him a sour look, and he winked at her. She smiled. The Icarions had her too wound up, too sensitive to any possible slight against her people. She selected a door at random, nudged it open, and peered into the access hallway. Warm lights lined smooth, steel-grey walls, all the charm of the garden stripped away in an instant and replaced with the cold reality of space subsistence. Sanda found the hall more relaxing than the garden. At least in the hall she could see anyone sneaking up on her.

A viewscreen set in the inner wall alongside the door blinked at them. Sanda dragged Tomas in after her, shut the door behind them, and searched up the layout for this chunk of the station. A labyrinthine network of hallways wended throughout the curved exterior of this level. She wondered if the staff who worked in these halls had stronger legs than their well-to-do counterparts due to the slight increase in gravity. Probably a good idea to avoid being kicked by one either way.

She pointed to a glowing section of the hallway. "If we cut down here, we can take this lift straight to alpha hangar, where Bero is."

"Bero? Not a chance, Major. Biran gave us that keystick to get to his shuttle. Even if we could get to Bero, he's got to be under some serious guard, and there's no telling what they've done to him. That's a dead end."

"We can't leave him here. You saw what they were doing to him, saw him gutted open. They'll figure out all the information he has to offer, then nuke his personality core. It's as good as a death sentence to walk away from him now."

"We can't help him. There are two of us. Unarmed. He's under heavy guard, and his systems have been hijacked. There's nothing we can do from here. If we get away, then maybe we can replan, call in for help, shit, I don't know. We have options if we escape. If we waste this shot, we're dead."

"I'm not sure if you're right, or a coward."

He stiffened. "I launched myself into empty space in an evac pod hoping to come across a ship that might lead me to you. What do you think?"

"We will come back for him?"

"Or do what we can to balance the scales, if it's too late."

That didn't sit right with her, but she nodded. It was the right decision. The kind of decision she should be capable of making as a newly minted major. The practical decision. The one with the least recklessness, the least possible casualties.

Tomas had probably trained to make decisions like this, in his role as a Nazca. Kind as he was to her, she had no illusions about who, or what, he was. No one spent their life infiltrating dangerous organizations to glean information without gaining a hard, honed edge. He'd be just as quick with a blaster as he was with a smile.

Poor Bero. If he could regain control of his faculties, he could free himself, but he was locked out of his own body. The feeling, she thought, was mutual. Her false foot clicked down the hallway as they walked toward the lifts to the dock where Biran's cruiser waited.

Maybe not entirely mutual, then. She still had her mobility, if not all her faculties. And Bero had been captured because he'd opened his doors to her. Because she'd taken Lavaux's bait and flown out to him on a Trojan horse.

She was pissed at him, sure. Wanted to punch him in his giant ramscoop of a nose. But she didn't want him dead. Didn't want him driven mad in isolation. He'd panicked. He'd acted poorly, dangerously. But what would she have done, in his position?

Bero didn't want to be a weapon any more than she wanted to be a Keeper.

"Here," Tomas said. The hall terminated in a bulb of a room lined with clear plex doors leading to narrow elevators.

"This one." He tapped the plex of a tube. "Going to be a snug fit for both of us," he said with a little smirk.

"I find I take up less space than usual." She gestured to her leg, revealed by the dress's high slit, and punched the button to open the elevator door. "After you."

He stepped in, turned around to face her, and she could see in the half second he went from warm smile to grave concern that he knew what she was going to do.

"Sorry, lover." Sanda hit the door-close button quick as a whip and keyed in the express line to the personal docks. Tomas lunged forward, palms striking the interior of the plex, mouth opened as he shouted something the plex kept her from hearing.

And then he was gone, whooshed away into the bowels of the station, set on a safer path than the one she meant to follow. She hoped he'd make it. Hoped he'd take the key Biran had passed him and burn hard out of this system. Make his way back to whatever system his Nazca base called home, report to his superiors, and go about some other, safer task without her.

Maybe it was the chip. Maybe it was just plain old Stockholm syndrome. Maybe she had a gunner's heart after all and couldn't make the call a major should. She didn't know why, not really, but Sanda'd be damned if she left a man behind without putting up one hell of a fight.

She stepped into an elevator and keyed it for alpha hangar.

CHAPTER 74

PRIME STANDARD YEAR 3543

THE WISDOM OF REPAIR BOTS

The elevator let her out at the edge of the hangar, just a few short walkways away from Bero. Sanda wished those walkways were longer. Then she might have time to figure out a plan.

Maintenance workers were absent for the time being, which was great, as she had no idea how she'd explain running around the hangar, without clearance, in a silk evening gown. She wished Tomas were with her—he was the spy, quick with answers—but pushed the thought away. He was safer making for Biran's cruiser.

Sanda followed a catwalk around the midlevel of the hangar, using wayward supplies and equipment to cover her from view as often as possible. From up high, she was better able to get a good, long look at the lay of the ground.

Things had settled down around Bero. The endless convoy of parts being dragged out of his cargo bay had stopped, the guards who'd overseen that work retreated for the time being. She couldn't see a single soul in the cavernous hangar, and that made her jumpier than anything. Just because she couldn't see them, didn't mean they couldn't see her.

It also stank, rather strongly, of being a trap. But if she turned back now, Bero was as good as dead.

She found a ladder down to the level Bero was on and half slid down it, landing in a soft crouch. The metal of her prosthetic foot echoed on the floor. Hangars weren't smoothed out for acoustics like the living and working areas of the station were. Here, where raw space was just a door away, every vibration counted, every noise could warn someone of something gone wrong. Not exactly keen sneaking-around ground.

Sanda tore a strip from the bottom of her dress, wanting nothing more than to make a joke to Tomas about being a heroine in an old CamCast, and wrapped it around the contact points of her foot until she could step without sounding like a mechanical army. She lost a little traction, but the leg was quick to adjust. She grinned and patted the coupling. At least it wasn't completely for show.

The way, so far as she could tell, was clear. No guards lined the ramp that bridged Bero's body to the hangar floor. Cameras must watch her every move, but unless she did something erratic, their security AIs weren't sophisticated enough to mark her as a threat, not now that she was ranked a major. She had the clearance. On paper, anyway. So sneaking around like a thief probably wasn't the best way to endear herself to those watching.

Sanda strode forward, shoulders back, head up, scanning the hangar as if she had every right in the galaxies to be where she was and knew exactly what she was planning on doing next. The champagne warming her system hopefully made her look more confident than she felt. Nothing like a little liquid courage when you were preparing to steal the most dangerous ship in the known universe.

She stepped into Bero's cargo bay, and the world closed in a little tighter on her. He wasn't here to greet her, to argue with her, even to lie to her. His voice had been silenced, and the hollow echo of her wrapped foot across his cargo floor sent shivers of rage through her. This was worse than anesthetizing a man and operating on him without his consent. This patient was awake, frozen, and silenced.

A muted, drawn-out beep made her nearly jump straight out of her fancy dress. She dropped to a crouch, taking cover behind one of the few mag pallets left behind, and waited. Nothing.

Then the beep again, a double punch this time.

"Grippy?" she whispered.

She'd last seen him hunkered down in the Hermes, hiding from the crew gutting Bero. The Hermes rested where she'd left it, severely lacking in cover now that most of the pallets had been hauled off. She forced herself to stand tall and walk straight over without a moment's hesitation.

The cockpit plex was hinged up, the system lights dimmed to power-saving mode. Grippy's little sonar eyes peered at her, and he hiccuped a double beep. He'd dragged himself into the backseat, scraping the pretty paint job on the ship in the process.

"I appreciate your redecorating, but you don't need to hide in here, little guy."

One short beep for *no*, which, considering the circumstances, could mean a lot of things.

"You think you need to hide?"

Beep.

"Huh. But you need to be in here?"

Beep-beep.

Grippy may have a brain the size of her fist, but hers wasn't much bigger, and she was sure his was more efficient. She leaned over the edge of the cockpit, peering into the low light in the backseat. Grippy was messing with the access panels she'd pulled the broken air filter out of, his thick clamps having a hard time gaining any sort of purchase on the handles. He must be trying to fix the broken filter. That was his purpose after all. To help fix up Bero. And with the big guy out of commission, it only made sense that his programming would move him over to the nearest damaged ship.

"You're not set up to fix the Hermes, and I need you to come and help me fix Big B, okay?"

Beep.

"Fine." She really didn't have time for this. "I'll figure it out on my own."

Beep.

"You don't think I can?"

Beep.

She reached to grab the bot. His treads hissed on the fake leather seat as he rolled out of reach, clamp-hand pawing at one of the panels like a cat trying to break into the food cupboard.

"Look." She hauled herself up so that her torso hung over the cockpit's edge and strained, grasping the handle on the panel. "Nothing but a broken air filter. You can fix it later, I promise."

She yanked the panel out. It wasn't the air filter panel, but a long, sleek brick of black metal. Frowning, she turned it to its side on the backseat, leaning so far forward that her feet lifted off the ground. A line of LEDs ran along the far edge, symbols etched just below them, all flashing green. She turned it over, trying to remember where she'd seen something like it before.

Tomas's signal jammer. The device he'd used to make sure they weren't overheard discussing the chip in her head. His was smaller, slimmer, but the structure was the same. The symbols beneath the LEDs almost a perfect match. A signal jammer of that size could easily silence Bero.

"Grippy, you're brilliant."

Two beeps.

She dragged it toward her across the seat, looking around for any ready tool to bash the thing in. There'd been wrenches stowed in the bay's side panels. Those would do.

"You're a long way from the party," Lavaux said.

Sanda dropped to her feet, pretending to have never seen the jammer, and stretched like she'd been going for a stroll. Lavaux walked up the ramp into Bero's cargo bay, a cigarette dangling between his fingers, one hand on his hip as he surveyed what was left in the bay. Maybe three meters stretched between them, the Hermes a physical barrier. She smiled, stepped away from the Hermes, and leaned against a wall panel.

"I've been isolated a long time," she said. "Needed to get a breather. I guess this ship still feels like a safe place."

"Really?" He flicked ash. "I would have thought it was more of a prison for you."

"It's complicated."

"I see." He circled toward her, slowly, pretending to look around the bay but drawing closer to her with every step. "They're looking for you. Wondering where their manufactured hero has run off to. Biran's a clever boy, but he can only stall for so long. Luckily my dear wife keeps tabs on everyone of consequence. It's why I married her, you know. Saves me the trouble."

"Have to keep an eye on a lot of people, do you?"

"Me? No. But it can be useful. At the end of the day, I'm only looking for one man."

"And who might that be?"

He was near enough to lunge for. Up close, his skin was eerily smooth. She slipped a hand behind her back, trailed her fingers across the cool metal of the wall in search of the panel's release mechanism.

"His name is Rayson Kenwick. I believe you've met."

She tried to keep her expression neutral, but she could see by the hungry gleam in his eye that she'd given away her surprise. Her fingers curled against the push mechanism.

"Never had the pleasure. We had better get back to the party. Maybe we'll find your friend there?"

"Your brother was not careful when he watched the message from *The Light*'s captain on my ship. Kenwick was here." He gestured to take in the ship. "And you, it seems, are the recipient of his misplaced gift."

"I don't know what you're talking about." Even she didn't think her tone of voice was convincing.

He tsked. "Don't fib, my dear. It's unbecoming of a major to lie to a Keeper." He twisted his wrist, and something dark and metallic dropped into his palm. "I think it's time you and I had a little one-on-one."

CHAPTER 75

PRIME STANDARD YEAR 3543

ONE MORE GOODBYE

The party swirled around Biran, indifferent to his pain. The smile he wore was tight, but natural enough to pass muster among those who did not know him. And no one at this party knew him. Not really. Those few of his cohort who'd finagled their way out of the Cannery and into the celebration stuck close to him only long enough to find someone older, more important, to drift off to talk to.

Biran couldn't blame them. He wasn't very good company. Every ounce of his willpower was funneled into not looking in the direction he'd last seen Sanda and Tomas go. Into not thinking about Anaia, locked up somewhere deep in the Cannery, unaware of the jubilation going on above her.

Did she even know he'd been successful in bringing his sister home? Would she care?

At the edge of the party, near the entrance the butler bots used to bring drinks and snacks out, Hitton approached Director Olver. Biran watched, grateful for the distraction, as Hitton leaned over and whispered something into Olver's ear. The older man's face wrinkled as he grimaced and nodded once, firmly, then set an empty glass on a butler bot's tray. He offered his arm to Hitton, who took it, and as they skirted the edge of the party toward the exit, Singh caught sight of them and followed as discreetly as she could.

Biran frowned.

Keeper Shun appeared out of the crowd, her young face bright with a real, happy smile. The most unfettered expression he'd seen in weeks.

"Speaker Greeve," she crowed with pride, placing her hand on his wrist while he struggled to watch Olver and the other Protectorate members over his teacher's shoulder. "I'm so very proud of you." Her smile widened to manic proportions. "I always knew you were special—your aptitude tests were the brightest we'd seen in decades, after all—but I'd never dreamed you would actually do it. That you'd bring your sister home."

She kept on talking, praising him with a fervent passion that would have made his cheeks turn scarlet under other circumstances. Now, he couldn't take his eyes—or his attention—off of the other members of the Protectorate, schooling together like fish toward the exit.

"Excuse me, Shun," he said, forgetting to use her Keeper title as he gently removed her hand from his wrist. "It is good to see you again, but I have something I need to see to."

Her brows pressed together in consternation. "Is everything all right?"

But he'd already slipped away from her, following Singh, Olver, Hitton, and Garcia out of the party and through the doors into the Cannery. They froze as a group, hearing the door open behind them, and turned around to face Biran. He said nothing, only crossed his arms and waited.

Olver sighed and shook his head. "We'd hoped to keep your nose clean of this."

"I am a member of this Protectorate." He scanned their ranks, swallowing as he realized Vladsen and Lavaux were absent. "And it seems we are not all gathered. What's happened?"

"Nothing's happened," Singh said, stepping forward with her chin tipped up. "We are going to execute our duties."

Something in the way she said *execute* made his skin crawl with sick realization. "Anaia. You're going to hear her trial."

"Trial?" Hitton shook her head. "There will be no trial, Speaker Greeve. You caught her red-handed acting as an agent of Icarion. The footage from the *Taso* has confirmed the fact, not to mention what we learned from the data scrub of her laptop. She's been feeding information to Icarion for years. We go to remove her chip, for Ms. Lionetti is no longer a Keeper."

Biran licked his lips. "You're going to kill her."

"We're going to do exactly what we've said," Olver countered. "You do not have to join us. A majority of the Protectorate is all that's needed to enact a removal."

"No. I should be there. Lead the way."

Singh looked like she was considering a protest, but Garcia caught her eye and shook his head, causing her to raise her hands toward the ceiling in a shrug before stepping aside to let Biran pass. Cloistered in the middle of the pack, he followed as they filed into the elevator. Olver scanned his wristpad over the level selection and tapped in a floor Biran had never heard of, let alone been to: B.

"We don't have a basement," Biran said.

"Correct. It stands for Beta. We rarely need to use this section of the Cannery, but all members of the Protectorate have access. Even you, Speaker Greeve."

"Though I don't know why you'd ever want to come here," Singh said, shivering lightly.

The door slid open. A dark hallway yawned before Biran, recessed lighting in the creases of the ceiling giving the grey-painted walls a sickly yellow glow. Sun-simulant lighting. The people kept down here weren't expected to leave anytime soon.

Olver led the way past a series of unmarked doors to the end of the hall. He swiped his wristpad over the lock and the light shone green, letting them in. It took Biran a moment to understand what he was seeing.

Four guardcore, in their black-plated armor, stood around the four corners of a chair. It was the same kind of chair he'd sat in to have his Keeper chip implanted, the body thick with soft padding and the back shaped into a cradle to support the head while exposing the brain stem to the technician.

A chair in which Anaia was strapped. Thick FitFlex straps wrapped her arms to the arms of the chair, the inner space of her elbow exposed so that she could be given an injection. Her skin had already been swabbed, the shine of antiseptic and bandage plastics revealing she'd already been stuck. Her grey-green eyes snapped up as the door opened, locking onto him.

He should want to squirm, he thought. Should be embarrassed—ashamed even—that he was standing here, free, while his friend faced extraction. The memory of her, bent over her laptop, that last look she'd given him that'd been real—and full of guilt—as he'd stumbled through her door haunted his every thought. His fists clenched.

"Has she said anything?" Olver asked as he took a tablet held out to him by a guardcore.

"No, sir," the neutralized voice said.

Olver sighed, flicked the tablet off, and crouched before Anaia to be on her eye level. "I won't lie to you. There is no undoing what you've done. Our technicians are combing every piece of correspondence you've ever sent. Every second you've ever been on video. We will figure out what you've sent to Icarion, and how long you've worked for them. That is only a matter of time. What we cannot figure out from the raw data, what we cannot know, is why? Why have you turned on your people, Ms. Lionetti?"

She slid her gaze away from Biran to match Olver's, and she smiled at him, slow and predatory. "Then that is what you won't know. That is what I'll take with me."

"Anaia—" Biran said, taking a step toward her. The guardcore shifted their stance, so he stilled and clasped his hands together in front of his abdomen, where they could see them. "I need to know. Please. Why would you do this? Why…" He swallowed. "What will I tell your parents?"

"Tell them whatever you'd like." Her pupils dilated, widening so that they chased out the green-grey he'd known most of his life and transformed her into the alien creature she'd become. When she spoke again, her voice was slow, slurred. The sedation injection taking root.

"Did you find Sanda?" she asked.

"Yes."

Her smile relaxed, lost its edge. "Good."

"She's ready," one of the guardcore said.

Olver pushed himself up, knees cracking. "Then there is no sense in delay."

Sweat gathered in the small of Biran's back as Olver turned and took a chip injection gun from a guardcore's outstretched hand. A click echoed in the room as he flipped a switch, transitioning the same device that implanted their chips—an only marginally risky procedure—to one that would remove them. It might as well have been a pistol aimed at the back of her head.

Olver stepped behind her. A guardcore reached out, gently pushing up the back of Anaia's hair. Her head dipped down, jaw slackening as the sedative ran its course.

Weight constricted Biran's chest. He closed the distance between them, dropped to one knee, and grabbed her hand—strapped down to the chair. He clung to the tips of her fingers. She forced her eyes up. Blown pupils reflected his own stricken face back to him.

"I'm sorry," he whispered.

"I know."

The gun fired. Her body jerked, spasming against the restraints. Her fingers dug into his, nails biting, eyes rolling back and then... Nothing. She went slack, head lolling to one side. Her chest rose and fell, breaths deepening, but those eyes slid shut and would not open.

Biran scrubbed the back of his wrist across his eyes, clinging to those limp fingers. "What now?" he rasped.

Olver handed the gun off to a guardcore. "She will be cleaned, given antibiotics to fight off any infection caused by the excision, and placed in stasis."

"Stasis?" Biran forced himself to look up at Olver, whose face was empty.

"Show him," Hitton said. "He should know where his friend will be buried."

"Very well." Olver gestured to the guardcore. "Prepare her. Biran, come with me."

He did not want to leave Anaia alone with those strangers. A stupid thought, he knew, but every instinct in his body screamed against him just...walking away while she sat there, unconscious and vulnerable. Not that there was any guarantee she was even in her own mind. There was no solid research on what happened to a brain once the chip was removed. A coma, sometimes death. He wished, bitterly, that she had died instead of fallen into the coma. At least then she'd know real peace.

Olver waited, the door half-opened. Reluctantly, Biran let her fingers come to rest against the arm of the chair and stood, hovering, wondering if he should say something. Wondering if she could even hear him.

"I'll see you soon," he whispered, patting the back of her hand once before stepping away. Somehow, that image of her—shocked and nearly vibrating with guilt—would not return to his mind. He saw her only as she existed in that chair. Limp, hollowed out.

He hoped, when they discovered he had helped Sanda escape with an illegal chip in her head, that the removal would kill him.

Olver took a few short steps down the hall before scanning his wristpad to open the nearest unmarked door. It blinked green and swung inward on its own. Yellow lights came up, flickering on down the length of a long, narrow room. And they just kept on coming.

"What...?"

His eyes adjusted. Rows upon rows of evac pods lined the walls of the room, stretching off into an indeterminable distance.

"How many?" he asked, when the silence had stretched as long as those lines of coffins.

"Dozens," Olver said quietly, as if he were afraid that to raise his voice would wake the sleeping dead. "Not all traitors, like Anaia. For some the Keeper chip did not sit well, their bodies rejected it, and we did what we could to recover them. Others...Catastrophically failed duties. Smaller betrayals. We all know the risks before we take the chip."

"And what will be done with them?"

Director Olver half turned, beckoning Biran back into the hall. Back to the party, from which Sanda was—if all had gone well— making her escape.

"That," he said, "is above my pay grade."

CHAPTER 76

PRIME STANDARD YEAR 3543

IF YOU CAN'T FIX IT, BREAK IT

Sanda hit the panel release just as Lavaux brought up his stunner. A crackling sizzle filled the air. The cupboard door shuddered under the strike. She choked on the scent of ozone, hacked up a cough, and grasped whatever she could get her hands on in the cupboard. Metal, cold and heavy. She clenched her fist and yanked out an oversized ratchet.

Before she could get her arm up to swing, Lavaux's stunner hummed to life again. She threw herself down, cursing as she rolled under the body of the Hermes and scrambled to her feet on the other side.

Lavaux laughed. "I appreciate your pluck, but you have nowhere to go, Greeve. The hangar is mine. The cameras are mine. It's just the two of us. And, I am sorry to say, it was me who put in the work order for that leg of yours."

A soft glow radiated from the back end of the Hermes, Lavaux's wristpad brought live. She heard the subtle shudder of haptic feedback, buttons vibrating under Lavaux's touch, and then her prosthetic went limp, dead weight. She swore and gripped the rim of the open cockpit to keep herself from buckling under the loss of strength.

"You're a sadistic sonuvabitch, Lavaux. I wonder just how many laws you're violating right now."

"Wrong question. You should be wondering just how many who enforce those laws will *care*." He stepped around the ship, faced her dead-on, and tipped the stunner back, resting it against his shoulder. Slowly, he strolled toward her, flicking ash from his cigarette. "One, maybe?" he mused, cocking his head to the side. "Your brother, no doubt, might raise some objections. But I've been at this a very, very long time. Do you want to know what your story will be? What the new headlines will say?"

"I have a terrible feeling that you're going to tell me." She struggled to straighten herself, hooked her elbow over the edge of the cockpit, and clung on for all she was worth. The stupid silk of her dress made it easier for her to slip back down.

"Major Greeve's mind"—he tapped his temple with the business end of the stunner—"shattered by Icarion torture. Hero driven to self-annihilation on the deck of the ship that broke her. That sort of thing."

"Not very catchy," she said, digging her fingers into the internal molding of the cockpit for all she was worth. If she could just get some purchase, some leverage, she could get a good swing in. He was in spitting distance now.

"Tragedy has never needed to be clever." He brought the stunner up, aimed it straight at her chest. A shot like that'd be enough to send her heart into a rhythm from which she'd never recover. She got the feeling this wasn't Lavaux's first dance.

But it wasn't hers, either. She gripped the molded interior of the cockpit for all she was worth and swung her body around on a pivot, slamming her chest into the hull of the Hermes as she brought the ratchet down on the jammer. Sparks exploded from the box, followed by a wisp of blue-grey smoke. Burnt plastic perfumed the air as, one by one, those little LEDs winked out.

Lavaux's shot scorched the floor where the bulk of her body had been just a second before. A low hum filled the hangar, vibrating deep in the metal all around them. Sanda grinned. Bero was waking up.

"Not just the two of us anymore, is it?" she said.

"You fucking bitch."

He grabbed her hair and yanked. Sanda hit the ground, her prosthetic bouncing against her good leg hard enough to leave a bruise.

She flipped to her back, got her palms on the ground and pushed, scrambling backward, away from Lavaux. His cigarette was gone, a tuft of her hair in his fingers instead.

She lashed out with her good leg, caught him in the shin and made him jump before he could get the stunner leveled. The ratchet was—she cast around—there, an arm's length away. She dove for it and gripped it in both hands, rolling sideways as she brought it around in a wide arc.

Her arms shuddered from the impact. A direct hit. Lavaux swore and dropped to one knee, the leg of his pants torn open over the shin where she'd hit. For just a second she saw a gleam of metal, of titanium-white, beneath his split flesh, a hint of red trickling out. Lavaux fired the stunner, grazed her hip. She juddered and jerked, vision going white at the edges, every muscle in her body flexing to the current.

Before he could take aim again she lashed out, aimed for his forearm. Something hard and brittle cracked under the force of her blow and then the stunner flung away—clattered beneath the Hermes, raining pieces. She laughed, spat blood on the floor.

"Think that's funny?" Lavaux said. Fucker wasn't even out of breath.

She pushed to her knee, bum leg dragging beneath her, and settled into the tightest crouch she could manage, ratchet poised to strike, every muscle that would answer her demand flexed and ready to uncoil. "Funniest damn thing I've seen in two years."

He smirked. Stood slowly, unfolding to his full height. She tensed, expecting a strike, but he just brought a hand up and pushed back his ruffled hair, set straight the collar of his dinner jacket.

"You'll find I do not need a weapon to achieve my goals. Though I tend to prefer cleaner solutions."

She got a good look at his leg, then. He gave her time enough to take it all in.

Where milky white bone should have been, a shaft of material she'd never seen before gleamed. Pale as titanium, reflective as chrome. Her own eyes stared back at her out of that horror show of a skeleton, but not for long.

His flesh crept back across the gaping wound, a network of synthetic vascularity weaving its way over the exposed bone. Muscle thickened. Oozed bright blood, but not at the rate a wound of that size should dump the stuff. The edges of his coffee-dark flesh quivered, hinting at their own reweaving.

"What are you?"

He smiled, flicked his torn pant leg to clean off a few specks of blood. "Humanity's next great leap forward. Or did you think there was only the secret of the gates to be found between the stars?"

"Found? You really are crazy."

She crept backward, putting space between them while the wound she'd dealt him reknit itself. Her leg dragged, metal squealing against metal, but he didn't seem to notice, or to care. That was what really unsettled her. Flesh regeneration aside, it was his blasé manner that gave her chills straight down to her perfectly normal spine. He behaved as if this were already a done deal. As if she were dead, the information he sought recovered, and everything else was a boring formality.

Bero hummed all around them, waking, but too slow. Then she realized. She'd thought Kenwick was a product of identity theft, of too-smooth plastic surgery. She'd been so, so wrong.

"Dios fuck. Kenwick. It wasn't a false identity. He was the same man, the same man through two hundred years. How? How is that possible? How are *you* possible?"

He raised both brows at her. "You didn't know, then? Hmm. I'd expected as much, but couldn't be certain." He cracked his wrist, popping it into socket after the blow of her ratchet. "Poor stupid Kenwick, to run so far so fast, only to die unknown, alone, at the hands of those who mistook him for a Keeper. Foolish, to be taken by a smartship of all things. I wonder if the Icarions ever realized what they held. What he was." Lavaux's lips curled with pure disgust. "Such wealth lies in your head, Major Greeve. And you don't even know how to use it."

"The coordinates," she said, then cursed herself for saying anything at all.

"You've seen them? Ah. That . . . That just won't *do*." He cracked his knuckles and stepped toward her.

CHAPTER 77

PRIME STANDARD YEAR 3543

SAFETY PROCEDURES ARE ONLY SUGGESTIONS

Lavaux struck so quickly she didn't have a moment to brace herself. Sanda gasped, pain radiating from her stomach as his first punch landed. She jerked right, threw herself to the side, and brought the ratchet up to strike, or at the very least, slow him down. He batted it away and grunted.

"Stop embarrassing yourself, Greeve. You're injured. Tired. Weak from malnutrition. You feel all that, don't you? Weighing you down?"

"Fuck yourself," she hissed. But he was right. Moving was like swimming through congealing amber. Whatever strength she'd felt after a few glasses of champagne and a handful of appetizers at the party was long gone. She needed rest. Food. And to get this deadweight prosthetic off her damn leg.

He grabbed her forearm, yanked her to her knees, and leaned down close to get a good look at her. Not her face. He obviously didn't give a shit about her. No, his other hand tangled in her hair and he pushed her head down, parting her hair with thumb and forefinger to find the telltale scar of a chip implant just above the base of her neck.

She took a swing at him with her free hand but didn't even get close.

"Remarkable," he said, mostly to himself. "I can't believe they got it to take. You must be very strong, Greeve. Thank you, for being a good host for my wayward friend's possession."

She heard the wasp-wing flutter of a pocket knife being flicked from its housing. Panic constricted her throat. The humming in the hangar intensified. LEDs lining the walls flicked through random reels of color. Maybe Bero couldn't find his way back to consciousness. Maybe the damage was already done. And even if he could, what could Bero do to help her, talk Lavaux to death? She had to stall.

"They kept his head," she blurted. "Kenwick's. As a trophy. Splayed it open like a butterfly and suspended it in the middle of their lab. He didn't look like you. He looked human."

He paused, grip tightening on her wrist. "I *am* human. And Kenwick was a fool. He took the coordinates because he believed what we were becoming was wrong, corrupted. If he figured out a reversal of the process..." Lavaux blinked, shook himself. "Never mind that. I've been waiting ages for this."

The tip of the knife bit the skin at the back of her neck. She jerked forward, tried to lean, to squirm away, but she was stuck. Crumpled on the floor, weakened, unable to use her deadweight leg. She might as well be a kitten drunk on milk, for all the fight she had left in her.

Blood welled. Trickled down the back of her neck. She gritted her teeth and strained anyway.

"Enough," Bero said.

Lavaux cocked his head to the side and smiled. "Ah. *The Light.* You've been a very naughty spaceship. You and I are going to have a good, long talk about what you've seen."

"Get out."

That tone was new. Deep. Not the panic she was used to.

"Clever ship you may be, but you don't call the shots here, Tin Man," Lavaux said. He sounded amused, like he was watching a child try to wheedle its way into getting an extra cookie.

"You are going to step away from Sanda and leave my cargo bay, or I will render this station and all its inhabitants to plasma."

Lavaux rolled his eyes. "So dramatic. Your engines have been cut off. I should know. I'm the one who gave the order."

"Your puppets forgot. I've been looking after myself for a long, long time."

Alarms blared, red LEDs flashing in gleaming arcs all across the ceiling and floor. The bland woman's voice was gone, muted forever if Bero had managed it, but Sanda didn't need the alert to know what was going on. Bero's engines fired into life, rumbling as they gained power. Even in Bero's cargo bay, so far from his engines, their piercing shriek pained her ears.

Lavaux lurched backward, dropped his knife as he brought his hands up to cover his ears. Sanda fell to the ground, covered her ears with her hands, and screamed above the wail of the engines.

"Bero! You've made your point!"

No answer. Metal screeched as Bero initiated the forcible closing of his cargo bay doors. Her stomach dropped. There was no way in hell she was getting trapped on this ship again. Not with Lavaux.

"Open the hangar doors," Bero said.

"You're not leaving this station." Lavaux got his feet back under him and made for Sanda. She swore and army crawled to the Hermes.

Bero said, "I am leaving. You have five seconds to initiate opening the hangar doors."

Dios. Bero's cargo doors wouldn't even be closed in time. She wanted to snap at him for trying to kill her after she'd removed the jammer that'd made him lose control of himself, but she needed every single molecule of air she could get.

"Don't be idiotic," Lavaux said. "You will damage yourself severely if you try to force those doors."

"One," Bero said.

Sanda was two meters from the Hermes.

"Two."

Lavaux screamed something, but Sanda's world was comprised of nothing but effort. All she could hear was the strain of her breath, the wail of the sirens, and the blood pounding in her ears.

"Three."

She grimaced, stretched out an arm, and gripped the Hermes's undercarriage.

"Four."

Halfway up. One knee bracing on the ground, her prosthetic dangling behind her. If Bero would just give her a few extra seconds, then—

"Five."

Bero's engines fired. He slewed around, pointing his nose at the massive doors of the hangar bay, and hit the throttle. He wasn't anywhere near relativistic speeds but, then, he didn't need to be to rip a space dock apart.

A concussive *whumph* deadened her hearing, all the complaints of metal and propellant reduced to little more than a cotton-stuffed whine in her head. As the ship turned, she slammed into the side of the Hermes, damn near lost her grip, cursed and gasped and tried to yank herself into the shuttle. Its air filter was broken. It hadn't been topped up. But it was something, anything, between her and the empty black.

Impact jarred her, rattled her bones and made her bite off the tip of her tongue. She turned her head, saw through the narrow opening in Bero's cargo doors debris wash away from him. Bits of twisted metal spiraled outward, a shredding hurricane, a cluster of junk was all she could see and then—the exterior of the hangar bay, and the hole blown straight through its doors.

Bero pulled away from the station. Black filled the view through the gap. Lights and alarms screamed about atmosphere and pressure, but Sanda knew she was already dead.

Her grasp gave out. She fell away from the Hermes and slid across the floor, unable to stop herself. One last burst of power from Bero, one sharp turn. What little cargo was left in the bay flung through that slit in one great purge. Grippy slammed into her chest. She wrapped her arms around him, held him close.

Fleet training covered getting spaced. She'd run the scenario until she was sick of the word. But, hey, here she was, and the training took over just as intended. Exhale everything you've got, and pray.

At least her leg wasn't weighing her down anymore.

CHAPTER 78

PRIME STANDARD YEAR 3543

NOT ENOUGH

Fifteen seconds.

The longest anyone's ever stayed conscious in a vacuum before blacking out, for sure, is fourteen seconds. But they weren't sure about the timing, the exposure was accidental, and so they came up with fifteen: That's all the time you've got in the void. Fifteen seconds, to say goodbye.

Fourteen seconds.

She'd been blown out backward, facing Bero as he raced away to an unknown future. Dents marred his body, long scrapes stretched along his once pristine paint. A survivor of a war he didn't want, didn't understand. Sanda couldn't bring herself to hate him for spacing her. He was beautiful to her, with all his scars. She hoped he found peace.

Thirteen seconds.

Grippy was cold in her arms. Metal gives up heat faster than skin in the void. His little LED lights winked at her. He didn't beep. Like her, he probably didn't know what to say.

Twelve seconds.

Bubbles burst along her tongue. They should hurt, but they just tickled. The pain should be immense, all-encompassing. She'd already evacuated herself, a sordid mirror of her awakening on Bero. But the pain wasn't coming. Nerve damage. That was never a good sign.

Eleven seconds.

Her trajectory locked in. She was headed back-first toward the hangar that'd trapped Bero. She'd never make it there in time. There was nothing out here to change her direction with. All she could do was turn her head, crane it over as hard as she could to get a look at the world she was leaving.

Ten seconds.

Ada Prime's Casimir Gate filled the sky. Only from this position, she thought, can one truly appreciate the gate's beauty. It was massive beyond her ability to articulate—even Keep Station, so large it housed hundreds of thousands, barely managed to eclipse a small stretch of the ring that was the frame of the gate. The light of it had always been Ada's guiding star.

Nine seconds.

The gates were humanity's greatest accomplishment. The bastions of their civilization. She thought of Lavaux, his leg, his words. The Keeper chip lurking in her skull hiding a secret not of the Keepers. She hoped Tomas would follow this thread. That he'd use his Nazca connections to discover what lay beneath the surface of a mystery she was only now glimpsing the edges of.

Eight seconds.

A gleam lay stationary in the space before her. A ship, a missile, a failing of her retinal system. Maybe this was the light, the narrowing of the tunnel, which many claimed to have seen before they died.

Seven seconds.

Vision began to go. She tried not to think about what that meant.

Six seconds.

How unfair, that she should not get the full fifteen.

INTERLUDE: ALEXANDRA

PRIME STANDARD YEAR ONE

PLUTO'S ORBIT

Alexandra Halston gripped the handle attached to the wall of the sleep pod and shoved, shooting herself "up" through the central body of the *Reina Mora* to the viewing room. Five years of travel, and the ship was bleeding the last of its velocity as it prepared to enter orbit around Pluto. When she'd been back on Earth drawing up plans, she'd wanted to orbit Pluto's moon Charon to be closer to the gate. That argument had been intense, but eventually cooler heads—mostly Maria's—had prevailed, and she'd acquiesced to getting as close as the Pluto orbit would let them.

All bitter feelings fled the second she'd woken that "morning" and gotten visual on the construction of the gate. Any closer would have been pointless, unable to see the full scale of the project. From this vantage, the gate—a Casimir, she was calling it, as a cheeky wink to the science she still did not understand—dominated the single viewing window of the *Reina Mora*.

It would be invisible to the naked eye, a thin line of black against the endless dark of space, if it weren't for the construction bots lighting it up. Most of the building payload for the gate she'd sent in anticipation of her own journey had arrived in only a few short months. Light packages riding massive solar sails flung out from the Elequatorial lift and, as the world eventually discovered, the Lunar elevator as well.

While Lex had stewed in the slow, but safer, transport, the bots had gotten to work, following the piecemeal instructions programmed into them to create the object described by the Sphere in full glory. They had been finished for weeks, now, all preliminary checks cleared. Waiting while the *Reina Mora* bled velocity, and the governments and journalists of Earth drove themselves mad demanding she explain herself.

A whisper of war hounded her heels. Larger nations rattled sabers at the smaller nations—Puerto Rico had declared its independence—that housed her facilities. Nukes were rumored to be pointed at the Elequatorial lift. At the moon. The nations of the world promised to arrest her the second her feet were back on terra firma. They, of course, hadn't a clue she had no intention of striding upon that blue marble once again. How could they?

They would see, she thought, as she kicked around, her short hair drifting in the zero gravity, that everything was about to change. That the petty squabbles of Earth would soon lose meaning.

"Ready?" Maria propelled herself into the room with a shove and gently play-collided with her, pressing her full lips against Lex's as they bumped into the window. They turned together, both stuck to the spectacle outside the window like glue. Lex traced her finger across the scar tissue on the back of Maria's neck, revealed by the lack of gravity lifting her hair, and smiled as she shivered.

"Yes. We only have so much time before we lose the view. It has to be now."

Maria squeezed her hand and flipped with the ease of a gymnast, pushing off the wall to clear the view for the cameras. This moment would be Lex's alone. Maria shifted around, adjusting the articulated arm that held their video camera in place. For the past five years, they and the crew of the *Reina Mora* had made Lex's location ambiguous. Many suspected she was on the *Reina Mora*, but they had never been able to confirm.

This time, Lex forwent the ties she'd used to keep her hair corralled, the tight clothes she'd worn to make sure nothing drifted. She faced the camera down, the Casimir Gate lit up in the window over her shoulder, and let her hair drift. Her clothes bunch. Whatever happened next, the subterfuge was over.

Maria flicked the broadcast button. Lex began.

"People of Earth"—and she flashed that charming smile—"I bid you hello from the orbit of another world. Behind me"—she gestured to the gate—"the fruits of my, and all of Prime's, long labor. You have questions, I know. But now is not the time for such things. Now, I bid you only: watch."

Perfectly concerted, the lights around the ring intensified, Lex turning so that her profile could be seen—but not obstruct the view—as the Casimir Gate began, slowly, to power up.

Her heart thundered so hard in her head she could hear nothing else. As the light increased, the rings began to spin, looping one inside the other, until they'd dissolved into a blur of grey light—something brighter, crackling and blue-violet barely discernible in the center.

"Bring up the POV feed," she demanded.

On a tablet Velcroed beside the window, the camera view of bot one snapped to life. A maelstrom of the visual spectrum assaulted the camera at first, a violent lash of color and chaos, and then, in a breath— calm. Serenity. The gates must be moving, power poured into them, but everything snapped into peace. Frozen in place, unmoving.

"Push it through," Lex said.

Behind her, the hesitant voice of Erik, "The readings aren't—"

"Now."

The bot's view shuddered as it was commanded to deploy its rockets. It flung toward the center of the gate in a burst of speed, its camera flickering as it got closer and closer to the gate. Then—grey—not the blue of a cut feed, but visual snow, mottled and crackling. Lex held her breath, pressed her palm against the plex window.

The image resolved. Space, black as anything, shot through with stars in an arrangement that tickled at her memory. She knew that system. She just didn't know it from this angle.

"Where is it?" Maria asked.

"Tau Ceti," Lex said, and burst into happy tears.

CHAPTER 79

PRIME STANDARD YEAR 3543

DAY FORTY-THREE

G et that damn robot out of here," Papa Graham said.

His voice jarred her out of unconsciousness. Sanda tried to open her eyes, but they were swollen shut, an unsettling liquid dribbling along her cheeks. Her tongue filled her mouth, cutting off air. She tried to take a breath through her nose but that was nearly swollen shut, too. She jerked, gasping, arms spasming as they tightened around the rigid body of Grippy.

"Forget the robot," Tomas said. Strange, that she would hallucinate Tomas hanging around with Graham, the grumpier of her dads. "Do you have a pressure chamber? A suit we could throw on her? If all else fails, we could stick her in the airlock halfway chamber."

"What kind of racket you think I'm running here? I've got real medical facilities. NutriBath."

"Then stop jaw-wagging and go prep the fucking thing," Tomas growled. The voices were muted, as if they were speaking through mouths stuffed with marshmallows. A tinny ringing persisted in her ears.

Someone stomped off hard enough to vibrate the floor she lay on. A mask was pressed over her face, hard plastic digging into the tender flesh of her bruised cheeks, and then a gust of cold, pure O_2 rammed itself up her nose.

"Easy," Tomas said. Grippy was pried from her arms. She fumbled, reached for the robot, the only thing she knew was real in her half-wakened state. Tomas took both of her hands in his. He didn't squeeze, but she didn't need the pressure to realize what was wrong with her hands. Her fingers were swollen, massive sausages with dried and peeling skin. Everything was cold. That realization came to her slowly. Not painfully cold—no, she'd gone beyond pain again.

She tried to part her lips to ask what had happened, if Tomas and Graham were real or the hallucinations of a dying mind, but her mouth was already opened. Her straining cracked her lips. Warm blood trickled along her chin.

"Hey, don't try to talk. We've got you. You're safe. I'll explain later. Just don't die on me, okay, Major?"

Safe. Hah. That was definitely a dying mind trying to comfort her, keep her from panicking. Funny thing, a mind trying to keep itself calm. It's not like it mattered. If she were going to die anyway, maybe she wanted to go out a screaming, gibbering mess. She settled on calm. It wasn't like she had the strength to try any other method.

Footsteps vibrated back toward them. "Gotta get her to the thing, it's a built-in."

"That's a shit design."

"Work now, complain later."

They lifted her. *No, no, no*, she wanted to scream. Her skin stretched to its limit, every limb and cavity a sloshing mass of fluid. She was a balloon set to burst, every slight jostle threatening to be the one to break her.

Okay. Maybe she wasn't dead yet. But she sure as shit felt like she would be any minute now.

"Take it easy," Graham growled.

"Likewise, old man," Tomas said.

Good to know the men in her life were getting along. Her head lolled, someone's hand darted in to support it, fingers brushed the incision Lavaux had made.

"Shit," Tomas said, "someone tried to crack her head open."

"Someone? We know it was Lavaux. I'm going to rip that bastard's testicles out through his ears and choke him to death with them."

She wanted to tell them not to bother, Lavaux was definitely dead. Unless they'd picked him up, too, he'd been spaced right alongside her. But then she remembered the flesh knitting back into place around his bone, and her head hurt too much to figure out if the vacuum was enough to kill a cockroach like Lavaux.

Her body shifted. A different kind of cold seeped up beneath her, around her, flooded over her and into her, soothing aches and cuts she didn't even know she had. Her head went under, the O_2 mask was taken away. Gel flooded over her face, seeped beneath her sealed-shut eyelids, crept into the cracks in her lips, swirled around her bloated tongue, and ventured up the broken paths inside her nose.

The human survival instinct was a good few thousand years behind technological advancements. She thrashed, tried to take a breath but sucked down NutriGel. Luckily, the medis who'd made the stuff had prepared for human folly. Sedatives washed through her. Consciousness slipped away.

CHAPTER 80

PRIME STANDARD YEAR 3543

A DAY TOO FAR GONE

He'd watched her go. He'd stood up there, beaming smiles upon a crowd of sycophants, and watched her take Cepko in hand and disappear into the garden. Into the night—into an uncertain future that had resulted in her battling for her life while he tried to keep too many in the crowd from wondering where she was, from noticing that she—their hero, their star of the hour—had fled into the black.

He should have been there.

Over and over again, the images replayed themselves. Plastered all over the news, there'd been no possible cover-up this time. Bero tearing the station's dock apart as he lurched for freedom. Sanda falling, falling, unprotected into open space, and then Graham's cargo hauler swooping in to snatch her out of the end of everything. Thank everything that ever was for Callie. She'd gotten through. She'd kept her promise. Underneath the table, he tapped out a quick text to her: *Anaia Lionetti. Look.*

He hit send.

Had Graham succeeded? Biran didn't know. Didn't want to know—because if Graham contacted him now, it would be to say he was coming home, or hiding out somewhere until things calmed down. There would be no good news in that call. In that call, Sanda was dead. There was no point in hiding, in secrets.

And so he prayed for silence. For unknowing. Because in uncertainty, Sanda had survived that fall.

What he knew—knew for certain—was that in her flight, Sanda had given him what he needed to survive his fall, too.

Big sisters. Couldn't help but look out for him, even when she was fleeing for her life.

"Are you listening?" Olver snapped.

"No," he said, truthfully. He'd been replaying that scene—Sanda's fall, the hauler's desperate flight—over and over and over again. Nothing the director had to say could ever be half so important.

Olver slammed his fist onto the table, making everyone gathered jump. The Protectorate, together again with General Anford. But not Lavaux. Never again Lavaux. Slatter had been right, there would be an opening on the Protectorate after all.

"God-fucking-damnit, son, I'm telling you you're dying. Do you understand? Do you understand what you've done?"

"Oh, yes." He held up a hand and ticked off the points one by one on his fingers. "Allowed unauthorized access to a Keeper miniMRI. Contributed to the destruction of the station's dock. Contributed to the escape of *The Light*..." He hmmed. "Am I missing anything?"

"Accessory to the death of Keeper Lavaux," General Anford said. She had the look of a woman who hadn't slept in days. Biran felt guilty about that. It was the only thing he felt guilty about.

"Ah, right."

"Murder, Biran. Murder." The director sat heavily, his shoulders slumping as he raked a hand through his hair. "Lavaux was a good man. He didn't deserve to be spaced."

"He attacked Sanda. She defended herself."

"That's not what the security footage says," Vladsen cut in.

Biran met his gaze steadily. "Such things can be doctored."

"Who would do such a thing?"

"I'll come to that," Biran said, and turned away from Vladsen, ignoring the concern pinching that man's face. He'd lost his leader and tried to cover up what his leader had done in his final moments. Biran would fix that, would set it all to rights soon enough. But now he needed to fix his situation. "But first, none of you are asking the right questions."

"We have all the information we need," Olver said.

"What questions?" Anford said, leaning forward.

"Whose chip?"

"What does that even mean?"

"You know my sister accessed my miniMRI and scanned herself. What you don't know is the nature of the data she recovered. I don't know that, either. But I know whose chip it was."

"A fake crafted by Icarion, no doubt," Olver said, waving a dismissive hand. "We pulled the data she accessed. It was a garbled mess. Meaningless."

"I doubt that." From inside his coat pocket, Biran pulled out an old manila folder. Sanda had always had a love for the old-fashioned nature of paper, and he was grateful for the feel of it now. The tactile, solid, truth in his hands. He laid it down upon the table, turning it so they could all see the name written on the front tab. "Rayson Kenwick. The chip was his."

"Impossible," Olver said, his face creasing with real confusion. "I know that name. Unremarkable man, died ages ago."

"Not exactly. He faked his death and fled. Did you know he was a participant in the Imm Project?"

"A botched affair."

"Maybe. Maybe not. The point is, he fled because the chip in his head wasn't a Keeper chip—it hid something else. Something we can't access, and something Lavaux knew about. Lavaux was looking for *The Light*, yes, but only because he believed it the last known location of Kenwick's chip. He switched gears when he realized the truth."

Vladsen stammered, "I-impossible."

Biran met his gaze again and felt a surge of power as the young-looking man shrunk back from him. "Far from it. And Lavaux was not alone in his search. There are others like him, others who know about these dark chips. Know that they contain hidden information. More like Kenwick."

"And what information do you propose these chips are hiding?"

"I don't know. But I intend to find out."

"You won't survive the next twenty-four hours, Greeve."

Biran leaned forward and flipped the folder shut, then laced his hands across it and stared General Anford straight in the eye. "I'm the only one who can do this job, General. I'm the only one with the contacts, with the drive, with the position. This is a security threat the likes of which the Keepers have never seen. This goes beyond the Protectorate. This is your jurisdiction."

She licked her lips. "And why are you the man for this job, Greeve?"

"My contacts—"

"No. Not politics. You. Why you?"

He leaned back, dragged his arms across the table and let them come to rest on the arms of his chair. Why him? Technically, he could hand this information over—had already done so—and Anford would pick up the thread. He had no doubt she could run a capable investigation.

But she believed in him, she just needed a push. Some confirmation of her instinct, and that couldn't be his curriculum vitae. This wasn't a job interview. It was a character assessment. She needed to know something real. Something...hard. Something true.

"I'm good at finding things," he said. He just wasn't very good at keeping them.

CHAPTER 81

~~PRIME STANDARD YEAR 3541~~

PRIME STANDARD YEAR 3543

IN A SYSTEM FAR, FAR AWAY

She awoke in light. Jules groaned, reached up to rub a hand across her face, and then jerked it away—expecting burns, expecting pain—but there was nothing. Just her skin, a little pink and puckered, peeking out at her from the long sleeve of a hospital shirt.

Hospital. That explained the white. Not the lab, then—she'd destroyed that—but she'd destroyed herself, too. Or had meant to. But if she were being honest with herself, a lot of the things she'd done over the course of her life had been with the buried intention to destroy herself. Those hadn't worked, either, so why should an explosion?

She sat up. Someone had decked her out in pale green hospital garb. A faint breeze tickled her head, and she reached up to rub her—scalp? Her hair had been shaved off. She shook her head, struggling to make sense of what had happened, of where she was.

Because this definitely wasn't a hospital. The walls were white, and the floor was the cheap composite that covered all government buildings, but the furniture was just...wrong. Her bed was something more like a cot, her room too small to allow a lot of medical staff in at once. Maybe it was a prison. But they wouldn't have put her behind bars until she'd woken up. She was pretty sure there were laws about that kind of thing.

A screen flickered on the wall, turning on the second her eyes skimmed over its surface. Some newscast from another planetary system—Ada, was it? She'd heard that name. There'd been a war there, hadn't there? The thing with Icarion.

She swung her legs over the side of the bed and paced the edge of the room, wary. No cameras that she could see—but that didn't mean much—and the door was most definitely locked. A small window inset in the door gave her nothing: just more white hallway beyond.

"Hello?" she called out. No answer, naturally.

Jules turned her attention to the news broadcast and almost fell over her cot. The image cut away from the broadcaster to some sort of party, a fancy gala in a garden the likes of which Jules had never had the pleasure to visit. Dignitaries and obvious Keepers mingled together, all happy as starshine to be welcoming some woman named Sanda Maram Greeve home—a military type, she gathered. Lost in the war but found. Hurrah.

But that wasn't what almost knocked her over. In the crowd, along-side some Keeper who looked like he spent more time at museums and parties than doing any Keeper work—what *was* their day-to-day job, anyway?—stood a whip-thin, pale woman. Her hair had been piled on top of her head, but it was the same woman. Jules would know her anywhere. The woman looked up, at the camera, as if she were staring straight into Jules's eyes.

"Do you think my hair looks better like that?"

Jules almost jumped out of her skin. Through the plex window, Rainier stood, looking much the same as she had when Jules had thought she'd blown her up.

"That's a recording," Jules insisted, though the voice screaming in the back of her skull knew it wasn't. "It's old footage. You're not... you can't be..."

"In two places at once? I really can't, you're right, you know. Because there are *more* of me, and so I can't ever just be in two places at once."

"You're insane."

"Well, of course I am. I am only a fraction of what I once was, after all. How can a mind ever be sane if it's been all broken up? There used to be so much *more* of me, glorious and whole. But that body was damaged and dying when my husband found me and saved me."

"He should have left you to rot." Jules backed into the cot, bracing her palms against the hard edge to stabilize herself.

"Oh, quite probably. But here I am—and there I am, and a few other places, too. It is nice, in some ways, to be distributed. The world is easier to understand when you can move through it, touch it, taste it, really experience it. But it takes so *long* for thoughts to pass from one body to the next. I don't know how you humans do it. Doesn't it get tedious?"

"What in the hell are you?" She breathed out the words, hands trembling as the Rainier Lavaux over her shoulder smiled brightly into the news cameras.

"How rude of me not to introduce myself properly! You've been healing so long, I can't expect you to remember our little chats from before. My names," she said, "are Rainier Lavaux. I am a ship. Or I was. I intend to be again, someday, you know. What do you intend to be?"

Jules couldn't get her brain around that, so she asked the only thing she felt mattered, "Where's Lolla?"

She blinked too-wide eyes at her. "Who?"

"The girl! The one at my crew's nest. You didn't kill her, so where is she?"

"Oh, the little one. She didn't take as well to the upgrade as I'd hoped. You had done so well, I thought it might be something in your environment. An unfortunate failure."

"Would you make sense!"

"The little one. She touched the agent. It didn't like her very much."

"What agent?" Jules paced the length of her tiny white cage to slam her palms against the door. "Who touched Lolla?"

"Why, the agent you brought to your nest, dear. Would you like to see her?"

Jules froze. She couldn't breathe. Her vision swam for a second and then she put her forehead on the plex, feeling the cold seep into her skin.

"Lolla's here?"

"Yes."

"Take me to her!"

Rainier eyed her warily. "Only if you promise to behave yourself."

Jules clenched her jaw. "Yes. Fine." She held her hands up, palms out. "You took all my weapons, anyway, remember? I swear to you, if you can bring me to Lolla, I won't try anything."

"Hmm, I don't *believe* you. But that's okay, isn't it? You really are no match for me. And besides, the walls here will shoot you if you try to hurt me. Keep that in mind, okay? Security here is quite advanced, and rather fond of this body of mine."

Jules thought back to the voice in the speakers at Udon-Voodun and the wispy, familiar voice she'd tried to forget she'd heard the first time she entered the lab. If even a sliver of what this woman had to say was true, her consciousness might be connected to the electronic systems of the building.

Not that it would mean anything, if Lolla was here.

"I understand," she said. She kept her hands up and her posture slouched to show she wasn't ready to fight. "Please. I just want to see her."

The door slid open, disappearing into the wall. Jules stepped into the hall hesitantly, arms up, scanning the narrow passage for any hint of where she was. Camera eyes watched her from every angle, the lenses not bothering to be inconspicuous. The halls were lined in the same silvery-white tile as her cell, but if there were any other cells like hers she couldn't tell, because not a single one of the other doors had a window.

The slippers she'd been given shuffled across the floor as she followed Rainier. She had to grip with her toes to keep them from sliding off, and the drawstring on the scrub pants they'd given her kept coming loose. She hated medical attire so much. Not just because it signaled vulnerability—you only wore this stuff if you were going in for something serious—but because it hamstrung her ability to move.

What she wouldn't give for her old boots and pants back, at the very least.

Rainier led her to a door and passed her hand over the lock scanner—no wristpad. That's what'd struck her as strange about the woman at first that Jules couldn't quite place. Though she wore a sleeveless dress, her arms were bare, no hint of a tan line where the pad would normally go. Jules's own arm was pale as dry sandstone in a large rectangle where her wristpad once lived. Her connection to the world, severed. She hoped like hell that the authorities she'd lured to the lab had gotten enough data to track Rainier down.

Jules followed Rainier through the door. A round room awaited her, the ceiling inset with pale white and blue lights, giving the room a frosty, cold feeling even though the temperature was the same as it had been in her cell. Jules shivered and rubbed her bare arms, shuffling forward as Rainier stepped aside. In the center of the room, on a dais meant to support a NutriBath, rested a clear-lidded preservation pod. Jules's heart lurched.

She knew what must be in that pod. Knew, too, that she didn't want to look. That every second her sinking feeling went without confirmation was another second Lolla was not in there. But the dais drew her forward, as if its mass were great enough to exert gravity upon her.

Lolla. Pale—paler than Jules had ever seen her—her fan of light brown hair spread like a spider's web in the gel medium of the pod. Her eyes had been closed—they didn't need to be, she knew, some went in staring—and her arms crossed over her chest. Based on the lack of tension in her face, the neutral set to her lips, Jules guessed that the girl had been asleep when she'd been put under. Good. No one should have to experience coming in or out of stasis conscious. She pressed her palm against the plex, trailing her gaze over the display inset in the top of the pod like a crown for Lolla. Her vitals were good, if elevated for sedation.

"What happened?" she asked, not daring to take her eyes from the girl lest she vanish in a blink again.

"Her body fights the agent. Not like yours. Your cells lapped it up like a sponge."

A silent sob wracked Jules's body as pieces clicked into place in her mind. Things she'd ignored—tried so hard to ignore—flooded her thoughts. The blaster wound. Her lack of need for food and sleep. Her body was changing, had been ever since she'd touched the wraith mother. But it hadn't been wraith mother at all. It'd been something else—this agent—meant for Keepers, or other beings. Not Grotta scum like her. Like . . . Like Lolla.

"Why? Why is my body accepting it when hers isn't?"

"Haven't a clue, but I mean to find out. Do you want to help her, Juliella?" Rainier's cold hand alighted upon her shoulder. "Do you want to save your little one?"

"Yes. Please. Yes."

"Then you and I, we have a lot of work to do."

"Anything," Jules said with more feeling than she'd mustered in ages. "Anything."

CHAPTER 82

PRIME STANDARD YEAR 3543

ANY DAY'S A GOOD DAY IF YOU WAKE UP ALIVE

Sanda woke screaming. She thrashed, arms ramming into the hard enamel of the NutriBath cocoon, leg jerking and kicking as she struggled to gain purchase against the slick bottom. She heaved forward, folded over herself and hacked lumps of gel into the pool still draining from around her lap.

"Hey, lass," Graham said softly. A hand, rough and familiar, closed around her upper arm and held her steady while she retched. "Slowly now, my brave girl. We're taking you out earlier than we should be, but you're stable. Wouldn't do to break an arm flailing around like that, now would it?"

"How long?" she demanded and wiped gel from her eyes, scrubbing at her lids with the backs of her hands.

"Six hours. We're through the gate. The vacuum really chewed you up."

Blinking the rest of the goo clear, she opened her eyes. The room lacked the antiseptic charm of Bero's medibay. Bare metal walls hemmed in a dingy storage room, mag pallets that had seen better days heaped high with haphazard boxes held in place with thick straps. Yellowish light gave the room a warm feeling, though she was shivering so hard she feared she'd bite her tongue in half. Again.

"Through the gate...We're in the Atrux system?"

"That's the place." Graham handed her a microcleanse rag, and she wiped herself down, then took the robe he offered. She was weak, but she had a much easier time dragging herself out of the cocoon this time around. At least this time she knew what to expect from her missing leg.

Graham gave her a hand and, when her foot was on solid ground, folded her into a hug so tight it took her breath away. She may have been weak, but she wasn't so worn out she couldn't hug him back just as hard. Sanda buried her face in his chest and tried not to cry. Luckily, she was severely dehydrated.

"Thought I'd lost you again," Graham said into her hair.

"I just keep getting harder to kill." She laughed, then fell into a rasping cough. "What in the hell happened? Did I really hear Tomas earlier?"

"Aye, the lad's here." Graham nudged her away from him, held her by the shoulders at arm's length while he took a visual inventory of any injuries she might have remaining. The NutriBath had done its job. She wasn't back to full health, but he nodded to himself.

It'd only been two years, but he looked older to her in the same way Biran had. He was still a mountain of a man, standing five inches taller than her, his skin taut around ropey muscles he'd gained from hauling cargo. He always was too impatient to wait for the hand trucks to warm up. Wrinkles mapped his face, leading the way to his fully grey hair. It did a number on your body, thinking your loved ones were dead. She should know.

Graham scrunched up his nose. "When Ilan and I came up for what we were calling your coronation, we knew something was funny. We're no strangers to Keep Station, all the guards know us, but we were getting waylaid at every step. Couldn't even grease the usual palms. Your brother sent a reporter down to tell us what was up.

"Ilan kept them busy while I slipped around and got to the dock where we keep this old thing. The ship was loaded, ready for a run out to one of the moons in Atrux, so I had good reason to be checking her out—and no one minded much, as I was far away from the party.

"While I was trying to find a way to Biran's place from the docks, I saw your man—Cepko—poking around Biran's cruiser. Thought he was going to steal it. Nearly bashed his head in before he was able to explain who he was." Graham grinned. "Your old dad's still got some moves.

"So I let him go and asked what he thinks he's doing, leaving you behind if things are so dire, then some bloke's voice I don't know comes over the speaker and addresses us by name—tells us we got, oh, five minutes to get over by the big hangar or you're going to be spaced. We took the cargo hauler, 'cause neither one of us understood all that fancy shit in your brother's cruiser, and were shocked as all hell to see you blown out the back of that big ship."

The storage room door burst open as Tomas barged in, looking rough around the edges. A purple-red bruise marred the side of his face, his broken arm hastily put back in a sling that was just dirty enough for Sanda to be convinced Graham rummaged it from somewhere on his ship. His color was pale, his brows knotted with worry.

"You're awake?"

"I really hope so."

"What's the rush, Cepko?" Graham asked.

"Bero's moving. You'd both better come see this."

Sanda put her arm around Graham's shoulders and let herself be half carried to the communications deck. The ship was an older model, one of Graham and Ilan's first acquisitions, from a time when they disliked having any human quarters outside of spin-grav. She found that affectation pretty annoying right now.

The deck sported a captain's chair, a second's chair, and a nav chair, all pointed straight at a smartscreen covering the entire forward bulkhead. On the screen, Bero loomed, a news ticker running beneath the image detailing the stand-off between Prime and Icarion's rogue ship. They didn't have the details; the reporter was babbling on about the Icarion ship wandering too close to the station and damaging the docks, but it was enough. Bero had spent the last few hours hovering just close enough to Ada Prime's planet, station, and gate to make taking any shots at him tricky. And now, he was moving.

"What do you think he's doing?" Tomas asked.

Graham got her settled in the second's chair while Tomas hovered at the nav podium, checking streams of data she couldn't make out.

"No idea. We didn't exactly have time to chat."

The newscaster's satellite camera followed Bero as he swung around, slowly, pointing his engines—and by proxy his weapons system—back somewhere closer to the star even while he pointed his nose out to empty space.

"What's he aiming at?" she asked.

"Running that now," Tomas said.

She gripped the armrests until her fingers trembled, watching the little glints of Ada Prime's gunners swoop in close to Bero. He was a big ship. It'd take them a long time to knock him down if they decided it was worth the risk to fire.

"Come on," she willed all those making decisions halfway across the galaxy from Atrux, "he's not pointing his weapons at Ada. Let him run."

"Got it," Tomas said. "Weapons pointed at an Icarion research station in orbit around Icarion's moon. Operations classified."

Tomas leaned back in his seat, letting his hands go limp on the controls he'd been fiddling with. He glanced over at her. They locked gazes, and he nodded.

"He's going to take out the station that made him," he said.

"What's on the other end? What's he headed toward? It can't just be the station. Those coordinates in my head, is he going there? Bero's powerful, but he's beholden to Newton just like the rest of us: For every action, there is an equal and opposite reaction, so if he busts that station, where will he end up?"

Tomas shook his head, waving expansively over the display. "I have no idea. As far as I can tell, it's all uncharted in that direction. And the coordinates you flashed me earlier from the chip aren't that way, either."

"So what? He takes out the station at the cost of flinging himself into empty space, to die a slow, degrading death?"

"Lavaux might order him destroyed anyway," Tomas said.

"Lavaux is dead." She paused. "Probably. Maybe."

"Maybe?" Graham asked.

She waved at him to shush; the newscaster's voice had lifted in pitch. She couldn't see the woman reading the cast—all the cameras were centered on Bero—but she knew panic when she heard it.

The newscaster said, "My s-sources indicate that the ship appears to be siphoning power into its engines. Sources inside Keep Station fear the ship, called *The Light of Berossus*, may be preparing to engage in combat. The safety of the station, and Ada, are, of course, top priority, and tensions are high on the memory of the bombardment."

"If they only knew," Sanda said.

"Oh. That's bad," Tomas said.

"What?"

"Chatter indicates damage abatement protocols. Lavaux may not be calling the shots, but someone jumpy is."

"They can't just—"

On the viewscreen, Bero flared to brilliant life, knocking out the cameras in a blast of radiant white light. Sanda lurched forward, arm extended, as if she could do anything at all to stop what was happening.

"Report," she demanded.

"Shit," Tomas said. "Trying to find alternate feeds. Hold on."

The light could have meant a lot of things. It could have been an attack, but it just as easily could have been Bero firing up his big engines and gunning for the empty black. She held her breath against the possibilities, tried not to snap at Tomas as his fingers danced across the controls, dialing up hundreds of news feeds and some not-so-public satellite imagery. A cackle hissed through the speakers. Tomas hit a button and pressed his earpiece in tighter.

"I'm into Prime secure feeds," Tomas explained, then held up a hand to forestall her questions. He was listening. Hard. "No shots fired," Tomas said. "No attack was made on Bero. Keep Station is running damage assessments, but it looks like Bero just took off."

"Took off? Did he alter course? There was *nothing* out there, Tomas, you said so yourself. That's a suicide run."

"Trying Icarion primary channels now."

An older man in an Icarion jumpsuit appeared on the screen, his eyes sunken and his collar yanked open and twisted askew. Over his shoulder, video of Icarion's largest moon dominated. Streaks of fire blazed through its thin atmosphere.

The reporter spoke in grave tones, gaze locked on the camera. "A research station in orbit around Moon-One has been damaged in the blowback from *The Light of Berossus*'s engines. We do not yet know at this time if the damage was a premeditated attack by Ada Prime using our own ship against us. Officials have confirmed that the loss of the station was total.

"We do not yet have a death count. Damage to moon habitats is so far superficial, but all residents are advised to take cover in appropriate shelter..."

The viewscreen flickered, this time to the face of the first reporter, nothing but empty black space green screened in behind her where Bero had once been. "It's gone," she said, bewildered eyes wide, sweat sheening her forehead. "*The Light of Berossus* is gone."

ACKNOWLEDGMENTS

I want to begin by thanking my husband, Joey Hewitt, who is my partner in all things. Whether he's offering feedback, making me tea, or listening to me mutter about random facts, my writing, and my life, wouldn't be half so rich without his support.

Thank you to the Murder Cabin Crew, Andrea Stewart, Tina Gower, Annie Bellet, Karen Rochnik, Marina Lostetter, Thomas K. Carpenter, Rachel Carpenter, and Anthea Sharp, for not yet killing me. I mean, uh, for your support and writerly friendship. Getting together once a year for a week of writing and scheming has been invaluable.

I am forever grateful to my local writer buddies who meet up with me for coffee, chat, and—eventually—work. Erin Foley, Earl T. Roske, Trish Henry, Laura Davy, Laura Blackwell, Vylar Kaftan, and Clarissa Ryan have all been instrumental in cheering me on.

And a very special thanks is needed to my editorial and publication team. To Sam Morgan, my agent, for his endless encouragement and good humor. To Brit Hvide for her razor-sharp editorial insight, and for geeking out with me over Mass Effect. To Kelley Frodel who is an absolute wizard at copy editing. To Nivia Evans, for her fresh set of eyes. To Sparth for his amazing artwork, and to Lauren Panepinto for her excellent art direction. And, of course, to all of those at Orbit who I have yet to meet. Thank you all.

extras

about the author

Megan E. O'Keefe was raised among journalists and, as soon as she was able, joined them by crafting a newsletter that chronicled the daily adventures of the local cat population. She has worked in both arts management and graphic design, and has won Writers of the Future and the David Gemmell Morningstar Award. Megan lives in the Bay Area of California.

Find out more about Megan E. O'Keefe and other Orbit authors by registering online for the free monthy newsletter at www.orbitbooks.net.

if you enjoyed

VELOCITY WEAPON

look out for

THE LAST ASTRONAUT

by

David Wellington

Sally Jansen was NASA's leading astronaut, until a mission to Mars ended in disaster. Haunted by her failure, Jansen now lives in semi-retirement, convinced her days in space are over.

She's wrong.

A huge alien object has entered the solar system and is now poised above the Earth. It has made no attempt at communication.

With no other living astronauts to turn to, NASA wants Jansen to lead an expedition to the object. For all the dangers of the mission, it's the one shot at redemption she always hoped for.

Yet as the object reveals its terrifying secrets, what began as a journey to make First Contact turns into a desperate struggle for survival . . . and one thing becomes horribly clear: the future of humanity lies in Jansen's hands.

PERIAREION

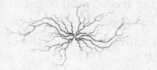

I t's a grand old flag, it's a high-flying flag . . . "

"The crew of Orion wish you back on Earth a happy and safe Fourth of July. We may not be able to set off any fireworks out here, for safety reasons, but we want everybody to know we haven't forgotten what this day means to America."

"That's right, Blaine. And here on Orion, we have two reasons to celebrate. Today we passed the orbit of the moon. Today we can officially announce that the four of us have now traveled farther than any human beings in history."

"USA! USA!"

"That's Mission Specialist Ali Dinwari holding the flag we're going to plant on Mars in just a few short months. Next to me here is Flight Surgeon Blaine Wilson, who's keeping us all healthy—"

"Keep it up, keep it up, twelve more minutes and then you can have a hot dog!"

"Blaine's a cruel taskmaster, but it's true—you see Science Specialist Julia Obrador back there on the treadmill, she's waving for the camera. We have to exercise for two hours a day each because there's no gravity on *Orion*. We need to keep our bones in good shape so when we get there, we can walk on Mars instead of crawling."

"You forgot to introduce yourself, Sally."

"Right! Good thing you're here to remind me, Blaine. I'm Sally Jansen, mission commander—"

"Gonna be the first woman to walk on Mars, what what!"

"—Ha, yeah—mission commander on *Orion 6*. We're going to finish this exciting special meal of hot dogs and fruit punch, and then we're going to get back to work. But we couldn't let the day go by without letting America—and everyone on Earth—know that we're—"

" . . . And forever in peace may you wave!"

"—right on course, headed for a historic moment on the red soil of Mars. Happy Fourth, everybody!"

"OK, *Orion*. Returning to normal communications. Great job up there—the media people are all smiling, which is a good sign."

"Thanks, Houston." Commander Jansen looked back at her crew and gave them a thumbs-up.

"You got it," Ground Control said. "Though—I'm getting a message. It looks like Julia has been neglecting her social media. Remember, you all need to post at least three times a day. If people back on Earth don't hear from you regularly, they start to worry about your mental health. It looks bad."

"Obrador?" Jansen asked.

"I'll do better, just . . . Jesus. Can I get off this thing?"

Blaine Wilson gave Obrador a nasty grin. "Another nine minutes."

Jansen shook her head, though. There was work to be done. "Forget it, you're done—and don't worry about InstaChat, either, we've got things to do. Wilson, I don't want to hear about it. Houston, this is Jansen, this is MC. Have you found an explanation for that anomalous reading I told you about? On my board I still have a red flag for blowthrough pressure in the number six fuel tank on the excursion module."

"*Orion*, we're assuming it's some kind of faulty relay. Those systems are all locked down for this part of the mission. Blowthrough was never requested, so there's no reason for a red flag, or any kind of flag. Everything else looks good, it has to just be a glitch."

"It's been showing red since we finished our orbital transfer burn. I don't like it, Houston. Maybe I'm being paranoid, but—"

"It's your call, MC. You tell me what you want to do."

Jansen glanced around the HabLab at her crew. They were in good shape, a little pumped from having a chance to call home, even if it was just a recorded message. "This is a good time to check it out. I'm asking for authorization for an EVA so I can evaluate the tank with my own eyes. We good?"

"You have authorization for EVA. Just be careful, MC."

"Understood, Houston."

SALLY JANSEN, ASTRONAUT: Are we really doing this? I don't want to talk about that day. I . . . OK. OK. Back then, NASA had us do pressers and media ops constantly. I mean, all the time. The Orion program cost billions, and they felt they needed to show American taxpayers what they were getting for their money. They wanted us all to be rock stars, to be TV people. I was never comfortable with that. Jesus. Can we take a minute? Just a minute, let me collect myself. The thing you have to understand is that July fourth, 2034, was the worst day of my life.

Wrestling into the extravehicular activity suits was hard enough in the close confines of the HabLab; climbing through the soft lock afterward was enough to leave Jansen breathing heavily. The HabLab module—where the astronauts lived and worked—was a seventeen-meter-long inflated cylinder made of two flexible walls with the ship's water supply circulating between them. The water kept the habitat cool or warm as

necessary, and provided shielding from the radiation environment of deep space, but the module bounced and shook every
time you shoved against it, like an air mattress, in a way that
did not inspire confidence.

The habitat's airlock was a narrow fabric tube that you had
to wriggle through in slow motion, every twist and turn careful
and premeditated so you didn't snag any of your space suit's hard
parts on the thin walls. One tear in the soft lock and they would
have to scrub the EVA until it could be repaired.

Somehow she managed to climb out onto the side of the
module, where she helped Julia, the mission's science specialist,
make the same transition. Obrador's face was white as a sheet
behind her polycarbonate faceplate, with sweat beaded across
her forehead. She gave Jansen a nervous laugh and clutched the
ship as if afraid she would fall off. It was no surprise she was
nervous—Obrador had done plenty of EVAs in simulators, but
had never actually been outside the ship since it left Earth. Jansen
patted her on the arm to reassure her.

Hell, Jansen wasn't exactly frosty herself. Around them the
universe stretched off in every direction, empty and dark. Jansen
fought down a sensation of vertigo. This time was different, she
thought. Different from all the EVAs she'd done on the Deep
Space Gateway station while she'd trained for this mission. It
took her a second to realize why.

There was nothing below her. Nothing on either side, nothing above her ... nothing at all, just nothingness ... forever.

In space, in microgravity, there were technically no such
things as up and down. Yet human brains were so well adapted
to gravity that you couldn't think like that, you couldn't ever
accept it. It had been easier on the space station because the Earth
was there, enormous and bright. The curve of the planet was
down, your brain could accept that. It could learn to accept that

you were flying, that the ground wasn't rushing up to meet you, because there was a down to point to. Not anymore.

Fifteen days out and the Earth was behind them, bigger than any star but far enough away that it offered no psychological relief. Jansen's head started to spin as it tried desperately to find a reference frame—and failed.

"There's always something to hold on to," she told Obrador, who nodded gratefully. "You never have to let go, OK? Just grab something and hold tight."

Inside her helmet, Jansen's voice sounded small and tinny, as if she were hearing herself over the radio. As if it were somebody else offering this good advice.

She looked at *Orion*, at the spacecraft, and somehow found her bearings. There were four modules in her ship, each with its own function. At the back was the service module, which housed the ship's main engine and its fuel supply. Forward of that was the conical command module, the only part of the ship that would go back to Earth once they were done on Mars. The long cylinder of the HabLab was wrapped in an insulating shroud of quilted silver fabric, dazzling in the sun, and then at the far end, pointed right at Mars, was the spherical excursion module, with its landing legs sticking out in front of it like the antennae of a bug. The lander that would set down on the red dust and was where she and Ali would live in close quarters for two weeks while they collected rocks and took meteorological readings.

That was still months away. If she couldn't find the source of the fault, if everything looked fine but the red flag persisted, she knew it was going to irritate her for the rest of the mission. Best to get it cleared up now.

"Hand over hand," she told Obrador as she climbed the side of the habitat module, pulling herself along. "Little by little."

She had to be careful not to go too fast, or she might launch herself right off the side of the ship. She wouldn't go far—her safety line would catch her—but she had no desire to find out what that felt like.

"Understood," Obrador replied.

Her helmet radio crackled and spit at her. Just noise on the channel, probably cosmic rays, charged particles hitting her transceiver as they blasted through the solar system at nearly the speed of light. If she closed her eyes right now she knew she would see green pinwheels of fire spinning behind her eyelids. They were exposed out here, practically naked to the invisible energies that filled what looked like empty space. But as long as they were back inside within an hour, they should be all right.

"Wilson, I want you to crack open the excursion module," she called. "I need your eyes on the inside to help me trace this problem."

"Understood," the flight surgeon called back.

"Where do you want me?" Dinwari asked.

"You head down to the command module and strap yourself in." He could keep an eye on their suit telemetry from there, and run the entire ship if he needed to. Putting him back there was just a safety measure, but NASA loved safety measures most of all. "I'm not seeing any damage to the exterior of the spacecraft. That's good. Obrador, how are you doing?"

"All good," Obrador called back. "You think this is a wiring problem? The bus that connects the ... the excursion module and ... the ... "

She could hear the fatigue in Obrador's voice. Every move you made in a space suit was exhausting. They might be weightless, but they still had mass, and every movement, every meter forward meant wrestling with the bulky gear. "Don't try to talk. Save your breath for the climb."

"Thought there would be . . . stars," Obrador said, ignoring her.

Jansen looked out at the black sky around them, the empty stretch of black velvet that could feel so close sometimes it was smothering you and at other times made you feel as if you were dangling over a bottomless pit. "You don't see stars out here for the same reason you don't see stars on a clear day back on Earth," she said. "The sun's light drowns them out." A wave of fatigue ran through her muscles, and Jansen stopped for a moment, stopped where she was and just . . . breathed.

When she'd recovered enough she started climbing forward again. She was almost level with the excursion module. "Blaine, do you have the forward lock open yet?"

"Just about," Blaine called back. "I'm equalizing air pressure between the excursion module and the habitat. It's taking a minute."

"No way to rush it," she told him. "OK. I've reached the number six fuel tank. I'm going to start a visual inspection." A broad, flat belt of metal ran around the excursion module where it mated with the HabLab. The fuel tanks hung off that belt like a ring of bells, each of them nestled in a tangle of pipes and wiring.

The tanks on the lander were separate from *Orion*'s main fuel system—they would be tapped only when the crew was ready to return from Mars. The hydrazine propellant inside them would be used to launch the lander back into Mars orbit, where it would reconnect with the HabLab and the command module for the trip home. For this outer leg of the journey those tanks were completely shut down and inert. They shouldn't be showing up on her control panels at all, much less reporting a low-pressure condition. It was a real mystery.

She could see most of the tanks from where she was, and they all looked fine. Some of them were obscured by the shadow of *Orion*'s big solar panels, though, and number six just had to be one of those. She sighed and switched on the lights mounted on her helmet. "Wilson, how are we coming along in there? I'll need you to crack open the FPI inspection panel."

"Uh," Wilson said, "FPI?"

"Fuel pressure indicator," Jansen said. NASA loved its acronyms, and there were a lot of them to remember. "The sensors are indicating that this fuel tank has lost pressure, which doesn't make any sense. I want you to open up the FPI panel and check the wiring in there, to make sure it isn't the sensor that's broken. There should be a diagram inside the panel showing how things are supposed to look. Just make sure the wires all match the diagram."

"I'm in the excursion module now," he told her. "I'm waving, can you see me?"

She wasn't close enough to any of the lander's tiny viewports to look inside. "Don't worry about me, I've got my own job to do out here. I—"

She stopped speaking. Everything went into slow motion. What she'd seen, what her light revealed—

"Boss?" Obrador asked from behind her.

Jansen licked her suddenly dry lips.

This was bad.

Number six tank was cracked. A big, jagged hole had opened up where it connected to the side of the module. Maybe a micrometeor had struck the tank, or maybe a piece of space debris. Either way it looked as if someone had fired a rifle bullet right through it.

She saw a pool of wetness all around the damaged area, a round, wobbling mass of liquid hydrazine adhering with surface tension to the excursion module's skin.

Then she saw bubbles form and pop in the middle of the glob of fuel. Air bubbles. Air that had to be coming from inside the spaceship. There had to be a leak—the same impact that tore open the tank must have cut right through the hull of the module. Hydrazine was leaking into the crew compartment of the excursion module. The module that they had just filled up with air. With oxygen.

"Wilson," she called. "Blaine, get out of there—"

"There's a funny smell in here," Blaine said, as if he couldn't hear her. As if she were in one of those nightmares where you shouted at someone to stop, to turn around and see the monster right behind them, but they couldn't hear you at all. "Kind of like cleaning fluid, maybe left over from when they sealed this module up. It's an ammonia-y kind of smell."

He was smelling raw hydrazine. Raw rocket fuel, which had aerosolized and filled the tiny module. He was standing in a cloud of flammable gas.

GARTH UDAHL, ORION PROGRAM FUEL TECHNOLOGIES SUPERVISOR: *Hydrazine is very hazardous stuff. It's a simple chemical, but it's incredibly corrosive. The smallest amount, if you breathe it in, can burn the lining of your lungs. It can also self-ignite, given the proper catalyst. Say a patch of rust on the inside of a panel. It's my opinion that once Dr. Wilson entered that module, he never stood a chance.*

"Wilson!" she screamed. "Move!"

She pulled herself along the side of the excursion module, pulled herself level with one of the viewports.

"Boss?" Obrador asked again. "What's going on?"

Through the viewport Jansen could see him burning. Hydrazine flames were invisible, but she could see Blaine smashing his arms against the consoles, trying to put out the flames. She could see his hair curl and turn black, could see his mouth open in a horrifying silent scream. He reached toward the viewport, reaching for her. Begging her for help.

Some cosmic mercy had killed his radio. She couldn't hear him, didn't have to listen to him burn. She saw him slam his hand against the viewport, over and over, maybe he was trying to break it, to get out, to get away from the fire—

In a second that fire was going to spread through the hatch. It would spread down into the HabLab. It could spread through the whole spacecraft. It wouldn't stop until it had consumed everything.

Somebody had to get the hatches closed, to contain it. But the only person close enough to do that was Wilson.

There was another way.

Sally Jansen had trained for a million different ways things could go wrong in space. She had drilled endlessly for every possible contingency. She knew exactly what to do in this case. It was right there in her brain, ready to access. All she had to do was open her mouth and say it.

If the two modules separated, their hatches would automatically slam shut. It was a safety feature.

It was the hardest thing she had done in her life. But she was an astronaut.

"Dinwari," she said. "Ali, can you hear me? Jettison the excursion module."

"Commander?" he asked, his voice very small. He might as well be back on Earth, shouting at her through a megaphone.

"Do it!" she said.

"I can't! Wilson's in there!"

Jansen had no time to waste arguing. She scrambled along the side of the excursion module, moving as fast as she dared.

She found an access panel between two fuel tanks and tore it open. Inside was a lever painted bright red, marked *CAUTION: EMERGENCY RELEASE.*

She pulled it, hard.

Explosive bolts connecting the excursion module to the HabLab detonated instantly, one of them going off right in her face. Light burst all around her and she was blinded for a second—a very bad second, during which she heard her faceplate start to crack. The explosion threw her bodily away from the module, swinging out into deep space on her tether, out of control and tumbling.

She could barely see anything as she went flying head over heels. She got only a glimpse of her spaceship coming to pieces.

A billowing cloud of condensing water vapor jetted outward from between the two modules, air rushing out of the HabLab. The cloud was cut off instantly as the hatches between the two modules slammed shut.

The excursion module tumbled as it accelerated away from the HabLab. The flexible habitat module sprang back and forth in an obscene motion that Jansen barely saw. She was spinning, spinning out to the end of her safety line, and then it snapped taut and she doubled up, her arms and legs flailing. She grabbed at the line and tried to stabilize herself, tried to get a grip as she looked back over her shoulder.

The excursion module was still moving, still flying away from them, tumbling wildly into empty space, its landing legs whipping around crazily.

Hands grabbed the shoulder joints of her suit, hands that pressed down and pushed her against the side of the HabLab, her cracked faceplate buried in the silver fabric even as ice crystals started growing across her view.

It was Obrador, crouching on top of her, protecting her from the debris that pelted the side of the HabLab all around her.

"Boss! What did you do?" Obrador screamed, but Jansen barely heard her. "What did you do?"

There was only one thought in her brain.

Jesus, God, whoever, please. Let Blaine die fast.

SALLY JANSEN: No. No. Stop—that's a lie. That isn't what I was thinking at all. I . . . I'm not proud of this, but if we're doing this, if we're going to be honest . . . my thought at that particular moment was just, you know. This is over. This is it. I'm never going to Mars.

TELEMETRY CHECK

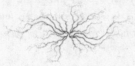

EXCERPT FROM AUTHOR'S FORWARD TO
THE 2057 EDITION OF THE LAST ASTRONAUT,
BY DAVID WELLINGTON

*I*t's my firm opinion that you can't understand what happened later unless you know what she was thinking, what she was feeling, that day in 2034.

When I was hired to write about the events of October 2055, I was told we needed to get the story on people's streams as soon as humanly possible. The public needed to know what had happened and what it meant. I was able to fulfill at least one of those goals. I did the research and put together a thing that looked like a novel and read like the instruction manual for an X-ray machine. The technical information was there, and the facts that were a matter of public record. Nobody understood what any of it signified, though. I didn't understand, myself. I'm not sure I fully understand it now.

I've been lucky enough to receive a lot of new information since then. Most importantly, I was given exclusive access to interview the people involved. I've included snippets from those interviews in the text of this new edition. I've also included the brief examination of the last day of the Orion 6 mission that you've just read. I think it may be the key that unlocks the true meaning of what happened during the mission of Orion 7.

But I've gone further than that. This is no longer a piece of journalism, no longer just a recitation of facts. I've tried to explore the psychology of the people who were there, even when this is, for various reasons, no longer possible. In many ways Sally Jansen's 2055 mission was not just an exploration of objects in space, but also a journey into the human mind. I feel the story is better for these introspections. You can judge for yourself.

Our story picks up twenty-one years later, when only one man in the entire world knew what was happening. I've done my best to examine what he was thinking, that day he jumped out of bed and onto a train.

Sunny Stevens pulled at the drawstrings of his hoodie. He wished he'd thought to change his clothes before he crossed half the country for this meeting. It had all been so last minute... When NASA actually answered his message, he'd basically just walked out the door. He'd never actually expected this to happen, and he hadn't thought to prepare.

Now it was time to make an actual decision. He could still walk away—say he was sorry, but he'd made a mistake. Take the train all night to get home and go to bed and pretend he'd never even thought of this crazy plan. Go back to work tomorrow at the Hive and hope nobody was monitoring his email.

Or he could go through with this.

He'd been sent through security, taken down a long hallway, and told to wait. Someone had asked him if he wanted a cup of coffee, and he'd said yes, because he hadn't actually been listening. Now he was sitting on a yellow leather sofa that probably dated back to the Gemini program, deep inside the maze of office complexes at the Jet Propulsion Laboratory. NASA headquarters, even since 2052, when they'd shut down the Johnson Space Center in Houston, after the flood.

A place he'd wanted to be since he was five years old. Back then, he'd wanted to be an astronaut. He'd wanted it so bad he'd devoured every piece of space news that came across his stream.

When Sunny was ten he'd watched Blaine Wilson burn alive in space, over and over.

By the time he was fifteen America no longer had an astronaut program.

Sunny had been devastated. His dream was shattered. Instead of flying through space he'd studied it through telescopes and become an astrophysicist. He would get out there, among the stars, one way or another. By the time he'd gotten his PhD, he'd accepted the fact that he was never going to pilot his own spaceship, never going to talk to Ground Control from a million kilometers away. He'd learned to live with that, to almost accept it.

And yet...now he was here. In Houston. For real.

He was thirsty, and he was hungry, but mostly he was worried that he wouldn't be good enough. That he wouldn't be able to make his case convincingly enough to even get NASA's attention. But his data was sound. It was good. There had to be someone here who understood its importance.

He'd been waiting for only about fifteen minutes when a man in an old-fashioned suit and a string tie came walking down the corridor toward him. The guy was white, maybe seventy, maybe seventy-five. He was what Sunny's mom would've called bone skinny. He was carrying two cups of coffee.

Here we go, Sunny thought.

"Dr. Stevens? I'm Roy McAllister. Associate administrator of exploration and operations." He handed Stevens one of the coffees.

"It used to be called human exploration and operations," Stevens said. He set the coffee cup down on an end table. He never drank the stuff.

"I beg your pardon?"

Sunny wanted to shake the man's hand, but he was worried his palm would be sweaty. "Your job. It used to be called human exploration and operations. You were in charge of manned spaceflight. Back when NASA did that kind of thing. You ran the Orion program. Now you're in charge of deep space probes."

McAllister's face was sunburned and weathered and hard to read. There was no missing the pinched annoyance there, however. Had Stevens already screwed this up?

"It's my turn to correct you. I'm not quite so old as you may think. By my time we called it 'crewed spaceflight.' Not 'manned.' "

"Right," Stevens said, closing his eyes in shame. "Right."

"At any rate, I believe I'm the person you wanted to talk to. Your message was a bit cryptic," the old man said.

Sunny cleared his throat. "2I/2054 D1," he said.

And that was it. The die was cast. No going back to the Hive, not now.

McAllister's smile faltered a little. "I'm sorry, I don't think I understand."

"That's its name. Its designation, whatever," Sunny said. He knew he was babbling, but he couldn't stop. "I haven't given it a name yet. I'm pretty sure I get to name it. I discovered it, after all."

McAllister nodded and pointed at a door a little way down the hall. "Let's go in my office and talk about this."

SUNNY STEVENS: *After the* Orion *disaster, NASA said they would take a couple of years to study what went wrong. Make sure it couldn't happen again. It took most of a decade, and with every year that passed NASA's budget got slashed, and slashed again. Congress invested, instead, in private sector space programs. After NASA went bankrupt in the forties, they had to break up the second International Space Station and drop its pieces in the Pacific Ocean. After that, commercial spaceflight seemed like the only game in town. So when it was time for me to find a job, I didn't even think of applying at NASA. By 2055, NASA hadn't trained an astronaut in ten years. It was still around; it takes forever for a government agency to die. Their mission had changed, though. No more spacewalks or golf games on the moon. Instead they put all their budget into two things: satellite surveys of the damage caused by climate change and deep space probes to the planets. Robot ships. Nobody declared a national day of mourning if a robot blew up in orbit around Neptune.*

McAllister sat down behind a cluttered desk and folded his hands together. He gestured for Stevens to take a seat across from him. "I understand you work for KSpace."

Stevens grinned and plucked at his hoodie. "What gave me away?" The hoodie was bright orange—KSpace's color—and there was a pattern of tessellating hexagons down the left sleeve. KSpace's logo.

It wasn't a logo that was likely to make him a lot of friends in NASA headquarters. KSpace saw NASA as the esteemed competition. NASA saw KSpace as the boogeyman.

"Yeah, I'm on their deep space research team, over in Atlanta." KSpace had its center of operations in Georgia, in a sprawling campus called the Hive. The place where Sunny had lived, played, and worked for the last four years. The Hive had some first-rate telescopes, so he'd liked it there. Until now. "Basically we do cosmology and astrophysics."

McAllister nodded. "The message you sent me contained the orbital elements of an...asteroid? Comet? Something like that. An object passing through the solar system. I had one of our people take a look, and they just about split their skin."

"I have more. More data I can give you," Sunny said.

For more than a year, Sunny had been tracking 2I. He had *terabytes* of data on it. He knew its albedo, its mass—he had spectroscopy and light curve analyses. He'd been building his case for a long time.

When he took his data to his boss at KSpace, he'd been told it seemed interesting. That the company would look into it.

That had been three months earlier, and since then he'd heard nothing. Not a peep.

Somebody had to do something. Somebody had to send a ship to go look at this thing. If KSpace wouldn't do it, then Sunny was sure NASA would. It would *have to*.

Except judging by the look on McAllister's face, NASA didn't necessarily agree.

"Dr. Stevens, what you're offering me is proprietary work product," McAllister said. He leaned back in his chair. "I'm not sure exactly how business is done at KSpace, but I imagine that any research you did for them was on a strictly work-for-hire basis."

Sunny nodded and looked down at his hands. He'd known this would be a problem, sure. But the data—

"Meaning that if you turn this data over to me, you could be sued for breach of contract. And NASA would be breaking the law by receiving stolen goods." McAllister frowned and fluttered one hand in the air. "Technically."

"I know," Sunny said.

"So why don't you tell me why you came here? What you want from NASA."

Sunny took a deep breath. "A job."

"A job," McAllister repeated.

Sunny opened his mouth to say more. All that came out was a laugh. It wasn't a fun laugh. It was a laugh of desperation.

"We're always looking for good astronomers, but if you want to apply to work at NASA I'll direct you to our hiring portal—"

"I want to quit KSpace and come work here," Sunny said. "It's... kind of complicated, because I'm still under contract in Atlanta. I want to break that contract. To do that, I need to be protected. From, you know, KSpace's legal team." Sunny winced. "It's a pretty good legal team. I want a decent salary, though that's, you know, negotiable, and health insurance, and maybe two weeks' vacation. I have one more demand, too, which is pretty big but—"

"You have a demand." McAllister's face turned very cold. "Dr. Stevens, I don't think you understand. I just said that I can't accept the data you've offered me. Which means I can't, in turn, offer you a job. I'm sorry you had to come all the way down here for this."

He started to rise from his chair.

Sunny had one last chance. Just one chance to save himself here.

Time to pull out the big gun.

"It's decelerating," he said. "Spontaneously. It's spontaneously decelerating."

Sunny had taken a pretty big risk, coming to NASA with this. He had hoped to talk to one of its scientists, not an administrator. His only hope now was that this sunburned bureaucrat had enough of a background in orbital mechanics to get the point.

McAllister didn't stand up. His eyes didn't bug out, and he didn't gasp for breath. But he did reach up and scratch the side of his nose, as if he was giving Sunny's outburst a little bit of thought. Finally he said, "All right. Maybe there's something we can do."

Maybe—maybe he did get it. Maybe he understood why this was so important.

McAllister studied Sunny in silence for a while. "Perhaps you should take off that sweatshirt before we go any further."

Sunny grabbed two handfuls of orange hoodie. "Uh, I'm not wearing anything underneath. Today's my day off. When your message said to come here, I just ran for the train. I didn't think about clothes."

McAllister reached up and touched the device clipped to his ear. Presumably he was calling an assistant or somebody. "This is McAllister. Yes. Would you do me a favor and find a man's shirt, somewhere? I know it's an unusual request. Just bring it to my office."

A staffer showed up a few minutes later with the new shirt—a white T-shirt from the JPL gift shop. It showed the old logo, a red swooping curve over a navy blue disk.

"Welcome to NASA," McAllister said.

Enter the monthly
Orbit sweepstakes at
www.orbitloot.com

With a different prize every month,
from advance copies of books by
your favourite authors to exclusive
merchandise packs,
**we think you'll find something
you love.**